DIRTY GIRLS

Erotica

for

Women

EDITED BY
RACHEL KRAMER BUSSEL

SEAL PRESS

DIRTY GIRLS
EROTICA FOR WOMEN

Seal Press
A Member of the Perseus Books Group
1700 Fourth Street
Berkeley, CA 94710

Library of Congress Cataloging-in-Publication Data
Dirty girls: erotica for women/edited by Rachel Kramer Bussel.
    p. cm.
ISBN-10: 1-58005-251-7
ISBN-13: 978-1-58005-251-1
    1. Erotic stories, American. 2. Women—Sexual behavior—Fic-
tion. 3. American fiction—Women authors. 4. Erotic stories,
English. I. Bussel, Rachel Kramer.
PS648.E7D57 2008
813'.01083538—dc22
2007039238

9 8 7 6 5 4

Cover and Interior Design by Domini Dragoone
Printed in the United States by Maple Vail
Distributed by Publishers Group West

Dedication

TO DIRTY GIRLS, PAST AND PRESENT—
AND THE MEN AND WOMEN WHO
LOVE AND LUST AFTER THEM

CONTENTS

DIRTY AND SWEET WRAPPED UP IN ONE

Introduction

" *I* can be dirty and sweet at the same time" reads my self-proclaimed motto on my MySpace page. When I wrote that, I meant that not so deep inside me lurks the soul of a highly perverted, kinky, dirty girl who can get aroused often by a single word whispered in my ear or a solid smack across my ass. Once someone gets me into that zone, I'll do anything, no matter how depraved, to be with them. I'll find myself fantasizing about all the wicked things we can do together throughout the day and night, waking from wild dreams with the wish that they were beside me. I'll see their name in my inbox and get instantly wet. I'll tell them in public exactly what I want them to do to me, and vice versa. Yes, that's what I mean by "dirty."

Yet I don't think my sexual interests make me any less of a well-rounded, kind-hearted, intelligent person. I'm "sweet" in the sense that I care about my friends and family, like sending cards and random gifts, strive to be a good person—also, I run a blog about cupcakes. I'm as likely to kiss a lover's forehead tenderly and offer to tuck them into bed as I am to throw them down on the floor and strip them naked. For me, the sweet-and-tender and down-and-dirty go hand in hand; I'm most turned on, and most slutty, when I'm partnered with someone who brings out my sweet side. Once I visited a boyfriend who was sick with a fever and did the one thing I could think of to make him feel better: I sank down onto his bed and took his cock in my mouth. Playing the slutty nurse, horny yet doting, is another aspect to my dirty/sweet motto.

I'd originally meant the phrase as a throwaway line, but more and more I'm realizing that everyone (or almost everyone) has a dirty and a sweet side. All too often we denigrate the dirty girls—the ones who dare to publicly show their naughty sides—as incorrigible sluts rather than realizing just how exciting it is to tap into our lustiest selves. Once you crack the surface of those who are seemingly prim and proper—the demure suburban housewife, the suited up banker, the quiet secretary, the curious bookworm, the shy computer nerd—you'll very likely find that the simplicity of the word "dirty" doesn't go anywhere near far enough to describe the kinks that lurk within them.

The women writing here don't apologize for being dirty. They know who and what they want, and they go after the objects of their affection in all kinds of different ways. Reading this collection—whether from start to finish or skipping around to your favorite authors or the most eye-catching titles—will give you a glimpse into what makes women wet, what makes us feel and act dirty, what makes us slick our lips and spread our legs. Maybe, just maybe, their stories attempt to answer Freud's infamously infuriating query: "What do women want?" To judge by the twenty-seven tales you hold here in your hands, they want to be worshipped, they want to be ordered around, they want to be sent spinning into ecstasy and then come crashing back down. They want strangers bearing ice cubes on a hot day, and they want to be a party favor passed around among guests. They want hot vacation sex, visits to peep shows, and a man who'll lick stinky cheese off their boots. They want power, and they want to give up power. They want sex at the office and in the great outdoors and on trains and airplanes. They want sex with the whole United States of America (or at least part of it). They want to be wooed, seduced, flirted with, taken. They want men, women, and sometimes both at the same time.

Of course, there's more to what women want out of sex than any one book could possibly capture. What I've done with this anthology is highlight some of the best erotic writing I've found from authors who show you exactly what makes their hearts beat and their clits stand at attention. What they're up to is, as Marie Lyn Bernard so aptly puts it, "Fucking Around" (which I briefly considered as a very fitting alternative title to this book). When I first heard Bernard read this story tag-team style at my reading series In The Flesh, I was blown away. She captures so much of the drama of sex—the high highs, the low lows, the awkwardness and the intensity—in a playful yet totally hot way. And when she writes about the Big Apple, it'll make you want to hop the first plane or train to get here: "New York fucks me. New York fucks me so hard that I cry. My pussy opens like the long throat of a flame-swallower. Her fingers make love to the inside of my belly button. I am sweating so much that our bodies glide against each other like fish underwater." You'll find yourself drawing a map of your own sexual conquests, marking your territory right along with Bernard.

But for every feisty babe here, there's another just in the process of discovering what turns her on. "Dirty" can be a state of mind just as much as it can be a description of one's bedroom antics. Carol Queen's peep-show-virgin protagonist, Abby, doesn't quite know what she's getting into with her new friends Daniel and Lila, but she desperately wants to find out. "Lila's lips covered hers right away, soft and wet, licking and nibbling in one of the most arousing kisses Abby had ever experienced," writes Queen. "Dirty" doesn't always mean depraved, either; these stories aren't all wham-bam-thank-you-sir (or ma'am) quickies. Many of them evoke the intensity of emotion that sex can bring with it, the ways having a lover know you literally inside and out can throw your life completely off balance, as if they can read your soul like a map, using fingers, toys, tongues, and cocks to navigate you until they own your internal compass. The thrill of giving yourself over to someone, of giving up control for that deliciously delirious sensation of pure erotic adrenaline, surfaces throughout this collection.

The women you'll find here are complex; they're by turns playful and bashful, horny and haughty. They want to share much more with you than just the details of their latest screw. They want you to know what makes them tick, who haunts their dreams, why they can't quite forget the man who fucked them senseless, even when they're with someone new. They like to watch and be watched, to take risks, to live out their long-held fantasies. Some are in loving, committed relationships, ones that allow them room to get their freak on with the person who knows just how to push their every button. Others, like my "Icy Hot" protagonist, don't even want to know their bedmate's name: "I forgot about the fact that I didn't really know him at all. Sometimes, in a city of millions of strangers, you just have to take a chance and let your body make the decisions for you, as I've learned over the years. And my body was saying *Yes, please, more, harder.*"

Dirty doesn't preclude poetry, the kind where the words roll off the page, roll from your tongue, so beautifully it's like they themselves are making love to you. Writers like Marilyn Jaye Lewis, Suki Bishop, and Melissa Gira probe the twisted places women go in search of sex—and themselves. In "A Prayer to Be Made Cocksure," Gira elevates the art of the blow job to new heights: "I sucked your cock as if it were the last cock. I trusted you to let me keep breathing, to never take that final bit from me, to tell me that getting any air at all was your choice just by reaching your hand down the length of your chest to me, to cradle the back of my neck, to run your fingers across my lips, softly, as you plunged suddenly and held me at the edge." She takes you right into that moment, where this intimate act is dissected, treasured, hoarded, and missed.

You'll find a range of motivations here, from women looking to spice up a lackluster relationship to single girls on the prowl, to kinky couples, daring Dommes, and sultry sirens intent on performing on a sexual stage of their own creation. You may read their stories and ask yourself: Would you ever write your name across your lover's cock? What about pick up a stranger at a rock concert or screw a doctor in a hospital? Get fingered at the opera? Go to a bondage club? These characters do all this and more, always making sure their wanting, lusting, panting, and perversions are met with equal fervor.

Take a hot and steamy trip with these writers as they unlock your deepest desires, or perhaps give you some new ideas to try out next time you shut your eyes and part your legs. From tender to tempting, sweet to sadistic, loving to lascivious, there's something for every reader who wants to go to bed with images that'll surely make you blush and just may spark some brand-new, unique fantasies of your very own.

Rachel Kramer Bussel
New York City
July 2007

FUCKING AROUND

Marie Lyn Bernard

New York

I told New York I loved her but she wouldn't say it back. We had just made love, and then I said it and she laughed. I felt like she was holding all my limbs together with her breath, and so when she laughed it felt like she was dropping me and pretending it was an accident.

NEW YORK: It takes me a long time, you know that, I told you that. But when I do say it, I'll really mean it. When I feel it, you'll know it all over.

New York fell asleep but I couldn't. I stood naked at the squashed rectangle of window in the corner of New York's bedroom and watched people spill out the glass doors of a hip restaurant. A man put his wife in a cab and then met a girl on the corner; she was pretty and looked happier than I'd felt in years.

NEW YORK: Come back to bed, baby, what are you doing? If you aren't doing anything, you should be sleeping.

I told New York I was going to start seeing other places.

NEW YORK: You'll come back.

Boston

I meet Boston at a retirement party for a professor I worked with. He is wearing a corduroy blazer and a red rugby shirt and has blue, shiny eyes and wide, benevolent shoulders.

BOSTON: What's your drink? Lemme guess . . . vodka cran? No—I take that back. Vodka tonic.

ME: Does this work with other girls?

BOSTON: Yeah, usually.

He talks about his family while I try to figure out how tall he is—I'm inspecting the heels of my shoes, the girth of his boots. I get drunk and give up; he sits on the couch, I lay my bare feet in his lap.

ME: I have very long toes, you know.

BOSTON: Oh yeah? What does that mean?

I press my big toe up the crotch of his starchy pants, and then I rest so his limp dick nestles into the arch of my foot, and then I shift my toes around until he gets hard again. I do this over and over. We giggle a lot. It feels good but temporary, like a hot shower. I miss New York a little, but New York never made me giggle.

Boston is enthusiastic. He takes me to his beautiful brownstone. He pushes me against the wall with comical force and begins to attack my mouth with his mouth.

Boston wants to pick me up and toss me about like his arms are rackets and I'm a buoyant shuttlecock. Boston aspires for earthshattering sex, the stuff of movies and wet dreams, but as soon as he gets my ankles on his shoulders and grabs a glimpse of himself in the mirror, he comes all over me.

BOSTON: That was good, huh?

ME: Huh?

I look at his shrinking cock. What a waste of a beautiful eight-inch cock, I think, with veins like a roadmap of everywhere he should have been.

Washington, D.C.

Washington, D.C., buys me four drinks in a hotel bar and then takes me to his apartment, which actually also looks like a hotel: pressed sheets, organized bath products, neatly folded cream-colored towels.

D.C. has Magnum King-size condoms ostentatiously placed on his bathroom counter. We rub against each other. I feel what I think is D.C.'s dick through his pants, but it turns out to be his T-Mobile Sidekick. I am disappointed to unzip his pressed and properly frayed jeans to find the smallest dick I've ever seen in my life.

WASHINGTON, D.C.: My girlfriend always got me those Magnums. So I just kept on getting them.

I know he must be lying, but I'm too worn out and ambivalent to argue.

WASHINGTON, D.C.: I'm gonna rock your world, sugar. You ever hear of a little something I call the rectal G-spot?

ME: Yeah, um, that's not really gonna work for me.

WASHINGTON, D.C.: Are you sayin' I'm afraid of hard work? I am not afraid of hard work.

D.C. is okay at first, solid but boring, and then he just keeps grabbing the wrong things, sticking his finger in holes that don't get wet or even feel good. I don't know why I think he might know what he's doing, and I start to wonder if he put drugs in my drink.

He wants to try again in the morning. He smells like coffee and Splenda, and I feel like I might throw up.

WASHINGTON, D.C.: Baby, I am excessively optimistic about your Big O.

I can't even call New York to talk about it. I know what she'll say.

New York: I can't believe you let yourself get fucked by Washington, D.C. Were you drunk? Were you stupid? Did he promise you something? He's not gonna do it, you know. He's all lip service.

Wisconsin and Michigan

Wisconsin and Michigan have been dating for five years. I think Wisconsin is cuter, even though she's a little chubby. It suits her, though, and I like how she licks organic yogurt from her spoon and how when she speaks it sounds like maple syrup.

WISCONSIN: Michigan's parents hate me. But I know it's not me they really hate. It's the idea of their daughter fucking me that gives them night sweats. We get along sometimes, at their cottage. We make love underwater while her parents grill hamburgers, which I don't eat, because I gave up meat.

I like the way she says the word "meat" and it makes me wish her tongue were on my pussy, eating me, getting even fatter if she wants to. I want her face between my legs and my face between her girlfriend's legs, all of us licking each other, sweet sap instead of sweat, I want her breasts on my face, I want to fall asleep that way. When I come, it won't be normal cum. It will be blackberry jam.

Time passes; it feels like it's been a week since I've slept anywhere but between these two beautiful girls.

WISCONSIN: Michigan told me that her ex-boyfriend would sometimes fall asleep with his cock inside of her. It made me jealous, you know? So I started falling asleep with my fingers inside of her. One, two, three. She sleeps like a log and comes in her sleep.

Wisconsin wants to use a strap-on, but Michigan can't stop laughing while Wisconsin tries to get it on. They tell me to put it on instead, but then I start laughing, and then we are all laughing, and I have a stupid dead dick wrapped around my waist. We decide against sex and eat ice cream instead.

After nine days, I need to leave them. One of us is getting attached, and it could possibly be me. I don't say goodbye, I just leave them a card with a poem in it.

Los Angeles

Los Angeles is either the best or the worst sex of my life. I meet Los Angeles on MySpace; in her photograph she is wearing a short skirt and a pink wig, and her headline is "I'm the Real Deal, Baby!" I am surprised when I meet her because she looks just like her photo.

LOS ANGELES: Why wouldn't I?

Los Angeles picks me up in a shiny yellow car. She also has shiny yellow hair that blows in the wind. I turn up the radio and let my mouth hang open, and above me is nothing but perfect blue sky.

LOS ANGELES: My husband is always out of town. It's like I barely know him! Wanna lay out?

Los Angeles goes to the bathroom to change into something more comfortable, and I look in her refrigerator for a beer. All she has are celery sticks and powders for protein shakes.

That is when I start to suspect that Los Angeles is a robot.

LOS ANGELES: I couldn't find my bikini.

She is naked behind me, and I am crouching by the veggie crisper, hunting for something identifiably edible.

I stand up and she stops me with her breath; just existing right behind me is enough to send me into some tingly place near plea-sure. She takes off my shirt with her fingernails. I turn to her. I'm not hungry anymore. I feel like she's feeding me with air.

She bites my lower lip, lets her teeth linger. She slips her tongue through my lips, briefly, then pulls back, places her palm on my jutting hip bones, and yanks me to her. I grab her hair in fists.

We make out and tumble onto her couch, made of suede and air. I think her fingers are battery powered.

LOS ANGELES: Make me bleed, I want you to make me bleed.

I do. First her back; my nails make tire tracks. She screams in delicious pleasure. Her blood is the color of Bing cherries.

LOS ANGELES: I had fifteen orgasms. How many did you have?

Whether she is being honest or not, I'm certain I could rewind and locate all fifteen crescendos. I tell her I had two.

LOS ANGELES: Only two?

ME: That's good, you know, two?

LOS ANGELES: Oh no, I always aim for the stars.

She orders expensive takeout, but I don't want to eat it, I just want to fuck her some more because I know she won't be there in the morning, I can just feel it. She's more heartless than New York. New York has a heart; she just chooses not to use it. I don't know if there's anything about Los Angeles that resembles a heart, but she sure is pretty. She eats fat-free Cool Whip off my nipples.

In the morning, she dresses for work and I no longer recognize her.

LOS ANGELES: The maid is coming at three. I'll be at work. If my husband calls, don't answer it.

I am curious about her secrets and her ugly heart, so I snoop around and find an old driver's license with her photo on it; she looks young and angry, and her name is not Los Angeles, it is Kansas City.

But I don't care. I like her plastic and fast and full of lies. I drink cock-tails by her pool all morning and leave before she comes home.

I can't tell New York about Los Angeles. She'll just kill me, I know it.

Detroit

Detroit just got lucky at the new casino, and he buys me a Coors Light, and I don't have the heart to tell him that I don't drink beer. Detroit looks older than he is. His skin is firm and sheet-white, and his eyes are a subterranean industrial gray, and he gets me drunk and makes me laugh so I let him drive me home.

DETROIT: Have you ever blown a guy who was driving a car?

ME: Have you?

DETROIT: Are you serious?

ME: What? Do you have something against gay people?

Detroit shakes his head.

DETROIT: College girls, fuck. You college girls.

I'm not even in college, but I don't bother to correct him.

I know I shouldn't; but I let him fuck me in the back seat of his car in the driveway of his mom's house, where he lives, and that's after I blow him in the front seat. His skin smells like ash and grease, and his jeans are fast and insistent against my damp cunt.

ME: I want you inside me.

DETROIT: Hells yeah!

I think Detroit might be good at something, and I'm hoping that it's fucking. Detroit rolls me onto my stomach. Detroit actually holds my damp panties to his nose and sniffs them.

DETROIT: You've got some ass for a white girl.

Detroit doesn't tease. Detroit has condoms in his glove compartment, and he makes me rip open the package with my teeth. It feels terrible/awesome.

Detroit plunges straight in and hard. Detroit is a lumberjack fucker and a spanker, and he plunges into me like he's taking something from inside of me to use again later.

DETROIT: Is that how you like it, you dirty little girl?

I squeeze my muscles around his short fat cock, and he comes. He tries really hard to make me come, first with his fingers and then with his mouth. He has the right idea, I think, but no follow-through. I tell him it's okay.

DETROIT: I was hopin' you'd say that. I sure am wiped out, I gotta tell you.

Detroit gives me something red and itchy. I call him, but his phone is disconnected, and when he finally calls me back, he says he got something from me.

ME: You're kidding, right?

DETROIT: Don't hate the playa, hate the game.

ME: What?

San Francisco

San Francisco takes me to an S+M party where everyone is wearing taut leather and has a lot of Opinions. I am surprised: I met her in the park, she had flowers in her hair and a vintage bicycle. Is she a top or a bottom? Does she want me to whip her? I don't understand.

SAN FRANCISCO: I like clothespins on my nipples.

San Francisco makes me nervous. A man wants to take us home, and she pinches my ass and says it's time to go.

SAN FRANCISCO: I'm sorry, it's just that—God, I just have all these—you know? Issues? About my body? And I'm trying to work through them, and this really helps.

The next morning Portland comes over with marijuana and bagels. He hugs me even though we just met. Portland is scrawny, and he loves disappearing behind San Francisco's flesh and Opinions.

That night, we all masturbate together and we all come. It's lovely. It really is. It's so lovely that I can't stand it. I tell San Francisco that I think she's hiding something from me, and she insists that she isn't.

SAN FRANCISCO: Okay, fine. I was a stripper once. For two years. During college, but it helped me write my thesis.

ME: That's the lamest secret I've ever heard.

Alabama

Alabama picks me up in his pickup truck—he opens the door for me, and then we drive to a bar where everyone knows his name.

ME: Okay, what do you really do? No more playing.

ALABAMA: I'm a poultry farmer. Where'd you think chickens come from?

ME: The egg?

ALABAMA: You're mighty fine, you know that?

His house is humid, but his sheets are plaid flannel. He has a body like Paul Bunyon. In the morning, he will tell me:

ALABAMA: You're the tiniest girl I've ever been with.

I'm a clean pink ballerina in his arms, graceful and slick. He pushes me onto the bed, and I lie with my knees bent at the edge, my feet square on the ground, and he takes off his belt and his pants and slides his cock out of his boxers.

ALABAMA: Stay there, darlin', stay right there!

I do. I spread my legs for Alabama's country-boy dick. He fucks me with the elemental intensity of a man who handles animals and land and dirt. When he comes, I hold him, and the look in his eyes makes me want to cry. I feel like he could be crying too, but he doesn't know it.

On his nightstand, there is a plastic cup from Dunkin' Donuts and a photo of his dog. I hear him on the phone with his friends; he sounds like an asshole.

This, I know, will be the best night of Alabama's life. I know he will call me just to talk, and I will feel guilty but I will not call him back. He makes me scrambled eggs and kisses me goodbye.

ALABAMA: Be safe out there, y'hear?

I don't have the heart to tell him that no one's safe anymore, or that I'm going back to New York.

New York

New York is three hours late to meet me, like she didn't even miss me. Her eyes are green rimmed with red. She looks sick and devastating and gorgeous. Her nails are perfect and glossy. Later, she will use them to trace the entire length of my spine with a spotted trail of blood, like I did to Los Angeles, but this time I will like it and it will remind me of hearts and love.

NEW YORK: I haven't slept in like, three days.

ME: Do you want to do this later, then?

NEW YORK: Why? No, of course not. What are we waiting for?

New York might not know that I can see her veins through her skin now, or the scar from the tattoo she got removed. I liked that tattoo, but I guess I'd never told her that out loud. I realize I need to hold on tighter to her if I want to keep her, really.

I kiss her and she tastes like toothpaste and cocaine. I can feel her shoulder blades like angel wings. Our bones clash together like drumsticks. She puts her iPod on shuffle and sticks it in the speakers and we fuck to Daft Punk and the Gypsy Kings and Miles Davis and k.d. lang and La Bohème.

NEW YORK: I've started taking Ritalin before we make love. It helps me focus. I've got a lot going on.

New York is wearing expensive underwear, and she lets me take it off with my teeth and then canvas her inner thighs with hot blushing kisses, and she squeals in a voice that sounds nothing like her actual voice. New York takes off her own bra and she apologizes:

NEW YORK: It's from Conway.

ME: All your dirty trashy bras are from Conway, and I don't care.

New York fucks me. New York fucks me so hard that I cry. My pussy opens like the long throat of a flame-swallower. Her fingers make love to the inside of my belly button. I am sweating so much that our bodies glide against each other like fish underwater. The mattress feels less and less like enough, and pleasure and pain race through my body like my veins are the passageways of a busted pinball machine. I can't tell if New York likes to hurt me or if she just doesn't care about me at all. New York's body is hard and thin but also strong. New York fucks like she's killing me with the understood secret that death is a long, divine orgasm.

NEW YORK: I love you.

ME: I—

NEW YORK: Shh. Don't ruin it.

When I come, it's short and pure; a star shoots straight from my pussy to my head and everything goes brilliant white for one second—maybe even less than that—but that split second of complete nirvana is worth it. I look at New York and wonder how she does it.

LIVE TONIGHT

Saskia Walker

aomi was aroused, because live music always gave her a sexual thrill. For Naomi, no other way of experiencing music came close to this, and this was like good sex for her, the best kind—hot and horny and unbridled, the kind where you can't wait to debauch yourself and get off. Something about the atmosphere and the way the music surrounded her, pounding up through the floor, really got to her. It flooded her senses and gave her a totally unique kind of high. Naomi often felt as if she were an extra instrument, as if her body was being played along with the instruments on the stage—and that sense of being played was what did it for her.

It had to be a public performance. She couldn't re-create it at home. The club scene was good, but not unique enough. She also liked smaller venues and pub bands but could never lose herself in the environment quite as well as she could at a large venue, and that was the key. Only there did the experience become so intense that her pulse pounded and her underwear got hot and damp within moments. By the end of the concert, she'd have to go to the ladies' toilets to wank before she made her way home. With her back up against one wall of the cubicle and her foot wedged on the opposite wall, she'd shove her hand inside her underwear and rub herself hard, forcing out all that built up arousal. She had to take that last step, otherwise she was a wreck by the time she got home, as if she'd been taken to the very edge of orgasm and left there, wired and yet incomplete. She was always close, fast at her peak, the complete high of the experience flooding out of her, running onto her thighs at her moment of release.

This rather intimate experience of live music was Naomi's secret thrill. She kept it that way because no one had really understood quite how intense it was for her. Though she had tried, with several men.

"It makes you feel sexy, I can dig that." That was the usual type of reply, delivered with a shrug and a grin. When she tried to explain that it was more than just "feeling sexy," that it was actually like having sex—that it was enough to make her come with the slightest touch—the subject usually changed fast, because most of the men she'd met would rather believe it was their presence that was turning her on rather than some extraneous factor. Maybe she was meeting the wrong type of man. She had hoped she would find someone who would understand her, someone who would play into it. Deep down she wanted to share it, like a sex toy or an aphrodisiac, but she'd come to the conclusion that she probably never would.

The nearest she ever got to a true understanding was with a rock guitarist. He'd listened, curious, as she tried to explain it. He didn't say much—he never did—but he didn't dismiss the idea. So she had asked him to stand at the end of the bed and play for her. He had the look: long shaggy hair, stubble, sleazy in that don't-give-a-fuck rock musician way. She squinted her eyes, pretending she was at an actual gig, and watched him, letting the music take control. She got hot, really hot, unable to resist stroking her breasts and thrusting her fingers between her thighs. He'd loved it, watching her writhe across the bedcovers and masturbate while he played. Her fingers stroked her clit and she shoved two fingers into her wet cunt in time with the music. Riveted, he sped his playing when he'd realized she was quickly coming, moaning aloud and gyrating her hips against her hand. Abandoning the guitar, he unzipped his fly and dove onto the bed with her, bringing her back to a second climax by fucking her hard, really hard, banging her into the bed as if she were the drum and he was pounding out his very own fierce rhythm through her body.

It was good, damn good. Although she suspected the hot

sex was more about his reaction to her "show" for him than what the music did to them. It wasn't perfect, but near enough for her to get hopeful. Alas, when they went to the actual concerts together, he preferred to schmooze, hanging out with the bands backstage then watching the live music from the side of the stage, hobnobbing with the other musicians. He'd tried to take her up there with him but she'd declined, because that wasn't what she was after. She even told him about the wanking in the ladies', but that had just made him rush her back to his place so he could get her flat on her back on his bed.

They'd shared several hot sessions with his guitar performance from the end of the bed, but now he was out there on a European tour somewhere, and she was back to trawling the music magazines for the perfect mix of music and venue. Like she had tonight. And what a night it promised to be. Whorl, one of her favorite-ever bands, and The Academy, her favorite venue. The perfect combo beckoned to her.

She tagged on the end of the growing queue, hugging the wall of the building. In the very early days, she used to come to these things with friends, but she had ended up frustrated. They all wanted to hang out together, somewhere where they could chat and watch, and get to the bar. What Naomi preferred to do was have a drink before she left home and then forget all about that lesser form of self-indulgence. She had something better in mind.

When she got inside the venue, she moved at will, seeking out her beloved bass pounding up through the floor. Before the band came on, or between the bands, when the place was brightly lit, she kept on the move to avoid pickups. Standing near a crowd of people was also good cover and kept those achingly bad chat-up lines at bay. There was no support band tonight, and that suited her well. The auditorium filled quickly, and she flitted about while the lights were up, anticipation running her ragged. Her heartbeat was already erratic, her core hot, and her pussy tingling with anticipation.

It was a hot night, and she'd dressed for comfort: Doc Martens, tight black vest, and denim miniskirt, her hair loosely tied up on the crown of her head. When the final few sound checks were made, she began to rock along with the DJ music, noticing how it was chosen to lead into the band's set. The lights dropped and the band emerged onto the stage—three guitarists, a drummer, and the singer, Carrie. Naomi lifted her arms, clapping and cheering with the crowd, unable to keep the grin off her face. Carrie was wearing a short skirt not dissimilar to her own. Her blue-black hair flew out from side to side as she moved to the first beats of the drum. She was a small, sexy woman, overtly powerful. The men adored her. Some of them even tried to reach up onto the stage and touch her. She'd sometimes put her boot on their shoulders and kick them away, flashing her red underwear at them, blatantly. Naomi loved it, but very soon, when she found her own nirvana, she wouldn't even be noticing stuff like that.

The crowd surged forward, and it was the time to stake her claim on a good spot. From experience she knew where the sound reverberated the most, weaving across the venue toward the spot. Skirting a pillar, she spied the place she wanted to be. There was a small gap in the crowd, enough for her to squeeze into. Focused on her target, she jumped when she bumped into another person leaning up against the pillar. The crowd was moving at the other side of her, and she staggered. A strong hand reached out and grabbed her around her waist, steadying her. She looked into the man's face. He smiled, inclining his head.

Somewhat unnerved, she mouthed "Thank you" to him. Even in the gloom, she could see that his eyes were narrowed as he quickly assessed her. He seemed to be alone. It wasn't very often that she saw another loner at a gig like this. She glanced back at the spot she was headed for. He followed her gaze and ushered her through, but when she looked back over her shoulder, he was still watching. The gig was under way, but after a few minutes she took another quick, curious look. Yes, he was definitely keeping his eye on her. He had short bleached hair, spiked and sexy. He caught her eye and returned her smile. Heat traversed her skin. His eyebrows were straight, decisive, almost mirroring his sharp cheekbones. With strong features and a quirk to his smile that suggested he was both cynical and adventurous, she couldn't help being aware of him. Normally she barely noticed the people around her. He was into the music as much as she was, moving to the sounds, his shoulders against the pillar seeming to ground him somehow. What a good idea, choosing that place to anchor himself. She couldn't help smiling and made a note to try out the spot next time around.

The band moved into the second track, one of her favorites, and she was drawn back to the experience, moving her body, her eyelids lowering as she savored the music pounding through the floor. The sound soared out through the airwaves, wrapping around her before diving deep inside, teasing her most intimate flesh. God, it was so good. Each delivery of sound across the frets or drums might as well have been played on her erogenous zones. Her nipples were hard inside her vest. With every movement, her body snaked, her thighs rubbing together as her hips swayed and dipped to the rhythm.

By the fifth track, her hair was beginning to escape its band, strands touching her shoulders. She swiped them away restlessly. As she did, she saw him looking over—the guy by the pillar. The stage lights swung over the audience, picking up his eyes, sharp and inquisitive. And he *was* watching her, watching with a knowing look in his eyes that felt as if he had touched her—like he knew exactly what she was feeling, and how she was feeling it. The lights moved and she danced on, enjoying the ongoing feeling of his eyes on her. Even though she couldn't see them anymore, she could feel it. Heat pounded between her thighs, her pulse tripping. He knew how turned on she was, she was sure of it. She glanced back. Yes, even in the gloom she could see that he was still watching her.

Lifting her head, she focused on the stage. A moment later, she felt movement against her back, fingers resting on the curve of her hip. Her eyes closed; she breathed deeply. She didn't even have to look to know. He'd made his way over. He knew.

"You really feel it, don't you?"

The words were said close against her ear. Deviant pleasure shot through her, and her head dropped back in sudden ecstasy. Her hand reached over his where it rested on her hip, squeezing him in identification. Glancing back, she nodded. "All over me, and inside."

Moving closer, he spooned her hips inside his, swaying to the sound with her, feeling each rhythm and nuance physically. They were locked into it, together.

"How did you know?" she asked.

He answered by hauling her closer still, and wedging her tight against him. She gasped when she felt how hard he was, the bulk of his cock against the crease of her arse through their clothes. Oh, but that was good. This is what she had wanted, a man who instinctively understood and played into the experience, and now the missing ingredient was right there, at her back, loaded and cocked for action. "This feels so good," she blurted.

He squeezed her waist in response, riding against her to the sounds. "Oh yes."

A heady thrill flared inside her when his hands roamed up and down her sides, stroking her body to the music. Her arms lifted as she swayed against him. His arms rose alongside hers, brushing against her with the hard sleek muscles of his biceps, enclosing her. Painfully aroused, she rippled in his grasp. He bent to kiss her neck. She groaned aloud, sensation snaking over her shoulders and back from the place his mouth had touched her.

"Come back to the pillar," he said. He nodded his head back at his previous viewing point.

She agreed, and he took her hand, holding it tightly. A couple of people in the crowd looked annoyed when they made their way back across their path, but she couldn't care. Her heart thudded while she watched him take up his position, pivoting his shoulders against the pillar so that his hips were right there for her to rest in. His booted feet were widely spaced, creating a niche between his legs for her to stand in. He smiled so wickedly that her mouth opened in anticipation, her breath catching in her throat. She didn't know the guy at all, and yet she felt instinctively attuned to him because of this shared sexy appreciation of the live music. He patted his thighs, beckoning her closer, his intentions clear. He wanted to explore this too; he wanted them to feel it together. And so did she. She wanted to touch him again, to have his hands all over her; she wanted to know how far they could push it, right here in the crowd, right now. They were two people with a shared need—to experience each other in this place, in this moment.

Nestling into position, she reveled in the feeling of his

strong, male body against her back. His aroused body. As his hands stroked over her hip bones, and then moved higher, to the soft underside of her breasts, her heart and mind beat out a fierce, direct response.

"Oh please, touch me, touch me everywhere," she said, unable to stop the words. She glanced back, unsure he'd even heard her amidst the layers of sound feeding out to them from the stage. But he smiled and moved against her, his head alongside hers, listening to her words as he watched the stage over her shoulder. She blinked and watched Carrie dancing across the stage while his hands moved on her breasts, squeezing, molding the flesh. It sent a loop of fire from her nipples to her cunt.

"Play me, feel me," she urged. The words were tumbling out; she was losing control, desire overriding decorum. Her strongest physical need was sexual release. And he knew. She could see his response, the tightening of his mouth, the inhalation of breath, the subtle shift in his shoulders.

"Concentrate on the music," he said.

When she rested back, he had his hands on the waistband of her skirt immediately, with his fingers drumming against the zipper. Torturously close to her hot spot, and yet not close enough. She reached under his fingers, flipped open the button, and lowered the zipper. He didn't even hesitate, sliding his hand inside the fabric, his fingers exploring her body. She moved against him, constantly aware of his erection, letting him know she was aware of it too. His hand moved deeper, under the line of her underwear. With his hand in there, her underwear was pulled tight against her buttocks, stinging her, making her squirm. Her groin was pounding with need, her sex clenching and releasing. He clasped her pussy firmly, massaging it, lifting her in his grip. Her clit pounded, locked tight in between her sex folds. This time, her hips moved, and it wasn't just the music, it was that and more—the sheer brutal need to feel that decisive touch on her clit.

Dizzy with deviant pleasure, she glanced about, watching the people moving around them. Any one of them could look their way, see them, point, or complain to security. But that somehow made it even hotter, dirtier and more dangerous. Right then, he pressed deeper with one finger and it slid into her hot, damp niche. His finger was right over her clit, stroking it, and she couldn't have stopped him if she had truly wanted to. He was wanking her off, right there in the middle of the crowd. The music was in her blood, he was tuning into it, and the thrill had her locked into the moment. Her body reacted, her head going back onto his shoulder, her shoulders pivoted against his chest. She reached her hand behind her back and squeezed the hard bulk of his cock through his jeans.

"Let me feel you in my hand," she said when the sound dipped.

He looked at her, eyebrows raised, with a tight, wicked smile. He hesitated only a moment, then moved his free hand under her fingers. Undoing his zipper, he shifted, and she felt the hot, silky surface of his erect cock against the palm of her hand. When she gripped and stroked it, he swore aloud and drew her in close against him, crushing her hand and his cock behind her back while he held and moved her with his hand locked over her pussy. His cock felt good, long and hard. The ridge around the head made her ache for it rubbing inside her, her sex clenching in response.

She was close, so close, her body trembling on the point of release. Then the music stopped, the band left the stage, and the crowd began to chant, clap, and stamp their feet, trying to bring them back out for the encore. His hand latched ever tighter over her mons, crushing her clit, pushing her on. A sense of urgency got hold of her; time was short, and she wasn't done yet. People were glancing around, chatting while they waited, and right there in the crowd, the back of her skirt was riding up against her arse, the front zipper peeled open to give him access.

Dirty girl, she told herself. *Horny bitch.*

Her head lifted, her moan escaping into the chants of the crowd. A sweet and sudden climax hit her, and her body shuddered. Her thighs turned to jelly, her neck loosening and her head dropping forward.

By the time she had grounded herself, the guitarists were back onstage, playing furiously for the encore. Empowered, she pulled his hand free, turned in his arms, and straddled one of his thighs, her hand clasping his cock again, stroking it swiftly as she looked up at his face.

The crowd roared. Carrie was obviously back onstage, but for Naomi it felt like it was for them, for their own performance. That thrilled her, and she had to bite her lip to keep her in touch with the world outside of the music, and him. Soon they'd have to pull apart, but she wanted to make him come first.

When Carrie's voice lifted and started, she moved in regular, swift strokes. She could see the restraint in his expression, feel it walled up against her. They'd come this far, right there in the middle of the audience. She rubbed herself against his thigh, making the pleasure in her clit sparkle and last. "This is so good, you feel so good."

His eyes closed, his breath coming fast. His cock reached in her hand. "I'm going to come," he said urgently. He rested his forehead against hers. "If you don't stop, I'm going to come, right here."

"Don't stop," she said. She squeezed his cock, massaging it fast, needing to trigger it, wanting to feel his release, wanting it all.

His locked eyes with her, and she saw it coming there, his eyes blazing. His cock went rigid and he came, his shaft jerking, fluid running down between her fingers. Thrilled, she suddenly realized the crowd was cheering again and the music had stopped. The lights went up, and he pulled himself together and acted fast, hauling her skirt straight, leveling her. Zipping his fly, he locked her against him again, holding her as if they were just having a postgig hug. He grinned.

Her underwear was gloriously drenched, and she let out a breathy laugh as she looked at him, doing up her zipper and button while the crowd started shifting toward the exits. "I wish you'd been inside me," she murmured, her desires speaking for her—she wasn't even thinking about what she had said.

"So do I," he said with a hoarse laugh. He pushed her hair back from her forehead and kissed her mouth for the first time; softly now, curiosity in that intimate touch. With her hands on his chest, she could feel the both of them rushing on the experience, their hearts beating hard as they stayed against the pillar, the crowd shifting away on either side of them. As they drew apart, she studied him. In the light, his looks were maverick, and she saw how attractive his eyes were as he scrutinized her. She wanted him; she wanted to see him again, but right then she didn't want him to ask for her number, in case it spoiled the moment. She felt the question rising between them and went to put her fingers on his lips, but he caught her hand and rested it back on his chest. It made her want, and need, all over again, and she rolled her hips into his.

"Are you going to be here for the Thursday night gig?" He lifted her hair from her shoulder as he asked, holding her with one hand around her hip as she moved against him.

He wasn't asking to see her again; he was asking to do this again. Pleasure rippled through her. "Yes," she replied without hesitation, not even pausing to consider who might be playing that night.

"In that case, I'll see you right here, on Thursday night." He stroked one finger down into her cleavage. "But, next time, don't wear any underwear." He reached to kiss her again, his tongue moving slowly, languorously, against hers.

When he drew back, Naomi chuckled softly, her blood racing. "Improved access, hmm?"

He grinned. "I figure it could work—you wear heels; I'll bring a condom."

Now she was getting hot all over again, starting to squirm. "All the way? In the gig?"

He nodded and pushed his fingers into her hair, tugging on it softly.

She grabbed him around the back of the neck and pulled him to her for one last kiss. "You're on," she stated as they drew apart. "I'll see you here, right here, Thursday."

As she strode out of the venue, she couldn't take the smile off her face, mentally calculating the hours until their next gig. Outside, in the street, the gig crowd clustered around the bootleg merchandisers, and she weaved through them, heading to the Tube. Glancing over her shoulder, she looked up at the sign.

Live tonight.

The words were never truer.

JUST ANOTHER GIRL ON THE TRAIN

Catherine Lundoff

*P*eople on the train always looked alike at first glance, she thought as she watched her fellow passengers from the corners of her eyes. It was a bad idea to look at them directly. She'd learned that her first year here, riding the subway to her job downtown. There was that time the crazy man followed her several blocks from the station, shouting after her. Then there was that other incident involving the missionaries and those copies of *The Watchtower* that kept showing up in her mailbox. No, best to watch covertly over her book, let her eyes slide past as though reading the station signs when she looked up.

You got to see all sorts of interesting things that way. The Chicano boy with the dreamy eyes watching his girlfriend sleep on his shoulder. The old women dozing over their shopping bags or books. The heavily made-up woman (or was she a man?) in the latex mini who kept checking her (or was it his?) watch and tapping one impossibly high heel restlessly against the train floor. She had a story made up for each and every one of them. That was the best part about riding the city trains; the stories never ended.

That woman across the aisle this morning, for instance. She must be worried about something from the way she sent nervous glances at the doors every time the train stopped. Between stops, she looked first at her watch, then at the floor, her thin brown eyebrows meeting in a scowl over her long nose.

Once, the other woman's small brown eyes met hers for an instant before they both looked away. The other woman's gaze told her nothing really, held no obvious reason for the clear anxiety she was feeling. But there had been something there, something she couldn't explain. When the woman got off at the next stop, she got up and followed her.

Why she did it, she never could say. But it was the beginning, this sideways path to follow strangers for a glimpse into their lives. Was it that it made her own life seem less ephemeral when held up to the mirror of someone else's? She couldn't or didn't want to answer that. She only knew that she was curious. That she needed to know something about this woman's life and why she was so nervous.

Up and out of the station she went, trailing a half block or so behind her quarry but still trying to look as if she knew where she was going. The crowds helped with that, swirling around to hide her from the woman, the woman from her. Something about the chase made her hot, made her think of the hottest, sweatiest sex she'd ever had. That part wasn't about the woman she was following, or at least she didn't think so. No, it must be about the hunt itself. She grinned a little to herself and followed the nervous woman around a corner.

Her quarry glanced around before slipping up the steps of a building, and she stopped to watch her go inside. Looking up, she noticed that there was a neon sign on the roof, blinking with the name of the hotel. The crowd swirled around her like a river while she wondered what to do next. She watched a group of teenagers walk by, one boy's hand stuck possessively in his girlfriend's jeans pocket. She looked back at the hotel and thought about sex.

Then she thought about following the woman inside. But then what? Instead she walked around the block, looking for a way to see into the rooms, maybe see what she was doing. She glanced down the alleyway that ran behind the hotel. It looked empty of rats and muggers and other urban perils. Somebody came out of one of the doors and dumped some restaurant trash in the bin, then stopped for a cigarette.

She waited until he went back inside, savoring the aroused ache that filled her when she thought about assignations in hotels, about steamy affairs that swept you away. The voice of her common sense warned her away, warned her back into the safe and familiar. She thought about listening to it for all of a single minute.

Then she walked down the alleyway, looking warily around her for unwanted company. So far, it looked deserted. She looked up when she got to the middle, wondering if she could see anything in the hotel. She stretched up on tiptoe, stepping back against the brick wall of the alley, heart thumping with anticipation.

At first, there wasn't much to see. Just maids cleaning the rooms and someone opening the curtains before they left for the day. She walked down a little further and found a tiny deserted courtyard between the buildings facing the hotel. She looked up at closed and shuttered windows, then walked over to press her back against the wall and stared up at the hotel.

The courtyard smelled like garbage and pee, and she had just told herself that she was nuts and needed to leave for the third time when the curtains on one of the fourth-floor windows opened. The woman from the subway looked out as a man's hands reached around her and started unbuttoning her shirt. She still looked anxious, gnawing her lip as he kissed her neck and shoulder.

Then her eyes closed, and from the alley, she could see his hands on her breasts, her blouse parting under his fingers. It was almost as if she could feel his hands on her own breasts, and she squeezed them experimentally, thumbing her nipples through her blouse and bra to feel something of what the woman in the window must be feeling. The unaccustomed sensation almost tore a moan from her throat. Clearly it had been a while since anyone had touched her like that.

She could see the man's hands unfastening the woman's pants, pulling them down, then bending her backward into a kiss. The woman in the window clutched at him, her hands obviously desperate, even from such a distance. A hot stab went through the watching woman, releasing the wetness inside her so that it ran down her thighs, so that she didn't think she could bear not being touched. She stuck her hand down her pants, her eyes fixed on the hotel window.

She was amazingly, wrenchingly wet and empty. Her fingers were never going to be enough to fill all that, but she did the best she could and slid them inside herself. Above her in the window, the man was working his way inside the woman from behind; she could see it on her face, even from here. The other woman's eyes were closed, her mouth open and gasping. She thrust back against her lover, taking him in.

For a moment, the woman in the alley closed her eyes too as she rocked forward on her fingers, picturing herself in the window. Her fingertips brushed her clit, and the sensation almost made her scream. She bit her lip, circling her aroused flesh with her thumb. For a wild moment, she thought about taking off her jeans, but that was too much. Instead she leaned against the bricks and rubbed herself to orgasm with a muffled moan.

Her legs hadn't stopped shaking when she looked up. This time, the woman in the window met her gaze. She could see the man reach around and slip his hand between her thighs. The woman frowned down at her before she caught her breath, before she turned back, yielding to the insistence of the man's hands and dick.

The frown had been enough to shake her back to reality. She zipped up her jeans again, feeling somehow elated and ashamed all at once. Then she walked away down the alleyway, her stride brisk and businesslike as she headed back to the subway.

That was the beginning of turning voyeur. At first she was afraid it might have come from some newfound phobia about being touched. Perhaps she just needed a good therapist. Then she worried that it grew out of a fear of dating and intimacy. So maybe she just needed a new lover. A week or so after that, she decided that she just liked to watch.

The night that she came to that realization, she followed a man out of the restaurant where she and her friends were eating dinner. She trailed him down darkened city streets to the edge of a city park. Then she found some bushes to linger in, out of sight, while he sat on a park bench. He looked around, and she watched as his eyes followed the taut firm asses of the young men who jogged past. She could almost feel him harden as he fidgeted on the bench, looking for the best place to arrange the erection she could see from her hiding place.

She thought about going over to him, about unzipping his pants and taking his dick in her mouth without saying a word. About licking and sucking him until he came, his hands hard and tight on the back of her head. But she didn't think it was her he was looking for, and she stayed where she was.

Finally one young guy jogged past, slowing down a little as he passed the bench. She could almost feel his gaze caress the sitting man's erection, the connection so hot it made her ache even watching it from here. She could almost feel the seated man harden even more as he looked over the jogger's firm ass, his sturdy, muscular legs. She watched as the jogger smiled a slow, secret smile then turned off the path and headed for a thicker clump of bushes behind the bench.

She saw the seated man stand up a few moments later and trail the other into the bushes. The thought of it, of hot and forbidden sex with a desperate risk of discovery, sent a jolt through her. She could picture their hands on each other's bodies, their mouths open and wet, pressed together in a kiss. She found herself standing up and walking toward another clump of bushes, as if pulled on an invisible line.

A quick glance around told her that there were other people nearby in case there was trouble, but no one close enough to see what she or the guys in the bushes were up to. She circled the clump, listening for the telltale gasp of breath, the soft moan that would tell her what she came to see.

After a minute, she heard it. The moan came just as she

found a gap in the bushes and behind a tree. She slipped into that gap, her steps nearly silent on the summer grass. She hunched over, ducking down so she'd be hard to see in the bushes, and glanced around the tree.

They were there, the jogger kneeling in front of the man from the bench. She could see the man's dick slip into the jogger's mouth, see the man lean backward against a tree, his eyes closed and his head tilted back. The jogger made a small slurping noise as his mouth took in the full length of the hard-on.

The breath caught in her throat, and she rubbed the seam of her pants against her engorged clit as she watched. There would be no time to get her hand down her pants, she could see that already in the standing man's face—the way his expression changed as he shifted toward orgasm. She rubbed hard, her fingers fierce and demanding against her own flesh. Her hips rocked forward of their own accord, the movement mimicking the men in front of her.

The cloth of her pants, of her soaking wet underwear, scraped against her sensitive flesh until she had to bite back moans of her own. At the same time, she was so wet, so empty, that it felt as if it would have taken both men to fill her. She pictured that for a moment, rubbing faster until her orgasm took her just as the standing man came. She missed watching that moment cross his face, because her knees gave way, and she found herself kneeling in the dirt, thighs shaking with release.

She stayed there, trembling in the aftermath, and watched

as the jogger wiped his mouth and stood. He reached out and gently touched the other man's cheek before he turned away, slipping through the bushes and back to jogging, as if nothing had happened. The other man looked after him, his eyes dark with longing and desire as he zipped himself up and followed. She stood up awkwardly and brushed off her knees. Then she left the park in the opposite direction, walking stiffly and carefully so as not to further irritate her already tormented flesh.

A few days passed, just enough to heal and whet her appetite for more. She went looking for what she wanted to see, watching for it wherever she went. It took time to find the right spot and the right couple, but eventually, they turned up.

She was at a bar with a date when she spotted them. Her date was talking about something, and she hung on his words until she saw the couple walk in and sit down. She wasn't sure that it was them she'd been watching for, not at first. But then, just then, the woman slid her hand up her man's thigh in a slow, sensuous gesture full of promise, and she knew she'd found them.

Her date knew he'd lost her and kept trying to recapture her attention until she finally pleaded a headache and bolted. Once outside, she circled back to the bar in time to see the couple go out on the dance floor. They were a matched set: all black silk and gothy, the woman's eyes made catlike with too much eyeliner. They kissed as she watched, the woman catching the man's lower lip in her teeth as they broke it off. He laughed.

She shivered just looking at them, the telltale scent of desire rising from between her legs. She followed them when they left the dance floor, headed into a hallway that led back into the rest of the building. She watched as they made out, their mouths wet and fierce against each other's, his hand reaching down to cup her ass and pull her hips forward against his. Her hands were wrapped tight around his neck, holding him in place as she opened her legs to let his thigh slip between them.

The watching woman felt a shock go through her, as if she were a part of their scene. She looked around for a place to hide and watch them, but there was nothing convenient. Instead, she found a dimly lit table with a good view of the hallway and an empty bar stool. She ordered a drink as she dangled one hand off the table, slowly and carefully feeling her way between her legs.

The couple had gone a little further while she'd been getting settled in, and she could see his hand under the woman's shirt now. His mouth caressed her neck, and even from here, she could see his teeth flash on her skin for an instant. Her own need was more urgent now, and she rocked herself against the barstool in a vain attempt at release.

"Hi there. You here by yourself?" The guy was standing between her and the hallway, and it was all she could do not to yell at him. Part of her noted that he was sort of cute. Nice body. Maybe enough to fill the ache inside. But she wanted to watch first. She murmured something about waiting for a friend, one who'd be showing up soon. He moved on just in time for her to watch as the guy in the hallway pushed his girlfriend against the wall, then lifted her up to hip level. Her legs wrapped around his waist as he pushed himself inside her, her mouth open and gasping, his face hidden in her neck.

The watching woman pulled her purse into her lap to hide the hand between her legs. She schooled her face to stay still, frozen as if listening to the music while she watched, imagining what it would be like to be taken in a public place. The thought got her wetter than she'd ever been, and despite herself, she gasped a little as her fingers found her clit through the thin fabric of skirt and underwear.

"That's some friend you're waiting for." The guy was back, standing behind her this time, so close that she could feel the heat of his body. "Can I help?"

She hesitated, her eyes still locked on the hallway. The couple was close to climax, and she found her head nodding like it was on strings. The guy stepped up to her, hand encircling her waist and face buried in her hair. He kissed her ear as one thumb slid slowly over her rock-hard nipple. She gasped and jumped as his other hand worked its way between her legs. In front of her, the couple in the hallway came, seemingly together. She could see the guy arch his head back, mouth open in a silent cry. The woman with him gave him a fierce smile, all desire and love and power.

The guy behind her ran his tongue down her neck as she came, silently shivering on the barstool. The couple left the hallway hand in hand while she was still shaking, and she didn't watch them leave. She could feel the man behind her, his hand still wrapped around her and his dick hard against her back. "Do you want to go over there?" He murmured in her ear, nodding toward the hallway.

She shook her head. "It wouldn't be the same now." She smiled at him over her shoulder and let him kiss her lips.

"Then I think I know another place that might work. Come with me?" She met his eyes for a second, then slid off the barstool and grabbed his hand. He grinned down at her and pulled her out the door with him. And she didn't watch anyone else for the rest of the night.

She was on the train again a few weeks later, the memory of last night's sex with her new boyfriend still sharp and clear in her mind. She remembered the feel of him inside her on his apartment balcony. She could sense his neighbor's eyes on her, watching as his hands pinched her nipples into diamond points, as her hand dove between her legs. Watching as she came, shaking and nearly collapsing but for his strong arms around her; as he came a moment later, his groan echoing down the side of the building.

It made her smile remembering it. It made the breath catch in her throat and her eyes darken as she sat on the subway. It was almost enough that she didn't notice the woman across the way watching her. The other woman's eyes were hungry, wanting something from her. She recognized that look and, all in an instant, knew what her answer had to be.

She pulled her face into a worried scowl and checked her watch, then her cell phone. She sighed impatiently. Her foot tapped on the floor, and when her stop came, she bolted out the door. She could see the other woman follow her, and she smiled as she dialed her boyfriend's number. She hoped the other woman would enjoy the show as much as they did.

BEAUTIFUL CREATURES

Kristina Wright

She was the most beautiful creature he had ever seen. Jon had watched her for over an hour as she sat at the hotel bar, nursing some tropical concoction the color of an ocean sunset. Her skin was pale and unblemished, and he wondered to what great lengths she went to keep it that way. Her bikini was royal blue, the matching sarong tied low around her hips. Her hair was a long, straight mane of several shades of blonde that were too perfect to have been God-given. He wondered if she was a natural blonde who simply emphasized her original color or if it was all an illusion. Whatever it was, it was beautiful, falling nearly to her waist in a shimmering curtain.

Ignoring the view of the pristine beach and emerald green ocean just beyond the wall of floor-to-ceiling windows, Jon kept his gaze on the beauty across from him. Her body had the hourglass curves of a 1940s pinup, her breasts plump and full above a narrow waist. Again he wondered if the look was natural or enhanced, though it didn't much matter, because the image, whether reality or fantasy, was stunning. He watched as she toyed with her glass, twisting the jaunty umbrella, running a flawless, French-manicured nail around the rim before slipping the same finger between her plump, delicate, pink lips. She could have been anywhere between twenty-five and forty, though he pegged her somewhere in the middle. Her look was bored and slightly jaded, suggesting she was well out of her twenties and that tropical paradise had long since lost its appeal. He was intrigued enough to move closer, circling around the nearly empty bar and taking the seat beside her. He could have left a stool between them, probably should have if he didn't want to scare her away, but he wanted to gauge her reaction.

Her response surprised him. He'd expected a smile, whether coy or polite, perhaps a nervous glance or an involuntary shift of her body away from him. Instead, she swiveled around to face him, her crossed leg bumping his bare knee. He noticed her toes matched her fingernails, the French manicure done to perfection on feet that would have made a foot fetishist swoon. He wasn't one, but even he could appreciate the delicate arch of her soles in their wedge sandals. The taper of her ankle and swell of well-defined calves and thighs only emphasized the pinup image, but there was something in her expression—something in the deep blue eyes that were only a shade or two lighter than her bikini—that suggested she was neither coy nor nervous.

"You've been watching me," she said. Her voice was cool, perfectly modulated, as if she'd had vocal training. "Now you're going to lay some smooth line on me about how beautiful I am and what a lucky man my husband is."

Jon hadn't missed the rock on her left ring finger; he just hadn't cared about it. Instead of retreating, as she clearly intended for him to do, he asked, "Is he?"

She blinked. She wasn't wearing makeup or, if she was, it was so artfully applied as to give her skin the appearance of unadorned beauty. Her tongue darted out to lick her bottom lip. "Is who what?"

"Is your husband a lucky man?"

He kept his voice as light and controlled as hers, not betraying even the hint of a smile. Again, the tip of her tongue darted over her bottom lip. He decided it was a nervous gesture, but the thought of her tongue gliding over the head of his cock had him rock hard.

"He used to think so." She said it without bitterness, but it was a little too flippant to ring true. She cared, she just didn't want anyone to know she cared. "I don't know now."

"What do you think?"

She shrugged, her shoulders raising enough to cause her breasts to sway. "Does it matter? He only cares about work—and that I am his to show off—perfect, presentable, untouchable to anyone but him."

He sensed she hadn't meant to say so much, but he pushed the issue anyway. "Is that what you want to be?"

Her laugh held the bitterness that was absent from her empty words. "What I want to be is fucked."

He still didn't smile. "Is that true?"

She ignored the question. "I don't know why I ordered this. I hate rum."

Jon didn't respond, waiting instead for her to steer the conversation to where she really wanted it to go. Despite her distaste for rum, she finished her drink in two long swallows. He watched her throat move and again imagined her mouth on him. The image was so vivid he could nearly feel her warmth. Her cold-as-ice exterior did nothing to cool his libido.

"I would love to get fucked," she said softly. She arched a pale eyebrow. "Are you interested?"

He didn't answer immediately. He sipped his beer, contemplating her offer. She was beautiful, but he needed more. He wasn't quite sure what the "more" was, only that he needed something besides the superficiality of physical beauty to entice him.

"Well, I guess that answers my question," she said, her expression closing down. She stood as if to leave.

"Sit down."

She hesitated, fingertips resting on the bar.

"I said, sit down."

She sat.

"Do you want me to fuck you?"

She licked her lips with her tongue again, making them glisten. "I don't . . . I—"

"It's a simple question," he said. "Do you want me to take you to my room and fuck you?"

She nodded, blonde hair shimmering.

"Gentle or hard?"

She swallowed convulsively. "Hard."

"You like it rough? Like to be tied up?"

She nodded again, blinking quickly.

"How rough?" He was trying hard to control his growing desire for the beauty in front of him, but the husky tone of his voice was betraying him. "How much?"

"As rough as you like," she said, lowering her eyes. "Tie me down. Use me."

The last had been said so softly that he nearly missed it. "What did you say?"

She looked up, meeting his steady gaze. "Use me."

Jon threw a ten on the bar and took her wrist. "Let's go."

She followed him wordlessly through the bar and across the wide expanse of the lobby to the bank of elevators. He pulled her inside an available elevator and pressed the button for the fifteenth floor. She stood beside him, gaze lowered, breathing a little erratic, a tiny smile on her pretty face.

"What's your name?" he asked as the elevator doors closed.

She looked up. "Pamela."

"Take your top off, Pamela."

The smile faltered and her eyes went wide. "What? Now?"

The elevator had passed the fifth floor and was climbing.

"Take your top off, now, before the elevator door opens, or I won't fuck you."

She stared at him, blue eyes startled, a blush creeping into her cheeks. Despite her dismay, there was something in her expression that let him know she was aroused at the thought of exposing herself at his command.

"Now, Pamela."

The elevator had passed the twelfth floor. Quickly, her eyes looking anywhere but at him, Pamela reached behind her neck and unknotted her bikini top. The material fell away, revealing her breasts. They were more impressive bare, the nipples dark and tight against her pale skin. He resisted the urge to reach out and pinch the tips between his fingers.

The top was still knotted in the middle of her back, and she hurriedly worked at it, but either the knot was too tight or her fingers were too clumsy, because the doors opened on the fifteenth floor before she could remove her top completely.

She was so intent on her task that she seemed unaware the elevator doors were open and that she risked exposure. Jon pressed the button to hold the doors open as she finally, almost triumphantly, handed him her bikini top.

"Too late," he said, letting her top fall from his fingers. "Too slow."

He heard her stumble out of the elevator behind him, but he ignored her as he strode down the hall.

"Wait, please," she said. "I'm sorry. I tried."

He stopped midstride and spun around to face her. She nearly bumped into him. "Put your top back on and go to your room, Pamela."

She looked at him with her sparkling blue eyes, tears glittering in her lashes. "Please, I'm sorry. Please. I need you."

He had no intention of letting her go at this point, because he needed her as badly as she needed him, but he had no intention of making it easy on her either. "What do you need, Pamela?"

"I need to get fucked. Please. Oh god, please."

"The next time I tell you to do something, you will comply immediately. Understand?" He emphasized his point by pinching one perfect nipple until she gasped. "Understand, Pamela?"

She nodded. "Yes, sir."

"Good." He turned, trusting she would follow. She did.

His hotel room was cool and dark, the blinds drawn against the harsh tropical sun. She followed him into the room and locked the door without being told. He crossed to the chair by the window and sat down.

"Come here," he said. He knew his tone was harsh, but he also knew she would respond to it. "Take off the rest of your clothes."

She slipped out of her shoes before walking toward him, undoing the sarong as she did. There was the briefest hesitation before she stripped off the bikini bottoms, but then she was naked. The lushness of her body was only emphasized by her nudity, the swell of her breasts balancing the fullness of her hips, the juncture of her softly rounded thighs meeting at the perfectly groomed pale blonde hair on her mound. He studied her, noting the few insignificant flaws on her otherwise perfect body: a birthmark on her hip, the two-inch-long scar across her right kneecap, the faint shimmer of two silvery stretch marks, one on each breast, as if she had developed too quickly during puberty.

"Tell me again what you want, Pamela."

As if sensing there was no turning back now, she took a deep breath. "I want to be fucked. Please."

"Good girl," he praised. "Now, touch yourself while you beg. Spread your legs and show me what a naughty girl you are."

She widened her stance, as if bracing herself for some physical onslaught. Sliding her right hand between her thighs, she fondled herself. "Please fuck me," she whispered.

"More."

Using both hands, she spread herself open before him, exposing the glistening folds of her vagina and her swollen, red clitoris. "I need to get fucked. Tie me down and fuck me. Do anything you want. Please."

It was something to watch a woman so stunning, so flawless, beg to be used. His cock throbbed, aching to penetrate her and give her what he desired. Jon stood up, pulling his belt through the belt loops on his pants. He doubled the belt in his hands.

"Hands over your head, Pamela."

Obediently, she stretched her arms up, her fingertips still glistening with her arousal. Her eyes shone with a combination of expectation and arousal, but there was no fear, no sense of apprehension. Quickly, before she could tense, he swung the belt at her breasts. The leather connected with a satisfying *whap,* followed by a squeaky gasp from her. She kept her arms in the air, even while a pale pink welt rose across the swell of her breasts.

"Good girl," he praised. "Keep your arms up."

She closed her eyes. "Yes, sir."

He swung the belt again and again, slapping her beautiful, pale tits until they were streaked with pink and red welts. She whimpered every time the belt connected with her delicate flesh, but she kept her arms in the air. Her only concession to the pain was when she laced her fingers together over her head, as if holding onto herself was the only way she could keep from protecting her tender breasts.

"Excellent. Stand up, Pamela."

It took her a moment to respond, her expression dazed. He knew she had slipped into her own little world, and it made him smile. When she stood in front of him, he ran his fingers along the welts he had raised on her skin. She shivered beneath his touch.

"Does it hurt?"

She hesitated, then shook her head. "I like the way it feels."

He pinched a nipple until she winced. "You like the pain."

"Yes," she breathed.

He nodded. "Bend over the bed. Legs spread. I want to see your wet cunt."

She leaned over the bed, hands braced on the mattress, legs spread. She was indeed wet, so wet he could see a trickle of moisture on the insides of her pale thighs. He ached to touch her, fuck her, but not yet. Soon, though. Very soon.

He whipped her ass and thighs harder than he'd whipped her breasts. He made her whimper and moan, her lower body twisting away from the contact with the belt, while her hands never moved from their place on the bed. He watched the pale skin streak and redden, and every three or four strokes, he asked, "More?"

Every time, her answer was, "Yes, please. More."

He knew she would take as much as he gave her. Knew instinctively that he could hurt her if he wasn't careful, because she was too far gone to know the difference between sexual pain and real injury. He stopped finally, sweat dripping down the small of his back—the sweat of exertion as well as arousal.

He put his hand on the small of her back and pushed her down on the bed. She collapsed without protest, as if she could barely stand. He sat on the edge of the bed and looped his belt around her wrists, pulling them together. She whimpered, but not in pain.

"Roll toward me on your back."

She complied, with difficulty. Once on her back, her hands pinned under her, he pulled the end of the belt up between her legs and over her crotch. She trembled at the contact.

"Did you like being whipped?"

"Yes, sir."

"Do you want to be fucked?"

She looked into his eyes. "Please, sir."

He yanked the end of the belt up between the lips of her cunt, pulling her shoulders back, "Good girl."

He stood, stripping beside the bed while she watched him. Her eyes lingered on his erection and her breath caught. Once he was naked, he stood there stroking himself while she watched.

"Beg."

"Fuck me, please, fuck me." She spread her legs, showing him how aroused she was, showing him what she needed. "Fuck me hard."

He knelt beside her on the bed. Then he slapped her between the thighs. She yelped, an expression of surprise and pain and lust on her face. He slapped her again, making a wet, smacking sound as his palm connected with her crotch.

"Please, please, please," she babbled. "Fuck me, fuck me. Fuck me!" He was on her then, inside her in one hard thrust, driving her halfway across the bed as he fucked her. She felt so good, so warm, wet and hot and tight. So fucking wet. Her arms were still pinned beneath her body, so he wrapped his hand in her hair and tugged, pulling her head back, kissing her lips, her neck, her shoulders.

She kept moaning and whimpering, words mingled in the sounds of her arousal. "Yes, fuck, god, fuck me, yes, hard, fuck me . . . " She sounded out of her mind with lust, and he knew the feeling.

He slowed his pace, unwilling to finish too soon. "I want you to come, Pamela," he said. "I want you to come on my cock. Do you know what I'm going to do when you come on my cock?" When she didn't immediately respond, he pulled her hair harder. "Pamela, do you know what I'm going to do?"

Her eyes fluttered open. "What?"

"I'm going to move up the bed and fuck your mouth until I come."

She moaned, mouth open, blue eyes staring into him. Then she came. He could feel her cunt tighten and spasm around him, and he pulled her hair tighter, fucked her harder. She wrapped her legs around him, arched her back as much as she was able, and pulled him into her wetness, moaning and whimpering as she came. She bucked against him, her cunt rippling along his cock as they rode out her orgasm together.

He pulled out quickly, while she was still coming, surging up her body until he straddled her breasts. With his hands clenched in her hair, he raised her head to his wet cock. "Suck," he gasped. "Suck me, Pamela."

She was still moaning when she took him between her lips. His cock glided across her tongue and bumped against the back of her throat. He started to pull back, not wanting to choke her, but she raised her head, and he felt her tongue ripple along the length of his cock. Then he was coming, coming hard, coming in forceful spurts into her mouth, down her throat. He clutched at her hair, unable to take his eyes off her as he came.

She sucked him long after he'd finished coming. Sucked him gently, her tongue lapping at the head of his cock as he softened. Finally, he pulled away and collapsed beside her on the bed. They were both gasping, panting, the sounds ragged and harsh over the soft whir of the air conditioner. His pulse throbbed in him, and where their hips touched, her skin felt hot, almost unbearably so.

Finally, after several long minutes, when the earth had stopped spinning and they were both breathing normally again, she whispered very softly, "Thank you."

"You're welcome, Pamela. It was my pleasure."

He rolled on his side and looked at her. She looked at him and smiled, as radiantly as any woman in love. He knew she wasn't in love, of course. At least not in love with him. She was in love with the sensation, the adrenaline, the pain. She was in love with the way he'd made her feel. He saw the tangled hair, the smudged eye makeup, the blotchiness on her neck and face where his beard stubble had irritated her skin, the red marks on her breasts that he knew were fainter than the welts on her ass and thighs and the puffy redness of her wet cunt. He saw her as she really was.

She was the most beautiful creature he'd ever seen.

IN THE NAME OF...

Isabella Gray

*I*t started with a black Sharpie pen, as we were lying in bed, drowsy and naked, watching TV. Theo and I had just finished making love, and he was basking in the well-deserved glow of his sexual prowess. "I wonder if I could write your name along the length of my cock," he mused. "Not like when I'm just getting out of the shower, but if my cock was really long and hard, right before we fuck."

I shrugged, and reached for the Sharpie on my end table. Sliding my hand between the sheet and our bodies, down his soft stomach to his cock, I nibbled on his ear. "Let's give it a try," I said.

It took a few tries to get it right. That first night, fumbling in the blue glow from the television, Theo used large, widely spaced lettering, and could only get half my name along the length of his cock. This initial defeat, however, did not deter him. It, in fact, made this whole thing a quest. Given his days as a teenager, when a good time was playing Dungeons & Dragons, there was nothing Theo loved more than a quest. He would persevere. I would humor him.

We revisited the subject a few days later, while I was in my office grading papers and Theo was sitting on the edge of my desk, playing with the pens and other detritus in my pencil cup. As I scribbled notes in margins and wrote "Great job," over and over, Theo unbuttoned his jeans and started jerking off. He found a red marker and pulled the cap off with his teeth. Once his cock had achieved what he deemed the appropriate level of length and rigidity, he began, in smaller script this time, to write my name along the length of his cock.

I paused, watching him over the top of the paper I was reading. "You're starting too far from the base," I muttered. He shook his head, but ultimately, I was right. By the time he reached the tip, giggling because the felt of the marker tickled, he had three letters left. I bit my lower lip and remained quiet, but I was thinking, "I told you so."

When I crawled into bed later that night, Theo was waiting with a blue marker, and in tiny script, he was writing my name on the opposite side of his cock. He accomplished his task, but the letters were so tiny that the overall effect was underwhelming. I kissed the tip of his nose before turning the lights out. "That's sweet, honey," I told him. He turned away from me, his shoulder muscles tight with irritation, his cock covered in blue and red ink. My man looked so sad and defeated that I closed the space between us, pressing my breasts against his back. I laid a line of kisses across his broad shoulders. He pretended to ignore me until I slid my hand up his chest, lightly squeezing his nipples between my fingers, throwing my left leg over his. Reluctantly, he turned toward me, his lips turned down in a small pout. I placed a kiss just left of his lips, then crawled on top of his chest. I slid my tongue between his lips and slowly lowered myself onto his cock and apologized properly.

Theo finally got it right when I took matters into my own hands. Straddling his thighs, and using a purple marker, my choice this time, I carefully wrote I S A B E L L A, with room to spare. When I was done, I took a moment to admire my handiwork, letting the ink dry, and then I wrapped my lips around the tip of Theo's cock, suckled softly and tasted a thin sliver of salty pre-cum. I worked my way down the shaft, humming so my lips vibrated until my lips were pressed against his groin. My throat muscles quivered in protest. Theo groaned gleefully. "I have no idea why this turns me on so much," he said. I tried to reply, but I was occupied and had long ago learned not to talk with my mouth full. He slid his hands through my hair and began rocking his hips back and forth. I could imagine the smug expression on his face as he stood there, the muscles in his thighs flexing against my cheeks as he made me swallow my own name.

Sooner than later, I was ready to up the ante. Writing my name on Theo's cock in different colors, across different areas, with different orientations, was well and good, but there wasn't a lot at stake. It was an exquisite secret that deserved an audience. Over coffee at a café near the campus where I taught, I stared across the table at Theo, running my sandaled foot up and down his calf. I wondered, not for the first time, what it would be like to see him with another woman. I wanted to see if I could go through with it, surrender that part of myself for a night, see if he would come back to me, see what he would look like thinking of me while fucking her. It was a dangerous idea—such things rarely end well, but I couldn't help myself.

"What are you thinking?" he asked.

I took a sip of my coffee, frowning at the bitter taste, and then I shared my suspect thoughts. Theo coughed and blushed, a light red rising from his neck up through the dirty blond roots at his forehead. He turned his head to the side in that endearing way he does when he's nervous and quickly looked around to make sure no one was listening.

"How do you come up with these ideas?"

I smiled, winked, and took another sip of coffee.

For a few weeks, Theo dismissed my idea, but my investment in the notion increased with each passing day. I began to look at every woman who crossed my path in a new light.

Theo always claimed that he didn't have a type, but even a casual inspection of the photo album where he kept pictures of his exes demonstrated a theme. It was obvious that he likes his women short, with dark hair, blue eyes, and just a touch of crazy. In restaurants, I would point out potential candidates, and Theo would either blush or roll his eyes. While we were having sex, I would offer suggestions from the eligible pool of our mutual acquaintances. When I was at the gym, hunched over the handrail of the elliptical trainer, trying not to pass out, I would stare down saucy minxes bending over yoga balls or stretching out on the mats, imagining what my husband's long body would look like bent over theirs.

Once I had found my "It Girl," I surprised Theo at work, slipping into his office and locking the door behind me. He grinned at me from behind his desk and loosened his tie. "I do love a working man," I drawled as I inched around his desk. Theo tapped his desk and closed the file he had been reading.

"It's a matter of approach."

"What is?"

"You know."

Theo leaned back in his chair, crossing his fingers behind his head. I stood behind him, massaging his shoulders, flicking my tongue against his ear. "I've found her and now it's only a matter of approach."

Theo opened his mouth, but I turned his chair around so he was facing me and pressed two fingers to his lips. "Shhh," I said. I dropped my coat, and, turning his chair as I walked, I hopped up on his desk, ignoring the papers and pens and the half-empty coffee mug. I slid my shoes off and perched my heels against his shoulders. "We should make the most of your lunch break." Theo arched an eyebrow and slid my skirt up around my hips. He hooked his fingers around the waistband of my G-string and slid them down until they were around one ankle. He slid those same fingers inside my cunt, and I gritted my teeth, wrapping my ankles around his neck and pulling him closer.

"Tell me I'm right," I said.

"Right about?"

Theo began licking my clit, twisting his fingers around in a languorous circle.

"Tell me I'm right that it's fucking hot that your boss is thirty feet away and your wife is spread open on your desk."

Theo groaned softly and stood, quickly unbuttoning his slacks. I slid my legs around his waist, and he placed his hands on my shoulders, thrusting his cock inside me, hard and deep.

"Tell me I'm right," I repeated.

Theo pulled me up, wrapping his arms around me, clasping the back of my neck as he kissed me, fucking me fast and dirty. I clenched my cunt muscles and sank my teeth into Theo's neck.

"You're going to leave a mark," he gasped.

I released my grip. "Tell me I'm right."

Theo's hips started rocking faster, and then he was coming, his breathing slightly ragged. "You're right," he said, over and over.

I held him inside me, enjoying the moment, enjoying the heat of his body and the shiver down my spine. "That's all I'm saying."

At home that evening, Theo sat down next to me on the couch and began tapping his fingers against his thigh. "So who is she?"

Her name was Francesca, and we had grown up in the same Italian neighborhood in Brooklyn. Back then, she wasn't much to look at, and admittedly, neither was I, but now, she was something else—deep olive skin, icy blue eyes, and jet black hair that cascaded down her back. Her features were sharp and angular in places, round and inviting in others. She wasn't perfect looking—her eyes set far apart, her lower lip slightly crooked—but she had a crafty smile, a loud laugh, and ass for days. These were all things Theo would enjoy, and I hoped she would be up for it—we were both recovering Catholic schoolgirls, after all. Francesca and I got together for drinks every couple weeks, so it wasn't extraordinary when I invited her to our place for dinner the following weekend.

I served veal saltimbocca, roasted green beans, a Caesar salad, and a good pinot noir we had picked up in the wine country last year. Francesca raved about my cooking, regaled us with a story about a disastrous blind date, and eventually noticed that neither Theo nor I were saying much. "What's up with you two?" she asked.

Theo looked at me, his eyes wide. I set my fork down. "Rather than be coy, I'll just come out with it. I'd love to watch my husband fuck you," I said. "A one-time thing."

Francesca coughed and refilled her wine glass. "You always were crazy, Izzy."

Theo reached for my hand, and I grasped his fingers, tightly. "Yes, but I'm not kidding."

Francesca nodded and traced the rim of her wineglass. "When?"

I cocked my head to the side. "Now?"

I sat in the armchair in the dark corner of our bedroom, wearing only my panties. I wanted it that way—to watch him without him watching me. I wanted him to forget I was there, lose himself until I found him again. There were candles on the end tables and the dresser—it would add to the mood, we had decided. Francesca brought her wineglass with her and sat on the edge of our bed, taking long, steady sips until there was none left. She unbuttoned her blouse, tossing it toward the doorway, and shimmied out of her jeans. In the dim light of the room, I felt a moment's panic as I took in her ample décolletage, her flat stomach, and the ass that wouldn't quit. Theo stood behind her, cupping her ass in his hands and squeezing. Then Francesca slid toward the center of the bed, crossing one leg over the other as she leaned back. Theo undressed quietly and brought me the Sharpie, hesitating as he handed it to me. I pressed the palm of my hand against his heart, then wrote my name on his cock. I wrote slowly and carefully, pressing the marker firmly into his skin. He leaned down and kissed my forehead, then I turned him around, and sank into the softness of my chair. I couldn't watch him walk away. I closed my eyes and ignored the tightness in my chest.

Theo stood at the end of the bed and shyly crawled up until he was kneeling between Francesca's legs.

"I can't believe we're about to do this," she said.

Theo looked back in my direction. "Neither can I."

He slid his hands between her calves, sliding them up to her inner thighs as he spread her legs. He kissed her navel and dragged his tongue along the undersides of her breasts. When he wrapped his mouth around each of Francesca's nipples, sucking loudly, she grabbed the sheets beneath her, drawing her fingers into loose fists. Blindly, Theo reached for the end table, where earlier he had set a condom. He ripped the package open with his teeth, and Francesca sat up on her elbows, helping him slide the condom over his cock. She smiled at him, her shoulders relaxing, and slid a long, manicured finger into Theo's mouth. He groaned—he loves that sort of thing—and holding Francesca's wrist, he pulled each of her fingers into his mouth one at a time, before placing a kiss on the inside of her wrist.

I leaned forward in my seat, my chest growing tighter still, my throat dry, my eyes curiously damp, and my pussy on fire.

Francesca sighed and slowly rolled over on her stomach, smiling back at Theo—an unexpected, surprising, and perfect erotic gesture. She arched her back, her perfect ass high in the air. Theo slapped it lightly. Francesca wiggled. "Don't be shy," she said. Theo splayed both hands across Francesca's ass, sliding his thumbs between her ass cheeks, before slapping her ass again, harder this time. "That's what I'm talking about," she encouraged. Theo alternated between smacking Francesca's ass and massaging her backside with his fingers until her skin was bright red and her thighs were quivering.

She looked at Theo over her shoulder, and he paused long enough to kiss her—a crushing, sloppy, hungry kiss that forced me to look away. Francesca reached for him, and he worked his cock inside her, my name sliding into another woman's cunt one letter at a time. I could hear how wet she was. The bitch was enjoying this. So was I. I also entertained the idea of each of the letters of my name circulating through her bloodstream and wrapping themselves around her throat, constricting with each breath and moan until she went silent.

At first, Theo teased Francesca, filling her to the hilt, waiting, sliding all the way out, rubbing the tip of his cock along the curve of her pussy before filling her again. He turned to me, smiling, and tapped his heart and pointed to me. Francesca's legs spread wider. She rocked back against my husband, urging him to stop playing games. "Fuck me," she said harshly. Theo grabbed hold of her waist and shoved his cock forward, deep and hard. They found a rhythm, the two of them, their bodies slapping together wetly, then coming apart, and back together again. Theo grabbed her hair and pulled Francesca's head back, her neck muscles straining. He slid his tongue in her mouth, groaning, the sound, I imagined, echoing into her chest and waiting there. He fucked her harder, the sound of her desire growing slicker, looser, my name reaching further into her body. I sat perfectly still, my jaw aching. My teeth had been clenched for some time. They looked good together—his pale skin against her darker tones, his leanness where she was round, their thighs pressed together, the undulation of their bodies moving in time, their eyes closed, mouths open. I felt myself disappearing into the walls of our home, the rest of the world falling away. And I felt the painful and intense pleasure of watching something I was not supposed to see. I hated myself for it.

"You like this, don't you?" Theo asked, punctuating each word with a slap on her ass. "You like it dirty."

"God, I do."

Francesca began moaning louder until she was practically shouting, her head and her long mane of black hair flying from side to side. She whispered, "I can't believe I'm going to come." She shrieked once and buried her head in a pillow, her body trembling. Theo kept fucking Francesca, steadily stroking her pussy with his cock. "I'm not stopping until I'm done," he said, lifting her hips higher. He fucked her until he came, his ass clenching as he gave her one final thrust, so hard that she slid up the bed, her head bouncing against the headboard. He lay on top of her for an uncomfortably long time, then rolled off when Francesca pushed him away and jumped out of bed. The room was filled with an awkward silence. I finally allowed myself to breathe deeply and pulled my knees to my chest, hugging myself.

Francesca started collecting her clothes. "I don't want to overstay my welcome," she said. "But that was wonderful."

Theo smiled and wrapped a towel around his waist. Once Francesca had dressed and composed herself, he walked her to the door. When he returned to the bedroom, I had blown out all the candles and was standing near the window, watching Francesca drive away. I heard the snap of Theo removing his condom and tossing it into the trash can. I couldn't look at him—afraid of what I might see there—not even when he wrapped his arms around me from behind, nor when he whispered, "I love you."

I reached back and squeezed his thigh. "I know."

"Are you angry?" he asked.

I shook my head, swallowing hard.

"You sure?"

I took his hand and pulled it around my waist, sliding it beneath the waistband of my panties. He parted my pussy lips with two fingers. I hissed, my clit throbbing and jealous and angry. I felt my wetness slide around his fingers while he stroked my clit. "What does this tell you?" I asked.

CHEESY BOOTS

L. Elise Bland

"*M*istress," the submissive mumbled into the phone during his initial interview. "I know this wasn't covered in your questions, but I do have one small request."

"Okay, what is it?" I asked, assuming my answer would be "No." There are certain things that clients ask for that I simply won't do or don't care to do, and these are always the interests that are brought up at the end of the conversation—sex, public humiliation that would get us arrested, brown showers, and worse. "Your question had best not offend the Mistress," I warned.

"Oh no," he stuttered. "It's really quite innocent. You see, I am into trampling. Not on my body, but on food. I would love to see you in your tallest, cruelest leather boots, the heels and toes smashing away at, say, a McDonald's hamburger. Or even better, a McDonald's cheeseburger with peanut M&M's on top. You would force me to watch you as you pulverize my dinner into a crunchy, greasy mess. And then you could make me lick it off the bottom of your filthy boots!"

He began to hyperventilate into the phone, so I cut the interview short. Weird, I thought. But fun. I was up for the challenge. I made a note of his special interest, intrigued over this refreshing new breed of foodie. After all, I was so tired of the pretentious food scene in my city—the snooty wine tastings, the overly analytical dinners, the endless debates over olive oil. Sometimes it seemed like everybody was missing the point, but here was a guy who was really ready to have fun with food, even if it was junk food. I thought about telling him to bring his own snacks to the session, but then decided to surprise him instead. After all, how predictable would it be to force-feed him exactly what he wanted?

My fridge is always stocked with an arsenal of exotic cheeses. It just happened that on that certain day, I had a gem of a cheese waiting to be shared—Vacherin Mont d'Or from the French Jura Mountains, also known simply as Vacherin. Best of all, this cheese was unpasteurized. *"Au lait cru,"* the cheese-monger had whispered to me when I bought it. "Raw, young, and ready to eat." Somehow, an illegal cheese, aged less than the requisite sixty days for its type, had made it under the customs radar and straight into my shopping basket.

The Vacherin is a gorgeous treasure, presenting itself in a round chipwood box complete with a lid, almost like a jewelry box. The cheese itself is something to behold. Inside is a soft, decadent cream that is held stable by a band of spruce bark, all topped off with a colorful, wrinkled crust. Vacherin looks warm and inviting, but given its smell, it is a far cry from traditional comfort food. This mountain cheese is sometimes popped into the oven to make the inside even creamier and more aromatic. Touch the top with a spoon and it cracks like a crème brûlée.

Before my guest arrived, I had already delved into my hot cheese pie and spooned out some of the gooey mess for my own pleasure. I had had my fill—as much as I could manage to eat while wearing such a tight leather corset—but there was still over half a wheel left, which was plenty to play with. I left it sitting in the oven, where it would stay warm until the time was right.

We had a good first session. My new sub showed up right on time, and we went straight into play. He was a handsome man in his fifties with graying hair, a well-kept body, fur all trimmed. He went through the protocol with ease and assurance, though I could tell he was the restless type who wouldn't fare well in a submissive role for over an hour. We did a lot of the usual—flogging, spanking, bondage on the cross, cock and ball torture and clamps. As wild as it all may sound to a layperson, the bulk of our session was nothing extraordinary. In fact, I can't remember much about him except for the frightened look on his face when I announced, "Eat."

I stuck the toe of my thigh-high lace-up leather boot (the exact boot he had requested) into the mysterious chipwood box. Aromas of leather and pasture wafted through the dungeon.

"Come closer," I said, grinding the toe deeper into the crust. He glanced nervously from side to side, probably searching for his Big Mac and trustworthy fries. To frighten him even more, I took my stiletto heel and stirred the fragrant cream, creating a long wet strand that extended from the tip of my stiletto back into the box like a stalagmite. Then I carefully leaned back on my stool and ordered: "Get over here, boot boy. I said 'Eat.'"

With hesitation, he crawled toward me, not quite sure what this foreign cream on my boot was. Once his nose was within a foot of the cheese, his face puckered into a highly unattractive scowl.

"That smells like feet!" he protested. "I have a food fetish, not a foot fetish."

"Hush that fuss," I said. "It's just cheese. Get down there and lick it off." I don't take kindly to bossiness, especially from submissives who have already made such extravagant requests.

"But where's my Big Mac? With normal cheese?" he whined. "I don't want to eat that nasty cheese!"

"What do you think I am? A drive-through?" I asked, kicking my boot out in anger. The warm Vacherin was dripping off my stiletto heel, waiting to be caressed and appreciated. At twenty dollars a pound, it was not going to waste. "This cheese is rare," I told him. "So rare that it is illegal in the States. Do you realize how lucky you are? How dare you even think of refusing my precious cheese? Lick it, you ungrateful slave!"

"Red!" he called. In the BSDM community, there are safe words—code words, as it were. When someone wants to stop an activity altogether, they say "red." To slow down, "yellow." He called "red," the firmest of all protests. As a responsible Domme, I respect all safe words, but I wasn't done messing with his head just yet.

"Okay, 'red' means we stop the session now," I said, my boot still playing in the box of cheese. "And you probably had some expectations of release, right? Oh, maybe of entertaining yourself in my regal presence at the end?"

"Yes ma'am," he muttered, looking down at his still-hard cock. His better half was begging for him to eat the cheese. "Go for it, bro. Don't do this to me! Just lick the damn boot!" His cock was screaming, pointing at me, panicked and braced like a rabid one-eyed animal.

"If we stop now," I said, "you will stuff your little mister right back into your pants and leave, hard or not. It's all the same to me. Eat or go."

I ran the boot up and down the side of his cock until his eyes watered slightly, and then gave his erection a playful kick. It bounced a couple of times and sprang right back into place. His nervousness made him more attractive and, quite frankly, saved him. Had I not seen that glimpse of true desperation in his face, I would have grabbed my money and sent him packing. Game over.

"If you're too chicken to eat this fine cheese," I told him, "then get over here and wipe it off." I tossed a rag at him, and once my boot was clean, I headed back into the playroom. Although I hardly knew the naked man on my floor, I could tell from the interview that he liked to lick. I dug through my box of dildos until I found the perfect toy, my blue-and-white swirled double-headed dildo. With its G-spot curve and a little nub perfectly designed to tease the clit, this toy was guaranteed to entertain, at least on my end, and that's what mattered the most. "Whatever the Mistress wants," the subs repeat to me mindlessly, as if this mantra should please me. They have no idea what the Mistress really wants, and when they find out, they don't quite know what to do.

"Okay, Mr. Picky Eater, close your eyes. I have something to whet your appetite," I announced, sitting back down. He knelt before me, cock still hard, eyes darting back and forth beneath his eyelids as if in a dream state. I pulled my thong over to one side and, with slippery ease, guided the toy deep inside me. Its firm curves immediately hit all the right spots, sending a hot chill down my legs and straight through my boots. On the one end, my pussy clamped, and on the other, my hard-on sprang up to mirror his. Swords drawn, we were ready for a duel.

"Open your eyes," I commanded, and when he did, there I was sitting before him with my thigh boots spread, stroking a sizable blue dick in between. With each movement, my end of the toy snaked up and around inside of me. Spellbound, he watched and waited. I licked my fingers and moistened my cock, making sure to swirl my long red nails around the head oh so sensually so that he might imagine I was actually touching him. But my gentleness didn't last long. With a firm hand, I gripped the shaft of my cock and gave it a good choking, a thrashing so violent I nearly yanked an orgasm right out of myself. I know my blue toy wasn't a "real" cock, but under my hand, it felt like one—skin tightening, head bulging. I was harder and hornier than any man ever could be. I pulled his head in between my knees.

He feigned a grimace, and then his inner drama queen emerged. "No, please don't make me lick that! Anything but that! No, no, no!" he whimpered, but "no" is not a safe word. When his mouth opened to form the final "no," I rammed my cock through his lips, and he didn't bother to spit it out. Instead, he launched into a flamboyant display of sucking, licking, and even vibrating my toy with his tongue. I could tell it wasn't his first time.

"Oh, so you'll eat dick but you won't eat cheese?" I asked, grabbing his thick gray hair. "Exactly how hungry are you?" By that time, I was so turned on I had almost—almost, I say—forgiven him for his cheese faux pas.

Without pausing for a breath, he worked pure magic with his mouth. I was so impressed that I let my guard down. I leaned back and even allowed him to touch my cock, and since he was, as many men are, probably a frequent masturbator, I knew I could count on him to do me right. After decades of practice, he knew just how to hold a dick, how to pull it and how to make it feel long and strong. Inside and out, my cock was raging, and I felt myself slipping out of Domme mode. Maybe it was the cheese, maybe it was the sub, maybe it was the distant intimacy, but whatever it was, it made me come. And when I did, my long tall boots shot out in straight black lines and knocked over the box of cheese. I didn't tell him I had actually come. It was really none of his business, but the spilled cheese most definitely was.

Postorgasm, my head was clear again. There was my prized cheese languishing on the floor. There was my new sub, now playing with his own cock—and without permission. Although still warm and wet, I was chilling as fast as the spilled Vacherin on the cold tile floor.

"Look what you've done now, you greedy little slave!" I said, waving my blue dildo in the air. "Not only did you refuse my cheese, but now you have completely ruined it!" I slammed my boot angrily onto the box and trampled it with all my might, piercing it with my stilettos and tormenting it with my sharp leather toes. I finished off my temper tantrum with an angry dance of tarantella. His eyes widened, and his hand withdrew from his cock. Most likely he had never encountered a Cheese Mistress before.

"How dare you make a mess of my cheese!" I shouted. "And to think I was going to take pity on you and let you get off today."

"Mistress, please . . . "

"No," I said, crossing my arms and tapping my cheesy boot. "Or should I say 'red?' It's my turn to call 'red' on you!"

"But Mistress, may I please have a second chance? Please?"

I looked down at him. His motives were obvious. "Why should I let you?" I asked.

Then he began to speak, more than he had during the entire session, or even the phone interview. "Because your cruel boots are so beautiful. Because I am not worthy to lick such soft leather or taste such fine cheese. Because now you have made me understand the true price of quality. I will never eat trampled Big Macs and M&M's again. Only cheese. Only for you."

Now he was speaking my language. I sat back down on the stool and stretched out my long boot. "So eat already."

With that final order, I guided his head down to my sticky, stinky boot and helped him acquire a taste for the French mountains—sharp and spiky, with a very creamy finish.

TRUCK STOP CINDERELLLA

Lillian Ann Slugocki

*G*racie Angelique DuBois drove to work that morning with the top down on her baby blue convertible, taking the country highway instead of the interchange and singing along to "Love to Love You Baby" at the top of her lungs. It was the beginning of a fine summer day, the sun just beginning its slow ascent over the ridges of the mountains. She was sure this was going to be her last summer slinging hash at Riddley's Truck Stop on Route 27. She knew she was meant for better things. The fact is that Gracie Angelique DuBois had all kinds of dreams: cosmetology, modeling, or even cocktail waitressing at a fancy bar in New York or L.A. Gracie was the kind of woman who believed in the power of rainbows and stilettos.

In the meantime, she always wore her tightest jeans to work, and her white high heels—even though, like Cinderella, she often went home barefoot because her feet hurt so bad. She did a survey once; she wore sneakers during a shift and averaged $15 an hour, but when she wore high heels, she averaged $25 an hour. It was hard to argue with the economics of that equation. Sex appeal and high heels provided a roof over her head. Gracie wasn't a stupid woman—she knew she was considered trailer trash, but she wore that as a badge of honor. Held her head high. Her mama and her mama's mama were trailer trash. But honestly, there wasn't anything trashy about her trailer. She had real wood floors, glass bookcases, and bright yellow curtains on the tiny windows in the living room that she had sewn herself. She got the idea from a magazine, using pillowcases and brass rings, and she thought, *Now isn't that clever.*

Her bedroom, which she laughingly called "the love nest" to her friend Sandy, was her pride and joy. Instead of blinds or shades, she hung a pink silk shawl she found at a swap meet so that it covered both windows. Any light that shone into the room was pink light, and Gracie knew this was very sexy. Her bed was covered with pink satin pillows with tiny bows across the front, and on her fake white marble night table was a crystal lamp and pictures of her mama and her mama's mama. Gavin, her last lover, had said, "Damn, Gracie, all you women are sexy."

She laughed out loud at this—Gavin McFitch was slight and very shy, with cornflower blue eyes, but his cock was a monster. He couldn't kiss, and he didn't eat pussy, but lord, she didn't care. She pulled herself together as she turned left into the parking lot of the truck stop. No sense thinking those kinds of thoughts now, not before she began her shift. Gracie was a true professional, and although it was a fact that every man in the diner dreamed of fucking her, she would never allow it, because it gave her an edge. Again, it was hard to argue with the economics of all those men who came back to the diner again and again, always hoping for a chance.

Grace adjusted the straps on her blue silk brassiere in the car. Were her boobs getting bigger? She hoped so. Her nipples were certainly erect. She scanned the parking lot and saw that all her regulars were there. The big rig over in the south corner of the lot belonged to Vinnie, a long-haul trucker from New Jersey who liked his burgers rare and his coffee lukewarm. To the right was a rig from North Dakota—Timmy was a strange man, but his biceps were girl heaven. Despite her very strict rules, she often found herself fantasizing about running her tongue—oh, never mind. Timmy was a nice man with a nice wife. She smiled when she saw Gus's beat-up Lincoln Continental. He was an old timer who lived ten miles down the road in a tiny little town called Possum. She just loved his crinkly brown eyes; sometimes they made her melt. Yes, all her boys were here today.

All eyes were on her as she sashayed across the parking

lot. Sometimes it's good to be queen—even if your kingdom is a diner in the middle of nowhere. The bells over the door rang sweetly as she made her entrance,

Timmy called out, "Well, now if it ain't our very own Cinderella, exactly ten minutes late to the ball."

Gracie replied, "Get off my ass, Timmy, unless you mean business."

The other men roared with good-natured laughter as she continued on into the kitchen. She knew what they were thinking: *Goddamn but that Gracie sure is* wild. *No telling what she might say to you.*

Oh yes, she was positive it was going to be a great day. Even Jeremiah, the cook, was smiling. She tied her white apron tight across her tiny waist, freshened her coral lipstick, combed her long blonde hair, and picked up her pad and pencil.

She licked the tip of the pencil because she'd seen other women do it in the movies, and she liked the look of it—thought it was sexy. Just then she heard the bells over the door ring. She poked her head out and saw three strangers enter, each one more handsome than the other. *Whew doggie,* she thought, *I'm gonna make some money from these boys.* She felt her nipples harden in anticipation. The key, she calculated, was to play it cool with them at first, practically ignore them. Circle around the tables a couple of times, give them ample opportunities to check out her tits and ass. When she sauntered out into the diner, she went straight over to Gus, who was sitting by the window.

"Hey, good looking," she cooed, "How's my favorite customer?"

Gus looked up at her adoringly, while she noted, with no small amount of satisfaction, that she had everyone in the room's attention, including the strangers'. In fact, the tallest of the three, wearing a red flannel shirt, was fixated on her tits, so she shot him back a long smoldering look.

Gus replied, "Just waiting to see my baby so I can start my day."

"Aw, Gus," she laughed, turning back to him, "that's so sweet; let me get a refill for your coffee."

"Hey, miss," the red flannel shirt called out, "we'd sure appreciate if it you'd stop over here with the coffee. We're mighty thirsty."

She turned and coolly responded, "Sure," even though her heart was beating faster than a rabbit in heat. Not only was he taller than any man in the room, his hair was blacker than a thundercloud in August, and his legs were like tree trunks. *Gracie,* she admonished herself, *you will not imagine those legs spread out in your pink sheets.* But *her* legs sure were shaking as she crossed behind the counter and grabbed the pot of coffee. She was about to turn around when she felt someone behind her. It was the stranger, whispering in her ear.

"Don't turn around," he breathed.

"I won't," she managed to say.

"You like me," he continued, "I know you do. I've seen other woman look at me the way you just did, and I know you make a practice of not fucking your customers. I know that you think that it gives you an edge, but I don't care about your edge, you forget about that—"

"—it's forgotten," she stammered.

"—because I'm going to fuck you before this day is over. Do you understand?"

"I do."

"Me and the boys," he continued, "are gonna eat our break-fast, scrambled eggs, toast, and coffee. Simple. Then I gotta go up the road, hundred miles or so, but I will be back. And you'll be waiting."

"I'll be waiting," Gracie agreed.

"Good," he said, "And to seal the deal, I want you to go into the bathroom and take off your bra—"

"My what?"

"Just do it."

Gracie turned to face him, looked deep into his sea-green eyes, and asked, "What's your name, cowboy?"

He replied, "The bra, Gracie. Take it off."

How did he know her name? She didn't care. She hollered to Jeremiah that she was taking a break and walked light-headed into the ladies'. As if hypnotized, she pulled off her tank top, leaned over, and unfastened her bra. Her breasts spilled out—she almost orgasmed right then and there but held herself back. She rolled it up, walked out, and handed it over to the stranger. He smiled slowly and, never taking his eyes off her, pulled back the waist of the blue jeans, and shoved it down deep, between his legs. Then he leaned over and whispered in her ear, "I'll be back at six. Make sure you're here, or," he threatened, "you'll never see your brassiere again." Then he flicked her pussy with his middle finger. He walked away, slowly and deliberately.

Her face aflame with both arousal and embarrassment, she placed his order and deliberately ignored him the rest of the time he was there. She flitted around her regulars, Gus and Timmy and Vinny. The poor boys were so jealous! She poured coffee and cracked jokes, all the while terribly, terribly self-conscious of her breasts bobbing up and down, right and left, like waves upon a storm-tossed ocean. She knew her pussy was dripping wet. But what could she do? A tall, dark stranger had her brassiere in his underpants and had promised to return at nightfall to fuck her senseless.

Hours later, after everyone left and she was refilling the salt and pepper shakers, she fantasized about who he was and how he was going to do it to her. *Maybe,* Gracie mused, *he's really a millionaire businessman with a private jet, and he's going to cover me in chocolate sauce and whipped cream and eat me up like an ice cream sundae. Or maybe he's a cowboy, and he's going to whisk me away to his ranch in the mountains and fuck me in a field of wildflowers til every muscle is my body aches. Or maybe,* she thought, *we'll do it down and dirty doggie-style in the back seat of my baby blue convertible.* She couldn't decide which scenario she liked best.

As the sun went down on the tiny roadside diner on Route 27, Jeremiah emerged from the kitchen, wiping his hands on his apron. "Well, that's it, Gracie, another day, another dollar."

"You got it," she replied, even though she knew nothing could be farther from the truth. The truth was she counted her tips and found an unbelievable $350. The most she had ever made on a shift was $150.

But that was the least of it. Innocently, she said to him, "Go on home, I got a few things to do. I'll lock up."

Jeremiah, who was no fool, said as he was leaving, "You come into work every day with your titties bouncing around like that and you'll be a millionaire before you know it."

"I'm with you on that one."

Once he was gone, she locked the door. After all, the sun was setting, and this was still wild country. She sat down to wait. It was ten minutes to six. He should be here soon. She waited and waited; she redid her lipstick, refilled the ketchup bottles, and then it was six thirty. The sun slid behind the mountains, and her elation turned to sadness. Her tall, dark stranger wasn't going to return—that only happened in fairytales. Shoot, she gave some fool pervert her brassiere for nothing. *Well, not for nothing exactly,* she reminded herself. She was a rich woman. The money in her tip jar was exactly half of what she needed to get out of town. Well, fine. That's how the cookie crumbles.

She slipped her high heels back on and turned off the lights in the diner as she prepared to leave. It was a twenty-minute drive back to her trailer park, so she went into the ladies' and almost fainted. He was there. The stranger. Leaning against the white cracked porcelain sink. He said, "It's about time, Gracie."

Her nipples were suddenly so erect it was almost painful.

"How did? Didn't you?" But she couldn't finish her train of thought; the words died on her lips. Because it didn't make sense. Hadn't he left eight hours ago? Hadn't she locked the door after Jeremiah left? Was she dreaming?

"We don't have time for explanations, darling. We only got time for this," and then he grabbed her, bent her over, and kissed her full and long and hot on her lips. She wanted to protest; she really did. Nobody kept her waiting. She was Gracie Angelique DuBois. Panting, she pushed him away.

"Hey mister, I waited a long time for you."

"You want me and you want me bad. Admit it."

"I guess," she replied resentfully. No man ever got the best of *her*. She had to keep her edge, stay in control.

"I got your number, Gracie, so you might as well give it up." Here his voice became softer than honey poured on blue silk; almost a whisper. "So get your ass over here." Then he unzipped his blue jeans and slowly, slowly pulled her brassiere out. "Get your ass over here, and put this on. Take everything else off. Except the shoes. You keep those heels on."

It was so hot in the room that the sweat was pouring down both their faces. But it didn't matter, she wasn't going to give in. She was going to strip whenever and wherever she wanted. So she started slowly, defiantly. She said, "I'll stay right where I am, thank you."

When all her clothes lay in a heap at her feet except her high heels, he pulled off his boots, stripped out of his jeans, walked up to her, and lovingly put her brassiere back on. He said, "Gracie Angelique DuBois, what am I doing to do with you?

She asked him, "How do you know my name?"

In response he twirled her around, forced her up against the wall, and fucked her from behind. She felt herself opening up to him, then devouring him. Their juices dripped down her legs, pooled in her shoes, and she was afraid they might slip and fall. But he didn't care, he entered her so deeply, so forcefully, she briefly saw stars. Then he suddenly stopped. Pulled out.

"No, no, no," she moaned, "put it back in."

"Beg me," he said.

"Baby, I'm begging you, pleading, put it back in."

"What will happen if I don't?" he asked, running his hands over her breasts.

"I'll die. I will. Now please."

She reached behind her, grabbed his cock and put him back inside of her.

"Never forget, darling," he breathed into her ear, as he started to move inside her again, "Never forget that I know who you are." Then he really started to fuck her, the way she liked it, not like the other farm boys, awkward and clumsy—but slow and hard and deliberate, each stroke masterful, finding her G-spot each time, like a hunter taking aim and never missing. Then, when she was breathing hot and heavy, he went faster and faster. The world started to spin, the lights flickered, and at that exact moment, he pulled out.

"Are you crazy," she moaned through parched lips. "Have you lost your fucking mind?"

But he interrupted her. "Suck me off, baby. Suck me off like I know you can." He pushed her head down to his cock, glistening in the fluorescent lights, slippery with her juices, and slipped her lips over the gleaming tip. Then she slowly licked the shaft, down to his balls, round and round with her tongue, enthralled with the power she had to reduce this cowboy to tears, because yes—he was crying. He was right, Gracie loved to suck cock— always had, always will. There was just something about that stiff slick rod in her mouth that pleased her enormously. When it started to pulse inside her, she knew he was about to come, so she lay down on the cold blue tiles of the bathroom floor and said, "Do me, baby."

WHEN SHE GOT HOME THAT NIGHT, she took a long hot shower, used up the last of her lavender bath gel, toweled off, and then, still naked, poured herself a glass of wine. Her face was glowing and her cunt ached—the truth of the matter is that Gracie was a very happy woman that night. She found $2,000 balled up inside of her brassiere, and if that made her a prostitute, lord, she didn't care. She finished her glass of wine and began taking down the yellow curtains in her living room. She was moving to New York City, and that's all that mattered.

THE CHANGE OF LIFE

Tenille Brown

*S*he looks likes she's been kissed, Doll thought as she stood in front of Bridgette outside the large brick building that would be her daughter's home for the next year. It was the way Bridgette's lips naturally puckered as she got ready to speak, the way her hair fanned out around her head when the wind blew. Of course, she probably had been kissed. In fact, it was probably that boy Thomas, from down the street.

But even if by chance Bridgette hadn't been kissed, she would be soon enough. She was a college girl now, and Doll would have much more than Thomas to worry about. There would be new experiences for Bridgette. There would be missed classes and booze. There would be drugs and boys and men.

"Want me to walk back up with you?" Doll asked.

"I'll be fine, Mama. You guys got me all moved in. You can go on back home, now." Bridgette touched her on her elbow.

"I know, but if you wanted me to help you get the comforter on your bed or stack your shoes, I could help with that." She was reaching now.

"The girl's gonna be fine, Doll, goddamn. Loosen the apron strings and let's go." Bernard's voice boomed behind them.

Doll's fingers grabbed at the seam of her pants. This kind of talk was what she was going back home to—and without her baby girl.

She handed Bridgette the bag lunch she had put together—fried chicken, sweet potatoes, and pound cake—though she knew she would just run out to McDonald's or something anyway.

Bridgette opened the bag and peered inside. "You're so country, Mama."

Doll laughed, though she wanted to cry. She leaned forward and kissed her baby girl on the forehead, though she wanted to snatch her up, throw her in the car, and take her back home. She stepped back, took hold of Bernard's hand, and waved goodbye.

IT ONLY TOOK BERNARD FIVE THRUSTS and three minutes to grunt and roll onto his side of the bed. Doll's hands clenched into fists at her sides, her lip folded under her teeth in dissatisfaction. She wanted to shake him awake, demand that he try again and get it right this time.

But what would she say exactly?

Bernard, honey, if you don't mind, could you kiss me a little more, and when you touch me, could you not stop at my breasts? And honey, if it's not a problem, could you let me get on top this time, do things my way?

But she couldn't say those things to the man who had been nothing but good to her, whom she had led to believe was satisfying her every need for the past eighteen years.

Maybe she had been foolish enough to believe that something would change, that after Bridgette left, sex would no longer be regulated to Saturdays after seven with the TV on and Bernard on top. That he would creep up behind her in the kitchen, ravish her over the sink while she was doing dishes, or lift her up onto the washing machine while the spin cycle was running. Maybe it was too late for things to change. Maybe this was what her life had become.

So when Bernard awakened and eased up behind her and whispered in her ear, "Wasn't that nice?" Doll rolled to one side, clasped her hands under her head, and spoke the words she *could* say.

"Bernard, I'm leaving."

DOLL STOOD ON HER FRONT PORCH, which was attached to her half of the duplex where she paid her own rent every month. She was admiring the pot of lilies she had brought home from work. She didn't feel much like fooling with them, but they kept her hands busy and her mind from wandering. Her mind wandered a lot lately since she had more time, seeing as how Bernard had finally stopped begging her to come home and Bridgette was still pissed about it and barely spoke to her at all.

It used to seem like Bernard never would get used to her being gone, calling every other day, stopping by the shop just to bring her mail when it wasn't even on his way to work. To hear him tell it, she was just going through "the change," but Doll had assured him that wasn't the case. Now things had changed; with the divorce almost final, he barely called at all, and she only saw him in town now and then.

Doll exhaled. She couldn't decide if she liked the lilies better in the front window or in the kitchen on the table. She debated to herself a minute or two and then decided it would be best to look at it from outside.

She stood barefoot on the wooden porch, cocking her head and studying the placement of the lilies. She heard the bustle of her neighbor, the man who had been renting the other half of the duplex for the past two months. The sound of his boots on the hardwood floor and the occasional clash of dishes in the sink were the only evidence of his presence.

The table, yes, they would look better there. Doll started back inside when she heard the creak of the screen door a few feet to her left.

"Evening, ma'am," came his voice, soft and deep. He nodded and smiled, one hand on the front door.

His hair covered his scalp in crisp, shiny curls. His temples were accented in gray, as was his freshly trimmed mustache. The pale blue shirt and crisp brown slacks looked good against his ginger-colored skin.

"Evening," Doll said, forcing herself to stand straighter, smile, and tug at her own hair, barely visible beneath her bright yellow scarf. She was suddenly aware of how plain she must look in her white t-shirt and baggy sweatpants.

He pointed toward the window at the soft, white petals. "You grow 'em?"

"No," Doll said, "Stella does, down where I work. I cut them, though." She didn't know what to do with her hands, where to put them when she wanted to reach out and touch his skin.

"I see. Then you must be . . . "

"Oh," she said, quickly wiping her moist palms across her pants. "I'm Doll. Doll Johnson." She extended her hand, and he took it, squeezing briefly, then letting go.

"Pleasure to meet you, Doll. I'm Manuel." He nodded and smiled, tipping his hat and placing it on his head before he walked away.

Doll repeated softly, "Man-*well.*" She stood inhaling the scent that lingered behind him and gave one last look at the lilies. *Yes,* she decided, her arms folded tightly across her chest, *they looked a lot better in the window.*

DOLL HURRIED TOWARD THE BATHROOM, leaving her clothes in a trail behind her as she discarded them. She plugged the drain and turned the water on hot, still shaking her head in aggravation.

Stella had some nerve, turning what should have been casual conversation into something that would follow Doll home and nag her until she found relief.

"It must get pretty lonely at night," she had said.

And Doll had simply shrugged, as if it hadn't even occurred to her, but now in the emptiness of her house, it was all she could think about, and Stella was a bitch for mentioning it.

She poured a capful of scented oil beneath the running water before she shut it off. She eased into the tub of hot water, the steam rising around her. The silence in the duplex was punctuated by Manuel's absence. He was late tonight, and Doll knew, because she always made sure to be sitting on her side of the porch or messing around outside when he came in.

Maybe he had a date. It was something she pondered more often lately since their exchanges had gone from friendly greetings to brief conversations peppered with mild flirtation. He was probably out with one of those cute little Latina girls she often saw around town. She had learned through their sporadic conversations that he was Dominican.

Over the weeks, Doll had disclosed to him that she was separated from Bernard, and she had learned that he traveled in the construction business. But what she wanted to know but couldn't ask was if he lay in his bed at night thinking of her the way she thought of him.

Doll spread lavender soap over her body, inhaling the scent as it covered her skin, and since she had become painfully aware that hers were the only hands that would touch her now, she saw nothing wrong with lingering on her breasts and paying close attention to her hips and inner thighs.

She stopped and let her hand rest between her legs, where warmth had found a place and gotten comfortable. She let the water cover her and let her hands find their way there.

Doll touched the places that hadn't been touched for far too long. She imagined her hands were Manuel's hands, his fingers cascading over her wet, brown skin, searching, then finding their way inside her. She imagined it was Manuel exploring her, awakening parts of her that had been left to rest. And when she found the spot that caused her body to tremble and her lips to part, she clung to the edge of the bathtub and waited for her body to settle.

Weak knees carried Doll to her bed, where she sat and spread lotion over her body. She stopped short when the sounds next door made her realize that Manuel had come home.

Had he heard her? But he couldn't have. He had probably just gotten in, and what reason would he have for listening to her bathe, anyway?

Doll heard the hard spray of Manuel's shower and then the

silence. She heard the springs of his mattress straining with the weight of his body, and then a rhythmic creak of his mattress followed by low moans.

Doll smiled, leaning in closer. She imagined patches of Manuel's cinnamon skin, still wet from his shower. She imagined his arms, toned from years of hard labor, gripping his dick. Her hand pressed against the wall, she listened as he pleasured himself, caressing grunts and groans from his throat. And when the moans came louder and quicker, only then did she crawl naked under her covers to wait for a sleep she was sure would never come.

STELLA'S EYES ON HER made Doll uncomfortable. It was as if she knew. She fretted with her bracelet and busied herself clipping tulips while Stella leaned on the counter, her back to the door.

"You look good today, Doll," Stella said finally.

"Thank you, Stella." Doll kept her back turned and her hands moving.

"New dress?"

Doll glanced down at the yellow sundress she had worn a dozen times. "No. I think you've seen me in it before."

"You seeing somebody?"

"No," Doll said, immediately deciding it was too quick, that she was letting Stella know too much.

"I'm just asking is all. You're still a woman, you know."

Doll sucked her teeth. She knew alright. And if she didn't know, then the heat between her legs and the sounds on the other side of her wall the night before had reminded her.

The bell signaling the open door drew Doll out of her brief haze. Manuel, walking toward them, encouraged her to stand straighter, beat the wrinkles out of her dress, and pull at her hair, glad that she had taken the extra fifteen minutes to curl it instead of pulling it back into her usual bun.

She cleared her throat, approaching the counter before Stella could turn around and throw her gap-toothed grin in his face.

"Hey, neighbor." Doll forced confidence where there was none. "You must be lost. I know you don't want nothing to do with no flowers."

Stella interjected. "Maybe he does, Doll. Maybe he's picking something up for a lady friend. We just cut some nice tulips."

Stella leaned over the counter, pressing her heavy breasts together with her forearms. She was shameless, downright pathetic, and Doll wanted to lock her in the broom closet.

"No, thanks," Manuel said, turning his eyes back to Doll. "I'm looking for something for me, for my place. You know, since I liked yours so much."

Doll liked the way Manuel's tongue rolled when he talked, the way everything sounded sexy leaving his lips. Doll wondered if he could see it, her desire. She wondered if it seeped through her pores and lay on her skin, if her eyes told Manuel what her lips could not. Her eyes rested on his hands, large and dark, the hands that had caressed moans from his throat, the hands that she had imagined on her body. And as she wondered now what those hands might feel like, she became warm—her face flushed, her palms moist.

But still, she spoke. "You're looking for some lilies, then?"

"Actually," Manuel said, leaning over the counter, his breath tickling Doll's bare arms, "I think I like those over there."

He pointed to a box of chrysanthemums just behind her. Doll turned around and reached for the plant, fingering the purple and red petals. "You like these? You sure?"

Manuel shrugged. "Of course, I don't know much about them. Think you could take a little time to show me? Say, this evening?"

Doll nodded. She placed his flowers in a small crate, took his money, handed him his change, and agreed to meet him at his place at seven. She smiled as he walked out the door, then walked weak kneed to a chair by the window and watched him drive away.

"WITH MUMS, YOU'RE GONNA WANT TO CHECK

for water every three to four days." Doll pressed the moist soil in the small green pot Manuel had provided.

"Uh huh," he said, his eyes on her face, her chest, everywhere but her hands.

"You know, since they dry out so fast."

"Okay," Manuel nodded.

The evening had been filled with easy conversation, silence only when Manuel sipped from his glass of scotch and Doll nervously gulped her wine. She had even taken a few drags from his cigar, even though the smoke burned her chest, but she decided it was something she could get used to.

"You taking any of this in?" Doll asked as her hands made sharper, quicker movements, turning the soil until she was ready to place the flowers inside.

"Not really." Manuel winked.

Doll pulled her hands out of the pot, shaking the soil off onto the paper she had spread over the table. "So what am I here for?"

"Company," Manuel said, bringing his glass to his mouth.

"You don't get enough company?" Doll said, never looking, sure that her eyes would reveal she was hoping for a "no."

"You ever see any?"

"I don't look for any. I try to mind my business."

"Well, do you ever *hear* any?" Manuel was closer now, his face directly in front of hers, his full lips curved in a smile.

Sweat sprang to Doll's forehead. She wiped at it with her forearm. The music suddenly seemed louder than before. The sound of the electric guitar tickled her ears.

"What's this we're listening to, anyway?" She asked.

Manuel's brows furrowed. "Carlos Santana."

Doll nodded, hoping her ignorance didn't show on her face. "Oh, I see. It's nice."

"What, you never listen to my man Carlos? *Mamacita,* we have got to expand your horizons." He reached around her waist and pulled her against him. "I'm going to teach you to salsa. I'm going to take you to clubs and make all my buddies jealous when I take you out onto the dance floor." Manuel wriggled his hips behind her.

Doll chuckled nervously. "Sure you are, Manuel. Now about these mums. They really could go outside, except it's pretty dry these days, and you'd have to be watering them anyway—"

"You hot?" Manuel interrupted, pulling Doll by the elbow toward the sink.

"A little bit," she said, shuffling beside him. Beads of moisture clung to her skin, ran down her neck, and disappeared down the front of her dress.

Manuel stood close behind her as she leaned over the sink. He turned on the faucet and held her hands beneath the cold running water. He rubbed his hands over hers, working the dirt from the creases in her hands and from beneath her fingernails. He wet his own hands and ran them across her forehead and along her neck and collarbone. He turned her to face him and loosened the top buttons of her dress.

Doll grabbed his hand.

Manuel exhaled. "That husband of yours, is he still a problem for you?"

"No," Doll said, her breathing becoming heavy. His face was close to hers. His eyes forced hers to stay still.

"Then," Manuel began, leaning toward her, "is this a problem?"

His ran his hand along her cheek, down her neck and over her breasts. His hand dropped to her belly and stopped at her waist.

Doll answered with her lips on his. Her tongue followed. He pulled her to him, lifting her dress. He caressed her hips and her thighs, then he hoisted her onto his hips, pressing her rear onto the counter next to the sink.

The oak was cool against her rear. She spread her legs to allow Manuel to slip between them. She rested her heels on the small of his back, her breathing growing heavy when she felt him harden and expand.

Then she looked down.

"It's pretty," she said.

She slapped her hand over her mouth. She didn't know what had made her say it, even if it was true. *Goddamn that third glass of wine,* she thought. She never could hold her liquor.

But Manuel only laughed. "I'm glad you think so, *mami.*" It bobbed up and down. "I think it likes you too."

He pushed the straps of her dress over her shoulders, leaving her breasts exposed. He took one into his mouth, slowly sucking and gently biting. Doll held the back of his head, her own thrown back in pleasure.

Manuel's lips left her breast and covered her mouth, his tongue gliding across her teeth and dancing with hers. He fumbled between her legs until her panties were in a bunch beside her and his pants were loose and resting around his ankles. He worked himself free from his cotton underwear and guided himself inside her.

She ran her tongue along his neck, darted it against the lobe of his ear. Her hands clung to his back as he pressed in and out of her. His dick moved inside of her as if on a mission, and when he found what he was in search of, he pressed in deeper.

Manuel groaned against her ear, pressing his fingers into her flesh. She clung to him, her legs bringing him as close as she could, and when she felt his warmth burst inside her, she relaxed, kissed his lips, and laid her head on his shoulder.

THIS IS MY LIFE NOW, Doll thought as she lay with Manuel in his bed. She had finally admitted to Bernard that she was seeing someone, and while he wasn't happy, he had promised not to stand in her way.

And Bridgette, well, she would understand. She was a woman now, and there would soon be things happening in her own life that would *make* her understand.

"You got the best hair," Doll said, running her hand over Manuel's scalp. "Where did you get these curls?"

He lifted his head off her belly, shifted himself between her legs. "You're just saying that." He leaned down, pressed his nose between her legs.

She arched her back, the aftershock of his mouth on her

coursing through her body. "No, really. And those lips, baby, where did you get those lips?"

Manuel smiled, one side of his mouth curved up. "Now that's a secret." He kissed her lower belly and pushed his hand up between her legs.

And suddenly Doll wondered just how many other pairs of legs he had lain between, how many other bellies he had rested his cheek upon. Had she been foolish to think she was the only one, to run off and tell Bernard she had a new man?

"Manuel, do I have anything to worry about?" She asked, suddenly feeling insecure.

"What you mean, Doll?" He spoke while still kissing and teasing her.

"Do you have anyone else?" She lifted his head so that his eyes were on her.

"I got you. Don't you think you're enough?" He began the kissing again, temporarily distracting her.

"I guess so."

She wanted to be. She didn't want to wonder if there was someone else there when she wasn't. She didn't want to listen for another woman's moans and screams on the other side of the wall.

And when he slid down her body and rested his lips on her sex, she opened her legs wide and let him kiss and lick her worries away. Her back arched in ecstasy, her bare ass rose from the mattress. She felt heat in her belly and tightness in her chest. And when she came in jerks and shivers against his lips, she didn't care who had been there before her, she only cared that she was here now.

DOLL PULLED THE SCREEN DOOR OPEN with her foot, balancing the bundle in her arms. She smiled at Manuel holding the phone on his shoulder, jotting something down on a notepad. She leaned over and kissed his inviting lips, then dropped her load of fresh clothes on his bed.

Manuel hung up the phone and turned up the radio. He extended his hand and lifted Doll off the bed, waltzing her around the room to Stevie Wonder.

"What's got you in such a good mood?" Doll found herself smiling along with him.

"It was a call about a job, baby." Excitement made his voice quiver.

"A job, really? Does that mean you're going to be sticking around? Are they working on something else around here?" She kept in step with him, her eyes searching his face.

"Nope. It's something upstate. They want me there the first of the month."

Doll cut their dance short and stepped out of Manuel's arms. "Upstate where?"

Manuel's brow creased in confusion. "New York City, baby. And it's long term. A year. Maybe even two." He kissed her lips and dipped her low. "You're not happy for me?"

"Yeah," Doll said, sinking into the chair. "Of course I am."

"Well, you don't look like it." He came over and sat on the arm of the chair. "Why so blue, Doll?"

"Well, how do you want me to feel? You tell me you're leaving and you expect me to waltz with you around the kitchen?"

"Yeah I do, 'cause I plan on taking you with me."

Doll lifted her eyes to his, looking for a sign that he was just talking, that he didn't really know what he was saying. "You want me to come with you?"

"Yep."

"To New York?"

"Yep."

She stood up then and reached out and took his hand and, holding each other close, they danced.

DOLL CRADLED THE CORDLESS PHONE between her cheek and her shoulder, lying across the bed on her stomach.

"I'm supposed to be there by now," she said, reaching over and fingering the petals of the chrysanthemum that now sat in her window. "Don't you miss me?"

"You know I miss you, baby. It's gonna be just a few weeks more. It was real hard finding a place once I got here, and the one I did get into needs some fixing up."

His voice still made her body quiver, his accent still made her toes curl, but she fought to keep to the subject at hand.

"I could help you with that, you know," she said.

"No," Manuel insisted. "I don't want you doing a thing once you get here except resting that pretty body of yours. But you can do something for me right now."

"What's that?"

"Lay back and spread those big pretty legs."

And Doll rested her head on her pillow and obliged, sending her hands and fingers where they were instructed to go, speaking to Manuel in whispers, reaching her peak in groans until she was spent and Manuel's soft voice sang her to sleep.

SHE FELT THE WATER when it hit her feet, soaked through her shoes, and pooled at her feet. The pitcher shook in her hand until she could no longer hold it steady, and it slipped from her fingers and hit the concrete floor.

Stella appeared as if called, her brow creased at the sight.

"What the hell is wrong with you, Doll?" She hurried to the broom closet and retrieved the mop, pushing it across the small puddle.

Doll placed the phone on its cradle. "Nothing," she said. "It slipped, that's all. I'll clean it up." She reached for the mop, but Stella nodded her head toward the front of the store.

"I got it. You just take care of the customers."

Doll exhaled and made her way up front, her saturated shoes sloshing with each step.

Temporarily disconnected . . .

She repeated the numbers over and over in her head.

"Can I help you with something, ma'am?"

No longer in service . . .

She had just spoken to him four nights ago, and he had whispered that he couldn't wait to see her, how she would love what he had done with their place, that it was just the post office holding up her ticket.

"I'd like to look at some of your pink roses, please." The older woman glanced around the shop.

"I'm sorry, ma'am, we don't have any." Doll felt unsteady on her feet, her stomach suddenly queasy.

"No pink roses?"

"No, ma'am." A mist of perspiration rested above her lip. "We have red . . . and white. I could show you those." She held on to the counter to keep steady.

"No, I need pink. How about your tulips then?"

"Red only."

"Only red?"

"Just red."

Doll's hands became fists on the counter. Her lips folded and her teeth pressed into them.

"Well, maybe some carnations, pink carnations would be lovely."

"Nothing pink! We don't have a damned thing pink in the place. There! Now, can I interest you in anything else?"

The words came before Doll could stop them, and by

looking at the woman's face before her, she already knew her answer.

"Yes, your manager, please."

DOLL COULDN'T BELIEVE IT. She had given the woman the courtesy of two weeks' notice and Stella had nerve enough to let her go when she still had a week left to work. Now Doll had a week left to do nothing, since her bags were already packed and her belongings sat in boxes, waiting to be shipped. She had told Bridgette how to reach her and Bernard where to send the papers after he had signed. The only thing keeping from her leaving was the ticket that Manuel had promised he would send last week.

She grabbed the stack of mail out of her box on her way into the house. Walking to her bedroom, she sifted through final bills, a sales ad, and a letter that she had sent to Manuel, stamped RETURN TO SENDER. She let the envelope fall to the floor, let her body fall onto the bed.

Her chest heaved rapidly and her eyes burned with tears that wouldn't come. Her body rocked and shook until there was nothing left to do but stretch out on the bed and sleep.

SHE FELT HIS HAND first on her forehead, and then her cheek. She opened her eyes, trying to make out the figure of the tall, dark man that stood before her. Then she sat up and straightened her blouse.

"Bernard . . . "

"The front door was open. You okay?"

"I'm fine. What's the matter?"

"Nothing, I tried calling, and, well . . . Bridgette will be home next week. She'll be working with me down at the plant this summer, answering phones in the front office. I thought you might want to know, you know, before you leave."

Doll stood up and tucked her purse underneath her arm. "We'll need to get things ready for her then. You driving the truck? If so, we can throw my bags back there. We can come back for the boxes."

"But what about you leaving? Going upstate with that new man of yours?"

Doll silenced Bernard with her lips. "Please," she said. "Just take me home."

HER KITCHEN SMELLED OF rosemary chicken. Doll grilled corns of cobs and tore up fresh greens for a salad.

Bridgette was coming home today.

Bernard crept up behind her and slipped his arms around her waist. He kissed her on her neck, tickled her ear with his nose. He did that often now, he even tried some of the things she suggested, like letting her get on top or doing it on the kitchen table. It was something she could almost get used to, except Doll knew things would eventually change. Somehow, they always did.

THE MILE HIGH CLUB

Kate Dominic

*I*t's too easy to get caught in the bathroom of a plane—especially these days. So, when I'm in the mood for airborne sex, I book myself a window seat on a cross-country red eye. The larger the plane, the better. People notice the passengers in the middle seats and ignore anyone on the far side of an aisle. The low lights, ubiquitous dark blankets, and generally somnolent atmosphere combine with the lull of the jet engines to create a late-night ambiance that almost insists people let down their guard and snuggle up like they're home in bed. Unlike the flight crew, though, I had no intention of encouraging my seatmate to sleep.

After four days of vendor demonstrations at a sex toy conference, followed by a frenzy of buying for the home-party franchises I was developing, I was already feeling particularly frisky. Unlike many of my counterparts, I never indulged at conventions. I was too busy wearing my professional networking hat. On the plane home though, I was like superwoman stepping out of her phone booth. I left the hotel shuttle and sashayed into the quiet of the airport with my TSA-compliant bag of tricks in hand.

Anonymity was an asset at times like this. I'd pulled my shoulder-length blond hair back in a softly woven scarf and dabbed on just enough makeup to highlight the green in my eyes and make my full lower lip look freshly kissed. I was wearing a peasant skirt with no panties and a loose flowing blouse and sandals. I'd considered going braless, but my nipples are so large that they'd be way too obvious when they got erect—which they always do when I'm ready to come. So I settled for a satiny front-hook bra and folded an attractive shawl into the large, open-topped, straw carry-on bag in which I'd also tucked my purse, a very small tube of hand lotion, and a steamy romance novel so well-thumbed it automatically opened to my favorite parts. I settled into my seat, pulled the shawl around my shoulders, and took out my book.

The young man who sat next to me just as the doors were closing was a bit of a surprise. Most of my fellow passengers were returning vacationers taking advantage of the reduced night rates. My harried-looking seatmate was dressed in an expensive, though slightly rumpled, gray Italian suit and sported a day's growth of blond stubble. He was probably ten years younger than me—in his early thirties, I guessed. He smiled apologetically as he shoved his briefcase into the overhead compartment and slid into his seat. The flight attendant was pointedly announcing that all passengers should now be in their seats with their carry-on luggage stowed and seat belts securely fastened about their waists so the plane could depart on time.

"Sorry," he muttered for the third time as he bumped me while resituating himself. He smiled politely as the flight attendant marched by on her final check, her eyes dutifully noting the seatbelt across his lap as he stretched his long legs under the seat in front of him and once more shifted his weight. I was fairly certain she hadn't noted the attractive bulge in his crotch nearly as closely as I had.

"We can lift the armrest after takeoff, to give you more room," I smiled, patting his arm casually as the attendant started reciting the standard emergency speech. I was amazed at how quickly the fates seemed to be smiling on me tonight. I let my hand linger, not too long, just enough for me to appreciate the strength in his forearm and to see he wasn't wearing a ring. A few moments later, the cabin lights dimmed. But rather than turn on my reading light as we backed from the gate, I gripped the armrest tightly. When my seatmate quirked an expressive eyebrow over his clear blue eyes, I muttered my own, entirely truthful, apology.

"I'm a bit of a white-knuckled flier." I grimaced, watching the lights of the plane ahead of us shoot past as we taxied out onto the runway. Despite my love of airborne trysts, I've never been that fond of flying itself—most specifically of the fact that I was not wearing a parachute. The smile that reassured me was tired, but it sparkled all the way to his eyes and warmed me down to my toes.

"My name's Jerry," he grinned, patting my arm like I'd done to his earlier. "I probably have enough frequent flier points for a first-class trip to Mars." As I nervously glanced out at the runway lights now moving rapidly by us, he laughed quietly and shook his head. "No peeking out the window! Relax and talk to me. Before you know it, you'll forget you were ever concerned." As we lifted off, I grabbed his hand. He chuckled and squeezed back. His fingers were warm and dry and surprisingly strong for someone in a power suit.

"What's your name?" he said firmly, giving our joined hands a little shake.

"Marla," I squeaked, mortified at my decidedly less-than-attractive vocal reaction. I clung to him until the plane leveled off, then took a deep breath and sheepishly placed his hand back on the armrest. Now that we were actually in the air, I was decidedly less embarrassed than I had been earlier and considerably less so than I intended to let on.

"That wasn't so bad now, was it?" Jerry smiled. He kept his arm next to mine, calm and reassuring. As I looked in his face, though, I could see the pronounced lines of exhaustion around his compelling blue eyes. I was getting second thoughts about seducing him.

"I'm much better," I smiled back. I explained to him that even though I was nervous, I actually flew cross-country every couple of months, to vendors and tradeshows and such. When I told him what my business was, he laughed and told me he was a marketing rep for a software systems repairs corporation, and that he'd just closed the biggest deal of his life.

"I feel like celebrating," he said tiredly. "But the deal closed so quickly, I'm getting back early. My wife and kids are still at her mother's for another week. I don't know that I'll call them for a couple of days though. Not that I don't love my mother-in-law." His sudden grin was mischievous. "But let's just say if I phone from the office, there's no way I can be shanghaied into taking an impromptu jaunt up to Connecticut."

Damn, damn, double damn. I don't play with married men unless they instigate it. I took a deep breath and smiled suggestively up at him.

"But if you were with your wife, wouldn't you be able to, you know, celebrate more privately?" I let myself blush; my Irish skin can do this pretty much on demand.

He leaned his head back into the seat and closed his eyes, smiling as he ran his hand through his slightly disheveled, though still impeccably styled, short blond hair. Even though I knew he was thinking about his wife, his tired good looks fascinated me enough to make my pussy tingle. When he opened his eyes, they were more than a little bit frustrated.

"Let's just say that at Stacy's mother's house, there's no such thing as a closed door, much less knocking on one. Between that and the kids running all over, privacy is not an option." I was surprised to see him blush as he smiled again. "I'll get more loving talking to her over the phone with a bottle of lotion in one hand and my cock in the other than I would sleeping next to her!"

He stopped, his whole body stiffening as he realized what he'd said. "I am so sorry! I didn't mean to be so blunt!" His deep red flush was absolutely charming. "Damn, I must be more tired than I thought!"

"Tired—and no doubt horny," I laughed, again patting his arm reassuringly as his eyebrows shot up. This time I didn't let my hand linger. If the fates were with me, Jerry would let me know. I didn't want to spook him. I settled back into my seat and wrapped my shawl around me. "If you get tired, I picked up a pillow and blanket on my way in. Since I'll be reading, I'll be glad to share."

His quiet "No thanks" was lost in the click of me flipping on my reading light. I opened my book. Jerry tipped his seat back and stared up at the ceiling, like he was trying to relax enough to sleep but not quite succeeding.

The well-worn page I'd opened to had the hero seducing the heroine with a frenzy of blood-boiling foreplay. Between that and the proximity of my attractive seatmate, it wasn't long before I was squirming. I slipped one hand under my shawl so I could rub my nipple to a peak through the soft, loose gauze and the form-fitting satin. As I sighed appreciatively, I flipped the previous page back with my other thumb so I could reread an especially hot scene.

Although my seatmate had his eyes closed, his tense body language and the significantly larger bulge in the front of his pants told me he wasn't asleep. I glanced obviously at him, taking a good, long look, like I was making sure he was asleep. Then I turned off my light, leaned my own seat back, and resituated my shawl to cover my whole chest.

There was just enough light for me to read the words I knew almost by heart. As I once more read the foreplay scene, I pinched and squeezed and rubbed my nipples, seducing my breasts until I was breathing hard. With a quick glance at my companion's now even more erect crotch, I slid my hand down my belly, moving gradually lower until I was pressing my skirt firmly into the apex between my thighs. I sighed, rubbing contentedly until I was wiggling in my seat. Then I picked up the blanket, draped it across myself, and opened my book again.

Before long, I was once more lost in the story. Not that I wasn't interested in my companion. I was actually fantasizing that he was the naked hero thrusting between the heroine's naked thighs. But I was getting so turned on that masturbating to climax in front of him would have been quite satisfactory.

I was so engrossed, I almost missed the flight attendants approaching with the beverage service. Only my companion's quick hand on my arm saved me from certain embarrassment. I quickly closed my eyes, pretending to be asleep with the book on my chest while my companion ordered a glass of ice water and quickly drank it down.

As the attendants moved on, I picked up my book and again settled myself for some serious reading. Jerry stretched his legs, resituating the now extremely obvious erection tenting the front of his pants, and leaned conspiratorially toward me.

"Is it still okay if I lift the armrest?" he whispered.

"Of course." I smiled demurely, moving slightly into the newly opened space as soon as he lifted the arm. He didn't look nearly as tired anymore. "I think we all like being able to stretch out a little."

I let my glance pass briefly but pointedly over his crotch. Then I lifted my book again. In my mind, I substituted the warm scent of Jerry's slightly sweat-tinged aftershave and his blond hair and blue eyes for the hero's attributes. Pretty soon, my fingers were moving again. I was getting so aroused that after a few shivering squeezes to my nipples, I kept my fingers on my clit as I turned the pages. My breathing quickened. I was getting so into the story and my fantasy of lying naked on a beach with Jerry that I jumped when his hand slid beneath my shawl.

"I've never done this before," he whispered, leaning toward me so closely that the warmth of his breath teased over my ear. "I mean, I haven't had sex with anyone other than my wife since we got married, and I've sure as hell never done it in an airplane." I inhaled as his strong fingers cupped my breast. "But my wife insists that adequate nipple stimulation is crucial to a good orgasm. She says it's my job to provide it. I'd be honored if you'd let me milk your breasts while you come."

As I shivered against him, his fingers competently flicked open the front latch of my bra. I sighed as my left breast fell forward into the warm cup of his hand. His thumb stroked my nipple. It hardened instantly.

"I'm an incorrigible breast man." He laughed softly, keeping his voice low enough that only I could hear. "I love the feel of a woman's breasts in my hands, especially ones with big sensitive nipples like yours. It makes me so hard."

My fingers stilled on my clit as he let go of the nipple he'd been stroking and picked up my other breast. I couldn't contain the soft moans that escaped my lips at the wonderful feel of his fingertips stroking first one, then the other nipple. I nodded breathlessly as he shushed me.

"I love milking a woman's breasts to orgasm." As his breath glided over my ear, his fingertips caressed the sides and undersides and down the tops of my breasts, caressing from the outside in, teasing all the way down to the tips until I was shivering. He laid his thumb and first two fingers just above my areola, pressing in and turning his wrist. He circled just above my nipple until my breast felt stunningly heavy and I was breathing hard.

Then he slid his hand down, catching my nipple, from the edge to the tip, tightly between the pads of his thumb and fingers. He stretched the skin out and twisted slightly, until the entire areola was pinched into his grip. Then he started a strong, rhythmic tugging. It felt like he was almost stripping sensation through my nipple. With each long, slow, twisting pull, I stiffened and panted, my pussy contracting in the flutters that I knew would lead to a blinding orgasm when I fingered my clit.

Suddenly Jerry froze, lowering his head onto his headrest and closing his eyes. His hand stilled under my shawl with my nipple pulled out and twisted hard. I had to fight to breathe evenly as the flight attendant walked by without so much as a glance in our direction.

When her quiet footsteps passed, Jerry opened his eyes and winked at me. He glanced quickly around the darkened cabin. The seat belt sign was off, but no passengers were up, and there were no flight attendants in sight. Except for a few reading lights sprinkled here and there throughout the cabin, everyone else in our section appeared to be asleep. With a quick grin, Jerry leaned against me and pulled the blanket up to his ear. As soon as his face was hidden, he lifted my shawl and lowered his head.

"This is milking too," he whispered. He silently, and with consummate tenderness, sucked my entire nipple into his mouth.

In all my life, I'd never been with anyone who worshiped my breasts the way Jerry did. First one, then the other, then back again. He drew my nipples deep into his mouth and suckled until my pussy throbbed in time to the rhythmic waves of his nursing. I frantically rubbed my clit, my hand gliding on my pussy juice.

Each time someone walked by, Jerry lifted his head and froze, looking for all the world like a peaceful, innocently sleeping husband resting his head on his wife's shoulder. And as soon as the interlopers were gone, he opened his mouth again. He sucked my nipples until they were so elongated and tender that just the softest flick of his tongue made me tremble. Then he lifted his head and pulled the blanket back up over my chest.

"You'll be tender tomorrow," he whispered. I jumped at the light brush of his thumb. He smiled against my ear. "You won't be so sore that you're really uncomfortable, just sensitive enough to remember me every time your nipples move beneath your bra." He scratched his fingernails lightly over my nipple, chuckling softly as I quivered. "Nobody but the two of us will know your nipples are a deep, dusky, well-sucked rose, or that just the touch of your bra makes you squirm." He pinched slowly, whispering "Shhhh" as I bit back a whimper. "But you'll know, Marla—and I'll know. We'll both blush each time we think about it."

I leaned into him, my face heating on its own accord as he milked me with his fingers until I was almost crying.

"Tomorrow, when I'm talking charts and figures and popping champagne with my boss, I'll think of how your beautiful nipples felt jutting out onto my tongue while I sucked you off. I'll remember how you trembled while I marked your lovely breasts with . . . "

Jerry closed his eyes in midsentence, breathing deeply and quietly against me as an elderly couple walked back toward the restrooms. When they passed, he once more turned toward me and ducked his head, this time sliding his hand under the blanket as well. His palm was warm and strong as it circled my other nipple then slipped under my skirt and moved slowly up my thigh.

With shaking hands, I held the blanket over his ear as he laved my excruciatingly sensitive nipple. His fingers inched up, his hand pressing my legs further apart until my pussy was fully exposed and he was gliding on my juices. He teased the edge of my cunt with his fingertips, licking my nipples, warning me what he was going to do. I glanced once more around. It was dark and quiet, and there was no one up. Jerry's touch was driving me insane. I lifted the heel of my hand to my lips and whispered, "Please." Just the one word.

His fingers slid in. I bit, my cry vibrating against my hand as my whole body shuddered. Jerry sank his fingers deep into my cunt, sucking my nipple all the way into his mouth. He suckled until I thought I would scream at the sheer intensity of the sensations exploding through me. I barely had time to bite my hand again before he pressed deeper, harder into my G-spot. He sucked my other nipple between his lips and I bucked up, stifling a scream as my pussy squirted into his hand. As I lay there panting, shaking to Jerry's incessant, tender licks, I looked back over the seat and saw the elderly couple starting back from the restroom.

I pulled the blanket higher and closed my eyes, drawing on all my willpower to hold myself still while they walked past, followed by the flight attendant, reminding them to rebuckle their seat belts as soon as they sat back down. Jerry gently and oh-so-tenderly licked and sucked and tormented the tender nipple beneath his lips until tears ran down my face. When every thing was quiet again, he lifted his head, smiling at me with swollen lips as he brushed the tears from my cheeks. He rested his mouth against my ear.

"I want to come in your hand, Marla." He was speaking directly into my ear, his breath soft and warm and not entirely steady on my sensitive flesh. "I know your nipples are terribly sore, but I still want to milk your breasts when I come." When I moaned softly, he smiled against my ear. "Thank you for sharing such an exquisite climax with me. I'm going to come so hard knowing I've serviced you the way a woman should be."

The blanket had fallen as he leaned into my ear. As he settled back into his seat, I spread the deep blue fabric over his swollen crotch, over the wet circle at the top of the stretched gray of his pants, and resituated my shawl over where my breasts hung sore and sensitive and free beneath my blouse. I slipped my hand beneath the blanket. Jerry shivered as I slowly slid his zipper down. I reached in his fly, unbuttoned his boxers, and pulled his iron-stiff, swollen cock free. Then I closed my hand around him and slowly stroked upward. He inhaled sharply.

"Oh, yes," he murmured. With his eyes half-closed, he slipped his hand under my shawl. I winced as his palms brushed first one breast, then the other. Then his fingertips were wrapped around my nipple again, tugging slowly and ruthlessly. I shook as he milked me.

"Yes!" he choked. I stared down at the blanket, stunned to feel his cock getting even harder.

Even though the cabin stayed quiet, the smell of sex juices was making people stir. A few rows in back of me, I heard a quiet conversation start. I gave one more quick glance around. The coast was still clear. Before I could change my mind, I opened my shawl and pulled Jerry's head down to my darkly swollen nipple. With a heartfelt groan, he latched on. As his cock spurted into my hand, Jerry suckled me until tears ran down my face and my pussy throbbed with pure, unadulterated pleasure.

I was still shaking when I glanced up. A flight attendant was working her way back toward us, a frown on her face as she looked up and down the rows of sleeping passengers. I quickly straightened my shawl, pressing Jerry's head up against my shoulder as he struggled to control his breathing. As he drew a deep, shaking breath, the attendant peered into our row. I couldn't quite close my eyes in time. I smiled weakly at her, determined to brazen it out and pretend I was just waking up. She looked around, her nose wrinkling instinctively as I turned my head and snuggled back into my seat.

She half smiled, like she wasn't quite sure what she was noticing, and looked down pointedly toward our covered laps. "Are your seat belts fastened?"

I carefully moved Jerry's "sleeping" head slightly to the side, dutifully whispering, "Yes, ma'am" as I peered quickly under the blanket. The corner of the shawl barely covered his still half-hard, sticky cock, but his semen-covered seat belt was securely fastened about his waist. As the musky scent of sex assaulted my nostrils, a man behind us snored loudly. The attendant turned to frown at him. When she looked back, Jerry and I were both "sleeping" soundly again. She pursed her lips and continued making her way to the back of the plane.

When she was gone, I reached under the blanket and cleaned Jerry with the inside of my skirt, smiling as he contentedly let me tend to him. He shivered when I squeezed the last drop from his shaft. When we righted our clothes though, Jerry stopped my hand, shaking his head when I tried to resnap my bra. I snuggled against his shoulder, resting companionably the rest of the way while he quietly milked my excruciatingly sore nipples beneath my shawl and licked the occasional tear running slowly down my face. No storybook heroine ever felt more cherished than I did at that moment. I left my book untended on the seat beside me and let myself shake in his arms until the lights went up and the landing announcements began.

Jerry held my hand when we landed, distracting me just as the wheels were about to touch down by quietly announcing that he'd changed his mind about going into work that day.

"Too tired, after all?" I smiled, knowing I was damn well going to catch a cab and grab a few hours of sleep before I made any of the follow-up calls on my agenda. I was surprised when he grinned and shook his head.

"Nope. I'm going straight to the ticket counter and catching the next flight to Connecticut." As I stared at him, his hand moved up my arm. I couldn't help my quiver as his finger brushed surreptitiously over the tender nipple beneath my blouse. Despite the dark circles under his eyes, he didn't look particularly tired at all anymore.

"You've reminded me just how much I love pleasuring a woman." He glanced around, then whispered in my ear. "And how much I love sucking a woman's nipples until she screams." I moaned softly as he lightly brushed the other nipple. "I'm going to get a baby sitter and drag my wife to a hotel room, just the two of us, the way I used to before we had kids and I started traveling so much." His lips gently brushed my ear. "I'm going to suck her nipples until they're so damn bruised, she begs me to fuck her. Then I'll pull her on my cock and suck her off until she comes!"

I was still laughing as the seat belt sign flicked off and we stood to leave. With my romance novel in my hand, I gave him a quick hug, hissing at the unexpected sting in my nipples, then blushing at his low, knowing laugh. But before he could say anything more, I shook my head and pressed the well-thumbed book into his hand.

"Give her this too," I said, "for the next time you're traveling."

The row ahead of us emptied. Jerry stepped into the aisle, subtly straightening his jacket over his now mostly dried crotch. He followed me out the door. I didn't turn to say goodbye. I had the sneaking feeling he'd remember me. And just by shrugging my shoulders, I'd realized I'd be remembering him happily for a long, long time.

LIKE A GOOD GIRL

Alison Tyler

*B*lack dress, black fishnets, white go-go boots.

My hair up in a high ponytail.

A velvet choker tight around my neck.

I stood in Jesse's bathroom and checked out my appearance as if seeing myself for the first time. This was my first day working at a prestigious salon in the heart of Beverly Hills. I knew that I'd be dealing with beautiful people all day long, and I wanted to do my best to blend.

"You know, it ought to be a collar," Jesse said, coming up behind me and putting one strong hand on my throat, covering the choker.

I stared at the two of us in the mirror. Jesse had a turquoise towel around his flat waist and nothing else. His dark hair was wet from his shower, and he smelled faintly of a spicy aftershave. As always, he was as handsome as his head shot. A movie star coming to life in front of me.

"Black leather," he said, "with silver hardware."

An interesting statement for the first day on the job, I thought but kept the observation to myself. I already knew better than to respond with some wisecrack comment. Jesse could be unpredictable.

"Buckled tight," he continued, dropping his towel now and stepping behind me.

I tensed immediately, not knowing what he was going to do.

"You're nervous," Jesse said, taking my hands and placing them gently on the edge of the pink ceramic sink. "Aren't you?"

"Yeah . . . " That was true enough.

"I'm going to make you forget your nerves," he promised, and I felt him slide the dress up in the back, revealing my bikini panties.

"Aw," he whispered, and I could hear the smile in his voice. "You wore white panties. Black and white, down to the core. Just like a good girl. Adhering perfectly to the salon's strict dress code." His warm fingers slid the panties past the tops of my thigh-high stockings. "But what's this, baby? You're breaking the rules?"

I didn't know what he meant, and I looked into the mirror once more, meeting his eyes as he gazed back at me. "Your ass is all black and blue."

Now I lowered my eyes as a shudder worked through me. The welts and marks from my most recent caning were only slowly fading. Jesse admired his handiwork for a moment before pulling my hips back hard against him. I didn't even think to resist—I simply gave myself over to him as he started to fuck me, smoothly, evenly, sliding his cock in and out at a hypnotic pace.

"You'll be at the counter, helping people, and thinking about how sweetly I fucked you this morning, and how hard I'm going to fuck you tonight."

And now my breath caught, because Jesse understood. Yes, I could come from being taken this way, but only if he dirty talked to me. "Normal" sex was never enough. "We're going out," he continued, slipping his hands up under my dress now and tugging my bra down to reveal my breasts. He twisted my nipples as he spoke. "You and me. We're going to a special place I know. And *they* have a dress code, too, just like your fancy high-end salon. But in this case it's 'Dresses optional. Collars mandatory.'"

He sped up the rhythm now, pinching my nipples fiercely as he fucked me. "So you think about that, Cody, while all the newness of your job makes you feel dizzy and off balance. You think about that, and tonight, I'm going to clear everything up for you."

And then he pulled out suddenly, unexpectedly, and gave my ass one hard slap before walking out of the bathroom.

I stood there for a moment, staring once more at my reflection, seeing an entirely different girl than I had moments before. I looked at my eyes, at the glow in the dark depths, looked at my flushed cheeks, and thought, *Jesus, they're going to know I just got fucked.* . . . But one thing was for sure: Jesse was right. I didn't feel nearly as nervous now.

THE SALON WAS THE BIGGEST PLACE I'd ever worked, with celebrities coming in hourly, often using a private elevator in the back. There was an espresso bar and an international newsstand and a whole bank of manicure/pedicure stations, their chairs facing a wall painted with a detailed mural of Paris.

"You understand that you never let a client off the phone without booking an appointment," Carmen told me. She was in charge of reception and had set aside the morning to train me. "If we can't book the desired stylist at that time, you offer another time. If the time is more important than the stylist, you find another stylist."

I nodded.

"And you're pleasant, even if someone is irate. That's the number one priority."

"But you can put them on hold," a pixie blond girl next to me grinned. "I'm Nina," she added, "and that's my favorite trick."

Carmen nodded. "As a last resort," she said, "because

they'll simply hang up and call back, but if someone's screaming at you, that's what we all do."

Screaming. People take their hair way too seriously in L.A.

The day flew. There was never down time. The phones rang without stopping, and the clients came in a steady stream. By six o'clock, I was whipped. At least that's what I thought, until I headed to my car and remembered Jesse and what he'd said. Quickly, I amended the statement in my head.

I wasn't whipped—*yet*.

WHEN I GOT HOME, Jesse was waiting for me.

"So you've never been to a club?"

"Sure I have," I told him. I'd been to clubs since freshman year of college. Coconut Teasers. The Whiskey. The Roxy.

"A *club* club," he demanded. "A *bondage* club."

I shook my head.

"Great," he said, once again placing his hand on the hollow of my throat, applying just enough pressure that the weight made it difficult for me to swallow. He pulled me close to him, his body hard against mine. "You're going to be on display tonight," he whispered, and now I sucked in my breath, visualizing the scene as he described it. "But don't worry, baby, it'll just be you and me, and two hundred of our closest friends." He faced me straight on then, moving his hand up my throat to tilt my face up toward his. "You're going to have to behave right tonight, Cody," he said in that soft voice, the one I found most menacing. "I know it's going to be tough for you. But I want you to try really hard for me. Can you do that?"

I nodded, and he immediately slapped my face, catching me off balance, then gripped my arms and stood me steadily before him again. The look in his dark eyes was fierce. "Can you?" he asked again, more menacing than ever.

"Yes, sir—" I whispered.

"Better," he nodded. "That's better."

JESSE HAD BEEN OUT at auditions for the first part of the day and then had gone to the gym. He told me to get ready while he took a shower. But I didn't follow his command. Instead, I sat in the living room with a glass of Jack, flipping the channels on the TV with the sound muted, not seeing a thing. My cheek stung from where Jesse had slapped me, and I had one hand against the side of my face, my fingers tripping up and down over the hot spot.

The JD in my glass got lower as the final rays of sunlight faded from the room, but I didn't get up to turn on a light or refill my drink. When Jesse finally entered the room, clad in black, he practically disappeared into the gloom. I felt him staring at me, but I didn't turn to face him. The glow of the silent TV was the only light.

Without a word, Jesse sat at my side. He took the remote from my hand and set it on the coffee table. I'd landed on some old black-and-white movie, and I stared at the screen rather than turning to face Jesse.

"You're scared."

I nodded. Tears were already streaming down my face. I wasn't just scared. I was terrified.

He took my hand down from my cheek and traced the tracks from my silent tears.

"We won't go tonight."

Now I looked at him, at the brightness in his dark eyes, at the serious look on his striking face. I wondered why he was taking so much time with me. I'd only known him a short period, but I'd thought I'd nailed him. A man who got what he wanted and moved on. Had he simply not finished with me? Or did he see something in me that held his interest a bit longer?

I knew my eyes were begging when I stared at him. I wanted to please him, but my whole body was shaking.

"We'll get there," he said, nodding, more to himself than to me. "Don't worry, Cody. We'll get there."

Now the tears came faster. I was letting him down. Visions of what he'd promised me flickered through my mind. Jesse displaying me. Cropping me in front of an audience. Hurting me. And while I wanted every single image that he'd promised, I was so worried that I'd let him down, fail him in some way, embarrass him.

"You make me want to move fast," he said, now bringing me up so that my legs were over his lap, cradled in a safe embrace. "You make me want to do everything at once." Again, I felt as if he were speaking more to himself than to me, as if explaining the situation out loud was helping him to process how we both were feeling. "But that doesn't mean you're off the hook tonight."

Had I started to relax? Had I let the whiskey work through me, the fire of it calming me?

"I promised you I'd take care of you tonight. I don't ever go back on my promises, Cody. Do you understand that?"

I hadn't spoken in so long that my voice was hoarse. "Yes, Jesse."

"Tonight I'm 'Daddy.' Can you do that?"

I closed my eyes as a fresh wave of fear spread through me. "Yes, Daddy."

"Alright, girl. Go get your pj's on and meet me back here."

I undressed quickly. Taking off my work clothes. Slipping into a silky short blue-and-white checked pajama set. I didn't stop to look at my reflection, didn't pause to guess what Jesse had in mind. I hurried back to the living room and then stood at the side of the sofa, waiting for my next instruction.

"Come here, Cody," he said, and there was no trace of a smile on his face or in his eyes. He'd turned the television off and lit the tall ivory candles that stood on the mantel. There were enough to create more light than the TV had, but the room was still dim and cavelike. "Over my lap."

I didn't look at his face again, simply crawled into position. Jesse's fingers caught the waistband of my pajama shorts and white cotton panties and pulled both down my thighs.

I thought he was going to start spanking me. My body was tensed for the first blow. But he didn't.

"Now, angel, I want you to tell me one of your fantasies. Can you do that?"

"Yes, Daddy—"

"Your favorite fantasy. One that you've never told anyone before, because you're embarrassed."

"Yes, Daddy—" I whispered, squeezing my eyes shut tight as I tried to think what to say. In my silence, Jesse ran his hand over my naked rear, and then right when I was about to start speaking, he tripped his fingertips down the crack of my ass, softly touching my asshole.

"Now—"

Oh, Jesus. He was going to be doing things to me while I spoke. I got that now. Shuddering, I did my best to tell him. "I'm in a school," I said, "like a private school."

"Mm-hmm," Jesse murmured, and now he had my cheeks spread apart, and I could feel him simply looking at me. I wanted to hide, to burrow into the cushions of the sofa, but I held myself as still as possible, and continued.

"And I've done something wrong—"

"Of course you have."

"Each time it's different. Smoking behind the building. Making out with another girl. Drinking beer in a car in the parking lot."

"What is it this time?"

"Reading dirty stories in a book that's banned on campus."

Now, Jesse had licked his fingertips and was slowly slipping one, then two, inside of me, gently finger-fucking my asshole. The pleasure was immediate, but I could feel my cheeks flaming at the same time. Shame floored me.

"And what happens to you?" Jesse coaxed.

I tried to be offhand. I was sure he could see where I was going. "You know, I'm sent to the principal's office—"

"Wearing what?"

"Scarlet and black schoolgirl skirt, white socks, patent leather shoes. White shirt, black cardigan." I could say it fast, because the outfit was the same every time.

"What does the principal look like?"

And now I lied for the first time. "You."

Jesse removed his hand and spanked me hard, five times in a row. He'd caught the flippancy in my voice. But I explained quickly. "Different each time," I told him. "I'll see someone at a store, or in a movie, or driving next to me, and I'll cast that person the next time I do this—"

"Do what?"

"Fantasize. Touch myself."

"Go on," Jesse instructed, but before I could, I felt something wet against my asshole and realized that while I'd been dressing, Jesse had gotten out a bag of toys. He slowly lubed me up, his fingertips skating around and around. I swallowed hard and then tried to continue.

"He says all the usual things, you know. I've been caught. Could be expelled. Whatever. Something clichéd, I know. But I don't hear a word, because on the desk is this wicked-looking paddle. Wooden, with holes in it. And I know from experience what that's going to feel like, how much it's going to hurt, how hard I'm going to cry. And I understand that I ought to be paying attention, but all I see is that paddle, and all I hear are my own impending sobs."

Slowly, Jesse began to slide something inside of me, and I stopped speaking. They were balls, on a string, and I found myself shaking my head, not wanting this. How gently he was touching me, taking care of me. How he knew that I'd like this, but that embarrassment, guilt, shame—all of those emotions—would build up inside me. I felt so exposed— revealing this fantasy while Jesse was just playing with me, teasing me.

"Don't stop, Cody. Keep talking. No matter what I'm doing."

"Yes, Jesse," I said, and then quickly, "Yes, Daddy—" I tried my best to focus. "He puts me over his lap and lifts up my skirt. He takes my panties down to my ankles, and then he spanks me, as hard as I've ever been spanked, with that cruel paddle. I'm crying from the very start—"

Jesse slipped another ball inside me.

"—crying so hard, and he says he's sorry he has to be so strict with me—with all of us girls—but that he does have our best interests at heart. He knows not to stop just because

154 ALISON TYLER

we're crying. He understands how to make a real impression, how to take us beyond our limits. Or where we think our limits are."

"And where are your limits, Cody?"

He wasn't letting me get away with anything. If I could focus on the story, I could forget that Jesse was sliding these balls inside my asshole, one after the other. But when he spoke, I was right back in the living room, upended over his lap, my pussy a lake of juices. My cheeks cherry-hued.

"I don't know—" I told him honestly.

"In your story."

"Oh, yes. . . . You know, it changes. Sometimes, I put my hands back to stop him, and he has to bend me over the desk, get something else to use. A cane. A crop. His belt. It depends on what I need . . . "

Jesse lifted me off his lap now, surprising me, and pulled my panties and shorts all the way off. Then he bent me over the arm of the black leather sofa and got behind me. I heard the sound of his buckle, and then felt the warmth of his cock against my skin. "What do you need now?"

As he spoke, he started to fuck me, and as he fucked me, he began to pull the balls out of my ass. One at a time, so that I couldn't even think. But I knew better than to stay silent. Already, Jesse was training me. My mind worked furiously, trying to figure out what he wanted me to say. What the right answer was. I knew that Jesse wouldn't be satisfied with a simple fuck session. God, I wouldn't either. But I didn't know what he expected from me.

"What I always need," I murmured, failing, I knew as I spoke.

Jesse laughed. His voice dark. He was slamming inside of me, and the beads were gone, and I felt emptied. I understood he was going to take my ass, and I also knew that wasn't the finale.

"Punishment," I said, my chin to my chest, words almost too soft to hear. "Discipline—"

Jesse agreed. "You do need discipline in your life. But what do you think you need right now?"

He'd know if I lied, if I told him something else. But I couldn't say the words. I just couldn't.

Jesse pulled out. "Spread your cheeks, Cody. Wide apart."

I'd been in this position for him before, but I knew he wasn't going to fuck my asshole. Not yet. He had some thin little switch, and before I could breathe, before I could beg, he was using it, right down the center, the pain cutting me, cutting through me. He worked with finesse, slicing that mean implement to the right or the left, before landing another perfect blow down the center, so that I felt as if he were splitting me open. And when he thought I was done, he dragged me over his lap once more, not for any teasing fingerplay this time, but for a ferocious over-the-knee hand-spanking that left me keening for breath. I was liquid as he positioned me finally how he wanted me, dragging me down on the carpet to fuck my ass, reaming me with his cock while I set my head on that soft old shag and wept.

"Does Daddy always know what you need?" Jesse hissed in my ear.

"Yes, sir," I choked out. "Yes, Daddy."

"Then you ought to trust me in the future." His voice was menacing. He was still on me, in me, holding me down with his weight. "I gave you a reprieve tonight, Cody. A get-out-of-jail-free card. I won't take pity on you again—"

He pulled out of me, and I thought he would leave me there, a mess on the floor, to pull myself together. But he didn't. He lifted me in his arms and carried me to his bedroom. He stripped the top of my pajamas over my head, so that I was totally naked, and then took off his own clothes.

"You'll go to sleep tonight with my cock in your mouth," he said, his voice so deep. "Like a pacifier. Suck it sweetly, girl, and I'll take care of you in the morning. Suck it like a good girl should."

"Yes, Daddy," I said, as I took up my position.

Like a good girl.

The words echoed in my head. Mocking me. But, hell, even if I'd never actually *be* a good girl, I could always pretend.

THE GARDEN OF SINN

Darklady

*H*is name was Sinn and he was beautiful.

Every week, his admirers gathered in a loose circle around him. No one remembered when it became the custom to do so. It simply happened, and having happened, felt as though it had always been the case. What better thing could there be on a Sunday afternoon than to watch Sinn bathe? What better feeling could there be than the torment felt in the gut and balls from knowing that this was the closest you would ever come to touching his deceptively soft skin? What greater purpose could exist than to arrive promptly each week and endure his maliciously innocent teasing?

Sinn was a gardener's assistant, and his light brown skin

was tanned to match the earth he smelled of. His hands were rough but delicate, strong enough to heave stone but sensitive enough to arrange a bloom. None of the men who assembled every week to admire his beauty knew much more than that about him. Few wanted to know much more. They certainly didn't want him to know anything about them, so there was never a word spoken between them and the young man whose nudity they admired and whose body they longed to touch.

Each week he came to this spot, this semiprivate/semipublic spot, to meditate after his week's labors, bathe his beautiful body, and pleasure himself. And every week the loose circle formed around him. The herbalist, the shopkeeper, the bank teller, the drunk Anglo with the tragic scar, and the old man who cheated at mah-jongg in the park took up their various places around the luscious boy—and imagined what it would be like to be his lover.

As usual, the herbalist stood in the shadows, stroking his cock and watching Sinn slowly remove his roughly woven garments, carefully setting them aside, knowing that his leisurely pace was infuriating to the men watching him. At night the herbalist would dream of kneeling before the boy and pressing his lips against his feet while running his hands along the strong calves, the knees, the firm thighs. He had been a weak child himself and as an adult had remained pale and gangly, unable to indulge in much physical activity. By stark comparison, Sinn's sculpted muscles gleamed with sweat, causing the herbalist's cock to stir inside his bony fist, slicking his palms with pre-come.

The last time the shopkeeper had seen Sinn, he had placed coins in the handsome young man's hand after he had purchased hard candy for some children. Siblings? Helpers? Neighbors? Offspring? He didn't know. His entire attention had been focused on Sinn as he had placed a piece of the newly purchased candy between his own lush lips—and sucked. Standing at the edge of the shade and watching the exquisite youth approach the water basin, he wondered what those lips would feel like wrapped around his cock and sucking the sweet cream from inside of it. For a moment Sinn paused as though listening, dipper of water poised over his nude body. The shopkeeper wondered if his thoughts had somehow been uttered aloud, and if he had been found out.

As always, the bank teller arrived later than the rest. He had no interest in watching Sinn undress or considering his mouth and its sucking skills. His eyes were entirely focused on the young gardener's firm, ripe buttocks. He yearned to grip each well-muscled cheek in his broad, soft hands. He was a big man, surprisingly big for a Thai. He never missed a meal and had little respect for those who did. He liked to imagine himself walking behind Sinn, who would be laboring hard in one of the various gardens of Bangkok. As he watched the youth bend to refill his dipper with bathwater, he pictured him bending over to straighten his work. Then the teller imagined seizing him from behind with his powerful hands, immobilizing him and plunging his fat cock between those fleshy mounds and deep into the dark, warm tunnel between them.

No one knew who the Anglo with the tragic scar was, or where he came from. Although the locals had been taking up positions for months, this man was new. Like the rest, he never spoke, never acknowledged that there were others. Unlike them, he could not blend neatly into the street scene once the final ejaculation was accomplished, the final dipper of water poured over Sinn's nude form. At more than six feet in height and with an angry red streak running from his left ear to the corner of his mouth, he was not anonymous, nor did he try to be. He stood in the sunlight, where Sinn could not possibly avoid his direct stare or pretend that he and his massive, exposed erection did not exist. In fact, his manner demanded that Sinn notice him, acknowledge his presence, attend to his needs.

Instead, the young man gave him only passing notice, focusing instead on himself, pouring ladle after ladle of cool water over his parched body, closing his eyes, and running his hands over his chest, his flat abdomen, his ass, his pelvis, pausing to cradle and stroke the fleshy prize that was beginning to stir between his thighs. As the men watched, Sinn's penis grew longer and thicker. Its pink, engorged head swelled, and the entirety of his member filled his palm. A slow, broad smile spread across his simple country face, and a sly look caused his dark eyes to twinkle. He pivoted his head to look out across the patio where the men lurked. Then he sat down on a decorative stool, confronting them boldly with his gaze, making the silent energy in the courtyard suddenly crackle with tension. All eyes were absolutely and entirely on him—and he knew it.

He scanned the assembled circle of masturbating admirers slowly and laughed with delight, licking his lips in anticipation of their inevitable orgasms and his weekly triumph over their otherwise respectable lives. For this brief time, in this magical place, he was no longer just the humble gardener's assistant; he was the god, the king—and his swollen cock was his scepter, the hot fluid it shot the addictive tonic that kept his subjects content and coming back for more. He palmed his inflamed dick, stroking it until it pointed stiffly skyward. Knowing that the men were watching him, aching for him, waiting for him to authorize their own ejaculations, made his erection twitch in his hand with pride and excitement. Who were these lonely, strange men that made their weekly pilgrimage to his quiet place? The mystery of the not knowing only served to further engorge him, pushing him closer and closer to the explosion that would signal the beginning of the end of the weekly vigil to the garden of Sinn.

As the cum began to tighten his balls and prepare for the trip up and out of his cock, Sinn caught sight of the old man who had for so long and so faithfully adored him from afar. He sat quietly near the bamboo, murmuring sutras to his own ancient but still vibrant staff, the withered skin of his body starkly soft in comparison to the smooth firmness of his twitching pole. As if sensing the youth's gaze upon him, the old man raised his head and looked into the eyes of his idol. For an instant there was a silent, visual connection between the two men—and then Sinn lifted his head in voiceless invitation.

Those assembled watched in confusion and amazement as the wizened old man rose unsteadily to his feet and hobbled cautiously toward Sinn. The young man smiled softly in approval, gesturing the elder onto the ground. Once stretched out, his back on the tiles, his wrinkled face directed toward Sinn, the youth leaned forward on his stool, directing his erection toward the stunned man. For a moment their eyes locked, then both turned their attention to the sensations beginning to wrack Sinn's body. The boy's mouth contorted, his eyes narrowed and closed, and his head snapped backward as a stream of hot come launched itself up and out of his shaft. Most of the white, salty liquid landed on Sinn's belly and groin, but a precious sample landed with strange precision on the old man's chest, above his heart. Within a moment, Sinn's substance was joined by that of the old man, running together down the elder man's side and onto the tiles below him. All around them, the other men likewise stained the ground or moistened their own skin.

The ancient one and Sinn rested for a moment, catching their breaths—and then looked at one another. Somehow they knew that this would be their last time in this life together, the last time they would share this aspect of mortality. Sinn rose to his feet, extended a slightly trembling hand to the man upon the ground before him, and assisted him to his feet. With eyes cast upon the ground, Sinn raised his hands, palms together like a closed lotus bud, until the tips touched his chin. Slowly he knelt before the man, sinking to the clay squares below, inclining his head in respect, raising his hands to his forehead and then to his chest. As he rose to his feet, he ran his tongue up the aged belly and chest of the man, tasting their combined essences.

As if by mutual agreement, the four other men stepped back and away, leaving the youth and the ancient standing a moment more, gazing into one another's eyes. And then, like so many times before, they parted—never to meet again.

BAG AND BAGGAGE

Teresa Noelle Roberts

*T*he closer they got to Paris, the more Jillian dreaded it. As the plane had cut through the transatlantic darkness, taking her and Michael toward what was supposed to be a romantic honeymoon, she'd squirmed in her seat, hashing over fears, memories, things she should have said and hadn't.

Some of those things she could still get off her chest. Better late than never.

For others, she was ten years too late.

Maybe it was chewing all night on those should-haves that had given her the hard knot in her stomach. Decade-old regrets and sorrows, things she thought she'd dealt with, gotten over except as the occasional dream, the occasional brief, bittersweet memory.

But the closer they got to Paris, the more she feared she'd been wrong about being over Colum. At least over him enough to face Paris.

She shifted again in her seat, trying not to disturb Michael. The longer he slept, the longer she could put off the conversation. Not forever, but for a few more minutes. A few more minutes before she told him the dream honeymoon he'd won for them in a raffle might turn into a nightmare.

But as the lights came up in the plane cabin and flight attendants began to bustle around, delivering coffee and stale croissants to groggy passengers, Michael woke up, annoyingly perky and bright-eyed. He leaned over, kissed her quickly, said, "How's my lovely bride this . . . shit, Jillian, what's wrong?"

"That obvious?"

He nodded, all the perkiness draining from his face. "Are you sick? Or . . . "

He didn't finish, but Jillian could tell what he was thinking. Not too hard to guess when you wake up the morning after your wedding and your bride looks like she's ready to cry or scream. "No, love, I'm not having second thoughts. Not about you." She kissed him with all the enthusiasm she could muster, which, as the kiss deepened, turned out to be more than she expected. She didn't just love Michael because she loved touching him, but that certainly helped at moments like this.

She pulled away, took his hands. Breathed deeply to calm

herself, looking at his solidly handsome, adult face—olive skin, dark eyes, sensuous lips, neatly trimmed beard—but seeing another one, younger and fairer, with blue eyes and wild reddish hair and an embarrassment of a goatee that never filled in properly.

"I'm worried about Paris," she said, realizing that the bald statement didn't make much sense but unsure how else to get started. "I thought it would be okay, but now I'm not so sure. Maybe it's stupid to be worried but . . . I went there with Colum on a trip from Dublin. The last place we went together."

"Great. Nothing like going on your honeymoon to a place full of memories of your first lover. Your *dead* first lover." His voice was controlled, flat. In contrast, emotions were washing over Michael's face so fast she was having a hard time keeping up: concern, anger (or at least annoyance), jealousy, frustration, and back to concern. "Might have been nice if you'd mentioned this before we were almost there."

She muttered an apology, looked away, out the window of the plane. They were over land now, although it was still too dark to make out much of anything except the lights of some town below them.

"Hey, I'm not mad. Alright," he conceded, "I'm a little mad. But I'm also trying to figure out what's going on—if this is just minor strangeness or a more serious problem we need to work through. So talk to me."

She sighed. "First of all, I'm sorry. The longer I didn't say anything, the more annoyed I figured you'd be, and the scarier it was to say anything. So I put it off longer. Dumb, I know."

"Human, though. But why didn't you say something right away, when we could have just made other plans?"

She made herself look at him, at the combination of worry and annoyance on his face. Half of her wanted to turn away again; talking might be easier that way. The other half wanted to snuggle against him, to bury her face on his shoulder, to whimper.

Neither, she knew, was a good idea at the moment. She just needed to get it out.

"At first, I was so focused on the rest of the wedding plans that all I could think was 'Yay, free trip!'"

There, that part was easy enough to say. She'd been stupid, but she wasn't the first bride who'd been too distracted to think clearly and who, as a result, did something spectacularly dumb.

But how to explain the rest when it wasn't entirely clear in her own mind?

She realized her nails were gouging her palms and forced herself to unclench her tense fists. "Then you were so excited that I convinced myself it would be alright. Ten years is a long time, and Paris is such a beautiful city. I figured you and I would go and have a great time, and at worst I'd have a few melancholy moments. No big deal. But the closer we got to actually going, the more anxious I got, but I thought that if I paid too much attention to it, it would make it worse, so I tried to ignore it. And of course, that didn't help at all."

Michael looked about as rattled as she felt. Touching his hand, she tried to reassure him, "I'm not still in love with Colum. If he hadn't died, he'd just be an old boyfriend, just a few funny stories I'd tell my friends on girls' night out, but he did die, and it left some scars. Maybe we should head down to Provence or something. I don't want to spoil things by being all morose. . . . "

"I'd like to think I can distract you enough that you won't stay morose for long. And I'm not going to let some dead guy come between us.' He squeezed her hands. "I love you, and Paris is one of my favorite places on earth, and I want to share it with you. Not with you and some Irish kid's ghost."

"Jealous?" Despite the haunted night and the sick feeling in the pit of her stomach, she managed a small laugh at the idea of Michael being jealous of the dead.

"No. Well, yes. This is weirding me out a little," he admitted. "I know you must think about him sometimes. That's normal. But it bothers me that he took you to Paris first. And it bothers me that it's bothering you now."

The flight attendant came around with coffee, which Jillian eagerly accepted. Its main virtues were warmth and caffeine, but she needed the caffeine—and the time it gave her to collect her thoughts. She drank a few sips of the potent-if not exactly tasty-black brew before she responded to Michael with, "It was a pretty miserable trip. In fact, I dumped him in Paris. It's wide-open for you and me to create some good Paris memories—but it's also likely to open up some old baggage."

His expression changed, losing some of the air of discomfort. "I'm not scared of old baggage," Michael said. "What's the worst that can be in there? Dirty socks? I love you, and you love me, and if things get strange, we'll deal with them."

Jillian wasn't convinced it would be that easy.

His answer had been too pat. Michael always said that no problem was insurmountable if they worked together, but he couldn't make every problem go away just by willing it. Not her memories, not his own worries about them. Oh, she didn't doubt they could get through it in the long run, but she doubted it would be pretty.

THE CAB RIDE TO THEIR HOTEL took on a surreal quality. On the one hand, she was snuggled against the familiar heat of Michael's body. He pointed out sights in the distance, regaled her with stories, and kissed her often, as if he was determined to distract her from any thoughts of Colum.

She didn't know how to explain that the kisses were double-edged, sometimes distracting her, sometimes triggering memories that weren't altogether pleasant—but not altogether unpleasant, which was in some ways more disturbing.

Arriving in Paris by train that first time—bleary-eyed, in lust, convinced they were about to embark on a grand romantic adventure. Colum had been half-drunk on a flask of cheap whiskey they'd brought from Dublin with them, and she'd not been much better off. Sober enough that she'd resisted having sex in the train compartment (which wasn't exactly private), but not sober enough that she didn't think about it for a second before telling him he was being unreasonable, that the conductor might come in at any moment.

Colum lifting up her skirt on the Eiffel Tower while she was distracted by the amazing view. And when she turned around, ready to slap him into next week, Colum yelling to the world at large that he was crazy about her, so crazy that he just couldn't keep his hands to himself—a grand gesture that got her to forgive him for the moment.

Colum in the fetid little room they'd rented, sated and grinning, with her beside him in similar happy shape.

The look on Colum's face—that last glimpse she caught when, after she swore she wouldn't glance back, she did anyway—as she stormed out of his life forever.

Good and bad, mingling together, strong enough that when Michael stroked her thigh, raising her skirt in the back of the cab, she caught herself saying, "Behave yourself!"

Jillian didn't tell Michael to "behave" when he wanted to fool around. Usually, she dove in and enjoyed, and if she wasn't in the mood, she'd say so, plainly. But the Jillian of Jillian-and-Colum—the girl who'd gone to Dublin on a scholarship from her Catholic college—had said it a lot.

Michael looked like he'd been slapped by her voice.

"I'm sorry I snapped," she quickly corrected herself. "I'm fried and still edgy, and I'm just not up for much besides cuddling and kissing until I get a shower and some real food."

He looked appeased—regretful, sure, but appeased—as he let her snuggle against him again. His touch was affectionate, but not sexual.

And it worked for a while. By concentrating on Michael—Michael's warmth and comfort—she managed to shut out most of the thoughts of Colum and get herself calmed down, almost convinced that a lot of her problem was simple exhaustion.

But when the cab driver pulled their luggage from the trunk, the zipper on her ancient leather backpack gave way.

Underwear and socks, a guidebook, birth control pills, her toiletry bag, and two novels fell out onto the dirty Parisian street. A bottle of aspirin rolled under the cab. The telltale odor of roses and vanilla told her that the perfume in her toiletry case had not survived the fall.

She cursed and started picking scattered possessions up, telling herself that it could be worse. Then, as she went to stick the first handfuls of stuff back into the bag, she realized it was worse. It wasn't just the zipper opening up. The leather itself had ripped, taking the zipper with it. She sat down on the curb and began to cry.

Michael sat down beside her, put his arm around her, and asked, "Are you alright?"

She sniffled, took a deep breath, forced herself to stop the tears. It didn't make her feel a lot better, but at least she wasn't bawling on the street anymore, which had to count for something. Dignity, at least.

"Colum gave me that pack. The one I'd brought to Dublin ripped partway through the term, and he figured a leather one would last longer than nylon. It sure did. It outlived him by ten years. And now it's fallen apart in Paris, just like he and I did, and I'm too damn tired to cope!"

Michael kissed her cheek but didn't say anything. He looked like he had a lot of things he was tempted to say—some kind and supportive and some less so—but apparently he figured it was safest to keep his mouth shut.

Great start to the honeymoon. So far, it was "Colum's ghost and associated baggage," one, "Jillian and Michael," zero.

A SHOWER IN THE GLEAMING HOTEL BATHROOM definitely helped Jillian's outlook on life.

She wandered out of the shower feeling pleasantly boneless yet still a bit restless. Michael was flopped on the bed, still naked, and he beckoned her to join him.

"No way," Jillian said. "If I lie down, I'm done for, and I want to see Paris." It was even true. No need to go into the memory of Colum in a similar pose on the far less appealing bed in their mangy hotel, trying to beckon her back in for round two, or twelve, or whatever.

She pulled on underpants and a gauze skirt, rummaged for a clean bra and the right shirt in the suitcase, determinedly not looking at the damaged backpack as she did so. "So what do you want to do today?" she asked. She already knew her own answer: *Keep busy. Make new memories. Focus on Michael, not Colum or her own thoughts.*

"First, more coffee and a real French pastry." Michael stretched, sat up, swung his long legs off the bed. "Then maybe just wander the Latin Quarter until we decide it's time for lunch. Go to Notre Dame." He snuck up behind her, wrapped his arms around her waist, whispered in her ear. "Do something silly and romantic and Parisian, but low-energy. Maybe a sightseeing carriage ride?"

His hands snaked up to cup her still-bare breasts. "See if we can show the carriage driver a few sights."

She froze, torn between the present—Michael's familiar body behind her, his breath tickling her ear, his well-loved hands caressing nipples that perked to his touch despite her odd mood—and shockingly vivid ten-year-old memories.

Paris at night. A smell of linden trees and rain and harsh cigarettes. Colum in a carriage, trying to force her head down to suck his cock. Not violent or rough, but pretty much ignoring her protests, which had started out giggly and were getting more and more furious as he kept insisting.

Jillian needed only a moment to push aside the memory and the mixture of anger and arousal that accompanied it. But Michael needed less than that to pick up that something was a little off. He changed position, moved his hands so he was cuddling rather than caressing. "Another Colum time bomb?"

"Yeah. I just remembered him mauling me during a carriage ride, trying to get me to go down on him."

"Did you?"

Jillian snorted. "Hell, no. I got really mad. We had a huge blowup, which probably embarrassed the carriage driver more than a blow *job* would have. And then . . . " Her voice trailed off.

"And then?"

"And then we went back to our crummy hotel and mated like minks." She said the words very fast and felt herself flushing, as if dredging up the memories dredged up her younger self along with them.

"Well, make-up sex can be hot."

Instinctively, she nodded.

Then she looked at the memories through the lens of what she knew now and made herself answer more honestly. "It wasn't just that. I couldn't bring myself to do the public blow job, but the idea of it turned me on. I couldn't tell him that though. I couldn't even really tell myself that. So I convinced us both it was make-up sex. Which might have been okay if it hadn't led to this stupid pattern of him suggesting something outrageous, me getting mad about it, and then having wild monkey sex later." She chuckled dryly. "And this happened all over Paris—I don't know if he'd been reading too much Henry Miller or what, but he turned into Mr. Exhibitionist as soon as we got here."

"Maybe we *should* just go to Provence tomorrow. It's lovely there, and we wouldn't have to deal with all this."

Lavender-scented hills untainted by memories sounded awfully tempting, but Michael sounded so forlorn that Jillian developed a new determination to stick it out and make it work. "I want to see Paris with you," she said, "through your eyes. I refuse to screw up the honeymoon any more than I already have, and I refuse to let this beautiful city be spoiled for me because of stuff that happened when I was twenty. I need to deal with this, Michael, and that means not running away.

"Besides—" this hit her like a beacon cutting through fog, putting some of her worries into perspective—"it's not all bad memories. He suggested some damn good fantasies that I wasn't ready to handle, so maybe something fun might happen if I end up in the same place, but older and wiser and in better company."

After a long pause, Michael said, "Maybe they're part of what you need to deal with, those things you've wondered about all these years. Not necessarily to do them, I mean," he added, evidently seeing the combination of heat and panic that flashed through her, "but at least figure out whether they're still scary."

She breathed a long sigh and threw her arms around her husband. She was scared but at the same time hopeful. Oh, she didn't doubt that there would be bad moments—either old grief or the memory of her own youthful stupidity coming back to bite her. But for the first time, she began to think it might be healing, not merely dreadful.

"Alright," Michael said. "We'll try this. Take it slow. But if it gets too crazy for either of us, Provence is just a plane ride and some credit card abuse away."

AFTER A LEISURELY STOP for coffee and pastry, they strolled through the Quartier, more or less toward Notre Dame. Michael took charge of the camera and snapped pictures of everything from street signs to cats in windows to women leaving bakeries with loaves of bread.

There was no groping, no suggestion of raunchy alley sex, not even as much kissing as usual. The occasional quick smooch. The occasional brush of his hand over her ass, seemingly accidental, but not really. The tender arm around her waist. Once kissing her fingertips in a doorway. Yet she could feel the sexual tension flowing off him like water.

And pretty soon, she was feeling it herself, a current that made her hyperaware of his body, his movements, his warmth, the subtle smell of him next to her.

Several hours and a stop for lunch later, they reached the Île-Saint-Louis, crossed the ancient bridge, and, like so many pilgrims before them, gazed in wonder at the facade of the great cathedral. Michael's arm was warm around her waist, holding her close.

"It's awesome—in the literal sense of the word," he said. "Pictures just don't convey it. I've seen it several times, but I'm always blown away."

"Maybe I'll get a better look this time, without Colum trying to convince me to fool around in a confessional."

Michael paused a beat, made a face that was half-appalled, half-amused. "He wanted to have sex in there?"

"Under the eyes of God' were his words." Jillian laughed softly, realizing as she did that the laugh didn't feel as forced as she might have expected. "That was almost the last straw. Almost, not quite. I told him we'd probably go to hell for even thinking it. But I've fantasized about it since."

Michael drew her into a kiss, the long, bone-melting kind that, against the backdrop of Notre Dame, made Jillian feel like she'd fallen into a romantic movie.

And it all but set her panties on fire.

She pressed herself against him, hoping for more. More kissing at least. A stealthy caress. Nothing major, just the little teasing touches she was used to from him.

Instead, he stopped, led her inside.

They entered the incense-fragrant nave, explored every nook and cranny of Notre Dame. They held hands much of the time, but Michael was so appropriate, it almost hurt.

Once or twice she thought about Colum, his beautiful Irish voice whispering obscenities into her ear in the cathedral. How appalled she'd been at the blasphemy—and how turned on.

It might be fun to have Michael do that to her. Not that she'd ever have sex in a church—but talking about it, now *that* could be exciting.

But he didn't. He brushed his lips against her hair, hugged her, acted like a doting husband—but not like a sex-crazed boy. And he didn't say a word that was even vaguely suggestive.

She was the one who broke, who whispered in his ear, "That confessional, over there. That was the one he wanted to use. Can you believe?" She couldn't quite bring herself to say more than that, not over the clamor of mixed feelings—self-reproach and arousal and guilt that the memory of Colum's naughtiness affected her one way or the other now that she was married to someone else. But all sorts of sacrilegious and sexy images flashed through her head.

"That's hot. Hot as in 'hellfire,'" he responded. "And I don't even believe in hell." He kissed her cheek lightly, then moved on. "Let's go see the bell tower."

They weren't even able to hold hands on the narrow circular staircase, worn concave by centuries of footsteps. He let her walk ahead and kept one hand on the small of her back—letting it stray down to her butt just enough to tease, then moving it back to the innocent area above it.

Only when they stepped out onto the open air of the balcony—still among a crowd of visitors but not exactly in the cathedral proper—did Michael pull her close, kiss her, meld to her with enough fervor that a few people cast scandalized (or possibly jealous) looks in their direction, whisper in her ear, "Now this is where I'd want to take you. Leaning over the railing, looking out over all of Paris. Not just under the eyes of God, but under everyone's eyes."

Her tangle of mixed feelings sorted itself out with remarkable speed: outrageously aroused but certainly not outraged; not guilty, because it was Michael saying it, not Colum's ghost.

And safe, which she'd never felt with Colum at such moments, no matter how wet some of his crazier ideas made her. She never really trusted him to listen to her boundaries, to know that "no" meant "no," or at least "not here, not now."

Michael, on the other hand, she trusted completely.

"Probably not a wise idea—I don't want to spend our honeymoon in jail," she whispered back, "but a really, really sexy one. Maybe a tease, though?"

Michael nodded, his smile slow and knowing and rich with desire.

Without putting his hands anyplace inappropriate or doing anything obvious to the people around them, Michael pressed his body against her, pushing his leg between hers.

Jillian bit her lip to keep silent as a small, sharp convulsion ran through her. It was just the kind of thing Colum would have loved to do but didn't have the skill or the discretion to bring off. Thinking of him didn't hurt or bewilder that time though. It was just a memory.

Their energy flagged after leaving the cathedral, and they went for more coffee. Over cups of excellent café au lait, Michael asked, "So, what happened with Colum?'

"Motorcycle accident," she said instinctively, knowing she

was ducking a question she'd rather not answer; she'd ducked it with everyone, including her best girlfriends.

"Not how he died—I know about that. I meant why you broke up with him."

She took another sip of coffee, wishing it were wine instead. The tale of the breakup didn't show either of them in a flattering light, but Michael deserved the truth. "It was spring. The term had ended, and pretty soon I'd have to leave Dublin and go home. Colum insisted that we had to visit Paris together, and I wasn't about to argue. Paris in the spring with your first love—what girl could say no? You already know that things didn't go exactly according to plan, but I still thought I loved him. Maybe I even did.

"The last night, Colum scraped together enough money to take me out for a nice dinner. Partway through, he pulled out this little box, and he said he had something to give me. The way he said it, I thought it was going to be a ring. It was Ben Wa balls in a jeweler's box."

Michael tried to keep his face composed and failed miserably. "They must have made your flight home more interesting," he said, barely keeping the laughter out of his voice.

"They might have if I hadn't thrown them in his face! I was so convinced he was about to propose. Instead he suggested I put them in and go for a walk along the Seine with him."

Jillian felt herself blushing. "I was too angry and disappointed to think straight, let alone to try to talk it through. So I stormed out of the restaurant in a classic college-girl snit and left Paris on the late train. We didn't talk again when we got back to Dublin—we were both still too mad—and I headed home the next week. That was in May. By August he was dead. Long before then, I'd gotten to the point where I could see the funny side of the whole mess, but I never had the guts to get in touch with him. So I never got to tell him I was sorry for being such a drama queen, or to explain why I'd been so upset."

She looked away, then looked back at Michael. "Or to say what I've wanted to say in the years since—that he helped me become more comfortable with my sexuality, helped me become who I am now. It was just a . . . delayed effect."

" . . . that I benefited from." Michael raised his coffee cup like a wineglass. "Here's to you, Colum, wherever you are."

She echoed the gesture.

"So, any ideas for what to do next?" Michael asked after a short silence. "Hit a museum, walk around some more?"

Jillian took a deep breath. "Maybe a carriage ride?" Seeing the startled but delighted look on her husband's face, she added, "If I could enjoy Notre Dame thanks to you, not to mention actually talk about the breakup, I think I'm ready for the carriage ride."

THEY DIDN'T ACTUALLY GET TO IT UNTIL DUSK.

Dusk, Jillian decided, was a good time for this kind of thing. The horse's hooves clopped patiently against the pavement, and Paris spread out around them, the colors softening and blurring together and the faces of pedestrians taking on a peculiar beauty as the light faded. Even the cars looked good.

Romantic. Definitely romantic.

She'd only meant to snuggle against Michael, kiss him, enjoy the comfort of his body. But all their talking had put other ideas into her head—ideas she'd masturbated to on and off for years but never thought she'd have the nerve to try.

Under the cover of a kiss, she dropped her hand into his crotch. Michael's cock sprang to life after just a few strokes through the well-worn denim.

She flashed again to that earlier trip, how when Colum had tried one of his naughty games, her nipples had perked up, her heart had started racing, and a great "fuck me" weight had gathered between her legs.

Just like she felt now. Only now she wasn't the same fearful girl.

She wasn't a girl at all. She was a woman with a man who loved her, and she didn't need to be afraid of her own desires.

She unzipped him. Michael's eyes widened as she arranged herself in the cramped seat and closed her mouth over his cock.

Iron-hard velvet. And oh, the smell of him, warm and musky and a little stronger than usual after the long day, rich enough to overpower the musty carriage seat. She wrapped one hand around the base of his cock and cupped his balls with the other, pressing into the magic spot behind them that would always get him off quick and hard. Much as she'd like to draw this out, it probably wasn't a good idea.

"If you keep that up," he whispered, "I'll be no good for you once we get to the hotel." His voice was already sounding a little strained.

Jillian looked up long enough to say, "I have faith. You'll take good care of me."

If she didn't explode right along with him, that is. Despite the awkward position, and wondering how much passersby could see, as well as the sneaking suspicion that the driver knew exactly what was going on—or maybe because of these factors—she was on fire, her underpants drenched, her sex throbbing blissfully.

She could feel him twitching beneath her—wanting to fuck her mouth, she guessed, but trying to fight the urge, knowing she didn't always like that sensation.

"Go on," she murmured around his cock. It came out more like, "Glug awn," but he understood. His hips pressed up off the cracked leatherette, pushing his cock deeper into her mouth. Almost too much to take, but she didn't care. She wanted to get him off—partly to avoid detection, but more because she just wanted his come filling her mouth. He pulled back, thrust again, and she worked with him. Again.

His hands closed in her hair. His cock twitched, and he exploded into her mouth.

She sat up, licking her lips and trying to look prim.

"Your turn," Michael said quietly, his voice still a little unsteady. "I'm not as flexible as you though, so you'll have to settle for my fingers."

"I can wait," she whispered nervously. Michael came stealthily—no noise, little change in facial expression—but she wasn't like that. If she came here, it would be obvious to anyone who saw her.

"I can't. Not much longer. But we can always head back to the hotel."

And something about his tone, the combination of urgency without pushiness, made her melt even further and mouth, "Yes."

"Yes" to his hand under her skirt, skillful fingers playing on her slick clit.

"Yes" to him half-lying over her, kissing and kissing as Paris passed them by.

And in the end, "Yes," out loud and only partly silenced by his mouth, to the orgasm that overtook her.

At that, the carriage driver did turn around. She smiled indulgently and went back to driving.

Blushing, but much less embarrassed than she would have thought, Jillian smiled back and arranged her skirt. As her husband sat up, she whispered to Michael, "I know what to do with the old pack. Sort of a Viking funeral, in honor of Colum."

And then she told him.

AT 2:00 AM ON THE NIGHT before they were leaving Paris, the Seine embankment wasn't quite deserted, but the few people there were either bums or people who would prefer not be noticed too much themselves: lovers, hookers, people enjoying recreational pharmaceuticals.

And one couple lugging a destroyed pack.

Stealthily, they found a trash can and shoved the bag into it.

Jillian had been wet on and off all day in anticipation, and Michael had stoked the flames with whispered teasing and surreptitious caresses as they'd taken a river cruise, wandered through Montmartre, enjoyed an amazing dinner. Then they'd gone back to the hotel and napped. Just napped, but she woke in Michael's arms with her nipples hard and her pussy slick.

When she'd left the hotel in a short skirt and no panties—something she wouldn't normally do—she'd gotten slicker yet. Michael, equally excited by anticipation, had needed to hold the bag in his lap on the Metro to hide what was on his mind.

Now they slipped into the shadows by the walled embankment.

Jillian leaned forward, bracing herself against the cold, rough stone. Over the hum of the city, she heard the small, precious sound of Michael unzipping his pants.

He raised her skirt. She shivered, drew a breath, parted her legs a little more. The heat of Michael's cock rubbing against her lips was almost enough to set her off.

And as he entered her, one hand on her clit, a surge of pleasure, not quite an orgasm but a teasing hint at one, made her clench and bear down on Michael's cock.

Michael, normally a patient lover, didn't hold back, disregarding all artistry and pumping into her hard and fast. Jillian let herself be swept up in the moment—the smells and sounds of the city around her, the cool night air on her skin, Michael driving into her, one hand gripping her hip, the other circling her clit.

The lights from a passing barge briefly illuminated the embankment, outlining their figures against the wall.

Jillian froze.

Glanced over her shoulder at the barge.

Came with a shudder that set Michael exploding inside her with a strangled, "Shit Jillian . . . "

And as they caught their breath, dabbed themselves off with tissues Michael had stashed in his pocket, rearranged their clothes, Jillian pictured Colum: a boyish face and lanky young man's body, a young man's curiosity and abundant raw sexual energy, a young man's heedlessness and occasional selfishness.

And then, with love, with regret, with joy that she was moving on with Michael, she let the image go.

ICY HOT

Rachel Kramer Bussel

I wasn't expecting to meet the sexiest guy in New York City during one of the hottest days of the year, but sometimes the best things come to those who wait—in line, at a bodega, in the middle of August. I could see the last bag of hard, cold, perfect ice just waiting for me at the end of the line, like my own personal pot of gold at the end of a rainbow, and my whole body shivered in anticipation. I clutched the magazine I'd been holding close to me to cover my nipples, which were sticking to my skimpy tank top. It had been too hot for a bra, too hot for anything but the barest minimum of clothing, hence the tank and a skimpy black skirt that fell loosely against my hips, exposing just the tiniest curve of my belly.

My short skirt clung to my body as much as the minimal scrap of fabric could, molding to my ass and hips as I stood there, sweltering. I tried to fan myself with a subscription card from the magazine, meanwhile fantasizing about jumping naked onto a pile of ice, the vision momentarily slaking a tiny bit of the heat suffusing my body. It was 105 degrees for the third day running, and everyone in town was feeling the burn. Like a fool, I'd taken an apartment without air conditioning back in January, figuring I could install it when I needed it. *Ha, I thought, no such luck.* By the time I could afford it, the heat wave was upon us, and an air conditioner was as rare as a pot of gold—or the perfect boudoir partner. I wanted that ice, and I wanted it bad.

Then something up front caught my eye. I couldn't help but notice the ripped hunk, the one in just a tight white tank top, frayed jean shorts, and sandals. His muscles were perfectly chiseled, sculpted into his arms as if planted there by the gods, not the kind one gets from copious, overdone workouts like those on so many of the bulging guys you see staggering down the street, as if the weight of their extra firmness is too much for them. His body was lean and natural, like he'd always been able to heft huge bags of ice—or swooning women—with ease.

Then I took a look as the guy swiped the chilly bag, my own personal treasure, scooping it into his arms as easily as if he were picking up a pack of peanuts. I kept looking as he took what was rightly mine, cradling the cold bag against his incredible body. For a moment, I imagined him cradling me in his arms in the very same way, then tossing me over his shoulder and carrying me off to his bed. I didn't know what to be jealous of more—the bag of ice, or him for getting to it before me—but one thing was certain: I wasn't giving up on either one. At that point, it wasn't just a matter of desire, but of survival. Everything about this hunk was perfectly proportioned, and when he wiped the sweaty swoop of hair off his forehead, I caught a glimpse of pale, piercing blue eyes. I shivered, despite the store's lack of air conditioning, then marched forward, as proudly as I could in my elevated flip-flops, wishing I'd worn heels that could click authoritatively on the tiles.

"Excuse me," I said, tapping him on the shoulder, "but I think you're holding my ice." I put my hands out, as if ready to accept it. I had absolutely no claim to the large bag of frozen water, seeing as he got to it before me fair and square, but I wasn't just hot and cranky anymore—I was horny. The heat felt different now, less oppressive and more sensual, like it was tempting me to melt into a puddle on the ground or strip off all my clothes.

He gave me a once-over, a very slow eye-fuck that took in every inch of my body, from my cropped red hair, freckles, deep brown eyes, and lightly glossed lips to the tiny gold hoops in my ears, my shoulders on display from the thin white tank top, and my nipples, which I knew were visible through the skimpy layer of white.

He kept on looking, moving on down to my loose black skirt, lingering there as if trying to figure out what kind of panties I had on (white mesh bikini, but he couldn't tell), and on to my long, lean legs, strong from hours of strolling up to Central Park from my East Village apartment and hiking across boroughs, reveling in the views from the Williamsburg and Brooklyn bridges. I'd always thought treadmills were cheating somehow, robbing walkers of the fun to be had from zooming through nature—even citified nature—in a new pair of sneakers. I was grateful for all that strolling as he took in my thighs and knees and taut calves before reaching my just-pedicured, magenta-painted toes, sitting prettily atop my flowered, pink, elevated flip-flops, which gave me a few more inches over my 5'7" official height.

I couldn't tell whether he liked what he saw, because he stuck out one chilled, dripping hand and said, "And what exactly is your name, my dear?" while keeping the ice hugged close to his chest. I looked up at him and shivered again, before I even shook his hand, because of the way his eyes seemed to read my every thought. When our fingers met, I gripped his hand tightly, afraid of staggering.

"Doris," I said, wishing, for the umpteenth time, for a sexier name, a Katerina or Veda or even a simple Amanda. I often wished I had the guts to simply christen myself anew each time I was introduced to someone I wanted to impress, but I knew I'd get caught in my own web if anyone ever tried to flag me down with my fake name. So "Doris" it was, even though I'd never really felt like a "Doris." I was a girl who'd do a cartwheel on the sidewalk, even now, at thirty. I was liable to flash my boobs at a party just for fun, run through a sprinkler in a new dress, or creep into a graveyard on a dare. When I was ten, I vowed never to be as matronly as my name would imply, and the contrast seemed to amuse him.

Without returning the courtesy of introducing himself, he said, in the huskiest voice I'd ever heard—part radio announcer, part Isaac Hayes—"Nice to meet you, Doris. Now, we have a little problem here, because as far as I'm concerned, this ice is all mine, and you know what they say about possession being nine-tenths of the law. . . . "

I stepped closer, resting one manicured hand on the ice, enjoying the chill that traveled through my fingers and digging my claws into the gleaming plastic. "I was never all that good at math," I said, laying my long-abandoned Southern accent on as thick as I could, "but I'm pretty sure that means there's one-tenth of this ice for me, isn't that right?" As I said it, I fished out a cube and held it in front of his eyes like a hard-fought treasure, a girl's pirate booty on our mini summertime ship. I took the piece of ice and slowly brought it over to my exposed chest, rubbing it against my hot skin and immediately feeling better, especially when I saw him stare intently while I dipped it down below the neckline of my tank top, taking a tour between my breasts before emerging back onto my visible skin. I rubbed it around my chest, then tossed my head back and stroked my neck with the quickly melting cube. I'd been dreaming about giving myself an ice-bath all day, though I thought I'd be doing it in private.

I had cooled myself off enough to slake that initial bout of heat that had been plaguing me since I stepped into the non-air-conditioned store, but another, better kind of warmth had quickly spread through me once I started talking to the sexy stranger—one that started from inside and spread outward; one that ice alone simply wouldn't be enough to chill. I had a small puddle with a tiny bit of ice, no longer a cube, still in my hand, so I just went for it—I held out my wet palm to his lips. "Want some?" I purred, my voice letting him know, if I hadn't already, that I was offering much more than water. Instead of using what I was sure had to be a big, rough tongue to lap up my offering, he took my hand, brought it up under his shirt, and pressed it against his chest. When I was done marveling at how strong and solid his muscles were, I thought I felt the beating of his heart.

He held his palm flat against the back of my hand as the water dribbled down his chest. Then he slid my hand along the firmness of his body, down his torso, and out from under his shirt. I let it drop back to my side as if in a daze, the chilly numbness matched by a special tingling through-out the rest of my body. I'd gone into primal, animalistic mode; all I cared about was getting the two things I most wanted in life at that very second—the ice and the man, but not necessarily in that order.

He stepped closer, and I had no idea what was about to happen, when the clerk cleared his throat in an unmistakable sign of annoyance. He didn't need to say a word to embarrass me. My cooled-down cheeks heated up again, and I stepped away from the man, who still hadn't given me his name. I snatched the bag and threw the three dollars down on the counter. I would have stalked out, but I was too turned on by my unexpected encounter with the ice man—plus I didn't feel it was totally fair to abscond with his ice.

Alright, the real reason I paused and looked over my shoulder was to make sure he was watching. I let the heavy bag drop down to my side. It's hard to feel seductive in the kind of sweltering heat that makes any attempts at fashion or hairstyling, or even smiling, pretty much futile by the time you get down the stairs. But he'd managed to make me hot in the best kind of way, and he—and I—deserved some kind of reward for it. He walked over to me—swaggered, really—his eyes boring into my body like he wanted to see inside.

He purposefully brushed against me so the ice touched my legs. "Ready to cool off . . . with me?" he asked, stepping around to stand in front of me and stare deeply into my eyes. I melted; again, his for the taking. And take me he did. He slipped a hand into mine as naturally as if we were a longtime couple off for a lazy stroll, but there was nothing lazy about the tingling our joined hands set off throughout my body. I almost didn't notice the blazing sun and thick humidity because I was so focused on touching the sexiest man I'd ever seen. I wasn't sure whether to look at him, or the ground, or straight ahead, and didn't even know what anyone else seeing us would think of me in my ratty clothes paired with this absolute hunk. I didn't really care, but it felt so surreal that I kept my head down and didn't say a word lest I stammer something utterly ridiculous and nix what promised to be the highlight of my summer.

Thankfully we arrived soon after. I was totally aroused but slightly nervous as well—not that he'd harm me in any way, but I just didn't know what to expect. What if the climax of our day, so to speak, had already happened as I traced myself with ice before his and the storekeeper's eyes?

I needn't have worried. As he led me into his apartment, I saw that it was simply but tastefully decorated, as welcoming as the man next to me. I was grateful to be out of the sun, and to see what would happen next.

"Relax, sit," he said, guiding me to a sumptuous chair, conveniently placed right in front of his working air conditioner, before whipping off his shirt. I got only a brief glimpse of his firm, muscular chest before I sank into my new throne and relaxed instantly, forcing any doubts from my mind. I shut my eyes and relaxed fully while he moved behind me. The next thing I knew, he was pushing my head forward slightly so he could massage my neck, his powerful fingers digging into my sweaty skin, pushing deep, their effect rippling through my body. It almost felt as if he were touching my pussy, and when his tongue brushed against the back of my neck, I shuddered, almost crying out as I gripped the sides of the chair. The chilly air blowing against me, combined with his magic hands and hot tongue, had my nipples hard.

I forgot about the fact that I didn't really know him at all. Sometimes, in a city of millions of strangers, you just have to take a chance and let your body make the decisions for you. And my body was saying *Yes, please, more, harder.* I leaned forward, offering him my skin, and he accepted, lifting my top over my head. I liked having my back to him; a sudden bout of shyness made me want to keep my breasts to myself for a few moments, to let him get to know them slowly. He took his time, leaving his hot breath on my neck and shoulder blades, suckling on each earlobe, until I felt once again like I was melting. Somehow—despite the fact that earlier that day I thought I was going to die from heatstroke—I wanted the heat that this man was causing inside me; I wanted him to make me burn with desire.

He kept going, saying little save for grunts, moans, and murmurs of approval as he wet my upper back with his tongue. "Put your arms on the side of the chair," he said, and I instinctively did as I was told. Simply responding to his order sent shivers all along my body as I waited to see what he'd do next. What he did was beyond anything I could have imagined. The first shock of it had me clutching the arms of the chair so tightly, I thought I might break them. He took an ice cube and began rubbing it against my skin, starting at my belly, right above the droopy waistband of my skirt. I squirmed, ticklish yet also overwhelmingly turned on, as he moved the melting cube against my belly, making trickles of icy water drip down my stomach. I didn't know if he was going to head south or north, nor did I know which I preferred. My entire body was calling out for this stranger's touch.

He let the chill settle against the cloth of my skirt, which was clinging to me, before taking the ice and running it up my stomach, between my breasts, and then around each nipple. My hard little buds strained forward; I looked down to see them anxiously trying to get his attention. Clearly, it worked, because he knelt down, balancing on his knees, and ever so lightly brushed his lips against one nipple and then the next before replacing them with the exciting, tormenting piece of ice. He stared at my skin as he made it pucker and goosebump, contract and retreat, reach and react. He kept going with that one piece of ice, which had now become the world's most powerful sex toy. He ignored my nipples and brought it up to my neck, then along the edges of my face, chilled streams of water trickling down my body. He rubbed the cube over my brow, then down my nose. My lips parted into an automatic O, my mind forming an image of his cock as I did so, but it wasn't his cock he fed me at that moment. He pushed the ice, along with two of his salty, sweaty fingers, between my lips, and I closed them, sucking hard. With each swallow, I tried to pull him in tighter. With the ice lodged against the roof of my mouth, I felt my pussy tighten as well.

I opened my eyes to see his staring right back at me. The air conditioner was blasting onto my neck, but I didn't care. He eased his fingers out of my mouth, then pushed them back in, slowly, clearly mimicking what he wanted to do to my cunt. He pushed gently against my tongue, and my body convulsed, the last sliver of ice sliding seamlessly down my throat as I let him invade my mouth. He had me, all of me, at that moment, as I opened up thoroughly for him. This was no longer about simple hot or cold, or ice or air, but about pure, raw, selfish desire.

He slipped his fingers out, and as much as I was tempted to clamp my teeth around them and keep them there as long as I could, I resisted. He turned, giving me a view of that firm ass again, the one I wanted to squeeze, but even though he hadn't bound my arms to the chair, hadn't given even the slightest order, I knew he wanted me to stay still.

He stepped away for a minute and returned with three ice cubes. He put the smallest one in his mouth and smiled at me the best he could. Then, taking one in each hand, he again started painting my body, treating each arm to a little ice bath before he moved in for the kill. He pushed my wet skirt up against my waist, revealing the panties that were little more than wet rags by that point. I was sure my swollen lips had to be visible through the fabric, had to be daring him, taunting him, begging him to touch them. He did, in his own way. With his left hand, he began rubbing one piece of ice against my nipple, which reacted immediately. With the other, he roamed along my inner thighs. I wrapped my ankles around the legs of the chair, curling my toes for good measure, spreading myself as wide as possible for what I hoped would be the ultimate invasion. He teased me so well, I thought I might break the chair. He went everywhere with that ice but where I needed him most.

While the softened edges of one piece of ice rubbed against my nipple, so cold it almost hurt—yet my pussy pounded out a plea for more—the other smacked against my inner thighs, darting up to the edge of my underwear, playing along my bikini line, teasing me with the promise of relief before dancing away, down to my knee, where it tickled. Once he'd made my entire inner legs momentarily wet—the water quickly drying against my skin while I remained in my spread-wide position— he brought the remnants of the other cube to my free nipple and pressed each bud against the ice with his thumb, mashing them against the cubes until I cried out. My face contorted in pleasure as his knee settled between my legs, my clit practically hugging it as he let those two cubes melt into oblivion.

But still he didn't let me have his cock. Apparently, he was going to make up for his ice-stealing antics by treating me to the finest in icy pleasure known to woman. With my nipples hard and dripping, my lips open, my legs spread, and my body primed, he surveyed me, looking at me with eyes that seemed to bore all the way inside me. He certainly didn't feel like a stranger, and it wasn't only because I'd given him my name. I didn't need to know his name to feel the powerful connection between us; even if it was "only" sex, it was the kind of soul-changing sex that I knew I'd remember forever. He took one of my hands and placed it on his cock, letting me feel exactly how hard he was. I stroked him slowly and silently, locking my legs even more firmly against the chair as my pussy clenched in anticipation.

Guiding my fingers with his, he used my hand to ease down his zipper, and one of the most beautiful dicks I've ever seen emerged. He shrugged off his shorts, standing totally naked before me, a perfect specimen of manhood. *What had I done to deserve this?* I marveled. I licked my lips, hoping he'd let me have a taste, but instead, he let me pump his cock, feel it pulse and harden, before he gently removed my hand. Then he tugged me upward so I was standing. He lifted up my skirt but didn't take it off, tucking its hem into the waistband so I was once again exposed.

He knelt and settled himself between my legs, then eased my panties off with his teeth. I closed my eyes to better savor the sensations and heard fumbling before more ice found its way to my belly, along with his tongue against the slight curve there while he let the water drip downward. He tugged on my skirt with his teeth, pulling it away from my body enough for the water to make its way toward my sleek pussy. I don't normally go totally bare, but with this summer's heat, every added bit of hair had felt like an unwelcome intrusion, and I'd grown to like feeling totally smooth. I was grateful for the decision as the chilled water made a beeline for my cunt.

Finally, the skirt came off, pushed down slowly with his strong hands as he followed the ice's path with his tongue. Cold and then hot, object and then flesh, had me writhing, bucking up against him, silently begging for more. He could have done almost anything to me in that moment, and I'd have craved it, calling out for more. "Yes!" I yelled as he dexterously shoved his tongue, ice and all, into my pussy. I couldn't help but sink slightly lower onto him, my hands going above my head, even though they had nothing to hold on to but each other, as my legs slightly bowed outward. He kept plying me with his tender tongue, the ice's burning cold sensation tickling my inner walls even as his tongue kept it moving, only giving each tender bit of flesh a momentary hit of its power before pressing into another needy part. And then the ice was gone, and it was just his tongue, fat, wide, and hungry. Then his nose too was there, nuzzling my clit while his hands made their way to my hips to steady me. He feasted on me like I was the answer to all his prayers while I stood there, letting the blessed heat of his tongue send shivers through my body. I looked down to see his head planted between my legs, but he wasn't thrashing all around; his tongue was doing most of the work. Then he eased it out and sucked directly on my clit, pulling it between his lips and then his teeth before shoving two fingers deep inside me, and I came so hard I thought I'd collapse, but he held me steady, flattening his tongue against my clit as he rode out my orgasm with me.

I should have been satisfied with that, but I wasn't. I was greedy and wanted all of him. "Please," I said, tumbling down to the ground and straddling him, pressing my heat against the proud statue of his cock.

"Wait," he said, pushing me back slightly, then reaching for another ice cube and making me watch as he ran it along his balls and up and down his dick. I'd never seen anything like the show he was giving me, and it was a sight to behold as the water dripped down his cock until it was totally wet and shiny. He offered me what was left of the ice cube, and I took it in my mouth before just going for what I wanted and taking his dick between my lips as well. He moaned the moment I let my tongue meet the underside of his cock, my mouth stretched wide in the way I love best. But I eased back, my pussy clamoring for some attention as well. With his eyes trained on mine, he slowly slid a condom over his hardness, then beckoned me forward.

When I sank down onto him, it was like fucking the perfect blend of hard, male cock and ice dildo. He was solid yet cool, and I tumbled forward while his hands went to my ass. We kissed while my still-hard nipples mashed against his. It felt like spontaneous combustion, a rocket boom, an explosion rocking my overwhelmed body, and it didn't last long. We were both so ready that when he bit my lower lip and said, "Now," his voice raw and gritty, I came, just like that, for him, for me, for this chance meeting.

Later, we dumped as much ice as his freezer could produce into his bathtub, and we laughed to ourselves as we competed about who could stay in the tub the longest. I stayed over that night and—wouldn't you know—the next day, the heat wave broke. It was down to a more manageable eighty degrees, and I left his place to return home, blasting my many fans, wondering if it had been a dream even as my pussy throbbed and my body remembered every second. I never saw him in the flesh again, but believe me, every time I fill my glass with ice, I remember what he did to cool me off, and I smile.

DREAMS

Marilyn Jaye Lewis

*V*eronica is asleep in the house of love. Lights off, always, 24/7. Even while her eyes are open, even while her lips move, soundly she sleeps. Roused only to a semblance of action by the pictures that are in her head. In cars, restaurants, bedrooms, bars, Veronica sleeps on.

Always, she's dressed in black. Daytime, nighttime—only the fabric differs. Her nightgown is black satin. Her underwear, black silk. Dresses, pants, sweaters, skirts: cashmere, cotton, mohair, wool. And clean—she is so incredibly clean. She smells like roses made of soap. Everywhere, all over her body. Roses made of soap.

In a car, she's game for kissing. She'll kiss like mad in a

car, concealing the part of her that wants to keep going. *Go further,* the quiet voice urges him, although the actual words never leave Veronica's lips. Never form a sound on the air that an ear might hear, committing her to her desire. For sure, that could wake her. So she relies on chance.

A hand between her thighs: "No," she says. A hand on her breast? "No." But she'll keep kissing. *Go further,* the silent voice urges him. *Try again.*

If he's too polite to try again, Veronica says goodnight.

They are almost always too polite to try again.

Here's an example of what she dreams of: A car. Four doors, metallic cream. Parked right there on the street, it glistens after the rain on a late autumn night. He opens the back door this time and says, "Get in."

She's game. This is roomy. This is unusual. She's in a black wool skirt. Not too short, but tight. It hugs her curves but doesn't cling. It keeps her ass untouchable. Undeniable, yes, but still untouchable. A black sweater. A pullover, cashmere, blanketing her breasts in softness like warm black snowdrifts. They are hard to resist like this, her tits. The urge to touch those blanketed mounds is nearly overpowering. Even to the eye of a quickly passing stranger, those tits are too inviting. There are the black stockings that stay put by themselves. They would feel smooth as silk if a hand were to touch the length of her leg, caress her thigh, where the heat rises. Her high-heeled pumps are shiny patent leather. In she scoots; across the back seat she slides. Closer to him. Impossibly close. This is what she came for: to kiss for a while.

At first, it's the usual. Kiss, kiss. *No, no.* But he persists. A hand on her thigh. *This is perfect,* she thinks. *We're going places tonight.* Her legs part; she dreams on. The hand inches higher.

Anyone might see them. Any face in an upstairs window in any house on the lonely street. At first, she's mindful of this. It informs her sense of propriety. She won't part her legs too much. For the moment, he gives up. His hand finds her breast instead, squeezes the fullness of it tentatively while they kiss. The cashmere is soft as kittens or baby lambs. Soft and warm like snuggling bunnies. The lacy bra he can feel beneath the sweater is almost too promising for words. It's packed tight with her tits, he can tell. His cock stirs like mad inside his trousers.

"No," she says. Thinking anyone might see this hand caressing her tit. "If we weren't so out in the open . . . " she says, her words coming out of her like soft breaths of innuendo, of everything she doesn't say.

"If we weren't so out in the open—what?" he inquires. "What would you do? If this were a dark car on a back road where no one could see?"

Not even me, she hopes. *Keep it dark. I don't want to see myself give in.* "You never know," she challenges him, practically saying, "Try me and see."

"Just one little picture," he persists, his hot mouth kissing her neck, her ear. His hand back at her tit. "Paint one for me—a picture of what you would agree to in the dark, when no one can see."

There would be a struggle, for one thing. There always is in her dreams; otherwise, it's not satisfying. She doesn't like to agree and give in, but she likes to feel her thighs forced apart, held open. She likes to feel the force of his thick cock shoving in. She likes to be pinned down in the back seat and forced to take it in front of everybody, all the eyes on the lonely street. *Just take it. Use your imagination and take it from me.*

He waits on her reply. When no words come, he scores. It's his point. As her punishment for not answering him, his hand doesn't leave her tit. In fact, he squeezes the concealed flesh more roughly through the cashmere sweater. His mouth finds her mouth again, latching on aggressively, nearly devouring her tongue, his mind sucking up her very thoughts amid the stifled protests in the dark car.

His hand goes up boldly under the sweater now; it's too exciting. The feel of padded lace, those warm waiting mounds. He wants the bra shoved up, the flesh out—the titties right there where he can see them, stark white against all the black. Everything black, black, black. Save for the white tits, with their tender nipples out there in plain sight, aching for a mouth.

If this were a back road with no houses and no faces in upstairs windows, he'd tell her to pull it up. "Go on," he'd tell her, "pull it up. I want to see." Making her lift it up herself, that sweater. Reveal the bra finally. The black padded lace that clasps in front. The soft white mounds bulging in the cups and almost spilling out. "Undo it," he might say, seeming a little bored with her, lighting a cigarette while she does it herself: pulls up the sweater, nervously unclasps the bra. Until there she sits, waiting for his attention. Shivering. Tits bared in a dark car.

No. Erase that. There are two of them now; two men in Veronica's dreams. Two rough, very insistent men. She wears the same outfit though. It's the same back road and dark car. But one of the men has her pulled up onto his considerable lap in the back seat; he's pinned her arms behind her while the other man yanks up the sweater, flips open the clasp on the bra. Her tits spill out, milky white, embarrassing her. The nipples stiff, too vulnerable. It's humiliating, how her tits hang there in the air as if they're up for grabs. Her nipples get even stiffer. She squirms in the big man's lap while rough fingers tug on her unprotected nipples. The more she squirms, the harder the cock gets, the cock bulging underneath her now, dead center under her cunt. Still, she squirms. She must. Her nipples are being tormented. It's merciless, what the other one does to her tits, what he's forcing her to endure with all his twisting and tugging.

So on she squirms, knowing that she's grinding down on the big man's lap but not able to do much about it. "Oh man, she's a *hot* one," the big man offers out encouragingly. And then both her wrists are held together in one of his huge paws, and she feels his other hand fumbling underneath her.

"No," she begs uselessly, knowing his cock is coming out. Feeling his fat fingers shoving aside the soaking crotch of her panties.

It will go right in, his fat cock, and give her secret away: just how wet she's gotten. She knows it. She wants it, both of them at once. Being this wet will prove it to them at last. It will not be long before she's on all fours, right there on the back seat. Her skirt shoved up, the panties shoved down. A fat cock stuffed in her cunt and another cock stuffed in her mouth. It's a back road, a dark car. Who's going to know?

You go, Veronica.

WHEN VERONICA IS ALONE in her huge empty house, she sleeps upstairs in her bedroom—the larger room—there on the left at the top of the grand stairs, the room whose bay window looks out on the flowering crabapple trees even in the dark of night. When she's sleeping alone up there, she sleeps fitfully, startling easily, waking at the merest sound. On those nights, her dream goes differently.

Let's check in on her sleeping brain. Ah. It's the "phantom intruder" dream, as usual. It goes like this: Her intruder is careful to be exceptionally quiet. He doesn't want Veronica awake until the final moment, when it's too late for her, but perfect for him.

Sometimes Veronica wakes with a start and sits up in bed, knowing that he's made his way into her room, but it's too dark to see him. She clutches the blankets tightly to her. The thin straps of her black satin nightgown slip wantonly down her shoulders. Her dark hair tumbles in soft waves around her face, her full lips parting as if she might scream. Terror becomes her. Her breath catches in her throat.

How lovely, he thinks. His cock stirs.

He's here for Veronica's cunt. No other woman on the block will do. He's been here too many times to count, always finding the iron gate unlatched, the door unbolted. He easily makes his way in the dark, up those grand stairs to her room.

He likes it best, though, when she remains asleep until the moment his hand clamps down on her mouth. That startled gleam in her eye, the moonlight streaming in and illuminating her wild look. That he likes best. But for that reward, he needs to be extra, extra quiet.

It goes one of two ways: Either he accidentally wakes her, or he doesn't. If he wakes her and she does the sitting up, startled, terror thing, he waits silently, patiently, and watches her torment. Just watches the terror build.

It's okay for him to breathe. The subtle sound of breathing adds to her confusion: Can she actually hear him breathing?

"Is someone there?" she calls out.

Someone's there alright, but he keeps that little surprise to himself. He refuses to answer, no matter how many times she asks the same question. He can't be fooled. The element of surprise is everything. Without it, the night's ruined.

He has infinitely more patience than she does. At last, she lies back down on the bed, her pretty head falling deep into the feather pillow. But she's not relaxed. She doesn't nestle cozily. No, she lies rigidly, ears straining in the silence. Someone's there. She's certain of it.

Not again, she thinks, her mind racing feverishly. She goes through a rapid checklist: Did she latch the gate, bolt the door? She can't remember. Her heart is pounding too wildly. It won't allow her an accurate account of such trivial things.

Black gloved fingers shoved up her cunt though—that, she remembers. Being told to turn over. "Spread your legs and turn over." The gloved fingers wedged in her hole make the movement difficult.

"Do it. *Now.*" Now it is, then. Over she goes. On all fours for a couple of gloved fingers up her cunt. It doesn't seem probable and yet . . . well, the memory is vivid, crystal clear. The fingers stuck up inside her, probing her hole rudely while she faces the other way and keeps her legs spread. It's humiliating.

That was the night she stopped sleeping so soundly. From that night on, she never slept quite the same.

And now here she is, disbelieving it could happen again, when in truth, it's happened too many times for her to count.

He's not wearing the black gloves though. Not this time. Tonight he's chosen something more obvious, the ubiquitous latex. He stands quietly against the wall, in the shadow of her towering antique walnut chifforobe, watching her in the dark. He's breathing steadily, biding his time. After all, the hard part—getting into the house in the first place—is over. He's here, he's ready. It's going to happen. Poor Veronica.

The intruder wonders how he will take her this time. It's not as if he plans every move beforehand. Certain things, yes. He already knows he will require that she do certain things.

For instance, when she's tied face-down across the bed, her head hanging uncomfortably over the side, he will jerk her head up by her hair and force her to beg him to allow her to suck his cock. To really beg him, too, to put a lot of feeling into it. He'll make her repeat the line over and over, until she gets the pitch just right and makes the emotion behind her plea seem genuine: "Please, *let* me *suck* it." That's how it should sound.

He might press his warm cock against the soft skin of her face, letting her get an unmistakable feel for its overall size, for how hard he is. He might even imply that if she doesn't ask to suck it in the most desperate, needful manner, it'll be going up her ass.

She'll know what that means; it happened last time. He'll grease her up back there, then slather his cock with the slickest lube. Since she'll be tied down by then, she won't exactly be able to resist him, will she? His slippery cock will push right up her asshole. It will go right in, regardless of his thick size, because the lube is made for that. It makes anal effortless—even for the novice. There she'll be, tied down, spread open, and taking his cock up her ass with ease. And he'll give it to her in no uncertain terms. Steady in, steady out; each thrust will go in deep, ensuring she grunts enticingly, creating the humiliating impression that she *likes* what he's doing to her back there. . . .

Well, to avoid all that (perhaps), she'll beg in the most convincing tones to let her suck his cock.

He might let her, he might not. It's the begging that he's after. Truthfully? He can get his cock sucked anywhere, and by women who are a lot more experienced at it than Veronica is.

IT MIGHT NOT SEEM LIKE IT at first, if anyone were to walk in on Veronica at this juncture—still dreaming and tied face-down across the bed, her legs forced open invitingly, the intruder with a sizable handful of her hair, jerking her head up awkwardly and insisting that she repeat the same line, "Please let me suck it," over and over. It might not seem like she's adept at it, and yet Veronica is an expert at begging. She can sound plaintive and desperate. Or she can sound ravished by the bottomless depths of her own sexual need. It depends on the circumstances, obviously.

For instance, that craziness in the car with the two men? It brought out a veritable panoply of begging styles in Veronica. Starting with the run-of-the-mill "No, don't," with her sounding timid and frightened, too vulnerable—that part where her sweater was shoved up and her tits were out. Then it gradually shifted to more of a whimpering "No, no," accompanied by that useless feeling; the fat cock about to go up her cunt and discover her wet secret. She was saying "no," but her heart wasn't in it. Clearly she'd given up moments before the word had come out of her mouth. Resignation. A "what's done is done" type of situation.

Where she really excelled at begging though—that happened after she was left to her own devices with those two men in the back seat of that car. By then, the big man whose lap she was adorning had his fat cock jammed way up her hole. Gravity being what it is, her own weight had caused her to sit right down on his shaft, and it went all the way up. In moments, the cock was wedged up her cunt almost painfully; it was really shoved up there. If it weren't for the considerable distraction being caused by what the other man was doing to Veronica's tits, she might have noticed that the cock inside her was too big, that her cunt was stretched tight, filled to capacity, and that she was in pain. But as luck would have it, her focus was elsewhere.

She . . . well, first, the story of Veronica's tits: They're large and all natural. They hang enticingly on her slender frame. When the nipples are erect, it's impossible not to want to grab them—even for Veronica, in fact. She loves her tits and can rarely find the self-discipline to leave them alone. Her nipples are plump, so easy to tug on, and unusually responsive. She can come from pulling on her own nipples if she keeps at it long enough.

So she's at a bit of a disadvantage now when it comes to thinking straight. That relentless tugging on her tits is making her feel like coming and not alerting her to the seriousness of the massive cock up her hole. Her begging style shifts noticeably to an urgent "Oh *god*," moving quickly into "Yeah, oh yeah," which only makes the guy tugging on her tits stop everything to hurriedly get his cock out of his trousers. He seriously wants to fuck her mouth, and she's all for it.

When his cock is out, she leans all the way over and practically plants her face in his lap. Mouth open, the cock goes right in.

Finally, the big guy lets go of her wrists. He's suddenly overwhelmed by the specter of Veronica's ass lifting up out of his lap, his cock still wedged in her cunt but starting to squeeze out. He wants a better angle. Not to mention that he wants to *see* everything. He flings open the car door and the overhead light goes on. The sight is beyond belief. Veronica is on her knees, ass out, legs spread, face-down in the other guy's lap. The big man shoves up Veronica's skirt—a tight-fitting black wool number that takes some shoving to get past her considerable hips. Then he tugs her black silk panties, the crotch soaking, down her thighs. They stop halfway, though, because her legs are spread.

That's a hell of a sight—that one right there. Veronica's pussy lips are slick and fat and swollen, almost hairless. Her cunt hole is pouting open, having been so recently impaled on a cock too large for the hole to comfortably handle. *It is such a gorgeous sight:* a slick, sopping cunt, fat with lust, spread and just begging to get stuffed again. But before shifting positions completely, before getting on his knees and really *fucking* her, the big guy spreads open Veronica's ass and seriously tongues her asshole.

At this point in her dreams, Veronica is delirious. It feels incredible, that tongue poking into the opening of her asshole. A muffled and very desperate begging ensues—sounding like, "Mm-hm, mm-hm," as her mouth rides the other guy's cock, her spit drooling down into his hairy crotch.

She is very worked up, her sizable tits hanging down and colliding with the cool leather car seat with every downward movement of her eager mouth as it sucks in the stiff cock. She is ready for some serious fucking now. When she comes up for air, she's begging the big guy behind her, "Fuck me, Christ, fuck me." And that's when the big man feels nothing less than compelled to comply.

SO . . . THERE'S THE KEY DIFFERENCE. How Veronica begs and whimpers when she's really wanting it versus how she begs when she's overwhelmed in a not so good way; e.g., the intruder in her bedroom and that whole scene. By the time the intruder has got her tied face-down across her own bed, she's already been zealously fondled in all her private places—even, in some places, rudely probed, as usual. It's been humiliating.

She's been stripped, of course, right out of her black satin night-gown. She doesn't wear panties at night, so she is stark naked in pretty much the proverbial heartbeat, leaving her nothing but oodles of time for begging and carrying on.

However, the intruder is unfazed. Her begging only registers when he has specifically asked to hear it. Otherwise, her pleas fall on deaf ears, and he keeps to his agenda, loose as it is.

Tonight's invasion had started out on shaky ground. At first it seemed as if Veronica would never calm down enough to drift back to sleep. What would be the next best tack to take if there were no element of surprise to rely on? *Was* there one? The intruder didn't think so. He opted for waiting as long as necessary. When at last it seemed, by her deep, steady breathing, that she was finally safely back to sleep, he crept over to the bed. This is where his patience really paid off. The creeping—he's totally soundless. And then the very slight, very careful sliding of the satin blanket, the satin sheet. It falls free of her shoulders, down past those promising breasts. It requires even more patience to lower the straps of her nightgown; luckily, they're loose-fitting straps. It doesn't take long before Veronica's tits are completely exposed. All the while, she imagines she's sleeping; that she's blissfully unaware of it, this free show she's providing to a total stranger.

The moonlight filtering in the bay window provides just enough light to discern those all-natural beauties. She's lying slightly to her right side, so the weight of her breasts squeezes them gently together, providing an attractive cleavage and giving the impression that the breasts are a lot larger than perhaps they actually are.

There are the plump nipples—so suckable. The intruder knows from experience just how susceptible to torment those nipples are. His gloved finger trails lightly over first one nipple, then the other. He repeats this featherlike, weightless caress several times, until the nipples stiffen undeniably. When fully erect, they protrude well over a quarter of an inch. Easily plucked. A single forefinger and thumb could readily grasp one of those stiff, protruding nipples—the left one, say—and lift the full weight of her heavy breast by it. However, doing it and not waking her are two very different things.

The intruder leaves her nipples alone for now and concentrates instead on sliding the satiny blanket and sheet down the length of Veronica's torso. The black satin nightgown offers no friction whatsoever. The sleek blankets practically tumble off her, it is so effortless.

The sight then is too priceless. Veronica's nightgown has worked its way up around her hips, and her legs are slightly parted. She's exposing herself. He retrieves the flashlight from his pants pocket. It's tiny, but its beam is powerful. He trains the beam of light between her bare legs, seeking the jewel. And there it is. Her clit. It's right there. He could reach out and touch it if he felt like it. Veronica keeps her cunt almost hairless. There's nothing hiding the tiny nub. It pouts out from between the smooth nether lips. It is too tempting, the urge to touch it or to run a gloved finger down the length of the inner lips. But he is on a greater mission. He leaves the clit for later, for when he can give it more-thorough attention.

The clit is the key to it all—when it comes to a girl like Veronica, that is.

One time, he had her in a collar and leash. A collar snug around her neck and the leash tied securely to the bedpost, giving her no leeway. She either sat still on the bed or choked herself. He pulled a pillowcase down around her head before turning the lights on and raiding her stocking drawer. All her stockings were black. Black, black, black. Some smooth, some lacy, some fishnet—but all black. With one black stocking, her wrists were bound tightly together in front of her, bringing her boobs together in a tempting proffered pose.

He took full advantage of that attractive offering, grabbing her tits in fistfuls and squeezing firmly. He'd worn black leather gloves that time. Her stark white boobs bulging in handfuls in the black gloves looked almost too enticing. He squeezed them more roughly, then tugged at those fat nipples and listened to her muffled groans.

That time, he kept the pillowcase on her head almost the whole night. Even though she looked ridiculous in it, he loved how she looked with the lights on. He'd used other stockings to secure her legs, to keep them open wide. A stocking tied around each ankle, then tied tight to the metal bed frame under the box spring. Her knees bent, thighs spread apart. She could not have looked more inviting if she'd had a sign around her neck reading TAKE IT—FREE. She looked uncomfortable as hell but nonetheless very inviting.

He sat on the bed, facing her. Making himself comfortable between her spread legs. He pulled those hairless lips open wider, forcing the clit to put in a reluctant appearance, to come out from under that protective hood. He could see everything when he held her open like that: the shy clit, the tiny pucker around the piss hole, and of course, the cunt hole—it positively gaped in this position. No virgin, she—he knew *that* already, from the best kind of experience.

What he couldn't get at was her anus, because in that position she was sitting on it. It didn't matter, though. He only needed her anus for those times when he wanted her complete attention, to drive home a point of some kind. And it worked well for that. He could get her to blurt out all sorts of unexpected promises when he had his fingers probing in the tight hole or, god knows, his cock fucking it. Mostly though, he came for Veronica's cunt, and in that position, for that whole night, he had it in spades.

Tonight there was no collar, no leash. It was going to be a bit of a high-wire act—getting her under his control without the assistance of something to choke her. But he was game for the challenge. There was still so much to learn about her and her journey up this ladder of sheer victimhood.

He put his flashlight back in his pocket. He had an idea.

He undid his pants and let them fall. He stepped out of them, out of his boxers too. His cock sprang free in the dark. He was so hard it was aching. Truthfully, he'd been hard for hours already. He pulled his shirt off over his head and then went quietly around to the other side of the bed, to where Veronica's dreaming head lay softly on the feather pillow. Lightly, he ran the head of his aching cock across her lips. He did this several times, letting his warm flesh just barely graze her while he teasingly toyed with one of her plump nipples. His hopes were that she would begin dreaming she was in bed with a lover, a favorite date, a boyfriend—anyone but the intruder.

Soon, she moaned sleepily, and her tender lips parted.

He gently but firmly pushed his cock past the parted lips. Nothing too drastic yet, nothing too suspicious. Just a steady in/out to get her saliva going while his nimble fingers taunted her stiff nipple.

His ears filled with her delicious moans. He could see plain as day that her legs were wider apart than they'd been only moments before. She was getting aroused. It was the perfect dream. The "phantom intruder" dream always worked well for Veronica.

Before she could move too far out of that dream state, however, he grabbed both her wrists, forcing her arms above her head, and he straddled her, planting his weight down on her chest. She was awake then. Wide awake, with his thick cock stuffed in her mouth and the thin straps of her nightgown cutting into her raised arms. Her huge tits were still hanging out, keeping the gown from fitting correctly. The whole scene was confusing to someone who'd been sleeping so soundly.

That's when the panicked squealing started. He had to get her past those unattractive sounds.

"Veronica," he warned her calmly. "Stop it. You know what happens when you get me angry." For emphasis, he stuffed his cock further down her throat, cutting off the annoying squeals.

When her body began writhing, he pulled his cock out of her mouth entirely, easing his weight down her body until her exposed tits were salaciously pressed against his chest and his cock was resting against her mound.

She was quieter now, breathing heavy and whimpering softly, which only got him more excited.

"Let me get in there, Veronica, come on," he coaxed her. "I only came for a quick one this time. Give me a quick one and I'll go away." He was lying, of course. He was prepared to spend the night violating her, but this was all part of the element of surprise. "Come on," he urged her. "Let me in there. The sooner I get in, the sooner I'm out and gone. Come on."

Veronica's whimpering continued. His grip on her wrists was too tight. But the thought of him gone appealed to her. She raised her legs for the intruder, spreading wide, her pelvis angling a bit and helping his cock find her hole.

It couldn't have been more perfect. Her cunt opened around

his cock and let him right in. He fucked her slow and steady, going in deep, keeping her off guard with his continued lies.

"That's right, Veronica, just like that. Open up and let me fuck it. Give me your cunt for a good fucking, and then I'll be gone."

He leaned down closer to her, his scratchy face against her tender cheek. His lips near her ear, he encouraged her quietly. "That's right, just let me fuck it, just like that, give me your cunt. It likes a good fucking, doesn't it, Veronica? I can tell by how wet you are already, your cunt likes to get fucked. Isn't that right?" He pauses a moment. "Veronica—isn't that right?"

At last, she breathes a quiet, "Mm-hm," her entire body taking in the full effect of the steady, slow fucking.

"I thought so," he whispers back. "You have such a naughty cunt. The memory of how much it likes to get fucked keeps me up nights. You want to go deeper, Veronica? You want to get your cunt fucked good?"

It takes a moment, but there is another breathy "Mm-hm" as Veronica dreams on.

SHOCKING EXPOSÉ! SECRETS REVEALED!

Carol Queen

*W*henever Abby traveled, she bought books. It was somehow more exciting to discover an interesting book when she was far from home, even the same exact book she might find in a bookstore in her own town.

Maybe when most people thought of San Francisco, they thought of sea air at bayside or delicious scents wafting out of North Beach cafés. But Abby thought about the mysterious mustiness of vintage bookstores or the clean-page smell of big bookstores like City Lights and Modern Times.

She was three stores into her shopping trip today—or, as she secretly liked to think of it, her "literary orgy." She visited at least a couple of favorites each time she came to San Francisco and tried to find at least one or two new bookshops to explore. She might manage to hit six or eight stores today if she timed it right, and then tomorrow she'd head home—clutching a cloth bag of treasures or lugging a box.

She'd only found one purchase so far, but it was a gem—in a tiny, dusty nook of a bookshop on Polk Street, she'd found an old picture book of strippers and burlesque queens. No photo in it was newer than about 1965, and some went all the way back to the turn of the twentieth century, where the women wore body stockings to create the illusion that they were nude.

What a find! Abby loved books best when they transported her somewhere else, and with this one, she didn't have to imagine the dancing girls with their sequins and huge feather fans—they were right there before her! She found the closest coffeehouse and sat dreamily sipping a cappuccino, carefully turning pages. She'd never been to a strip club, but the filmy outfits and racy high heels fascinated her. *Look at this one,* she thought. *If my grandmother had been a burlesque dancer, she might have looked like this.* Or what if she herself had been born in another era? That might have been Abby herself onstage, opening for beautiful blonde Lili St. Cyr.

San Francisco just made her feel this way—that anything was possible. After her reverie had faded, she finished the last sip of coffee and walked the few blocks to Kayo, a bookstore she'd never visited before. Stepping inside, she gasped—this shop seemed to have nothing but old pulp paperbacks!

From every shelf, glamorous dolls and bitchy babes gazed or snarled out at her. A few were menaced by monsters, a few were being ravished by pirates, but most of them were the focus of the cover all by themselves—or, in the lesbian section, in twos. They were redheads and blondes and brunettes, slinky in evening gowns or seductive in lingerie. They were gorgeous! Abby began making her way through the endless stacks of books, mostly fiction but interspersed with some midcentury pop psychology.

Shocking Exposé!

The World's Oldest Vice!

Transvestite Secrets Revealed!

What Every Young Wife Must Know!

Innocent No More!

Even the Kinsey Reports and Bulfinch's *Greek and Roman Mythology* had been published with lurid illustrations.

Abby walked sideways down a whole row, reading titles and drinking in the brightly colored covers. Almost every one had a gorgeous woman on it. Just change her clothes and she switched from *Amazon Pagan Queen!* to *Sorority Sis Unleashed!* The bookstore had been deserted when she came in, except for the guy behind the counter, so she almost dropped the small stack of paperbacks she'd picked out when she got to the end of the row and nearly bumped into a small, smiling woman, who stood as if waiting for Abby to reach her. A man stood behind her, smiling too.

"Oh! Excuse me!" gasped Abby. "I didn't see you there."

"I guess not," said the woman with a grin. Her sweater was buttoned tightly over curves. "You're the biggest bibliophile in town." She said it like it was a kind of tasty fetish.

"Yeah, we've seen you in the last three stores," said the man, who had on cuffed trousers and a vintage rayon shirt with a little tiki face embroidered where another shirt might have a pocket. Abby noticed disconcertedly that his nipples showed through the soft fabric.

"We're bibliophiles too," said the woman. "But we're taking a break and going over to North Beach now. Want to come along?"

Abby blinked. "Are you going to City Lights?"

"Nope, the Lusty Lady. You should go. You'll like it. I saw you snagged that excellent old stripper book down on Polk Street."

Abby flushed. "Have you guys been following me?"

"Oh, sorta," said the smiling girl. "I'm Lila, by the way. This is Daniel. C'mon, pay for your books. We'll get a cab."

Out on Post Street, a Veteran's taxi waited, with Lila seated inside and waving her in. Daniel held the door. Abby felt a little like she was heading through the looking glass, but they seemed okay. Actually, "okay" put it way too mildly—they were both really hot. Abby climbed in—once Daniel had seated himself, squeezing her against Lila, she told them her name.

"Want a drink first, Abby?" asked Lila. "We can take you to Spec's. Or Vesuvio! Kerouac's old hangout!"

"No," said Abby, feeling like she'd had a drink already. "Let's just go."

She expected a club with seats. But the Lusty Lady had nothing but booths. Abby looked around in confusion, but Lila took her hand and pulled her into a corner booth. Daniel followed them in and locked the door, then pulled out a ten and fed it into a machine on the wall. The kind they have at the Laundromat, thought Abby—but that thought seemed so incongruous here; she didn't say it out loud.

"It's a peep show," Lila explained. "We just watch through the window, see?" The window slid up with a whir when Daniel put the money in, and Lila pointed to the stage on the other side, where the women from the pulp covers seemed to have come to life—big hair, high heels, lingerie half-on, half-off. They sashayed around the stage just like the women on the books would do if they could move—like they owned the place! Some of them made slow, seductive dance moves, while one curvy blonde woman just stood and ran her hands across her pale skin. It looked like she might be about to masturbate.

Abby's eyes grew wide—there was a Hooters back home, but absolutely nothing like this.

"I used to work here," said Lila. "The dancers love it when women come in, and couples. Daniel and I come here a lot to show off for them. I thought you'd like to see them, and if you feel like it . . . "

" . . . you can put on a show for them too," Daniel finished for her. "Some of them like to watch."

"Anybody'll get into watching," said Lila, "if you give them something to see."

Lila began unbuttoning her tight, clingy sweater. A black lace brassiere slowly emerged, and she wiggled her shoulders just a little in the crowded booth, just enough movement to get the sweater off her shoulders. This caught the eye of a dancer, who drifted closer to their window, looked in at the three of them, smiled, and began to dance.

Abby didn't know which way to look. The dancer wore almost nothing—just high black heels and a black boa made of fuzzy Marabou feathers. She teased her nipples with it and pulled it oh-so-slowly between her legs, so it covered, and then revealed, her neatly trimmed pussy. Abby had never seen anything so sexy. Except maybe Lila—who stood right next to her, breathing warmly on her neck and leaning back into Daniel for support. His hands came up and caressed her lace-covered breasts, making Abby want to reach for them too.

"You can touch," Daniel whispered. "I told you, they like it when we put on a show."

Lila's breasts felt heavy and warm against Abby's palms. She'd never touched a woman like this—except a thousand times in her mind. She'd gone to girls' school with Colette and had adventures in Paris with Anaïs Nin; she'd read *Herotica* and let her fantasies run in every direction. With Lila's breasts in her hands, Abby felt somehow ready to have them there. She slid her palms in tiny circles until she felt Lila's nipples come up, until Daniel got involved, working his fingers swiftly to remove Lila's bra.

Lila threw her head back against Daniel's chest and sighed deeply. He bent down to kiss her, and she pulled her skirt up to her waist. The tiny room was so tight that the back of her hand caressed Abby's pussy on the way down—she couldn't even tell if Lila meant to do it. By now, Abby felt wildly overdressed too. "Can you help me get out of some of these clothes?" she asked, and Lila and Daniel both helped pull her sweater over her head and off. Then Lila unbuttoned Abby's jeans. Over her shoulder, Abby saw two more dancers come to join the first one, who still looked into the booth as if waiting for the show to start.

But just as Abby turned to see who else had arrived, the window began to close!

"Damn!" said Daniel. "Has it been this long already?"

"Time flies when you're having fun. . . . " said Lila, dreamily.

Abby burrowed in her jeans pocket for cash. She still had at least a twenty. "There!" she said when she'd managed to fish it out. "My turn!" She fed the bill into the slot, which sucked it smoothly away . . . and the window rose again.

There was the sensual blonde, still touching herself. There was the small-breasted girl with the Marabou boa. A Latina with long, wavy hair peeked over her shoulder, and Abby could see a statuesque African American woman across the stage, looking over their way.

"Abby, when you said 'My turn,' what did you mean?" asked Lila in that dreamy, turned-on voice. "Do you want to play?"

Abby nodded—she would have said something too, except Lila's lips covered hers right away, soft and wet, licking and nibbling in one of the most arousing kisses Abby had ever experienced.

"Abby," came Daniel's whispered voice right next to her ear, "open your eyes!"

Doing so, Abby saw two of the dancers kissing each other right through the window, almost like they were mimicking the show they saw in the little booth. Also, impossibly large and close up, Abby saw Lila's lashes, the waves of her dark hair. She let her hands range along Lila's body, touching everywhere she could reach, her hands sometimes finding skin and sometimes the texture of Lila's clothes. She could fit the cheeks of Lila's ass into her palms—they seemed just a little bigger than her breasts—and she touched naked skin when she cupped them, because Lila wore no panties. Behind Lila stood Daniel, his cock hard beneath the fabric of his pants. Abby touched him too. How much could they do in here? She whispered the question.

"As much as we have room for," said Daniel. "We might not actually have quite enough."

"But we live right around the corner," said Lila.

"That way we don't have to worry about running out of money for the machine."

So Abby gave herself up to the pleasures of touching them, and feeling two sets of hands on her, until the time she'd bought with her twenty ran out. They left a little gaggle of dancers bending down to wave through the slowly closing window.

Lila and Daniel really *were* bibliophiles. Their apartment was a tiny warren of bookshelves with a big bed. Abby dropped her book bags inside the door and stepped inside.

AUTHOR'S NOTE: The Lusty Ladies now own the place! As of July 2003, the exotic dancers at the Lusty Lady Theatre (where I used to work, back in the day) are San Francisco's newest worker-owned cooperative business. Congratulations to them!

TO DANCE AT THE FAIR

Donna George Storey

NAKED

Whenever I stand up to speak before an audience—be it a ballroom full of steely-eyed colleagues or the semester's first class of yawning kids—I think of Sally, and I feel strong.

Because, of course, Sally Rand—the sensation of Chicago's Century of Progress Exposition during the dark Depression years of 1933 and 1934—stepped onto the stage wearing nothing but two ostrich feather fans and a dusting of pure white powder. As the dance progressed, she would swirl her fans, teasing the audience with a flash of nipple or a glimpse of buttock, until, at long last, she would spread her wings to reveal everything. And then, in a flash of light, she was gone, before anyone could really know—had they really seen Sally nude, or was it all an illusion?

This afternoon it was especially fitting to conjure Sally's ghost as I took the podium. I was giving a paper on her and her sister performers, entitled, "'Enough Nudity for Anyone's Fifteen Cents': Sally Rand, the Crystal Lassies, and the Roots of Internet Porn at the Century of Progress Exposition." I brought plenty of slides, and the ballroom was packed. Sally has been dead for more than twenty years, but she still knows how to pull them in.

Novice that I was to burlesque, I was lucky not to be facing my audience alone. On my left was a dark and very handsome man named Mario Carbone. He had written a paper on "primitive cultures" exhibits and fantasies of empire specifically to join me on this panel. The lean, fair-haired man to my right with the intriguing air of melancholy was Christopher Hansen. For my benefit, he had tweaked his customary focus on FDR into a discussion of the perfect marriage of corporate capitalism and the New Deal at the interwar world fairs.

Although we now teach in different parts of the country, the three of us have been best friends since the first week of grad school. Our professors dubbed us "the inseparable threesome," and the other students openly laid bets on who got to be in the middle during our all-night fuckfests.

Mario, Chris, and I laughed it off, because we were sure

our bond was purely platonic, founded on mutual intellectual admiration. We wouldn't be honest enough with ourselves to go to bed together for another fifteen years.

CITY FATHERS

The stripper and the schoolmarm. On the surface, it would be hard to find two women more different than Sally and I.

Born in 1904 in the Ozarks and christened Harriet Helen Beck, Sally longed to be a ballerina from the first time she saw Pavlova dance the dying swan in Kansas City. At fourteen, she ran off with the carnival. Her wits and her blond good looks took her as far as Hollywood, where Cecil B. DeMille himself renamed her, thanks to the Rand McNally atlas that caught his eye. The advent of the talkies proved disastrous for Sally—she had a lisp—and the Depression hit her as hard as everyone else. It was out of desperation for work that she first walked onto the stage in Chicago's Paramount Club, naked but for her trademark feather fans.

Something more than desperation made Sally a star. Chicago was to host a world's fair, and she dreamed of a share in its riches. She applied to perform through official channels, but the city fathers turned her down. City fathers: I always imagine plump, sober-faced men atop Louis Sullivan skyscrapers, spraying the metropolis with semen, their dicks as fat as fire hoses. No doubt most of them sported tent poles in their trousers when Sally crashed their gala opening ceremonies as Lady Godiva on a white horse. The acclaim for this daring display of nudity forced the worthy gentlemen to authorize her show at the Streets of Paris. Most sources agree that Sally helped the fair turn a profit. She didn't do so badly herself. By the end of the summer, her salary had soared from $125 to $3,000 a week.

But Sally was more than a naked body, more than a clever manipulator of male fantasy. Another reason she rode as Lady Godiva was to protest the publicity shots of city matrons in their gala gowns, a callous gesture when so many working people were starving. One night that summer, she refused to let her friends be bumped from the best table in the house by FDR's son and his wedding party. Either the friends stayed put or she wouldn't do the show. As always, Sally got what she wanted in the end.

I, on the other hand, was born in a prosperous northeastern suburb more than sixty years after Sally. I never ran off with carnies. I never earned my keep exposing my small—but, to my lovers' delight, very sensitive—breasts. I never endured an arrest on obscenity charges—much less four in one day, like Sally. I did put on plenty of performances for my teachers and advisers. And I pulled off an impressive masquerade for my father-figure husband, who seemed, with the twenty-year age difference, to be the perfect partner for a scholar of mid-century American studies.

He wasn't.

Now I'm on my own again, my fortieth birthday looming. I'm supposed to be courting the tenure committee with the same old song and dance. But I find myself thinking of Sally and itching to be as daring and shocking and free.

THE HISTORY OF DESIRE

After we gave our papers, fielded questions, and kissed the requisite asses of the powerful eminences in our field, Mario, Chris, and I went off to do what we really came to the conference for—a long-awaited reunion dinner at a charming Italian place on M Street.

Things had changed in the two years since we'd last seen each other. Mario was being courted by Columbia and was complaining about how slow they were to make an official offer—rather bad form, since he's scored tenure and Chris and I are still waiting for the decision. Chris made dour jokes about his ongoing search for the right antidepressant. He made no secret of the fact that estrangement from his daughters after his divorce tore him apart. I leered at the young waiter, then regretted it. I didn't want it to be too obvious that I hadn't had good sex with anyone other than my hand in quite some time.

With the help of a few bottles of chianti, however, we gradually found our younger selves still very much alive beneath the older, tougher skin. We laughed and said clever things and confessed that we'd never found the same fellowship with anyone since. It was Mario, of course, who made the first light-hearted reference to another dinner à *trois,* some ten years before. A piece of history, I must confess, that was on my mind as well.

MARIO HAD JUST TURNED IN his dissertation and was flying off to take a plum job at Duke, while Chris and I still languished in the bog of research. Of course we were glad for him, glad to celebrate with pasta and wine. We were lounging about afterward on throw pillows on the orange shag rug of his apartment when suddenly Mario took me in his arms and kissed me.

It was more than a goodbye. It was a real kiss, slow and soft and piquant, with red pepper and Côtes du Rhône. The kind of kiss you feel in your pussy, or rather, the kind that makes your whole body feel like a pussy, tingling and melting and hungry for more. It took me by surprise, for Mario had been unfailingly faithful to his harem of bubbly undergraduates, all blonde and busty with a fuck-me-now wiggle to their hips, all very different from me. Fate would have it that the phone rang, and the voice of his latest young conquest trilled through the answering machine. We jumped apart, and he went to pick up the phone with a regretful shrug.

I turned to Chris, my lips pleasantly sore, my cheeks hot with arousal and shame. I was wearing Bill's engagement ring. Chris's wedding to Shannon was two months away. I suppose I was expecting to see judgment in his eyes for my sluttish behavior, but I met instead the second surprise of the evening.

Call me easy, and some have, but a man gets inside me first with his eyes. That silver flicker of desire sinks straight into my belly, and—if I want it to happen—he has me right then and there. The rest of it—spreading my legs with his knees and pushing open my wet, pink cunt lips with the swollen knob of his cock—is pretty much an afterthought.

Desire is exactly what I saw in Chris's eyes. He wanted to fuck me, fiancé or no. And I realized I wanted to fuck him. More than anything in the world.

Mario came to the rescue. His girlfriend needed him to come over right away. She was freaked out about an exam, and the newly minted Dr. Mario had the cure. We all rose, smoothed out our clothes, and left to be with the people we were supposed to be fucking, our bland smiles promising we would forget everything that had just happened.

But I still remembered very well that Mario and I kissed. And I remembered even more keenly, with the yearning of ten long years, that Chris and I did not.

WHY NOT?

In fact, Chris and I had been exchanging wary, questioning glances all evening now that both of us were free, or as free as two people with battered hearts can ever be. But Mario saved us again. His cheerful chatter lubricated our path from the restaurant to my hotel room, where the party continued. We raided the minibar and talked on through the evening. Midnight found me sprawled on my king-size bed, my feet in Mario's warm lap as he rubbed the arches with his strong thumbs, sending sweet, electric twinges running up my legs. Chris, who'd been nursing the same glass of well-watered whiskey all night, had crawled onto the bed beside me, joking that he was waiting in line for a massage too.

"You're looking tired, Chris, my man," Mario said with his lovely smile. "Don't you think you should be getting back to your room?" Though he'd put on weight and his lush hair was touched with snow at the temples, Dr. Carbone was still very easy on the eyes.

"Hell, no, I'm waiting for you to stagger out of here first so I can finally make my move."

I gave Chris a sidelong glance. He winked at me, to let me know that was a joke too.

"Then I guess Elizabeth will have to choose which one of us gets the boot."

I wiggled my foot against Mario's thighs. There was a bulge there. Through the alcohol haze, I realized I was glad.

"Why?" I murmured.

"Why?" Mario echoed. "Because Chris won't be a gentleman and admit defeat."

"No, I mean why do I have to choose? I want you both to be with me tonight."

"I think she's kidding," Chris said too quickly.

Historians spend a lot of time asking "how," which inevitably leads to "why," and there was, no doubt, a tangle of complex reasons why three middle-aged academics were about to engage in group sex on this particular night. But there, in the moment, the decision—and it was mine—to finally do a three-way with my two best friends was frighteningly simple. Because the real question that stokes the engine of history is not "why," but "why not."

Why not, indeed.

I sat up and put on my most seductive smile. Sally's smile. "There's obviously a lot you don't know about me."

My gaze flitted from one to the other, to make sure I had them where I wanted them, jaws slack, their eyes fixed in that primal, my-god-is-she-really-going-to-let-me-do-it-to-her amazement. I slowly unbuttoned my blouse. Their eyes followed, as if bound to the movement of my hands with steel cable. I pulled my shirt down over my shoulders with a shimmy and, still smiling, I traced the lacy edge of my bra with my fingertip. Could Sally have done better?

Mario's face had gone scarlet. Chris was up on one elbow, staring. He swallowed with a wet, slightly strangled sound.

Sally would have teased more. Sally would have them howling with their tongues on the floor before she gave any more, but the world moves faster in the twenty-first century. I unclasped the bra and let it slide over my arms, then took my breasts in my hands and arched my back, offering myself to them.

Mario whistled softly, like a distant train. Chris's face was tight, as if he were about to cry, but he was still staring.

"She's not kidding," Mario said.

Chris nodded.

"Come on, boys, get yourselves out of those clothes before I change my mind."

It was then they pulled their eyes from me and looked at each other.

What do you say, mate? Are you up for taking turns fucking our old friend Elizabeth in full view of each other?

Mario rose and began to unbutton his Oxford shirt. Chris pulled off his sweater. I watched them unbuckle their belts and wriggle out of their khakis. Mario wore briefs; Chris, boxers.

I pulled down the sheets and lay down in the middle of the bed. My friends joined me, one on each side.

Something wasn't right. In the lamp's glare, it was all too clear that Mario had grown a paunch, that he was too hairy for my taste. Chris had the smooth skin I prefer, but his ribs stood out like Jesus on the cross, the body of a man who'd endured hard times. I'm sure I disappointed them with my scrawny form. For all my feelings of sisterhood with Sally, I doubt anyone would ever pay to see me naked.

The three of us lay quietly for a moment, listening to the sounds of traffic rising twelve stories from the street below.

But history has its own momentum.

I nudged Chris to turn off the light.

The darkness made it easier for the show to begin. For Chris to reach over and cup my left breast gently. For Mario to trace my collarbone with his finger, then press his lips to my neck.

It tickled a little, and I laughed. They laughed too. Two male voices, one female, filling the room with the sound of pleasure entwined with disbelief.

DREAMS BEFORE BEDTIME

Before I get to the good part, I have a confession to make. The truth is, I'm used to crowded beds. Just the week before, I'd treated myself to a group encounter. There's nothing like it for a good night's sleep.

I'd been making good progress on my paper for the conference with a close reading of the text for Sally's Tru-Vue photo poster from 1933. The caption writer had indulged his own fantasies with a description of Sally's "proud, arched body . . . floating among the moonbeams . . . gliding, turning, skimming."

It got worse. "Bewitched by her own beauty." Sally spread her feathery wings for the finale "fluttering wildly, heart racing madly—pulses pounding." And then her joy was over, and she was serene again.

You don't have to have a PhD to figure out we're talking 1930's euphemisms for masturbation and orgasm, as if the male voyeur were observing her subjective pleasure and not merely projecting his own. This fantasy of orgasmic flight, I decided, would make the perfect conclusion to my talk. Couldn't it be seen as a symbol of the audience's desire to escape the grim realities of the Depression? That would explain why they gave Sally their money and their love, men and women alike.

Bewitched by my own cleverness, I shut down the computer and crawled into bed, my brain still flickering with images in vintage black-and-white.

It was then she came through my bedroom door, so lightly and gracefully, "skimming" might indeed be the right word. She perched herself on the edge of my bed and smiled. Her flesh gleamed white in the shadows. I smelled her powder and the faint musk of female sweat.

I should have been tongue-tied in the presence of my idol, but the words gushed through my lips like a fountain, the question no interviewer ever asked her, the question I longed to have her answer before she flew off again. *What was sex like seventy years ago? Tell me. Make me feel how it was for you.*

Sally's smile widened, but her eyes looked sad. Of course she could no longer tell me. She hadn't come to give me something. It was her turn to watch the show.

On cue, two more bodies climbed onto the bed. Male bodies, dressed in antique clothes. Slowly, their faces shifted into focus. They seemed like old friends.

The name of the sturdy young man in the worker's cap changes, depending on the night—Stan or Paolo or Johann—as does his job, one he's lucky to have—meat packer, baker, WPA construction worker. Maybe he helped build the fairgrounds. But he always lives in a boarding house. He's in love with the landlady's daughter and is saving every penny to marry her. He used to think of her white hands kneading bread when he lay on his narrow cot at night, pumping his cock in his fist, wiping himself guiltily afterward with a rough handkerchief.

But the summer of the World's Fair, all he thinks of is Sally.

The young man stretches out beside me and holds me in his arms, pulling me into his skin, so that suddenly I'm with him—I *am* him—wandering through the midway at night. He saunters under the sixty-four-story towers of the Sky Ride, past the Toboggan Glide and the Slide for Life, a ticket to see Sally clutched in his calloused hand. He takes his place in the back of the club. The front tables are for the rich men and their fancy ladies, even a few society wives who come to be titillated. He hates these men who spoil themselves with luxuries while so many starve, but he likes this place, because here, he knows he is their equal. When Sally appears, every man here will feel the same liquid flame shoot straight down his spine, melting his kneecaps, turning his cock to aching wood. A poor young worker can never have her for his own, but neither can the bosses, try though they may to clutch at her with their pale, fat fingers. For Sally's beauty, glowing with an opalescent sheen that reminds him of the drops of semen on his belly in the moonlight, belongs to everyone. To a future where all will enjoy her bounty in an endless feast of image and light.

Now the second man moves behind me, pressing his hard-on against my ass. His hands encircle my waist, and he tugs, tugs me out of the young workman's skin, into his own body, sprawled on a café chair, half-drunk on champagne, close enough to Sally to touch her. His name? Usually something like William B. Worthalot III, son of one of the city's most prominent men of business. Young Worthalot was at the opening gala, one of the first to spring a woody at the sight of Sally as Lady Godiva.

He's been to the Streets of Paris many times since. Once he brought his favorite mistress, a shop girl so lovely she needs no corset to mold her body to perfection. Afterward, William convinced her to pose for him like Sally, wearing nothing but feather fans, and later nothing at all. At first he had to coax her to show herself—*You have such natural beauty, my dear, you're a born star. Show me. Let me see you as you really are.* In the end, he could tell it aroused her, those rosy nipples standing up so stiff against the creamy white of her breasts. It made him hard too, very hard, a condition he could no longer rely on as he once did.

Tonight he has brought college friends from Denver. More than the fan dance, he enjoys their discomposure when Sally swishes by the table, as well as their moist-lipped gratitude when he offers to guide them to his favorite brothel after the show.

He himself observes Sally with a cool eye. On the face of it, she's no different from Chicago's other favorite daughters who bare all—Margie Hart, Ann Corio, Sunya "Smiles" Slane. How has Sally put herself above the rest? A certain twinkle in her eye, a secret swivel of the hips? The answer eludes him, which is why he keeps coming back, to grasp that thing and understand her strange power. And as much as I dislike him, I recognize myself in him, a man of untold riches who will never be satisfied.

I looked to Sally, watching us watching her.

Did I get it right? I asked.

She bobbed her head lightly—in assent or farewell—then vanished into air.

HOW THESE THINGS REALLY HAPPEN

In dirty stories, threesomes are always the same: three sets of mouths and hands and asses and whatever combination of cocks and cunts joining in every possible way so you're no lon ger sure what belongs to whom, which is probably the idea.

In fact, I wouldn't have minded seeing Mario bend Chris over the bed, then vice versa, or picking up a few insider tips as they sucked each other's cocks, or being witness to the most forbidden turn-on of all: a slow, loving, man-to-man soul kiss.

But it would have taken a lot more wine—and a lot more honesty—for us to go there.

Not that I should complain with a man on each side focused solely on my pleasure, an abundance of hands and lips and the heady scent of male flesh. But it wasn't at all like the fantasies in one crucial respect. My friends had divided my body in two, North and South Korea, and stretching from my neck to my clit was a DMZ that neither would cross. So far, our frolic was less a threesome than two one-and-a-halves on the same bed.

I would have to be the one to get the peace talks moving.

I sat up and turned, positioning myself between them, studying their cocks openly for the first time. Mario's rose red and thick against the dark curls. Chris's dick was longer and curved, reminding me oddly of the parking brake in my car, smooth and pale golden, eternally erect.

"What beautiful cocks," I murmured and leaned over to suck Chris. He filled my mouth with heat, the spices of male crotch. I started to hum. At first he laughed, then sighed.

For Mario I showed off some tongue tricks. Quick little figure eights just below the head, long gliding ice cream licks from root to tip. I saw Chris watching with narrowed, glittering eyes. Lust made him a stranger. It scared me. And it turned me on.

"Elizabeth, please stop now," Mario begged. He tugged me down and rolled me over to face Chris to make a nice Elizabeth sandwich. I heard a condom wrapper tearing, the snap of latex. He pushed himself inside me so quickly I cried out.

"You're on breast duty, Hansen," Mario called over my shoulder.

"With pleasure," Chris replied and scooted lower to take a nipple in his lips.

Mario pulled my leg up and over his thighs and began to thrust, all the while whispering in my ear. About how beautiful I was, so beautiful and smart he'd been in love with me forever. There was no woman in the world like me, with a pussy so hot and wet.

I closed my eyes and let the sensations flow through me, Mario filling my cunt, Chris flicking his tongue over one nipple, stroking the other with the pad of his thumb. But best of all were those words, so soothing and sweet.

My belly was on fire, and I was dying for Chris to rub my clit, but I sensed they'd drawn that boundary again. Still, I wouldn't give up my dreams of world peace. I reached down and took Chris's cock in my hand. It felt good, good to hold him and stroke him, and for that moment, we were like the fantasies, all of us connected, cock to cunt, breast to lips, hand to cock again, in one pulsing circle.

Suddenly Mario grunted and pushed into me with gliding, rhythmic strokes.

Chris looked up and met my eyes with a frown, my question mirrored in his eyes.

Did he just come—already?

We both smiled. Mario always managed to cross the finish line before we did.

CLIMAX

But Chris and I were never far behind. While Mario disposed of the condom, Chris coaxed my body across the bed so my hips rested at the edge and then knelt between my legs.

"I believe it's your turn to take the top half, Mario, my friend." He grinned to let me know it was a joke.

But that is exactly what happened. While Mario fed me

slow kisses and tweaked my nipples in a steady rhythm, Chris began to make love to me with his mouth.

I could tell right away he had a knack for it.

First he kissed his way around my swollen lips, then treated me to long, flat tongue strokes that felt like rolls of hot, wet silk rippling over my vulva. Then he teased and dallied, carefully avoiding my sweet spot until I pushed up against him and groaned in frustration. It didn't take him long to find the right rhythm, quick up-and-down flicks in the little groove to the side of my clit. Except he'd stop now and then, just to make me squirm and moan my disappointment into Mario's mouth. When he started up again, I moaned louder, because it was magic the way our mouths were joined in a column of flame running straight through me. By sucking my juices through my red lips, one pair for each, they were kissing each other too.

Chris pushed one leg up to my belly and held it there, opening me, stretching me so tight my ass seemed to lift off the bed. My thighs were trembling, and I knew I would make it. Relentless now, Chris's tongue lashed at my clit, and I sucked Mario's tongue like a cock until I couldn't anymore, I could only roll my head back and forth, sobbing my pleasure to Mario's soft coos—*Come for us, Elizabeth; that's right, let us watch you come*—and that's exactly what I did.

I looked down at Chris, still kneeling at the edge of the bed. He smiled up at me, his chin dripping. For the first time that evening, he looked truly happy. The golden boy of old.

"Let me do something for you," I said.

Something in his eyes clicked shut again. The gold faded to gray. He shook his head.

Under the circumstances, it didn't feel right to press the matter.

CURTAIN CALL

Again, Mario did just the right thing. As we pulled on our pants and buttoned our shirts in mildly uncomfortable silence, he suggested we meet for breakfast the next morning, a final celebration before he caught his plane.

It was smart, the only thing to do really: make everything the way it was before as best we could.

At the door, Mario tilted my chin up and kissed me gallantly. Chris and I hugged, our usual goodbye, but he added an extra reassuring squeeze. It struck me then that we still hadn't ever kissed on the mouth, the old-fashioned way.

Once they were gone, I turned and caught a glimpse of myself in the mirrored closet door.

To my surprise, I looked pretty. My eyes shone, my skin glowed with a twentysomething bloom. I gave myself a victorious smile. I'd done it. I'd become an adventuress, a breaker of taboos. It didn't happen quite the way I thought it would, but it never does.

On impulse I yanked the rumpled sheet off the bed and draped it around my shoulders, the best approximation of a "white heron in the moonlight" costume I could manage.

I wondered what Sally would do to ease herself to sleep if she'd just had sex with a man—or two—that satisfied her flesh but not her heart. I wondered if she'd be a little sad to finally understand why Mario's relationships never lasted too long. Or if she'd struggle with her own fantasy that Chris really was The One, and though we'd both married the wrong people the first time around, we had plenty of hot times ahead if only he could wean himself from those antidepressants.

What *would* Sally do?

Of course she was a realist. She knew fantasies were powerful. They could push the boundaries, change your life so it would never be the same, make you richer than you ever dreamed possible. But you never let them catch you or hold you down.

At the end of the show, there was only one thing to do.

I stretched my arms out and turned slowly, then faster—gliding, turning, skimming, whirling—around and around, my white wings outstretched, until I swear I was flying up and away.

THE FIRST DEADLY SIN

Gwen Masters

W hen I was a kid, I was coerced into wearing dresses with starched skirts and Mary Janes, ordered to sit in a hard pew and not squirm, and expected to listen to tales of fire and brimstone handed down from the pulpit. I grew up, not unexpectedly, believing that one detour from the straight-and-narrow would land me in eternal flames.

If you had told me then that I would be fucking in a church, I would have contemplated you with contempt and swore you were going to hell for the mere thought of such impropriety.

Then I married a Catholic.

Our marriage had gone on for years, but it was usually too much work and not enough play. As a consequence, our vacations were short, but they were memorable. We had planned this one for months, and we were determined to get the best out of every minute. We left the cell phones at home and eschewed the map for our own sense of adventure. For three days, we belonged to the open road—and each other.

The first day set the tone for how things would be. We had driven all day, stopping at interesting places along the way, often pulling over to make love in a secluded grove of trees down some lonely side road. Now we were shopping for antiques in one of the quaintest little towns we had ever seen.

We parked the car at the end of a strip of antique shops and set out walking. We weren't looking to buy, only looking to look and to be with each other. Throughout the afternoon, we browsed through old postcards and ceramics, played with antique wooden toys molded by the hands of a hard-working farmer, and studied old quilts. Adam chuckled often at my enthusiasm, even though he had seen it all before. We didn't even notice as the sun began to hide behind dark storm clouds.

We were pulled out of our absorption with each other when a shopkeeper announced in a pleasant voice, "I'm so sorry, but we're closing now."

Adam and I held hands and hustled to the door, only to find that it was pouring rain outside. The storms had finally moved in.

"I hope I rolled up the windows," Adam murmured, looking out at the rain.

"Too late now," I said.

The shopkeeper allowed us to stay for a few minutes, but it quickly became apparent that the rain wasn't letting up anytime soon. In fact, the heavens seemed determined to drown everything beneath them.

I finally turned to Adam and smiled up at him. "Wanna run through the rain?" I teased him. "Just like we were kids again?"

Adam grinned down at me. "We're not that old yet, are we?"

"You didn't seem that old last night."

He laughed. "Why not?"

We raced out the door, holding hands and giggling like schoolchildren. By the time we were a block away from the store, we found that our plan had a little hitch—this wasn't a gentle rain. It was hard and punishing, the drops stinging like needles on our bare legs and arms. Our laughter soon disappeared, and we huddled together under a tiny awning that didn't provide much protection.

This was not a storm. This was a flood. We watched as the water rose in the street. It climbed over the curb and churned down the cobblestones. It was a "forty days and forty nights" kind of downpour.

That's when I looked up and saw the church.

St. Joseph's Cathedral. Like all enormous Catholic churches, it was imposing and far too grand for the little town in which it resided. The soft glow through the stained glass indicated that we might find shelter there. The large rough bricks that built the facade were quickly darkening as they

THE FIRST DEADLY SIN 255

absorbed the moisture from the clouds. The door was huge, solid wood, and welcoming.

"Adam!" I yelled over the rush of the water flowing down the storm drains. "The church!"

He didn't hesitate. We raced across the road and up the steep stairs, ducking our heads against the fury of the raindrops. He grabbed at one of the doors and pulled. Nothing. The second door swung wide and easily on large hinges.

Cool air flowed out of the church as we stepped into the vestibule and stood looking at each other. Water dripped from Adam's hair and down his nose, ran down his chin, and dripped onto his chest. Puddles began to form under us.

Adam sighed and shook his head. "Look at us," he laughed, holding his arms out from his body. Water dripped off of him in constant little plops.

"At least it's dry in here," I said. Adam reached for a choir robe that hung on a nearby hook, looking around to see whether anyone was watching.

"Shhhh . . . " he said to me as I took it from him and used it to dry off as best I could. Adam found another robe and used it to dry himself, then we hung them neatly back on their hooks. Somewhat presentable again, we walked from the vestibule into the outer chamber.

We stood in silence, awed by the power of the place. The ceilings were three stories high and arched with solid oak beams. The ceiling was covered with a mural of the Virgin Mary, and the stained glass windows on either side rose two stories before joining the mural in a cacophony of color and priceless artistry. Even the pews were lovely, obviously hand-carved out of expensive woods. Three steps led to the altar. An imposing crucifix hung as the focal point in the massive church.

Adam automatically dipped his fingers into the holy water at the back of the church and genuflected. He murmured something that was foreign to my Southern Baptist ears. His eyes were wide as he took in the church.

"It's beautiful, isn't it?" he whispered.

"Absolutely," I praised.

"Let's sit," he prompted.

The pew was surprisingly comfortable. Adam always kept a small rosary in his pocket—it was like his guardian angel, he would always say—and now he pulled it out of his pocket and played with it, turning it over and over in his hands as I lay my damp head on his shoulder. We didn't speak, content to just look around for the longest time. I listened to the silence.

"Is anyone in here, you think?" I asked him.

"I'm sure someone is nearby."

I trailed my hand up and down his thigh. Adam quietly fingered the beads of his rosary while I stroked his leg. Maybe it was the heathen in me that my Baptist preacher never could quite talk away, but I found myself growing wet at the very thought of fucking Adam in a church.

I don't know where the idea came from. Maybe it was that

polished table that boasted a long sentence in Latin, then below it: Do this in remembrance of me.

"Adam?"

"Hmmmm?" He seemed to be almost asleep.

"I want you."

"To do what?" he asked.

I snickered. "No, silly. I want you."

He looked down at me, still not understanding. I made it very clear.

"I want you to fuck me in this church."

Adam started to laugh. I didn't. He sobered very quickly.

"You are serious," he stated flatly.

In response, I took the rosary from his hand and pressed it hard to his crotch. He grew hard almost immediately, despite his wide-eyed look of astonishment. I moved the smooth beads around the outside of his shorts, then slid them up inside the leg of them to press the rosary against his balls. Adam's hand covered mine to pull it away, but he hesitated as I slid the beads up his hardening shaft.

I circled my hand around his cock and laced my fingers through the beads. I slid both up his body, and he exhaled the breath he had been holding, groaning softly into my neck as he opened his mouth and bit down. I chuckled in pleasure as the wetness started to grow between my thighs.

"This is wrong," he protested halfheartedly.

"Do you think so?"

I slid my hand up his shaft and pressed one rosary bead to the opening of his cock. Adam's hips jerked, and his hand clamped down hard on my wrist, holding me there. I spun the little bead and he cried out, the sound muffled against my neck. I pushed the little bead deeper and then played with him, pushing it in and out of that little slit on his head, fucking him with the cool hard pebble.

Suddenly Adam lurched up and yanked my hand away. He hauled me roughly into the aisle. He tried to push me to the carpeted floor, and I resisted, pulling the rosary out of his pants and sidestepping him. My reflection looked back at me from the bowl of holy water. His eyes danced from me to the rosary as I reached in and dipped the beads into the liquid. Adam's mouth fell open in surprise. I walked to him and yanked down his shorts, suddenly exposing him to the angelic faces looking down from the ornate walls.

"What are you doing?" Adam hissed, his voice a frantic edge in the silence.

I was wrapping the rosary around his cock. He groaned aloud as I pulled it tight, circling it snugly around his hard tip, then rolling it down like a condom. Adam gasped as the beads rolled down to the base of his cock.

"I want you as hard as you can be," I whispered, leaning forward to drink the drops of holy water that slid down his balls. Adam thrust upward toward my mouth, and his hand found his cock. He began to stroke, and I smiled mischievously.

"Isn't masturbation a sin?"

"You're a temptress," he replied in his own defense. He squeezed his cock as I sucked one of his balls into my mouth. I ran my tongue over it, feeling it roll between my lips. Adam moaned—and even though he was quiet, the architecture of the place didn't seem to care for vocal decorum. The passionate sound resonated from the high ceilings and back down.

"Someone could walk in on us," he protested.

"Would you like that, to have a priest walk in on you being fucked?" I taunted. In answer, his fingers found the rosary beads and pulled, making them tighter around him.

"Would you like to show a prim and proper nun what a real cock looks like?" I asked him. Adam stared down at me with eyes that were alight with desire.

"How about showing her what a real fuck looks like?"

I stood and wrapped my fingers around his cock, then gently pulled. Adam followed me obediently to the altar, and as I turned to him he sank his hands into my hair.

"The altar?" he asked with an air of amazement.

I sank down to my knees and opened my mouth over him, taking him down in one long stroke. Adam's soft cry echoed from the ceiling. I sucked him in until the rosary beads rolled against my mouth. Then I began to slide my mouth up and down, sucking his head, licking the first drops of salty moisture and sliding down to taste the last of the holy water between the rosary beads.

Finally I slid my mouth all the way down his cock, circling

my lips around the rosary. I caught the beads with my teeth and slid them slowly up. He was bigger now than he had been when I put the beads on, and they were a bit difficult to remove. They squeezed tightly around his shaft.

I pulled them off and let them fall into my hand. My tongue flicked that spot right under his head. My teeth nibbled gently. I took the wet rosary beads and slid them down his balls, all the way back to his ass.

Adam tensed. I slid the beads up and down the cleft of his ass, letting the warm beads caress him, letting him get used to the idea. I sucked hard on his cock and then removed him from my mouth long enough to whisper to him.

"Relax."

I pushed the rosary against him. I pressed one bead against his puckered ring. Adam whimpered and moaned on a deep breath as he let his body relax as much as he could. I gently pushed, and the bead disappeared, sucked into his ass as he clenched it against the feeling.

"Oh . . . oh god . . . " Adam groaned.

He had completely forgotten about being quiet. I slid another bead to his tight hole and pushed. His body sucked it inside. I licked his cock with long strokes, sucking hard as I repeated the action with each bead on that rosary. Adam couldn't decide whether to buck his cock into my throat or push his ass against my hand. I kept it up until only the small cross on the circle of beads was left outside his body.

Adam looked down at me. His eyes were cloudy with pleasure.

"You are a heathen," he murmured, breathing hard.

"You're Catholic," I said. "Which is worse?"

Adam offered me a quirky, sarcastic smile.

He lifted me to my feet, and his hands found my shorts. He pulled hard. Seams ripped as he yanked them down my thighs and I kicked them off. I was wearing nothing underneath. Adam lifted me to the offering table, settling me on the cool polished wood. He climbed onto it. Bibles and a few candles fell to the floor with a thud. He pushed me up, then spread my legs wide and sank his cock into me with one fluid motion.

We were both on the edge already. He began to pump in and out, harder and harder. I slid my hand down his back and found that cross that was lying against his ass. He angled his strokes right against my clit, the way that years of lovemaking had taught him I liked.

I came with a low, deep moan. I bit my lip to keep from crying out. I stared at the mural on the ceiling, watching the angels that hovered protectively above.

I circled my hand around the cross and began to pull. The beads slowly popped out of his tight hole, one at a time.

He slammed hard into me, shoving me up the table, and I yanked hard on the beads. His cock throbbed inside me and he groaned again, this time with his hands buried deep in my hair. He kept coming as I slid the rosary out. Adam seemed to hold his breath for an eternity, then he sucked in great breaths of air and collapsed on top of me.

"My god, my god," he said over and over, like a prayer.

When the shaking subsided, Adam lifted me from the table and carried me to the front of the church. He stepped onto a platform that held the enormous crucifix.

I had a sudden sharp moment of doubt. This was so wrong—wasn't it?

All thoughts fled my mind when he lifted a long purple sash from the nearby pulpit and looped it over the arm of the cross, then around my wrist. He lifted another sash and did the same thing with the other arm. Then he unbuttoned my shirt and stepped back to look at me.

I was bound to the cross, my feet spread on the platform below me. The wood of the cross was rough against my back. Adam touched me with one finger as I looked out over the rows of pews. His finger slid down my body, circling each nipple before running down my stomach and over my curls. He paused to run the pad of his thumb over my hips before sliding his hand up again.

"Please, Adam," I moaned.

"I'm thirsty," he said softly. "Will you feed me?"

Adam knelt between my thighs and spread them wider. His fingers touched my clit, and I bucked up into him. The bonds around my wrists cut into me with a sweet, gentle pain. Adam quickly replaced his fingers with his tongue. He licked slowly at my clit, then slid his mouth down to delve into my cunt.

"Give me my seed," he murmured. "Do it, love. Give it to me. I know you can."

I tilted my head back. It thudded hard against the cross. I squeezed my inner muscles, rhythmically, hard. Adam groaned in approval. The sound echoed through the church. Adam caught the moisture on his tongue. He licked and sucked and played until my knees were weak.

"I can taste us both," he whispered.

I cried out as his tongue touched my clit and pressed hard. I squirmed before him. He licked and then sucked, alternating, keeping me on the edge.

"Come for me," he whispered. "Come for me in this church. Come for me on this crucifix. But while you do it, I want you to pray the rosary."

"I don't know how," I whined breathlessly. I was right on the verge.

"Hail Mary . . . " he prompted.

"H . . . H . . . Hail . . . Mary, full of . . . grace . . . "

His lips closed around my clit. His teeth sank down, and I suddenly couldn't breathe. He bit down slowly, threatening me with the possibilities. I was riding a thin line between pain and pleasure.

Adam bit down harder.

I came viciously, my body convulsing on the cross, the pain overtaking me with pleasure. My hands clenched hard on the rough wooden arms, and the sharpness of a splinter sliced into my finger. My body throbbed. I moaned sense-lessly as my orgasm waned.

Adam kissed me as he gently loosened my bonds. I fell into his arms, and he lifted me from the crucifix, carrying me down the stairs and the altar like I was a new bride.

"Where are we going?" I whispered.

He stopped in front of the altar and pulled out a small drawer under the remembrance table. I looked down as he set-tled me on my feet, and I laughed at what he pulled out.

It was a Communion cup.

"You have to be kidding," I said.

He looked at me with the most serious expression he could muster.

"You need to take Communion."

I stared at him. He nodded. I sank to my knees before him.

My first long lick made Adam arch into my touch. The sec-ond made him groan. He hadn't come while he was licking me on the crucifix, and the sweet torture he inflicted on me had made him more than ready. I closed my lips around him and began to lick at the sensitive spot right underneath the head of his cock. I flicked my tongue across it. Then I gently sank my teeth into it.

He gasped and began to writhe under my ministrations. My hands found his balls, and he almost laughed when he felt the cool beads of the rosary press against his soft skin. I circled the rosary around one of his balls and pulled gently. Adam's whole body jerked, and I tightened the grip of the rosary while my hand slid up to circle around him.

Holding his balls like that, I began to jack him off. Hard. I squeezed him with my hand on the upward stroke and let up on the pressure as I slid down. I twisted the rosary until he moaned. I flicked my tongue over the head before sucking him into my mouth again.

"Oh god . . . I need to come," he moaned.

I pulled down harder on the rosary, and he yelped. When I gave him a hard upward suck, Adam began to tremble. He cried out as he began to come.

I took the first shot into my mouth, then quickly squeezed his head hard. Adam moaned loudly in both pleasure and pain. I slid my mouth off of him, licking gently, and released his balls. The pressure in his cock was enormous. I pressed the Communion cup to the tip of his cock and let him go. His cock spurted out a few more times and into the cup.

"Wow," he muttered, as he braced himself on my shoulder to keep from falling over.

I held up the Communion cup, and he grinned.

"Is this for me?" I asked him. He shook his head.

"For you?" I asked.

"Get dressed," was all he said.

I slowly dressed before him while he pulled up his shorts. We walked toward the back of the church. Adam took the Communion cup from my hand. With a wicked smile, he stopped before the basin of holy water.

Before I could say a word, he tipped the cup and dumped his semen into the water. He swirled it around with one finger, then offered that finger to me to suck.

I was speechless. I watched the water drip from his finger-tip and slowly moved toward it, as if in a trance. I licked the tainted blessed water from his hand.

"Forgive me, Father, for I have sinned," he intoned slowly, and that broke the spell. I laughed out loud. Adam opened the door and looked back at me with an expression of wry irony.

The rain had stopped.

Adam chuckled and shook his head, surely remembering his childhood as an altar boy. I was thinking of the fire and brimstone raining down from the pulpit. We voiced the same thought at the same time, reading each other's minds:

"We're going to go to hell, aren't we?"

TE ENCANTA
EL MAR

Sofía Quintero

*M*ercedes followed him from the Hamaca Coral hotel to the beach. She expected that when she invited him to rendezvous with her in the sea he would resist, but that was always the case. That initial hesitancy always came with a glint in the eye and a flex of the cock, and Mercedes savored that reaction. It made her pussy sweat and sparked a burn that only the waters of the Caribbean Sea could quench.

She took a sip from her cup of iced water. Mercedes always loved the water for the way it loved her. As she walked to the beach, Mercedes recalled how her lifelong affair with the element began. It had to have been as a child in the tub with her favorite toy—a plastic starfish filled with a purple gel, scented with lavender. By the time she turned thirteen, Mercedes graduated to hot showers and the vibrating sponge she stole from her older cousin Nurys while visiting her family in *la capital*. She liked to slather the pink sponge with baby oil and tuck the pulsating sphere between the tops of her soapy thighs. With her clit quivering, Mercedes faced the hot stream and caressed her soapy nipples as the showerhead drummed water on her belly.

The summer of her *quinceañera*, she even lost her virginity in a hotel Jacuzzi tub. For over three months, Mercedes had teased her first love—a wiry boy named Sancho. They were among a group of kids who had snuck into the hotel's pool. Until that night, Mercedes only let Sancho stroke her tits above her halter and dry hump her in the *hamaca* behind her aunt's house. They would grow so horny that she would wrap her then-skinny legs around his waist. The hammock rocked until hooks squeaked, and Mercedes's aunt flooded the back porch with light. The hot teens had to spring apart before they could get caught.

But that night Mercedes let Sancho fingerfuck her in the hotel pool. Even as the chlorine clouded her vision and burned her eyes, she could not resist him in the water. They were wrestling in the pool as Mercedes scrambled for the ladder, and Sancho chased her. She reached it and tried to climb out, but he grabbed her by the waist and pulled her back into the water. Mercedes fell, splashing onto him, and Sancho's hand grazed her ass. He rushed to apologize and braced himself for a wet slap, but Mercedes took his hand and guided it beneath the bottom of Nurys's hand-me-down bikini. She grasped the sides of the ladder and spread her legs while zealous Sancho plunged one and then two and eventually three digits in and out of her juicy pussy. Mercedes gyrated her hips against his cocoa-colored fingers until she exploded. Then she dropped back into the water, grabbed Sancho's dick, and rubbed wildly until it fired several shots of come through the pool water. Of course, he suggested that they steal behind a bush and finish what they had started, but Mercedes refused, although not for long. The memory of her short-lived resolve caused her to giggle like she always did sixteen years ago.

A half hour after their escapade in the pool, she had stumbled onto the hotel's hot tub on her way to the ladies' room. Mercedes slipped in as a pair of female American tourists left. Inside she found the middle-aged women's male companions. They eyed her as she slipped into the carpet of bubble, and one attempted to speak to her in university-taught Castilian. Look-ing back now, Mercedes realized what she did not understand at fifteen. These men had mistaken her for one of the native women who strolled across the hotel grounds, offering to fulfill tourists' fantasies for a price.

Except to roll her eyes, Mercedes ignored the men until they gave up and followed their wives. Once gone, she began to play. She removed her suit bottom and straddled a jet. In the solitude, Mercedes felt free to grind and thrash and moan as the jet gushed past her lips and to her clit like a waterfall over rocks. After bribing a porter to let him into the spa, Sancho found Mercedes cooing as the bubbles rode over her tingling body. He tore off his trunks and jumped into the tub. Mercedes and Sancho clung to each other amid the rough waves, kissing, moaning, and rubbing until Sancho pushed Mercedes against the edge of the tub and drove his throbbing cock into her tight pussy. The bubbles pounded against them as he bucked into her, until they both cried out in Spanish. Sancho and Mercedes fucked and came and fucked again until the same porter discovered them and ordered the teens to leave.

LOST IN HER SENSUAL RECOLLECTIONS on her way from the hotel to the beach, Mercedes lost sight of him. When she reached the crowded beach of Boca Chica, however, she easily found him. Amid the pale Europeans sunbathing across green hotel chaise lounges and the sienna Dominican vendors selling johnnycakes and cornrows, he stood out. At least he did to Mercedes. Like her, he belonged here, and like her, he did not. She and he, they were like the locals, and yet they were different, and that was one reason why Mercedes desired him above all the others.

With a loose grip on her olive and rust sarong in one hand and the sweaty cup in the other, she made her way across the cool sand toward him. He sat on a blinding white towel he had borrowed from the hotel and skimmed through a trade paperback with an English title through prescription sunglasses. She reached him, casting her shadow across the page dense with text. He looked up, and Mercedes smiled at him. She gestured toward the towel, requesting permission to join him. He granted it. She felt him watch as she slowly loosened her sarong and slid it off her now full hips. As she curled it across the sand beside him, Mercedes gave him a lengthy view of her sun-kissed cleavage.

Once Mercedes sat down, she asked, *"¿Es de los estados unidos, verdad?"*

"Sí." He put aside his book and looked at her. She tried to look past the slightly tinted lenses of his rimless sunglasses, into his eyes.

"¿Es misionero?"

And as she expected, he laughed. He removed his glasses, and Mercedes fixed her gaze on the flecks of brown in his hazel eyes. "No, I'm not."

"So why are you here?" For a moment, she considered attempting another accent, but decided against it. Her natural one would do. "Are you alone?"

He shook his head. *"Soy antropólogo, y viajo con un grupo de colegas."*

"Oh." She drew up her knees and wrapped her arms around them. "And where is your group?"

He shrugged. "I don't know." Then he gave her a sly smile. "And right now I don't care."

She grinned back at him and offered her hand. "Mercedes."

He took her hand and kissed it. "Roberto." Unlike the others, Roberto posed no stupid questions, like "Did you know you're named after a car?" Instead he asked, *"¿Y qué haces? ¿Es estudiante?"*

"Claro que sí," said Mercedes, her eyes traveling freckle by freckle across his broad chest. She gazed from the wide cleft between the muscles of his chest down to the dark tuft of hair that speckled over his taut belly. "I study you, and I learn many interesting things."

"And what have you learned about me?"

"I know what you like."

"And what do I like?"

Mercedes tilted her head toward the water as it rolled blankets of turquoise and cobalt over bathers. *"Te encanta el mar."* She rose to her feet and offered Roberto her hand.

Roberto scanned the beach until his eyes fell on a trio of men who stood several yards away from them. A dirty blond in his early thirties haggled with an older woman attempting to sell him a beaded necklace, the r's of his Spanish flattened by a New England accent. The much older man to the blond's right watched in amusement, his blue eyes bouncing between them. Meanwhile, the gentleman to the haggler's left latched his arms across his wrinkled chest as he muttered, "No, grassy-ass, no De Niro, no, grassy-ass."

Roberto snickered at them as he pulled off his sunglasses. After putting them aside, he took Mercedes's hand.

Once on his feet, he took the lead, taking confident strides toward the water. Mercedes glanced back at the Americans. She knew she could have any of them if she so desired, and that they could offer her things that Roberto could not. That each of them harbored fantasies of pounding between her thick mahogany thighs and knotting his pasty knuckles in her mass of dark curls. As Roberto and she neared the sea and the sand grew cool and wet underneath her toes, Mercedes surveyed the beach for her sisters. She found many of them in the company of male tourists, accepting their spiked *batidas,* teaching them how to flirt in Spanish and laughing at their unfunny jokes.

"*¿Estás bien?*" Roberto's voice coaxed her back to the sea.

She smiled at him. "*Claro.*"

They waded deeper into the crystalline waters and attempted to steer away from splashing revelers. Finally, they stopped where the mild and tepid waves tickled her rib cage. Again, Roberto looked around them, wrinkling his brow at the nearby bathers. Mercedes sensed his nervousness. His colleagues remained oblivious on land, and the other bathers were far away enough, but it would only take a stray Frisbee to disrupt their groove. That possibility—and the apprehension it caused him—made Mercedes forget everything but what she'd wanted to do since she found Roberto on the beach.

Mercedes buoyed toward him until her hardened nipples grazed across his dripping chest. She rested her hands on

Roberto's shoulders and pressed her lips against his. He tasted like a cocktail of salt, sand, and *naranja*. Roberto slipped his warm tongue into her mouth, still cool from the iced water. They flirted with their tongues, their eyes closed as the sun warmed their lids.

Suddenly, Roberto stopped and turned his head. He looked around them, and then over Mercedes's shoulder toward the beach. She had to do more to keep his mind off his peers and his desire on her. Mercedes dragged her hands from around his neck, down his chest over his nipples, over his hard stomach, and to his waistband beneath the water. Then she reached for the hems of his swim trunks. She stroked his thighs, feeling the long hairs whisk back and forth with the sea.

"What are you doing?" he asked.

She just grinned at him and began to glide her hand up his leg until she could grip his cock. Mercedes stroked it, the salt of the sea grinding between the pocket of her wet palm and his thickening shaft. Roberto moaned and placed his hands on Mercedes's hips, running his fingers under the knots of her bikini. With one finger he traced her pelvic bone down to the top of her mound. Anticipating his next touch, Mercedes quickened her strokes, pumping Roberto's dick against her belly through the nylon of his trunks.

His wandering finger slid down her mound and between her legs, her lips now slick with wetness much thicker than the sea. Roberto and Mercedes swayed with the gentle waves as they rubbed each other under the water and buried moans in one another's necks.

"*Ay, sí.*"

"*Asííí . . .* "

Roberto fingered Mercedes's clit like an oily pearl while she milked his rod as it pulsated in her tight fist. Their pleasure rode the waves that lapped at their hot bodies. Mercedes wished she could drop to her knees and take Roberto into her mouth. She imagined it, feeling the sand scraping against her knees and her hair flailing in the current. Mercedes stroked, listening to the hollow of the sea engulf her and envisioning herself pulling down Roberto's trunks until his thick cock waved before her parted lips. She stroked along to her fantasy, virtually feeling his salty head as it slid into her mouth and thumped rhythmically against the soft lining of her cheek.

Then Mercedes saw Roberto join her under the water. He gestured for her to turn around. She leaned back, fluttering her legs toward him and swirling her arms like a synchronized swimmer until she was floating face down. Mercedes gazed at the white sand beneath her as she felt Roberto stretch her suit bottom to the side and snake his tongue in between her legs. The underwater waves wrapped around her moans and muffled them. As Roberto licked her clit, Mercedes legs drifted wider and wider, and her cries of pleasure bubbled to the surface.

"*¡Vírate, mami!*"

Roberto's voice brought Mercedes out of her fantasy with

her nipples aching and her clit throbbing with desire. She heeded his command, turning around and pressing her plush butt against his rod. Roberto gripped her waist as Mercedes widened her stance. He plunged into her, splashing the water around their waists. Under the veil of the sea, Roberto fucked Mercedes, the weight of the water adding depth to his thrusts.

"¡Así, papi, así!" She looked over his shoulder at Roberto. His eyes were closed as he tilted his head back into the beating sun. His chest rose and fell with the rhythm of the tossing waves and Mercedes's pulsating cunt. The band of his trunks rubbed against the backs of her thighs under the salty water. *"¡Asííí!"*

On the verge of climax, Mercedes dug the balls of her feet into the sand to keep from drifting. Roberto growled and wrapped his arms around Mercedes's waist. "Errrahhh!" Visualizing Roberto exploding inside her triggered Mercedes's climax, and her beating pussy poured her juices into the sea. As the waves of orgasm rippled from between her legs and throughout her body, she felt Roberto release his grip. Mercedes submerged herself into the sea, imagining herself enveloped in the salty waves laced with their desire.

When Mercedes returned to the surface for air, she realized that Roberto was gone. She waded her way back to the beach, searching it for him once again. She spotted him just as he reached the shore. When the water reached her shins, Mercedes lowered herself until she was kneeling on the sand with the sea hugging her waist. The sea caressed her as she watched

Roberto saunter back to his towel. As he picked it up and whipped it around his shoulders, his trio of colleagues rejoined him.

As the waves lapped Mercedes's breasts, she observed Roberto's friends as she had him. The oldest gentleman stroked his bald spot, the skin red and flaky beneath the Caribbean sun, and said something to Roberto. The other two men traded remarks to one another as they ogled three Dominican girls who swayed past them. Just as Mercedes hoped the girls didn't notice their rudeness, Roberto broke his attention to the elder to scowl at his peers. The elder pointed to his watch, signaling them that the time had come to leave Boca Chica.

After Roberto had gathered his towel, eyeglasses, and book, he followed the older man with his other colleagues in tow. He took a few paces, then paused to look over his shoulder, searching the water for Mercedes. She blew a kiss to him, and he waved back at her.

Mercedes watched Roberto and his colleagues until they were out of sight. Only then did she make her way back to the beach. She took her time returning to the hotel so she could dry under the sun, savoring the way her skin tingled with salt, heat, and satisfaction. She almost did not want it to end, but she knew better things awaited her.

She entered the lobby of the Hamaca Coral Hotel and strolled past the sign that read WELCOME TO THE MEMBERS OF THE AMERICAN ANTHROPOLOGICAL ASSOCIATION'S ANNUAL CONFERENCE: CHALLENGE THE BOUNDARIES OF ANTHROPOLOGY. Mercedes waved to the housekeepers and porters she encountered on her way to the elevator and on to her floor. When she entered the hotel room, he was in the shower. Mercedes peeled off her damp sarong and suit by the door and let herself into the bathroom. She pulled back the curtain and stepped in behind Roberto. Mercedes wrapped her arms around his waist and kissed her favorite freckle on his shoulder.

Roberto turned around and pecked her on the forehead. Again, he motioned for her to turn around, and when Mercedes did, he began to lather her back. "That was amazing," he said.

Mercedes hummed in agreement. "Didn't I say you'd like role-playing?" Then she said, "I really don't want to go Peter's presentation." She gathered her salty curls and piled them atop her head.

"Yeah, how many times do we have to suffer through that paper?" Roberto kneaded her shoulders. "But you have to go, *mami*. You don't want to risk having the chair of the department noticing that you skipped his lecture right before you apply for tenure."

"I have to go?" She sucked her teeth and twirled her neck. Mercedes turned around to face Roberto and give him a sassy grin. "If I have to go, so do you."

They loved to play like this. After spending three long days maintaining a professional demeanor for their colleagues, Mercedes and Roberto enjoyed stealing away together to be who they really were. He was the Dominican boy from Corona,

Queens, and she was the Dominican girl born in Williams-burg, Brooklyn, who both struggled—spiritually as well as financially—to earn their doctorates. Both of them felt that they belonged here, this being their ancestral land. And yet because of their privileged citizenry, both Mercedes and Roberto understood that neither of them belonged, either. This was one of many reasons why, although she could have whomever she wanted in her department, she chose him.

"Was Pete asking you where I was while you guys were at the beach?" Mercedes asked.

"Of course," said Roberto. "You know that ol' man is dying to see you in a bikini. All of them are."

And just like at the sea, Mercedes did not want to think about her colleagues except for the one standing in the steamy shower with her. Who lusted for her because he loved her for who she was, and not for how he fantasized she would be. The one who was as enchanted by the sea as she.

"Okay, we'll go to Pete's lecture, but let's skip the rest of the conference," she said. "Just for today." Mercedes slid her hands across Roberto's hips and squeezed his soapy buttocks.

"Okay. What do you want to do?" Roberto grinned. "Stay here in the hotel room?"

"No!" She slapped his butt and nuzzled her nose against his. *"Regresamos a la playa porque se qué te encanta el mar."*

FLIGHT

Suki Bishop

I. ASCENT

Sophie is trying to find something wonderful. She wants to believe that she can go anywhere and make it her home. She imagines that freedom means movement. She thinks of the migratory patterns of birds and imagines herself embarking on a long, continuous flight. All she has to do is spread wings, take to air, let it carry her.

The college is filled with boys more than half her age. Sophie sits under a tree and watches their young bodies, a cerulean sea of muscle and bone. Shirtless, they show off their ribcages, pelvic muscles that barely hold up pants. They are grotesque, skeletal. A crass display of anatomy beneath skin, the elemental human form. Sophie runs her hand over her belly. How round. How smooth. She closes her eyes, imagines the tallest one, the one walking alone now down the path, kissing her belly—his angular chin, his lanky, hesitant body.

II. PERIAPSIS

She has begun to hate painting, but as a visiting artist, that is what she is here to do. It is always waiting for her, always ready. It requires something of her she does not want to give.

Sophie sits in a leather chair, legs draped over the side. She is surrounded by artists: The blond, who has let down her hair, talks to the man who is all mind, no body. The blond leans in, mouths the man's words with him. A beautiful woman sits at the edge of a chair across from Sophie. Sophie lifts her foot, places it against the woman's crotch, presses with her toes. The woman's eyes close; she smiles, then lifts her hands and says to a nearby man, "Look what she's doing to me." Sophie feels embarrassed, but keeps her toe where it is, presses harder. Voices rise like garbled tongues, louder and louder in Sophie's ear.

Is she dreaming? Is she drunk? Someone who is probably Sophie stumbles out of the room.

III. MERIDIAN

This place. Sophie doesn't understand its landscape. She doesn't understand its quiet. Too much quiet bursts the ears.

She must remember what she came here for. She must gather herself and set her life in motion. She has come here to find something, to forget. She thinks maybe the little pocket of sunlight on her bed will save her.

IV. ORBIT

The second time Sophie sees him, she is startled by his voice. It is too deep for such a wrangly boy.

"Excuse me," he calls out. She has not had her coffee yet, and she walks a fast, New York City pace. She hears his voice like one hears an alarm clock through foggy sleep, registers it only on the level of bird sounds, passing cars. When she finally turns around, she feels exposed. As if she was trying to run away and he has caught her.

"Hi." She tries to remember what it feels like to be in control. She has done this a thousand times. Sophie the seductress, the love artist.

But her hands betray her. They are fluttering monarchs, a rising dance of nervous energy. One hand grabs the other, fidgets.

"I saw you in the big field yesterday." He nods toward the tree.

"Yes, I was there." She will play it cool. She is ready to kiss him now, take his wiry jaw in her mouth and press into him. She wants to fuck his mouth with her tongue, make him female, make him small at her touch.

"My band is playing this weekend. Here—" She takes the piece of paper, information in chicken scrawl. His name. Max.

She gathers herself and touches his arm lightly. "Maybe I'll see you there."

She wants to look back at him as she walks away, but she won't; she knows to trust her touch.

She will not see his band. She has to wait. She could get him, she is sure, if she is blunt, but she might lose interest if he is too easy. So she will choreograph her own desire. She will make the seduction difficult by not getting his last name or number. She knows she will run into him again—it's a small campus—but she wants to see how he will do it. This silly game— this hunt and peck. She hopes he will surprise her, that he will not be entirely predictable.

V. COMPRESSION

When she gets home she discovers she is locked out. She slams the door with the butt of her hand. She sits on the porch steps, is forced to listen to wind through trees, a hornet dipping in and out, insects like percussion rising up in high trills around her. She could cry or scream. Instead, she calls campus security, is told twenty minutes. Suddenly, she cannot wait for anything. She wants that boy. She wants him to wrap his fingers around her throat, push her head back, make her open and vulnerable. She wants him to push her to lash out, thrash around. She wants him to stop her breath, feel her pulse through his hand on her neck until her lungs collapse, soft butterfly wings folding in on themselves.

VI. VELOCITY

Max stands at the edge of an outdoor party. Sophie can hear music—grungy, incomprehensible guitar—echo across the green as she leaves the library. She doesn't let on that she sees him. Instead, she takes off her sweater, feels the warm night air hit her skin. She takes out her cell phone, walks slowly, and pretends to text someone.

A group of girls, like starved hyenas, swallows him. They have no shame. They throw themselves at him like raw meat, carcasses ripe for the mouth to pulverize. She imagines taking a fistful of hair—the little redhead with the bob—and pushing her face-first into the stone facade. Sophie would sink her teeth into the plump flesh of an earlobe, tear at the perfumed skin. She would make the girl come without even fucking her. She would break her down, show her how to ache so deeply she crumbles.

As Sophie walks past, she sees Max bend as the redhead whispers in his ear. She sees him tilt his head back, take a swig of beer, look out over the sea of girl heads, find her. Sophie meets his eyes, walks on.

She turns the corner, walks the straight path toward the parking lot. Hears footsteps behind her. She will not turn around. She will listen for his footsteps to quicken. She will wait until she hears his breath upon her. Then, only then, will she turn toward him, run her hand down his chest, feel the cotton T-shirt against her palm.

VII. LIFT

He leads her by the hand into the old gym—down the dirty stairs, into the dark basement, past an old, ripped, pool table, past walls painted black for a makeshift sound studio, white graffiti etched into surfaces. Into the dark bathroom. Against the wall. Not very original—a bathroom—but she is impressed that he knows it is there. He kisses hard. She could teach him, pull back and offer lips only when he learns to take them slowly, sensually. But it is these first kisses she prefers, the awkward fumbling, the darting, sloppy tongue, the boy trying to be a man.

She wants the lights on. Wants to take in the doorless stall, the rusted metal, the broken tiled floor. Wants to see his face in the mirror as she leans over the sink, lifts her skirt for him. What will he do?

He will become serious, concentrate as if about to take an exam. She watches his eyes travel over her, like they could burn through her, feels his hands rest on the small of her back, run over her ass, pale and exposed in the harsh fluorescent spotlight.

He will kneel on the hard floor and pet her like she is some kind of caught animal. He will breathe her in, wet her with his tongue, find her with his finger. She will forget the mirror, bow her head to his clumsy, divine touch.

VIII. SUBSONIC

When she was twelve, Sophie's neighbor called her a slut. Sophie felt the word in her chest. She thought, *I have something to hide,* though she had never even been touched.

When she lay on the floor of a boy's basement room, years later, her legs spread, her skirt hitched up, she did not think of her neighbor. Instead, she felt the plush carpet beneath her, took in the stale smell of basement and boy sweat. She felt vindicated—of what, she didn't know.

IX. DESCENT

Max has a girlfriend. She discovers this at the campus center when she sees them together at the far end of the hall. His arm around her. Her puppy dog gaze. The quick peck on the lips goodbye. Sophie darts into the bookstore, buries herself in racks of college sweatpants and tees.

Max doesn't know that she knows. Sophie wonders if he and the girl talk about her. Maybe the girl tries to make herself older, believing that this is what he wants. Maybe she fashions herself into what she thinks an older woman would be. What was it Sophie imagined becoming when she was young? She would never have seen herself becoming the kind of woman who desired boys. When she was a girl, boys her age seemed awkward and annoying.

Maybe the girl feels superior to Sophie. Maybe Max tells her intimate details about Sophie—how her breasts hang slightly when he unhitches her bra, how sometimes she cannot come when he goes down on her, how she likes it when he's rough. Maybe the girl asks him if she is better than Sophie, and maybe he says "Yes." Sophie hates to think of herself as the kind of woman who can't handle a complex situation. The girl draws Sophie closer to him, makes her want him even more. Not just because someone else desires him, but because he has a secret, or at least thinks he does. Because he is capable of leading a double life.

Still, he is such a sweet boy. Maybe that's it—he has secrets and yet has not been eaten away by them.

X. FUSELAGE

Max likes to meet Sophie between classes.

Tuesday—The library. He feels her up in the philosophy stacks. Like she is a schoolgirl. Like she is all breasts and hard nipples. Her nostrils flare from dust and the smell of musty books. Someone flips pages. A cough echoes. The elevator door opens. Sound of footsteps. *Hush.*

Friday—The empty classroom. *Shut the door. Turn off the lights.* He hurries, fumbles with his belt buckle, can't undo it. *Fuck.* She laughs. *Shhh.* He wants her quiet. She moans loudly, then laughs. She likes that he is nervous. She takes the buckle, unzips. Wraps legs around his back. Pulls him into her again and again with her heels digging into him. She is bestial: a rodent clawing its way out of a hole. Teeth gnashing. Strong jaws breaking through skin. Muscle torn from bone. His slender skeletal form hits hard against her. Hip bones jab. Ribs bruise soft flesh as they slam against her. So fast now the table will break, the plaster walls will surely cave, the building itself will collapse, a tornado of dirt and rubble around them.

Monday—On the way to the apple orchard. As soon as they are off campus, they walk down the middle of the empty road. Clasped hands swing back and forth. A car turns the corner. They walk straight at it. *Chicken.* Who will release the grip and run? Who will pull the other out of harm's way? The driver lays on the horn, weaves to the side, a near miss.

XI. FORCE

Maybe it is anger or jealousy that makes Sophie do it. Maybe that irrevocable line that was crossed—though she doesn't want to admit it—when he took another lover. Or more accurately, when she found out he had taken another lover, for who knows when it all started or how many lovers he might have.

She hadn't exactly sought him out, this new one. He was there, really, as if in answer to a call she didn't know she'd made. He stood in front of a dorm one night as she and some of the other artists stumbled home drunk.

She remembers this: the flicker of a lit cigarette, its firefly play, its now-you-see-it-now-you-don't dance, a hand carving space in air. Perhaps she watched the flicker too much, let it mesmerize her.

She remembers this: an after-rain kind of wind, its sudden rush through trees, the way it spilled rain from their branches, the muggy aftermath.

She remembers this: not the color of his eyes, not their shape—oval or round—not his lips or nose or chin, not his face, but the glint.

She remembers this: an invitation, her voice, her address, a time—tomorrow, midnight—a nod, hand touching a hand.

The body finds its way home, through darkness, through drunkenness. A centripetal pull toward a center. What does it mean that her center is this: dark road; flash of car lights; dull rising ache from between legs to lungs to heart; a door; a handle that turns only with a hard thrust; an interior lit by a warm yellow lamp; a staircase leading to a room; a soft bed; dreams spun by storm wind; shaking, bending, rattling trees.

XII. ALTITUDE

She should have stayed in bed today. But no, some ticker inside goes off and she gets up, still drunk, and goes to her meeting, tries to act normal. She's not. On the walk there, she almost trips on the pitter patter of her shoes. How funny they sound. Then, *Oh, look—Butterfly! Trees! How pretty.* She's babbling away to herself. *Shut up, Sophie. This is a very serious day. Be quiet. Shut your mouth.*

XIII. THRUST

Sophie cannot decide whether she wants him to come—this new boy with the flickering flame. Did she imagine the encounter? The invitation?

She doesn't call Max today. Maybe she's afraid she will weaken once she hears his voice. Instead she waits. She goes through the motions of the day: the laying out of paints, large careless gestures on canvas. Through it all, she waits to see if she will know what to do.

She drinks wine before bed. She means to only have one glass. But she has two, then three. Maybe it is the wine that makes her lie naked on the bed, over the covers, with the window open, the shade up, a candle burning on the dresser. She feels the breeze on her skin, hears the uneasy lullaby of cicadas. She falls asleep afraid and aroused.

XIV. ACCELERATION

When the boy comes in through the window, he pushes her down on the bed, hand against her throat, thrashes fingers against her face, smearing her own saliva. He flips her over, rams three fingers, then four. She cries, spreads wider, lets him knock through the barricade.

This boy is angry. She can feel something in him bigger than she can hold. But she can't stop herself from provoking it. He is an army of thieves and horses, mouths foaming. In his eyes she sees a sea of emptiness. He is a stranger, an enemy, a ravaging wind sweeping across a landscape, ripping leaves off trees, pillaging.

Why did she leave her window open? Fall asleep to fear, to dreams of empty houses—shutters falling, paint peeling, doors opening into rooms filled with broken windows, curtains blowing, wind that whips right through her? Maybe she wanted to punish Max: *See what you made me do? You made me open myself, and you did not come to me, you did not come to me as I wanted you.*

XV. ZENITH

Max wraps his arms around her waist, nuzzles his nose into her neck. *But that other girl.* Doesn't Sophie want Max to be happy? She knows it is absurd to think of her and Max as a couple. She is sometimes embarrassed by things he says—"What does 'repressed' mean?" he once asked her. And yet she loves him. If only she did not know the things she knows—things that create an abyss between them. They seem to love each other through glass walls, through water; theirs is a muffled, muted love.

XVI. COMBUSTION

She takes Max to a party. What good are secrets when your body gives them all away? She is bursting at the seams. She will pretend, for the night, that he is hers and hers alone. She grips his hand when they enter. Introduces him as her lover. He seems to like it. He stays by her side.

Someone suggests tequila shots every twenty minutes. They look at their watches to set the time. Sophie doesn't have a watch. She looks at her wrist, wonders why twenty minutes keeps coming up so quickly. They don't have salt, but they butcher a lemon with a butter knife to get rough slabs. "We have to lick our hands anyway, in honor of the salt," one of them says. They lick their hand beneath thumb and forefinger, imagine the salty taste, then down the shot.

She hears the party's bubbling chatter-hum. She entertains her colleagues, says something with wild hands. She catches one staring at her through the conversation ebb.

They file into a back room. Too many people for such a small space. "This is for you, Sophie!" There is a line of coke. She is unsure how to take it. Max shows her how, does the first line, the bigger of the two. She takes the rolled dollar, snorts, nothing comes up. "Just snort it up, do it harder." She does, and this time the little white line disappears.

She gets angry when she sees Max talking to one of her colleagues. He is *her* find, *her* bad behavior. "Let's pass him around," someone jokes; he should be their little student pet. Sophie is seething. Her hands shake. She digs her nails into her palms.

It doesn't matter that Max isn't part of this talk, that he is just talking; she hates him right now. She stumbles out the hallway, up the staircase, finds an open door. A colleague lies in bed. Sophie stumbles through the dark, cuddles up to him, her body merely rehearsing memorized lines: *This is the way*

I fit against a chest; this is where my head goes; this is the way my body bends into another's. The small comfort of habit. The body's memory after the mind has taken flight from too many tequila shots and a tiny white line.

Suddenly there are footsteps, a bang on the door. Max has found her. Sophie runs behind the door as it opens. "You're an asshole," he says. By now he's as drunk as she is, and as angry. He leaves the room, and Sophie runs after him. They fight in the hallway. Sophie lunges for his throat. They fight the scattered catfight of drunkards. Sophie runs; she doesn't know where she's going. Outside. Down a dark path, past a streetlamp, the shadow of trees. Then suddenly she's back in the room, wrestling with Max, who won't let her leave again. She has lost track of herself. They have lost track of each other. They stumble to find the other in their drunken haze. Eventually, they find sleep instead, in somebody's empty bed.

Sophie wakes up alone to a headache, a dry mouth, fragmented images. Last night feels like a movie someone told her she watched but she can't remember seeing. She knows there was no happy ending.

XVII. GRAVITY

Sophie sees him on the other side of the green. Walking away from her. Will she call out to him? Ah, but the girl is there, holding out her hand. Sophie feels alone, like a child. Except she is not a child. This girl has her whole life ahead of her.

Her cheeks are pink, her breasts perky. She can talk to Max about classes. She can sit casually on his dorm bed among their common friends, pass a cigarette between them. What can Sophie give?

XVIII. RADIUS

Sophie opens her bedroom window, lights the candle, strips down. She sets herself upon the covers, ready for the stampede. There is no breeze, as if the night has sucked air from the sky.

She closes her eyes, falls into an uneasy sleep. Dreams of worms burrowing into soil; they rip apart, regenerate, become hundreds of slick bodies beneath her feet.

She wakes to sunlight, a cacophony of birds outside her window, the candle's small flame struggling in a sea of liquid wax. And here: this same body, with the scar along its knee, the thick, fleshy thighs, the gaping black hole at its center.

XIX. SPEED OF SOUND

She's in the back seat, head against the window. Some colleagues have offered to take her to the city. They drive for hours, it seems, take numerous wrong turns. They pass silos and monasteries and fields so green she almost can't believe it. Why do the fields now seem oceanic, why now do they resonate inside her? She feels a sudden desperation. If she could, she would stick her arm out the window—this window that only rolls halfway down—and dig her fingers into the earth, claw it as she drives by, bury it under her nails, take some deep, sedimented part of this place with her.

But the car is speeding, passing other cars in the lane. Sophie is already on the move, despite her involuntary attachments. She must leave this all behind; it does not belong to her.

LILY

Tsaurah Litzky

I would never have made it through my first week at Kenny's Bar without Lily Santiago, the waitress Kenny assigned to show me the ropes. Lily was six feet tall, with boobs big as gallon jugs and legs so long they seemed to reach her neck. She could beat all the busboys at arm wrestling. They loved her.

It was December 1969, and on my first day on the job, I spilled a chef salad on a famous actor who was playing a six-foot-tall dildo in a hit Off Broadway play. Lily helped me pick the salad off him, all the while leaning over his arm, pressing her mammoth tatas into his chest to make him feel better.

Then she pulled me back to the waitress station. "If you've done this before, I'm Jackie Kennedy," she said accusingly.

"You're not Jackie Kennedy," I told her. "I lied about having experience." I told Kenny that I waited tables at the Bluebird Café in Santa Fe, but all the waiting I did there was outside the entrance, panhandling for spare change.

For a minute, Lily looked stern, but then she laughed. "You're a hustler, a little hustler," she said approvingly. "Don't worry. I'll help. I'll take you under my wing."

She taught me to fold the napkins just so, to brush the crumbs from the table between the main course and dessert with a menu. She told me to make the hem of my black waitress skirt six inches shorter. "Bend over a lot," she advised. "It's good for tips." One night I watched, amazed, as she balanced six big trays, three on each arm. Later, I asked her how she did it. Was there a special trick?

She looked around. The bar was packed, but the dinner crowd had cleared out. "Let's take a break," she said. She led me into the ladies' room. All four stalls were empty. She chose the one furthest from the entry, shoved me in, pushed in behind me, and locked the door. Lily put a hand inside her blouse, into her bra, and pulled out a pink handkerchief with an elaborately crocheted border. She opened the handkerchief and took out a little glass vial filled with white powder. The vial had a tiny spoon attached by a delicate chain to the cap.

"What's that?" I asked.

"Baby, you got a lot to learn," she said. "This is my vitamins, my magic snow, the white gold of the Andes, cocaine." I had sampled enough LSD to send me to the moon, but I had never tried this fabled drug. Lily loaded the tiny spoon and shoved it into her nostril, sniffing deeply. A happy smile spread over her face.

"I'm Wonder Woman now," she boasted. She loaded the spoon again, held it under my nose. "Come on, " she said. "It's your turn, breathe deep." I took a big sniff. My nasal passages grew deliciously icy and cold. The air around us brightened until Lily and I were bathed in crackling light. She hovered above me, her eyes sparkling like black diamonds.

"You like?" asked Lily. All I could do was nod; her voice was ringing like chimes in my head. "Have more," said Lily, then we both had another spoon. Lily wrapped the vial up in the handkerchief and put it back into her bra.

"That's a nice handkerchief," I told her.

"Thanks," she said. "My mother made it. Here's something else you'll like." Suddenly Lily bent her head down and kissed me hard, pushing her tongue into my mouth. Her breath smelled like Dentyne. I had never been kissed by a woman before. Her big, soft lips over mine felt so nice. I sucked on her tongue like it was a lollipop, the juice rising between my legs. I felt her hand creep under the waistband of my skirt, under the elastic of my panties. I pulled back.

"Don't be afraid," she coaxed. "Haven't I been a good teacher?" She slid her fingers down my back to my ass crack and entered, caressing me with one thick finger. My tits swelled, my juices heated to a rolling boil. Lily must have felt my resistance drain away, because quick as a lightning bolt, she lifted me so my feet were on the seat. My back was against the back of the stall, and I was half-crouching, half-standing.

She kept that hand in my ass while she used her other hand to pull my panties down to my ankles. Flakes of snow started to fall all around us, warm gentle snow. Lily pushed her fingers into my cunt and started to fuck me there. A giant bubble of pleasure rose up in me. It was about to burst, but Lily stopped. She pulled her hand out of my snatch, leaving me open and hungry.

"Sweet little cooch," Lily whispered. She took my hand in hers and guided it under her skirt, into her twat. Hot lava whirled around my fingers, but I wasn't scorched. I found her clit, thick and hard as a bullet, and started pulling it the same way she was pulling mine. We came at exactly the same instant, sighing, moaning, and melting into each other.

There was no soap in the bathroom, so Lily washed her honey off my fingers with her tongue. I cleaned her fingers the same way, and then we went back to work. We went to the ladies' room to share her vitamins often after that. I enjoyed our pick-me-ups, but I told Lily I also wanted some cock between my legs. She understood, because she liked men too. Ivan, the master chef, was her boyfriend. He gave her porterhouse steaks that she smuggled out of Kenny's in her pocketbook.

"Hook up with one of the other chefs," she suggested. "You'll get plenty to eat and plenty of takeout." I told her none of the other chefs appealed to me.

ONE DAY GRACIE, another waitress, asked me to work her Saturday night shift. She was going to a music festival upstate in a place called Woodstock. Lily had the day off and was going too. I didn't care about the music festival. I was thrilled to be getting a chance to work the most lucrative shift of the week.

When I showed up at four on Saturday to do the setup, there was a bartender behind the bar I hadn't seen before. He was dark, tall, and wiry, with flashing eyes, a nose like a hawk. He was washing glasses, and his strong hands moved so gracefully, shadowboxing through the air. I was fascinated. I wanted him, those hands on me, those long fingers.

The night manager, Irving, took me over for introductions.

"This is Aldo," he said. "You two will be alone until seven, then Margot is coming in." Aldo looked me up and down. He didn't waste any time. He was very direct.

"You look good," he said, "like a cherry." I was surprised. I was expecting the usual "Nice to meet you."

Standing in front of him, shifting my weight from leg to leg, I wondered what Lily would have said. Finally I came out with, "Is that supposed to be a compliment?"

"Take it any way you want," he answered, and then he turned back to the glasses.

It was very busy. I was glad when Margot showed up. A few times, as I was dashing around, I thought I caught Aldo looking at me. Maybe it was only wishful thinking, but maybe not. At the end of my shift, when I was cashing in my tips, he asked me to have dinner with him.

On Monday, Lily showed up all excited about Woodstock. "You should have been there," she said. But then I wouldn't have met Aldo. I asked her about him, told her I had a date with him Wednesday, my night off.

"Yeah, him, he just works Saturday nights," she said. "He makes that much in tips. Be careful," she warned. "I hear gossip, lots of gossip. I hear he's a heartbreaker, a killer in bed with a twelve-inch pinga." I promised myself I would be cool and tough on my date with Aldo. I would be a killer too.

Aldo took me to Forlini's on Houston Street. We drank daiquiris. I told him about my poetry; he told me about his time in the Merchant Marines. We ate quickly, glancing at each other. We both knew our idle chatter was the prelude to our time between the sheets. After dinner we walked east on Houston Street to his building, on Fifth Street off Avenue D.

The halls and the stairs all the way up to his apartment on the top floor smelled of pot and piss and rice and beans. I thought his place would be dark—a cave, a bandit's lair—but his living room was light and airy, with white walls, natural burlap curtains open on the big windows, a scruffy yellow sofa, a pine coffee table.

"Sit down," he said, pushing me toward the sofa. I sat. "Take off your shoes," he commanded, "Get comfortable." He vanished through a door at the end of the room. I kicked off my sandals, but I wasn't comfortable. I was nervous; the lobster fra diavolo Aldo had just bought me jumped around in my belly like it was alive.

Aldo came back carrying a tray with a couple of glasses and a bottle that held a green liquor. He put the tray on the coffee table, sat down next to me, and filled our glasses. I was conscious of the heat of his long legs so close to mine. His elegant black trousers were just tight enough to show the outline of the bulging package at his crotch.

"Go ahead, drink," he said. "Don't expect me to toast. I'm not that kind of guy."

I reached for the glass. "What kind of guy are you?" I asked, hoping my nervousness wouldn't bleed through into my voice.

"The kind of guy you need," he shot right back as I was taking my first sip.

The bittersweet stuff scorched my throat all the way down to my bush. I sputtered, gasping for air. "Green chartreuse," Aldo said before he drank his down in a single swallow. "One-twenty proof."

He got up and went to a desk that stood in a corner. He took something out of the top drawer. Then he sat beside me again, showed me what it was: a little blue velvet box that might hold a ring. For a crazy, dizzying moment I thought he was going to propose. Then he opened the box. On a bed of white satin, two shiny red pills shaped like lozenges glistened next to each other.

"Want to take a moonwalk with me, cherry?" Aldo asked. "Like the astronauts did last month, but we won't need a spaceship."

"I don't know," I answered, trying to play it cool. "Do you have an astronaut's license? Let me see it."

He grabbed my hand and put it right on top of the bulge in his pants. "It's right here," he said. His groin seemed to swell, pulsing beneath my palm. I could feel the love patch between my legs moisten. Despite myself, my fingers began to stroke him. I wanted him so much, too much.

Again I tried for that elusive cool. "What are the pills? I like to know what I'm putting in my body," I said, aware I sounded like the prig of the century.

"Horse tranquilizers," he snorted sarcastically. "Do you think I'd offer you anything but the best? This is the world's best LSD, with some other very special ingredients. Trust me or not," he spat out. "Yes or no? Make up your mind!" I knew I wanted him, but I was frightened of the effect he had on me. I couldn't stop looking at him, especially his mouth. Lily had warned me, but I didn't care. Hadn't I learned from my trips to the ladies' room with her? Nothing ventured, nothing gained.

"Yes," I told him. "Yes." He stopped frowning. "That's my girl," he said. We swallowed the pills down with more green chartreuse. "It won't hit right away," he told me.

"You like working at Kenny's?" he asked. I told him I liked the job fine, and we started to talk about our eccentric customers.

I was telling him about the Elvis impersonator who gave me my first hundred-dollar tip when the room began to wobble and shake around us. Aldo's face elongated in front of my eyes like I was seeing him in a funhouse mirror. I looked down at my hands; the same thing was happening to them. The plants by the window suddenly grew into giant leafy trees; the couch I was sitting on reached up and engulfed me. I was alone in a little boat floating on a blue river that sparkled like sapphires. Flowers, orchids, and giant roses grew in the trees on either side of the river. Aldo called my name, and then there he was, standing on a rock in front of me.

He wasn't wearing any clothes. Between his legs was coiled a glistening purple snake with one shining emerald eye. The snake winked, then stuck out a tongue that was forked with flames. The water everywhere around me caught fire, singeing my long hair, but Aldo saved me. He reached out to me, grabbing me up in his arms. The next thing I knew, I was in Aldo's arms, and he was carrying me away. My head was against his chest. I could hear his heart beating, *tum, tum, tum.*

He carried me into a small room that was dominated by a big bed covered with a silky sheet. An antique bureau stood against one wall. He put me down in the center of the bed, and I noticed my clothes were gone. The snake had vanished too. Now Aldo had something else growing between his legs, an enormous purple cock. The underside was bisected with a pulsing red vein; the engorged head was bigger than a baseball. I had never seen one so big. I had to have it. I spread my legs wide, inviting it inside.

A heady smell spread out into the room. It was my cunt stink, rank and fishy like a muddy pond. I was ashamed of how bad I smelled.

Aldo sniffed the air. "I like your perfume," he said.

Then he reached down and started pulling roughly on my tits, my nipples; pinching, hurting, pulling my desire higher up in me, sending it out into every corner of my body until I was only a pulsing vacuum wanting him, making me forget about my smell entirely. I heard a voice that was too soft to be mine beg, *please, please, please.* His massive cock head was big enough to tear me in two, but somehow I was not afraid. I was so wet I was flooding, and the monster glided in easily. I rushed to meet it, bucking, pushing myself at him, trying to grab it, catch it, and suck it down into my hungry hole.

"Don't thrust yourself at me," Aldo snarled. "Give it to me, give it to me!" He pulled out; his face above me was like a thundercloud. Destroyed, I sank back on the bed. No way I'd ever be cool. I'd always be a nerdy, needy girl.

"Relax," he said. "Take it easy." Then he put his hand over my snatch, stroking me there, bringing me back. He bent his head, put his lips to my breast, and started to suck sweetly on my nipple, nursing like a baby. Bit by bit, he drained the tension and fear out of me until I was like a sieve, a sieve of skin wanting him. Then he mounted me again, my skittishness all gone.

I surrendered, I moved, following him, opening to him, until his cock melted right into me and became a wave carrying me down the river.

He made me come so many times I lost count. Just before he shot, he pulled out and came right on top of me, leaving a white ribbon across my chest like a flag. The walls were shimmying, dancing around us. He wrapped his arms around me, and we slept.

When I woke up, bright sunlight was coming in the window. I was on my back. Aldo was snoring, his body curled and facing me, his legs stretching down to form a question mark. I was sticky all over, and my bladder was full. I wanted to empty it, rinse in a shower, and come back to bed and lie beside him.

I noticed a door beside the dresser, maybe the door to the bathroom. I lurched to my feet and stumbled across the floor. There was a pile of loose change on top of the dresser, a large pocketknife with a devil's head carved into the bone handle, and a swatch of pink that was somehow familiar. I looked closer. It was a pink handkerchief with crocheted edges—just like the one that belonged to Lily Santiago.

OPERA GLOVES

Maddy Stuart

*I*t wasn't for sex that I'd saved my pennies for so long, not even for a look at beautiful European bodies. The vacation I'd envisioned consisted of leisurely days over a melange and evenings at the Vienna State Opera, all spent in solitary. It was going to be all about me and my music, completely free from the stresses and awkwardness and posturing that interaction with other people brings.

So it was with some amount of distress that I found myself, on the fourth night of my trip and during a highly anticipated performance of *Der Rosenkavalier,* unable to take my eyes off the woman with the gloves.

She sat by herself in one of the boxes, head tilted slightly, completely absorbed in the performance. The dimness of the hall put her in soft focus, with the light from the stage giving her skin a muted glow. Her black evening gown would have been enough to make me salivate on its own, but what really made me stare were her long dark gloves, slinking over her elbows, making her exposed shoulders seem risqué. I couldn't remember a time when I'd seen someone actually wearing opera gloves to the opera, and I was fascinated with the way they made her arms look like two charmed snakes.

How was it that she had the box to herself that evening? I don't know even now, and I doubt she'd have told me. I thought then that she must have been rich or very well connected to have that plush, sumptuous space all to herself in a theater stuffed to bursting with people. But even if she was simply rich or well connected, why was it that she was attending the opera by herself? Perhaps her motives were like mine—perhaps she simply wanted to see the opera, to hear music she loved, to be entertained without having to do any entertaining. Imagining that she had something so close to my heart in common with me made me desire her all the more.

The first intermission arrived, and I had scarcely heard a note of the performance. As the lights went up, I saw the woman with the gloves rise from her seat and vanish into the darkness of the box's cloakroom. With a beating heart I counted how many boxes lay between her and the stage—five—and bolted from my standing-room spot, not even bothering to leave something there to mark my place.

I found the box nearest stage left and counted—one, two, three, four, five. My plan was to see her up close when she returned, to examine those gloves and those shoulders. I found an inconspicuous spot, leaned against the wall, and began to daydream while scrutinizing the milling crowd of people. Would she be disappointing up close, her eyes lacking the clever glint I dreamed of finding there? Were her arms as long, her shoulders as bright as I'd imagined them?

And then, all of a sudden, there she was, and my unprepared stomach turned to iron. She was returning to her box, absently slipping a silver cigarette case into her evening bag and turning her head this way and that. When I regained my bearings, I gorged upon the details that the darkness of her box had blotted out during the opera. She was wearing plum-colored lipstick and sparkling earrings, and the shoulders that had commanded my gaze so insistently curved into collarbones that gently accented her neck.

Then I saw her gloves in more detail. These weren't the black satin evening gloves I'd seen for sale in so many department stores. They clung to every bend and indent in her arms, with a surface impossibly smooth and almost gaudy in its glassiness. I suddenly recalled the window of a shop I'd seen back home, where a mannequin with pacifier nipples posed with a thrust-out hip and a riding crop. The mannequin had been wearing black gloves just like hers, with a matching bustier. "Sale on PVC," said a sign above her head.

Surely this woman didn't get them from a place like that.

Suddenly she turned and looked directly into my saucer eyes, so deliberately that I thought she must have noticed me staring. My mouth opened, sputtering for an explanation, unable to find either German or English words to excuse me. She paused for long enough to aggravate my discomfort and said, simply, "You are English?"

I could only nod while my mind frantically made an inventory of my appearance, wondering what had given me away. Terrified, I averted my gaze while she insistently maintained hers.

"Where are you sitting?" she asked, her voice lilting with the soft accent of singer's German. She didn't bother asking my name.

"Stehplätze," I croaked, surprised I had remembered the German word for "standing room" on a trip when all the German I'd learned in music school had rudely deserted me.

She looked at me a few moments longer, as though considering something. Her eyes ran up and down the dress I'd brought for concerts. It was rumpled from being stuffed in a suitcase too many times, and in that instant I thought she'd finished with me.

"You must be a music lover," she said, and smiled. "Come with me, you will be able to see much better from my box." She turned her back, and I watched the movement of her shoulder blades as she opened the door to her private room. It wasn't until she turned slyly back to me, lifted her arm—the glove made it seem miles long—and beckoned with a reptilian gesture that I understood she wanted me to join her.

She held the door open for me. My breathing staggered as I walked past her into the dark cloakroom and listened for the sound of the door clicking shut. With the sound of that click, the entire opera house seemed to fall silent. From the box I could see the other patrons ambling in and out of the hall, peering into the orchestra pit, and holding conversations, but all their voices were mute to my ears. The only voice I could listen to belonged to the woman with the liquid black gloves.

She gestured to one of the empty seats, pushed it to the front of the box, and angled it toward the stage. I took the seat she had prepared for me and found that she was right—the view of the stage was much better than it had been in standing room.

Just then the lights in the hall dimmed, and she took a seat beside me. She rested her gloved hand on the inside of my elbow, giving me goosebumps. Leaning in close, she whispered in my ear: "Listen closely to the performance. You will never hear anything like this again."

Her advice came as something of a disappointment, for I'd hoped that she'd brought me there for something other than a concert. And, I thought, it was quite a strong statement to make. A Viennese woman might be expected to feel strongly about Viennese music, but . . . "never hear anything like this again?"

Perhaps it was snobbery; perhaps she imagined the orchestra wasn't any good where I came from. Or perhaps she was simply given to hyperbole. It would be fitting for someone who would wear such dramatic gloves to the opera to make equally dramatic statements. *And where had she bought those gloves? Surely not at a department store.*

When the music started, her hand was still resting on my elbow, and she began to lazily stroke the inside of the bend of my arm with a single finger. I shuddered. Soon she settled into a rhythm and, though she was distracting me from the opera just as much in her box as she did in standing room, I became aware that she was stroking me in time to the music.

Her coated finger felt like a toy, something I'd want to put in my mouth and lick up and down. I was sitting perfectly still, my hands still resting in my lap, but the insides of my thighs were shivering, and I was overcome with the desire to turn, touch her as she was touching me, make her burn as I was burning. But the instant I shifted and turned my head, she made a hiss of displeasure.

"Listen to the music," she told me.

So, disappointed, I returned to listening. What performance of *Der Rosenkavalier* could possibly be more interesting than being petted in a box seat with long, glassy gloves? I didn't even particularly care for *Der Rosenkavalier*, not that part of it at least. The music just churns along, bumps along, and . . .

I caught my breath. Suddenly, out of all that churning and bumping arose a melody so beautiful that I was completely taken by surprise. Had it always been there, waiting for me to hear it? Somehow, in the recordings I'd listened to before, it had completely eluded me. In a moment I grasped that she was hearing it too, for her hand was moving up and down my arm as though she were conducting the orchestra herself. The melody rose, and so did the hand; it paused, and so did she. I was caught up in the intensity of her listening and found my ears hungering for the next note and the corresponding touch it would bring.

The melody ended, but the opera continued, and it became clear that she knew every note of *Der Rosenkavalier*, every breath and every bar. If an interesting moment or beautiful harmony offered itself, her fingers pointed it out to me, and every resounding chord came with a tantalizing squeeze.

The love duet approached, and I anticipated its arrival with increasing desperation. Not only was I drinking in the length and breadth of the music, but I was also reveling in the more carnal feelings my conductor had unearthed. In my own sex life, I had never wanted to play music during sex. Each one distracts from the other, I had thought, and I usually found the combination irritating. But this time, it seemed like my entire body was simmering along with the horns and the strings.

The stage, too, suddenly seemed transformed into a pleasure garden. I found my eyes lingering on the singers, their breasts displayed in low-cut gowns and swelling up with breath. One had slender, feminine legs displayed in masculine breeches; the other, a throat lit up with jewelry. And when they sang, their jaws hung loose, as though they were at the brink of orgasm.

The stage lovers moved closer, and the hand that had danced around my arm suddenly slid downward. The feel of her glove was electric, and I was ready to cry out in excitement. It felt smooth and cool, with not a hair nor jagged nail to interrupt the silkiness. First it caressed the top of my thigh, then my knee, and then finally she pulled it inward, gently nudging my skirt back and brushing the sensitive bare skin between my legs.

I wanted to take hold of her wrist and plant those black-coated fingers where I wanted them, but I knew that to do so would be the equivalent of shouting requests at the orchestra. So I let her stroke and explore while listening intently to the swelling music, hoping that when it reached the point of bursting, she would bring me to that point as well.

She pulled inward and inward again as the music rose, until at last she reached the fabric of my underwear. I spread my legs to accommodate her, and her fingers soon pushed aside the fabric and slipped behind it. The soprano onstage drew her breath, making her breasts appear to expand like balloons, and I felt the touch of a slippery finger against my clit, seeming to hum along with the strings, moving in circles as the music spiraled to a climax.

And then a beautiful high note floated from the soprano's mouth across the air, and her voice felt like it was coming from between my legs, the waves of pleasure running through me, attuned to her vibrato, as fingers entered and stroked my insides. My orgasm—does my memory make it seem more synchronous than it was?—lasted precisely as long as she held the note.

It took me some time to come to my senses, filled to brimming as I was with her smooth toy fingers and the sumptuous music. She did not move her hand, leaving one finger inside me and her palm against my mound.

The opera continued, although I felt as though the stage sets might melt before my eyes, as my body seemed to be doing. My companion continued to illustrate the music to me as before, but more gently, applying subtle pressure and small caresses. In my postorgasmic haze, every note seemed coated with the same glowing smoothness of her wrists and fingers.

I never saw her again. She didn't even stay for the third act, excusing herself for a cigarette at intermission and never returning to the box. But even after she left, the music still glowed. It was a quality in the music I spent months afterward trying to recapture with recordings and performances and a wide array of sex toys before realizing that she was right: I would never hear anything like that again. But after that, I never hesitated to bring my lovers to the opera, and I never again found it irritating to turn the music on when I took them to bed.

PARTY FAVOR

Andrea Dale

So I've told you about him before, my boyfriend (boyfriend? play partner? master? just *him*), the big time rock star, the one I signed a contract for, swearing I won't tell who he is, but I can walk away from him and his kinky fetishes anytime I want.

I just haven't wanted to yet. Not hardly.

He's spanked me backstage, kept me bound with a teasing vibrator between my legs on the tour bus, shared me with his even more inventive wife. But until now, he's only threatened to share me with the rest of the band.

It's him I crave, but I'm willing to be shared if he's the end result. Still, the idea of the whole group is . . . daunting. Little did I know just how much he'd planned.

First, there was the outfit. We had to try it out ahead of time, you see, to make sure it worked properly. He and his wife had a delightful time with the remote controls, seeing how far they could push me before I came, and then how many times they could make me come, watching me the entire time.

The party was a small one, just the band members and the manager and the publicist and various wives and girlfriends. Drinks, hors d'oeuvres. A caterer had prepared everything, but I was to keep the drinks refreshed and the canapés circulated.

Sounds simple, right? Not with what I was wearing . . . and what the party game was tonight.

He and his wife brought me into the living room after everyone had arrived. The murmurs of appreciation at my outfit (and how I looked in it) were nothing compared to the approval in his eyes.

Red leather, all carefully constructed just for me. Tight, low-cut top that zipped up the front, with a bit of stiffening at the tips of the breasts, reminiscent of Madonna's famed bra. Short flared skirt. White lace collar around my throat, and a scrap of apron around my waist.

"She'll be serving tonight," he said. People smiled, laughed. "Well, I was talking about drinks and food, but you're right about that too," he went on. And he went on to explain the game.

He held up the evil little controller.

"Her outfit is fitted with a number of vibrators," he

explained. "Very quiet ones. Listen." He twisted the controls, one at a time, and I quaked, but I knew the rules of the game already and did everything in my power to stand still, despite the delicious torment.

He turned them off. I knew it was going to be a long night.

"One set of vibrators are clamped to her nipples," he said. "There's one on her clit, and one vibrating dildo each in her pussy and her ass." He had me bend over, hands clasped to my ankles and legs spread, so he could flip up my skirt and show them the harnesses.

One of the wives oohed, and everyone laughed.

"Here's how it works. Throughout the evening, I'll turn on one of the vibrators. The first person who figures out that one is buzzing, and announces it, gets to guess *which* one is on. If they guess correctly, they win a prize."

"What's the prize?" the drummer asked.

He smiled. "Why, she is, of course. You can do something to her, or have her do something to you. The only rule is that you can't make her come. She can only come when I say so."

And so the party started. Even without the vibrators going, I was constantly aroused by the clamps on my tender nipples and the dildos stuffed inside me, sliding against me whenever I moved. I did my best to walk normally, smile pleasantly. I wasn't unknown—I was a familiar presence backstage—and everyone was friendly.

That is, until he set the vibrator on my clit abuzzing.

I'd thought I was prepared, but he'd waited long enough that I'd let my guard down. I had three drinks on a tray, and the glasses jingled together.

"Now!" shouted the bassist, who tended to be exuberant under any circumstances.

"Good job," he said. "Now, which one?"

The bassist pursed his lips, staring at me. I stood as still as I could, giving away, I hoped, nothing.

He guessed right anyway, and chose to spank me.

I was positioned over the arm of the sofa, my skirt flipped up. The various straps that kept everything in place criss-crossed around my thighs and waist, leaving my ass exposed.

He used his hand and was granted ten strokes.

Musicians, be they guitarists or keyboardists or drummers, have strong hands. These weren't light birthday slaps on my flesh, oh no—they were hard, and they fell true.

I hadn't known how well I responded to spanking until I met him. It had been just playing before that, but with him, I'd learned how the pain could mutate into pleasure. It didn't help that he didn't turn off the vibrator while the bassist was heating my ass. By the tenth slap, I was squirming and already on the edge, the dildos slipping inside me as I got wetter.

The buzzing on my clit stopped abruptly, just in time.

I rose shakily, and his murmured "Well done" gave my weak thighs strength.

The bassist tried again fifteen minutes later—damn his

alert ears!—when my nipple clamps went off, but he guessed wrong. I didn't know whether to be relieved or disappointed.

A short while later, the dildo in my ass sent tremors up my spine.

"A vibrator's going off," someone said immediately. "The one between those rosy cheeks of hers."

It was the woman who'd oohed and ahhed at my harness. I'd had a suspicion she was anal, and not in the retentive way. I, on the other hand, had something of a love/hate relationship about anal play. I mentally recoiled from it, but I couldn't deny how my body responded, no matter how much I wanted to.

He clapped. "And your prize."

She smiled coyly and stood on tiptoes to whisper in his ear. He cocked a sardonic brow (you've seen that expression in his videos, you know) and turned to speak quietly to his wife. She laughed and nodded, and the other woman took me by the wrist and led me off to one of the bedrooms.

She shimmied out of her jeans and turquoise La Perla thong and stretched across the bed. My role was obvious. I knelt at the edge of the bed, parted her thighs, and breathed in her spicy scent before setting to work with my lips and tongue.

I'd grown to love doing this, although at the same time, it frustrated me beyond belief, because I was usually doing it while being denied my own pleasure. Usually my release was dependent on how well I performed on his wife.

I had no doubt that my skills tonight would determine my reward or punishment.

The entire time I worked on her, coaxing her closer and closer to orgasm, the vibrator purred in my ass, reminding me who really called the shots.

My juices oozed around the leather harness even as her juices flowed, allowing my fingers and, soon, most of my hand inside her. I turned my palm upward, crooking my fingers. I sucked her fat clit into my mouth and hung on as she writhed and clenched and came.

My cunt clenched in empathy around the vibrator there.

After she recovered, she slid on her jeans and thong and fluffed out her hair. Then she surprised me by taking my face in her hands.

The tenderness in her kiss, her lips soft and her tongue pointed as she licked her own juices off my skin, was almost enough to make me come right there.

But I knew better.

It was harder a while later, when the manager and publicist simultaneously made the right guess. He opted for a blow job, while she chose to administer another spanking at the same time.

The game continued on late into the night. Sometimes the guests didn't notice that one of the insidious vibrators had started humming; other times someone clued in but didn't guess the right one. But often enough, both criteria were met—after all, they had a 25 percent chance of pegging the right vibrator.

Math was pretty much the only thing keeping me from pitching over the edge by that point. So it was with both fear and trepidation that I put down the drinks tray and came over to him when he called for me. My hands were bound together and then looped over a convenient hook in the ceiling.

The guests formed a circle around me, most crowding in front so they could see my face. He and his wife were right in front of me, of course.

He handed her the remote control.

"Whenever you want," he said, and I knew he was talking to both of us.

She didn't let me come right away, oh no. She toyed with me, taunted me. One vibrator at a time, just for a brief moment. All of them, but on the lowest setting. Gradually increasing until I was almost there, then suddenly turned off. On high and immediately decreasing.

I had no doubt it was for the guests' pleasure and not mine that she finally took pity on my predicament.

Awash in sensation, I didn't care who watched, who applauded, who heard my cries. I cared only that the agonizing arousal was building inside me, a crimson spark burning behind my eyes until it ignited and flamed and roared, consuming me in its head.

They released me after that, sent me off to peel out of my

leather garments, remove and release all of the vibrators, take a long soak in the hot tub.

"You did very well," he said, his breath ruffling my hair before he sent me away. "I'll reward you later."

The night wasn't over yet. Not hardly.

CARN EUNY

Madelynne Ellis

*C*arn Euny—I first came here years ago, back when my parents were still together, my brother and I were still speaking, and my grandparents were alive. It's the only family holiday I remember having truly enjoyed. There was something peaceful about that week, camped out in our hideous 1970s floral-patterned frame tent in some field with no amenities. We were each given a trowel at the start of the week. I found a hoard of coins and pottery shards with mine and went home with constipation. Robert, my brother, spent most of the week sailing his through the sky like an X-wing. I didn't enquire into the state of his behind. He's never respected it—gay ape. I hope he's happy with Tom.

It's early November. The sky is dreary, grey with the threat of thunder—the sort of sky that has Americans running for shelter, expecting a twister. I expect only rain. Rain is good. Perfect for keeping everyone else at bay, because I like to know I'm surrounded only by ghosts when I come here, not tourists. I want solitude, not the high-pitched cackle of children darting among the fallen houses and clambering over the grass-grown walls.

The wind nips at my nose and fingers as I trek up the mud track from the car park. By the time I get my first glimpse of the ancient village, it has started to drizzle. This place is haunted with memories. Mine are just a few shallow whispers. The earth here has seen countless lifetimes. The people of Carn Euny—what were they like? I like to sit in the remains of the narrow eighteenth-century cottage and imagine I'm the owner, looking out on my Iron Age neighbours.

I step over the stile. The place is so still—blissfully silent. I soak up the atmosphere, walking from house to house around the village perimeter. There are ten houses in total; indistinct circles of greeny-yellow where the grass has worn thin, surrounded by low stone walls. I finish on the steps by the cottage at the southwest end of the village, facing my favorite part of the tour.

The *fogou* is a dark tunnel of indeterminate use. The rain is lashing against my face as I approach, running off my Cagoule to leave soggy stripes across my trousers. I pause for just a second, then plunge on in. The tunnel smells of mulchy earth. Stones crunch beneath my feet as I cross a tiny passage that branches off the main tunnel, which I know from my childhood quests is barred at the farthest end. I reach the tree in too few strides, the tree that, like a silent sentinel, guards the underground chamber that is my ultimate destination.

The first time I came here, my brother charged ahead of me. Robert was forever charging headlong into everything. Nothing has changed. The last time we met, he charged out of my life with my boyfriend in tow. Still, despite his clumsy jig on that first visit, I remember that moment as one of utter stillness and chaotic noise. Coming here was like wading straight into my collective unconscious. "Shhh!" I hissed at him, putting my finger to my lips in a primary school fashion. "You're disturbing it."

"Don't be silly, Jo. It's not alive."

A swallow swooped past his head at that very moment, sending the silly fool hurtling into the sunshine, much to my twelve-year-old self's amusement. I think I ate my sandwiches down here in the semidark while the rest of the family slowly crisped above ground.

I did the same on the day he announced he was gay. We'd come as a sort of tenth-anniversary road trip—Robert, Tom, and I. Mum and Dad were arguing their way through the courts, Gran had died the year before, and Grandpa was languishing in a home, dead in all but name.

I haven't come here to think about them today though. I've come here to forget, to escape them.

But everything is going wrong, because as I emerge into the cavern, I realise that *he* is here, and that I'm not alone.

I have no idea who *he* is. He looks as if a hippie Dormobile snatched him out of the city and tossed him out down the road. He's wearing muddy cowboy boots, a pinstriped suit, and something that looks suspiciously like my gran's old traveling rug.

He's gazing into the shallow space that so resembles a hearth as I enter. Some fool has probably burned twigs there again. Mind, with twenty-four-hour public access, I'm surprised there aren't bottles, cans, and fag ends littered about the place. I guess the scary drive up here—along windy roads barely one car wide—puts people off, as well as the silent echo of the ages.

I fold my arms and glare daggers into poncho-man's back. How dare he be here? I planned so carefully.

"It rained the last time I came here too," he says.

Fantastic, I think. *Not only does he have the audacity to actually speak, his conversation is utterly banal.*

"It was just before my wedding. Two summers back. But that's all over now. Signed the papers yesterday."

"Oh dear." My response comes out rather flat, and instead of sympathetic I sound like an utter cow. *Maybe it'll scare him off.* It certainly makes him turn around.

"I drove three hundred miles to be here."

Hell. He's staking his claim. I'm so flustered that I can't manage anything more noteworthy than a grunt.

"I'm Sam, by the way." He lifts his satchel from the floor.

It's a grubby green thing, the sort we carried about at school covered in graffiti. "Do you want a drink?" He pours a mug of something black and steaming from a thermos.

"Brought my own. Thanks," I add as an afterthought, although I carefully omit giving my name. Actually, I brought something a little stronger than tea. Scotch, of the supermarket brand variety. No point in wasting the good stuff on being maudlin.

"A sandwich?"

"No—I'm fine. Got those too."

He swigs his tea . . . coffee, and I watch him as though he's the exhibit, not the round chamber in which we stand. The patter of the rain on the iron girder and turf roof has grown improbably loud. Fat heavy raindrops pierce the grate that normally funnels in light from above. It could be midnight down here.

"Sounds as though we're stuck here awhile."

I'm almost tempted to run out into the storm in response. His presence is overwhelming. It fills the tiny room, blotting out the voices in my head, the memories, the aeons of pleasure and pain.

"You're not screwy, are you?" he asked.

I guess I must look pretty wild to have prompted that question. I pat my wet hair to see if it's standing up Medusa-style, but it seems fine. Mind you, I have been staring at him since the moment we met. I guess that's freaky. Strange then, that when I turn away, I can't actually remember his face.

"My wife was." He walks around the chamber so that we

are facing again. I guess he really wants to talk. Poor sod. I'm nobody's first choice of a breakup counselor. There's still an exclusion order out on me, barring me from seeing Tom. I only wanted to know what I did wrong.

"I know she wasn't well," he continues, "and that you have to make exceptions, but when she tried to bite my ear off . . . " He falls temporarily silent. "You see? You understand, don't you? I couldn't go on like that anymore. Even her barmy dog never tried to savage me like that. He was happy enough humping cushions and virgin teddy bears."

He bows his head, and even in the dim light I can make out the scar tissue running around the top of his right earlobe. For a moment, his pain blots out the turmoil of my past. Damnit! He's forcing a crack in my bitter heart. I suppose I can share for a short while.

I give him a nervous grin. "Here." I take off the screw top and offer the scotch.

He swallows, only looking at the label after the third draft. "It's good. Thanks." He hands the bottle back. The neck is warm from his grasp. I take a swig myself. He's right. It's not bad. Okay, it's no ten-year-old island malt, but it's passable for a rainy Thursday.

We sit facing on the picnic rug that Sam unraveled from around his shoulders. It's traditional tartan with a tasseled fringe that makes me want to crack jokes about stealing old ladies' skirts, but like thick lumps of cinder toffee, the words stick in my throat. I can't open up to this man, this stranger. Though god knows, I want to talk. To let all the bitter gnawing hatred spill out and melt into the ether of this place. It feels safe here. I don't think my bile would leave much of a residue.

Tom. How could you?

I'll never forget the way you left. You never once looked back.

"What shall we talk about?" he asks.

Sam is all smiles again as he tucks into a doorstopper egg and cress sandwich. What is it about men and food? What is it about company and eating? I unwrap one of my own petite triangles and stare glumly at it. I have no appetite for celery and cream cheese, only a taste for the bottle.

"Sex," announces Sam, just when I'm starting to warm to him—maybe it's the whisky. "It's more exciting than the weather."

Men and sex, it must be like a perpetual buzz in their brains.

"When's the last time you had any, and was it good?" he asked.

I'm going to kill this one . . . so dead.

"Saturday, with my twelve-inch, multispeed, pump-action supervibe." Next question.

"Shit!" he says. "You win. February. Lousy breakup shag on the kitchen floor." He finishes his sandwich, leaving a smear of egg across his upper lip, which I helpfully wipe off. "Your thing sounds good. Does it have one of those anal-ticklers that lets you do both doors at the same time?"

"Ur-no! Perv!" I remark. "Is that why she divorced you? Cause you're a closet gay?"

"The ear thing," he reminds me, turning his head to show off the bite marks. "Why do you think I'm a closet gay?"

I shrug. Cross my arms.

"'Cause I mentioned anal play?"

"No." I bite my lip.

"Yes, it was."

"No, it wasn't."

"Tell me then." He clasps his hands around my upper arms. His grip is firm, but not aggressively so. I look into his bronze-flecked eyes, and it's as if I'm staring into the past. Tom had the deepest hazel eyes, with flecks of gold around the centre. I fell into those eyes the first time we met. Fell out again, the night I came home to find him screwing my brother. I'd suspected it for so long. Ignored the signs, pretended it wasn't real. Tom was my world; Robert, my baby brother. My own eyes are shining too brightly. I can't help it. It hurts too much.

"Hey, maybe you've had enough." Sam pries the bottle from my hand. "Don't go soul-searching in there; the only thing you'll find is oblivion."

"Got a better idea?"

He hugs me to his chest. I rest my head in the crook of his shoulder and sob.

"Sh!" he says, stroking my hair. "Hey, shh!" The ghosts of the past press in around us; Mum and Dad squabbling until dawn, Robert and his X-wing, Tom chasing me through the *fogou*. They stifle me with their voices, their screams for attention and release.

I don't realize that the noise is my own keening until Sam's lips close over mine in a silencing kiss. A last ditch attempt to stop the hysteria, I suppose. It certainly beats being slapped. Still, I pull away immediately. Stare at the red heat of his parted lips. They are plump, sensual, expressive lips, curved like a perfect bow and rendered oblique by his faint smile.

Tom was my first love, my only love. I know all about Tom. All his sensitive bits, all his secrets. I may have kissed a boy or two, way back in primary school, but none of them made a lasting impression. I can't conjure names and faces. I never slept my way around campus in my student days, never touched another living being except Tom.

And now Sam.

He raises a hand behind my head, and draws me into the kiss. At first, I taste only the whisky flames on my tongue—bitter, peaty oranges. Slowly, I taste him too—sugar sweet, with a jalapeño fever. It's a gentle kiss despite the flames, a getting-to-know-you kiss. So soft it makes me shiver.

I'm so pleased we're kneeling, because what would he think if he could feel my legs trembling.

We part again, but I can't bear to lose the contact completely, so I rub my thumb across his mouth. His teeth close over the tip, and his tongue flicks back and forth.

"Oh, shit!" I say, wondering if he's imagining my nipples or my clit. "Are we gonna fuck?" My voice is a slurry hiss. Suitable, I suppose, since I'm terrified. *Will riding his cock solve any more problems than the scotch?* I wonder. I take a swig for luck. Sam snatches the bottle from my grasp and chucks it across the chamber. As it falls, the rest of the amber liquid sloshes from the bottle in a perfect arc and is quickly swallowed by the ground. *The ancient gods are thirsty,* I think.

"Been there, done that, put on a different t-shirt," Sam says. "You won't find tranquility in the bottom of the bottle."

"I'm not sure I'm going to find it having sex with a stranger on a mud floor." *How did we get to this point? I've known him what, twenty minutes, half an hour?*

"Love hurts; it's a given." He wipes the silver tears from my eyelashes. "Casual sex is just that. It doesn't have to come with emotional baggage. You enjoy it and move on."

It's a nice solution . . . for him. He's gone without for months. What's he got to fear from a stranger? Clearly, I'm less psychotic than his ex-wife. For my part though, I'm not sure I can remain that emotionally detached. What if I fall head over heels and he just walks away? I don't even know where he's from. Three hundred miles. Where does that take you? Bristol, Birmingham? Further north than that—Dundee?

Sam licks the stolen tears from his finger like he's supping honey. He's not looking at me, but his attention is mine. He's aware of every breath, every tiny motion I make. I wonder if he can feel the tension crackling along my arms. It's growing so intense . . . I have to do something. Have to react. I bow my head and consider walking away.

No! I cannot leave this place. Not yet. I refuse to run away.

I find myself fumbling with the zip of my Cagoule. Not a good move, since now it looks as if I'm undressing.

Sam's gaze locks onto the open neck of my zippy fleece. There's a hint of shell-pink flesh between the metal teeth and the shadow of my cleavage.

I went half-crazy when Tom left, convinced myself that I was unattractive. Losing four inches from my waist didn't help. To compensate, I went on an expensive lingerie shopping spree. I suppose I thought having my breasts balanced on a Balconette and wearing skimpy knickers with cute ribbon ties would make me more attractive to the opposite sex. Not that they ever got to see this exquisite lingerie beneath my clothes. It was meant for Tom, the one person it was never going to work on, since he was now batting for the other team. Anyway, having fried my credit cards, it was all I had left. So yes, even for a rainy visit to the wilds of Cornwall, I'd dressed in my birthday best.

Sam's fingers sneak beneath the fleece and trace the underwire support of my Sou bra.

I bite my bottom lip, pressing my teeth down hard until the soft flesh feels swollen. His palm slides up over my breast, cups and squeezes. The nipple, he captures between his forefinger and thumb.

I can't look at him. I'm still not sure this is what I want him to do. Then again, maybe it's too late for this kind of hesitation. Is it ever too late if your knickers are still on? What happens when he teasingly undoes the pink silk ties? How will he react when he sees them?

My lips . . . my whole throat tingles with anticipation as he moves closer, lifts my chin, and kisses me again. His hand stays between us, working the nipple until sparks shoot down to my cunt.

This time the kiss is sloppy and dirty. His stubble chafes my chin and lips. It leaves my mouth feeling grazed. Still I rub against him, unable to get enough. I clasp him tight, both hands locked around his head. I want to disappear inside him and hide from the pain.

We pause for breath—panting, but unable to stay apart. Sam's hands wander from my breasts to my shoulders, from my stomach to my butt, and then back to my breasts. This time he's not content to fumble between layers of cloth. He lifts my fleece, ready to rub his face in the plump softness of my breasts, but he hesitates when he sees the bra.

His whole face lights up.

"That's very pretty underwear." He sucks his thumb then traces it along the wheat design all the way to the upper edge. "Shame it's gonna have to come off."

"Are you gonna buy me another one if it gets muddy?"

We're in a cave, I remind myself. It's damp and dark, and

there is rain coming in through the skylight. We're going to get filthy. And of course he's not going to buy me underwear. We both know we're going to walk away from here afterward and never come back. I love this place, but maybe it belongs in my past. Maybe I have to give it up to move on. Is that what happened to the people here all those centuries ago? Did something change? Did they have to leave the familiarity of the past behind and learn something new?

"Hey." Sam rubs his nose against mine. "Do the pants match?"

I want to cry, or laugh. Maybe both.

Sam tugs the waistband of my trousers away from the skin and tries to peek.

I have to laugh at that. His cross-eyed expression is too humorous. It turns this besuited stranger into a foolish, lovable boy.

"Do they? Do they?" he asks.

I shimmy the trousers down until the tie-sides are revealed. My fleece falls over my bust in the process, so I lean forward and capture it between my teeth to pull it up again.

"Whoa, boy," Sam hisses.

My gaze flickers down to his fly. He catches me looking and sucks his upper lip into his mouth in a predatory smile. "These are just a little bit of nothing." He lifts one ribbon end between his thumb and forefinger—pulls.

"An expensive little bit of nothing," I say.

"Good job I don't have to rip them off you."

The bow unravels.

For a frozen moment, we just stare at one another, then we're locked together and his hand's inside my pants. The buzz is intense, the evidence of my arousal plain upon his fingertips. The sensation on my clit is slippery and raw. My hips jerk instinctively with the motion so that I ride upon his index and middle fingers.

We topple onto the tartan blanket. The smell of arousal mingles with that of the earth. And somewhere in the tangle of limbs, I manage to unfasten his shirt and peel the jacket from his back. The hair on his chest is darker than that on his head. It's sparse across his chest, thicker around his loins.

I avoid touching him there.

I desire him, but still I hesitate. The guilt of betrayal stings in my throat. I feel I am being disloyal, even though it's been over seven months. *Tom is gone,* I tell myself, *forget him.* Sam is here and now, and he has pecs and an arse to die for.

His two pert peachy globes fill up my hands. I knead them in time with the rhythm of his caress.

Breathless, I straddle his hips.

"So, you're an 'on top' kind of girl." He peels my bra straps from my shoulders, lets them fall around my upper arms. My breasts, he tips out of their high-rise support and raises himself up to suck upon them.

His mouth is unbearably hot. I push him back down and

twist around so that I am facing his toes, leaving him with open access to my cunt, which he dutifully licks as I tease first his inner thighs and then his balls.

He slaps my butt. "Are you always this big a tease?" The second of the silk ribbons comes undone and seventy quid's worth of pink thread lands upon his chest. Sam scoops it up and drops it upon his face. Sniff-tastic! In return, I drag my tongue along his cock from tip to root and grin inanely in response to his sharpening breaths.

High on this animalistic mingling of texture and scent, I leave my lollipop, shuffle forward, and slip him inside.

It's a crazy thing to do, and I know it. But I'm too far gone to care. Whatever the consequences, I'll deal with them later. Right now, I'm healing. I have a man whom I desire, who desires me.

I sink onto him real slow. A man is nothing like a vibe. You can't poke him in at any old angle and hope for the best, or turn him off when you decide you'd rather just sleep instead. I've slept a lot recently. It's far from my mind now. Instead I'm chasing a fleeting shadow, a crazy belief that an orgasm will make things right, but my urgency makes us uncoordinated and arrhythmic.

"Easy. Slow down, butterfly." I like the way he calls me butterfly, though I feel more like a moth.

Sam clasps my hips, and slowly, we fall into sync. He sits up behind me, supported on his elbows at first, and then so his stomach caresses my back. One hand quests downward to my clit, the other cradles my breasts. We're together, but still so far apart.

"Turn around." Sam's breath burns the back of my neck and sends rolling shivers down my spine. I hardly dare face him. Part of me is still in denial. Part of me is still pretending that this is familiar, that maybe, just maybe, this is Tom. If I turn, I have to accept the truth, that I'm sharing my body with a man who doesn't even know my name.

All the same, I do turn. I let him slide in deep again while I bounce upon his lap. I ravish him with hands and mouth, lips and teeth. I scratch and trace his contours. The heat burns my skin. It rises between us until each thrust is accompanied by the liquid sounds of orgasm.

Something breaks inside my head as I ride the peak of a ferocious wave. Something has changed. Sam jerks inside me with a fevered intensity.

The comedown is slow.

We lie together on the rug until the rain has gone, dreaming of forever tomorrows. The sun peeps through the overhead grate and licks gold across our bared skin. Not until we hear voices do we part.

I dress, minus my ribbon-tie knickers, which Sam hands to me and I push inside my bag, along with the empty scotch bottle.

The voices belong to a troop of OAPs, old age pensioners, who totter into the chamber, waving sticks and clutching their backs until we are all squashed together and there is no room to breathe. They feel no resonance for the place, I realize. All their conversation is about where they've already been or are yet to go. I'm tempted to yell, "Silence!" at them, the same way I once did to Robert. Instead, I turn to Sam to share a disgusted smile, only to find he's already gone.

I leave the *fogou;* search the village from my central vantage point, but it's too late. I never even told him my name. Stupid pensioners. I feel like kicking their sticks out from them. Instead, I nod and smile politely and make the return journey to my car, which is hemmed in by their tour bus.

I make the discovery as I hunt for my neglected sandwiches. There's a whisky bottle label coiled up in the pink silk of my panties. Scrawled across it is an unassuming line of digits and a message.

Call me when you're over him.

I punch the number into the memory on my phone.

Soon . . .

A PRAYER TO BE MADE COCKSURE

Melissa Gira

*B*eing stretched along the length of you in that bed that'll never get slick with us again, curved so full into your belly, my cheeks pressed against your thighs, your cock sliding so sure down my throat, possessing me, possessing you, I sucked your cock as if it were the last cock. I trusted you to let me keep breathing, to never take that final bit from me, to tell me that getting any air at all was your choice just by reaching your hand down the length of your chest to me, to cradle the back of my neck, to run your fingers across my lips, softly, as you plunged suddenly and held me at the edge.

So many edges.

You wanted me to swallow you whole, and I did my best, and it would never be just right, and you keep on taking me anyway.

With my eyes gone out from the shelter of your skin and my body so near to crushed by you, my body so nearly becoming you (as if we've traded, one calling out for the other with one's own name), we are a single coiling, sliding mechanism; one animal desire; one fused being. I'm so fucked, so good, and you fuck my mouth with a confidence not just in your cock, which is an easy thing to believe in, but in me, who then had given you no reason to believe anything.

Yet.

Yes.

THE BLOW JOB STARTED in the suite that neither of us knew we'd end up in yesterday, and today is Sunday. Today is now, and I write this now, as it is happening, now. Now, Sunday, and I am listening to church happening across the way, and I don't even have to tell you to take of my body, because you are already coming toward me.

Before I met you, before you took me (which took the span of less than a day, but spanned at least two cities and two beds and two other lovers between us), I was sure that I was over blow jobs—that word, those two words, neither of which I am living up to with you inside me. After we stopped fucking, and maybe for good, because it was always possible, you still had me desperate to get a cock back there, where you had been.

I had to take a plane to do it right.

Coming for you, I was crumpled into my seat on an enormous

and classic sort of jet, in those headphones that shut everything out, struggling to stay under a too small blanket. The plane was so big and aisles so wide, it was as if I were onstage, my own spotlight overhead and very near to rows and rows of potential audience. As I was rubbing cool cream into my fingers, I felt my cunt clutch and ache, my hips rock along under me all the way to the back of the seat, and the scent of lemon balm coming off of my skin in the stale air burst me wide-open, the scent of lemon from the cream I kept always in my purse, the cream I nicked from the hotel—the hotel where I washed my neck and my breasts and my hands after sucking your cock, the hotel where I left your cock—and I came big and smooth into my seat a thousand miles up and far away, where everything is quiet and perfect and, like my body, can just go on forever.

And I am flying back to that blow job, the first blow job. The immaculate blow job. Before. There is a great "before" that lovers can never return to, that time that starts before they meet, so by definition, it can't be measured, unless one counts one's birth as the beginning. "Before" ends with your mouth. "Before" ends at the edge of the bed. "Before" begins in one hotel and ends in another.

There are things about your body that, as much as I know everyone watches you, I want to think only I know; things that I started. I may have created the way you snap back your shoulder against the down and flatten the covers as your nipple is being nearly clawed right off your chest in the half-light and hum of a laptop. I could have discovered how, on your back in the bath filled with sage and lemon, your calves just fold into your thighs and collapse so softly onto your chest when my fingertip grazes the base of your cock and the cleft of your ass. It was me who made the gasps at the back of your throat with my hands and the tears falling from the far corners of your eyes. I made your eyes make that look too, hot and almost done completely.

The blow job, though, is ours to make, and this is:

How I love for my cock to be sucked:

When my cock is sucked in the daytime, the red behind my eyes from the sun streams in as I come, and so I am coming through the color red of cock and the red of lips and the red of your nipples and the red of my nipples in your fingers and the red of my fingernails down your throat, the lacquer and the pink of my cuticles and the pale red-white swirl of your spit and your blood strung between them.

How you love for your cock to be sucked:

"You suck my cock so good," you say into the night air that hums between two phones too far. "You suck my cock so good, and I am not flying down there to fuck you," and your voice is heavy, like I like. "You are so fuckable, and I am not flying down there to fuck you. You suck my cock so good. I am not coming down there. I am not coming. I am not."

I can hear your body warm and rise with the repetition that I know from the cadence of every fetishist I've ever done.

So this "not fucking," then, is your foreplay.

I WAS ALREADY ON MY WAY somewhere else, to someone else, preparing myself for the fuck that would carry me past the end of our own. You are so temporary like this, when you only exist to me between breaths, and as soon as my lungs are emptied, my capacity has grown and so I must replace you, you and the space I have gained from taking you into me in the first place. Really the throat is just an escape route.

The city that I landed in was not like our first one: cold, and comfortable with its cold, and never once did the sun make it all the way up in the sky. No day and no sleeping set me to spin almost immediately, so that walking in thick tights and tall boots made the places where all the hems met, from my skirt to my waist, hum and vibrate, a waking wet dream in the dry of the gray.

I walked the streets with my phone and the dawn for company at the edge of sleep, at the edge of the day, knowing you were there close at the other. When you showed up immediately when I called out with a text (and I love how tight a text must be to work like this) to request your warmth, your words were back in my hand on the screen so fast, the speed and the heat going right to my cunt immediately. Still I was fairly surrounded, again, Sunday morning, and everyone off to goodness, and then, us.

So there was something deeply kinky about standing on that cold bridge in the middle of it all and listening to your warm voice in my ear with my legs wrapped around the metal and sliding the plastic where you reach me closer, and this is how we are, this is how we are.

And who is getting what, and who is giving what, and you get to come and I only get to hear and I need there to be connection here, but aren't you just getting off, and this is what I crave when I don't have you, and am I what you crave when I'm not there, and do you want to fuck or do you want to fuck *me*?

It's okay to not know, now.

Because I am willing to make mistakes again—mistakes that I would never give myself the chance to make if I weren't so wet with you still: messy, fucked decisions and unfinished, raw love affairs, and cocks to make so hard and drained, so perfectly flawed.

I am a good mistake to make, I think.

Because even if we break this, the whole of creation is reborn each day, and that creation in the first place came about from an entirely sensible act of sex. Fucking in tandem, a boy and a girl, still at the start of it all, come every word, every fold of flesh, every loop of sound, every bit of data and sperm and sorrow, every wing that takes me away and every text and every tone that brings you to me, every vulgar bell and puff of smoke, every prayer and every curse, every kiss and every motherless child, everyone, everyone there under their legs, flowing from their legs, a great river—and if their pillows could talk, what would they say, that bedless bed a river of tears and cum?

A girl and a boy are doing this every day, and like *us,* there is a *them* that goes on fucking, even when they're through.

I don't know what "through" looks like, so if you see me here, still acting like it's the end of the world without you in it, in me, I hope this explains why.

Because even if it's been over for ages, still we will just start again tomorrow.

WHEN YOU TOLD ME TO come see you, you asked what was I waiting for. *For enough.* For enough time to pass. That seemed reasonable. You said to come for days. In a few days. To come now if I wanted. I didn't break from hearing you go so hard then, as I do, feeling so far now. I didn't have enough of me break, the way I do, now.

And if we collide, will your skin still reach me, open, and open with me? If I reach you, will you bear into me; will you give me those eyes I give you?

And I am still so near, nearly not breathing, with a ring of wet around my jaw and dripping down my neck, drenching my hair before I know (and will only know when I sit to brush it out, later; when I pull my fingers through it as I lift my face still with your taste on me), before I felt just what's been done to me, become of me. My tears, my sweat, your come—are all here; are one and the same there. For a moment, spelled out on my skin, shaped with my own mouth, the fuck I want, the fuck I could contain, so still, so full, so held, so here.

Of this fuck and mouth, of all of this, I am, and I have become, and cocksure has always been one of my favorite words.

ALL ABOUT
HEARTS

Sage Vivant

Gil wasn't often detained at the hospital, but when he was, she did her best not to make him feel guilty about it. After all, how could you begrudge a guy who was late because he had to save a life?

"Could you meet me in the operating amphitheater?" he had asked her. She'd seen him perform surgery before, and it was the most potent aphrodisiac she could imagine. She was always proud of him anyway, but seeing him in action evoked a special kind of awe that made her heart—as well as other organs—swell.

The theater wasn't open to the general public, so she had to check in with the receptionist, a young woman she'd met at some hospital party or other.

"Hi, I'm supposed to meet Dr. Atkinson in the amphitheater. May I just go on in, or do I need to sign something?"

"Oh yes. He mentioned you'd be coming. I think he finished operating sooner than he planned, so you can just go into the operating area." The woman smiled and nodded toward the direction Petra was to take.

When Petra entered the anteroom, where doctors prepped for surgery, all was pristine. It was hard to believe it had just been used for open-heart surgery prep. *Wow,* she thought. *Doctors sure run a tight and sterile ship.*

She walked through the gleaming prep room, then opened the door to the theater. What greeted her was so unexpected, she froze as her mind tried to absorb it. Rather than the clear white fluorescent light focused on a supine patient, candlelight in many shapes and sizes dotted the space. A round table draped in white linen and adorned by a small vase containing a single red rose served as the room's focal point. Immaculate white china marked two place settings. Gil, dressed in a sports coat and crisp white shirt, sat on the operating table, holding a glass of champagne.

"Good evening. Glad you could make it," he said.

Her surprise morphed into excitement. "You devil! I can't believe you did this!"

She practically skipped to him and threw her arms around his neck as he laughed with satisfaction.

"I thought it was time to take you somewhere you'd never been for dinner."

"Well, this would be it, alright!" She kissed his freshly shaven cheek.

"You look especially beautiful tonight," he told her. She sensed his sincerity and loved him all the more for it. She had heard that compliment all her life, but whenever Gil said it, she always felt it came from a truer, more genuine place—a heart that knew her and loved her for more than her beauty.

"Thank you. This is all so wonderful, sweetheart."

"Wait until the dinner arrives."

"Oh? Where is it coming from?" She was intrigued.

"You'll see."

"Oh come on now! Tell me! I'm already surprised by everything else."

"The best surprises come in threes."

"They do not. That's just urban myth."

"No, I believe that would be an old wives' tale."

"Gil!"

"Seriously. You will find out soon enough. It will be here in a few minutes."

She pursed her lips and looked at him with suspicion before she sighed. "Okay. You win."

He poured her a glass of champagne, smiling as he did so. "It isn't wise to argue with a doctor, you know."

"I'm learning that," she said, bringing the glass to her face. She squinted slightly as the bubbles leaped onto her nose. As she let the liquid slide down her throat, Gil walked behind her and spoke softly in her ear.

"How about a back rub?"

"Mmm, definitely," she replied, taking another sip of the bubbly.

He massaged through her silk blouse, yet his fingers honed in on her most sensitive areas. Surgeon's hands— delicate, probing, accurate. He knew where her pain resided, and concentrated his efforts there. Tonight was no exception. He followed the knotted path along her trapezius from shoulder to neck, applying the perfect amount of pressure and massage to weaken her knees.

"Oh," she moaned. "That's perfect."

She'd often tried to explain just how sublime his touch was. Never had she enjoyed anything quite like it, and there truly were times when it alone sufficed for the sensual communion she needed with her husband. It wasn't that she didn't adore sex with him, but he massaged her so well that he delivered an afterglow that actually rivaled traditional copulation. How many men could do that? Her own experience told her "not many," yet she had to be careful not to use his incredible massage techniques as a substitute for sex. *If only he wasn't so damn good at making me feel fantastic,* she thought wryly.

He moved his hands slowly down to her rhomboids, using his thumbs to circulate magic close to her spine. Without thinking, she began to unbutton her blouse. He helped her slip it off her shoulders, as the heat from her skin rose up to express its thanks.

There were no barriers now between his miraculous, soothing hands and her grateful, waiting skin. She felt his lips on her shoulder blades and swept her long, thick hair to one side to keep his palette clear. His breath warmed her ear as he spoke.

"Want to lie down on the operating table? I can get at your lower back much better that way."

Her eyes fluttered open in half-conscious concern. "But what about the food? Won't it be here soon? We'll just be interrupted."

"Lynelle will ring me when it gets here. You'll have time to get decent."

Lynelle. That was the nurse's name, Petra noted to herself. Next time, she'd have to make a point of using the woman's name.

As she considered the wisdom of moving, topless, to the operating table, he pressed his erection against her ass and rubbed wordlessly from side to side.

"You drive a hard bargain," she said quietly.

"Thanks for noticing."

She giggled. He then guided her to the table, where she carefully laid herself down and surrendered fully to his gliding fingertips. Just as they made their way along her vertebra, more of her back relaxed. She suddenly became aware of the heat in her pussy and the way it flowed through her body, alternately exciting and calming her. She trembled and sighed, wondering what sensation could possibly feel better than this one.

She heard the door open and barely flinched, so firmly entrenched was she in the ethereal world created by Gil's hands.

"Alright, you two. On your feet. This ain't no stinkin' massage parlor, you know."

Petra's eyes sprang open, and Gil stepped away from the table. A tall, good-looking policeman faced them with a no-nonsense stance that didn't invite discussion.

"Officer, there must be some misunderstanding. I arranged for the use of this amphitheater. This is a private party, and I've obtained all the necessary approvals," Gil explained.

Still on her tummy, Petra looked from one man to the other, simultaneously frightened and bemused. *Which of these two strong-willed characters would win this match?* she wondered.

"I don't care who said you could fornicate in here, buddy, but I'm responding to a complaint by a decent citizen who wants you to find another place for your party. Now let's move along, eh?" Petra liked his Brooklyn accent. She didn't budge from her place on the table.

"May I call the nurse on duty and confirm my story? She'll show you that my signature appears in the book that hospital staff uses to reserve this room."

"The only person you can call is a lawyer, pal. I don't care what you signed. You wanna have happy times with your lady, you do it at home. Let's go! Jeez—doctors!" He practically spat the word. She found him more adorable by the second. He cut a striking figure in his dark blue uniform, but there was something in his eyes that betrayed the confidence he wielded about.

"Officer, my wife is a little shy. Could you look away while she gets up, please?"

"What, she's suddenly shy now? You doctors think cops are pretty stupid, don't you? Ma'am, just think of me like a doctor and get up nice and easy. I've seen it all before, trust me. No sudden moves, now."

She grinned and knew her eyes sparkled. "Like a doctor? Really? Is that how you want me to think of you?"

"Well, not like *this* doctor," he said, nodding upward at Gil, disgust on his face. "Look, lady, the quicker you get up, the quicker this will all be over. I'm sure Daddy Warbucks here's got a fancy lawyer to get you out of this mess, so you two will probably be free in a few hours. Then you can do whatever rocks your boat. Right now, I need youse both to get up and get dressed."

Gil had gotten her juices flowing before the cop had entered, and now this strapping young law enforcement professional had her thoughts flowing with equal speed. Slowly, she lifted her torso from the table, never letting her eyes stray from the New York policeman. She'd modeled for too many years not to be able to sense when the impact of her beauty made an impression. And as the cop's gaze lingered over her slim, half-naked body, she knew who was truly in control. She ran a hand through her lustrous hair and moved it to cover one breast. He stared at the other.

"We weren't hurting anybody, officer. How could anybody even have seen us? They'd have to have been spying on us to have been offended!"

"Nevertheless, ma'am. I got my job to do." His voice wavered slightly.

She squeezed her breasts together and grinned at him, wondering how far she was going to push this flirtation before he slapped cuffs on her.

"I understand. Is it alright if my husband helps me dress?"

"Whatever, lady. Just make it quick."

Petra winked surreptitiously at Gil, who seemed instantly to understand what she was up to. She got to her feet, stepped out of her shoes, and Gil reached around to unzip her skirt. As she wiggled, he tugged downward on the fabric. The skirt pooled on the floor, leaving Petra in only a black lace thong.

"What the hell are you doing? I told you to get dressed, not undressed!" The cop exclaimed, stepping closer to the couple.

"Oh! I'm sorry. I guess I'm so nervous, I misunderstood."

As she spoke, she got on all fours, and Gil stationed himself behind her but facing the policeman. Petra heard her husband unzip his fly and grinned as their visitor tried to decide what to do. Being naked in front of this stranger and about to be fucked by Gil had her pulse racing. She heard Gil fiddle with something on the side of the table, and soon, the table's height was being lowered just a few inches.

"Am I gonna have to call for backup, people? This ain't helping your case, you know."

Gil slid his cock into her pussy, and she spoke to the cop. "Maybe not, but it's helping my cunt immensely." She closed her eyes, savoring the disturbance she was creating as much as the fleshy thickness between her legs. Gil pushed into her forcefully, and the sound of her wetness echoed in the stark amphitheater.

"We had plans for this room, officer, and I'm afraid we're going to see them through. Now, you can either call for backup if you think you need it, or you can enjoy the festivities."

"And what's that supposed to be? Some kind of bribe?" The policeman meant the question to be a rhetorical one, but as it hung in the air, to Petra it sounded more like an honest inquiry.

"It's not a bribe, officer. It's an invitation," said Petra. She licked her lips like a porn star and stared boldly at his crotch.

Gil increased his speed behind her, and she felt like the most wanton, reckless harlot any movie had ever depicted. She knew her ass was up in the air, and that the curve of her back would be irresistible to any healthy male with a functional penis. She made eye contact with the befuddled policeman and held it, using the unspoken lure in her eyes to convey her desire. When he stepped forward, she knew she'd achieved her goal.

He stood only inches before her now, his uniformed chest at her face. She felt his internal struggle and knew it was time to speak.

"May I touch you, officer?"

Gil rammed her extra hard, as if to punctuate her question. She yelped softly.

The policeman didn't move or speak, so she reached out to cup his package through his pants. When he still didn't flinch, she used one hand to urge his zipper down. When his fly was completely open, she reached inside to find one exceptionally hard, commendably large cock. Its heat gave her the rest of the permission she needed to extract it from its boxer shorts nest.

She admired it briefly, noting its deep, even color and exquisite shape. Gil's would always be her favorite, but if she was going to be sucking another, this one was a mighty fine substitute. As Gil's palms caressed her ass cheeks, she flicked the tip of the cop's knob, eager to taste the tiny droplet of come that sparkled there. She didn't look up at his face—it was just as much fun to imagine the discombobulation there as to actually witness it. He tasted clean, as if he had recently sudsed up with some manly brand of soap.

His somewhat spongy head felt like velvet as her lips spread over it. Stopping just below the ridge around its underside, she kept her lips capped around him as she ran her tongue around the smooth head. He groaned. She got wetter.

Gil, meanwhile, had positioned her so that her hole was precisely where he needed it. She didn't need to spread her legs at all, because he burrowed into the spot where both their pleasures awaited. The walls of her pussy gripped him and creamed with every thrust. To the extent that she could, with the officer's cock between her lips, she slammed back against Gil to drive him deeper inside. As she moved, the small diamond heart pendant around her neck bounced up and down, hitting her chest every time he drilled into her.

The policeman's groans became constant, and his hands held her head. She moved her attentions downward to take more of his meat into her mouth. She slid up and down the length of him, and in her ardor, he occasionally slipped out, smearing her saliva on her face. His thick meat slapping against her cheek and banging into her nose only fueled her need for more, and she found herself lapping and sucking with uncharacteristic abandon.

"Oh, baby, I'm gonna come!" rasped the policeman.

Gil immediately pulled out of her pussy, which distracted the cop, who took the movement as a sign to pull out of Petra's mouth. She was left with two hungry holes and two men dangerously close to orgasm. What did Gil have planned?

"You don't get to come until you satisfy her like a man," Gil told him.

She wanted to laugh like a mad scientist at her husband's bravado. Without commentary, she waited for them to switch positions, swaying her ass from left to right to suggest the urgency of her need.

The cop took Gil's place behind her, but the table was somewhat low for him—he was a good five inches taller than her husband. Gil gestured toward the button on the side, and the table rose slightly to accommodate her new lover.

The cop gingerly fingered her slit, as if to sample what he was about to enter. He didn't slip his finger inside, though, which she was grateful for. She didn't want to have to explain that she was a cock-loving woman who didn't want to waste time on manual stimulation unless she was by herself. It wasn't long before his swollen thickness pushed itself into her. He used her hips for stability as he pumped her with a slightly faster rhythm than Gil had.

Gil beamed at her when he stood before her. She smelled the aroma of her pussy on his cock and licked at it to taste herself. He pointed his dick at her so that the beautiful head tickled her nose. Happily, she slid as much of him down her throat as she could. She'd always been delighted to suck Gil's cock and did it whenever possible, but there was something extra special about sucking Gil's cock while a handsome, well-hung man in uniform fucked her relentlessly from behind.

The cop came even sooner than she expected, spewing great streams of sperm across her back and onto the scrubbed white floor. Just as he yanked himself out of her, she too began to spasm and buck, yelling her cries into Gil's hard cock. In response, he let go into her mouth, flooding her with hot, gooey goodness.

The room, scented by the pervasive aroma of sex, amplified the threesome's heavy, recuperative breaths. Petra lay on her stomach, the corners of her mouth twitching with restrained joy. Gil, still at half-mast, had already fetched a towel to wipe the semen off her body. The cop leaned against the edge of the table, mentally regrouping as he tried to regulate his breathing. Finally, he walked around to the other end of the table so Petra could see him again. To her disappointment, he'd already zipped up.

Languorous and rested, she eyed him with playful challenge. "So, really, officer, how did you know we were here? Who reported us?"

Gil and the policeman exchanged glances. Gil broke into a wide smile, and the man in uniform chuckled. Without further comment, the cop strode out of the room, only to return within seconds, carrying a large insulated bag emblazoned with the name of a local food delivery service.

"I almost forgot. You need to sign this, doctor, and I'll be on my way." He presented a check to Gil for his signature. His police persona had evaporated completely.

"Dinner's here, sweetheart. You can get dressed if you want," Gil said, winking at her as she sat up, gaping with surprise. "Thanks so much, Tony. There's a little something extra in there for you."

"Thank you, sir," he said to Gil. "And thank *you*, ma'am. I hope you enjoy your dinner!"

He swaggered toward the door, and just before he left, he shot Petra a final, conspiratorial grin.

She turned to her husband and laughed. "You surgeons just never stop operating, do you?"

THE NEXT THING

Gina de Vries

*L*et me tell you about now. Now means not being in San Francisco—now means being stuck in Massachusetts. Now means that the only dykes for miles are earnest, just-out baby gays, and Lola and I both prefer women who are older and tougher. I wish I could tell you Lola's *real* name, because it's so perfect for a dyke like her, but I can't. So I'm calling her Lola instead, because that's almost as good. "What did my parents *think* I'd grow up to be?" she asked me once, exasperated. "I mean, *they* named me. If you call your baby Lola, and then you're shocked when she looks like a lesbian prostitute, you've got some problems with reality!" Lola is skinny and doe-eyed, with a snarly grin. She wears baggy cargo pants with lacy bras and camisoles, tall boots, and a leather jacket, and she always looks flawless doing it. I'm round and short; I do femme in a more vintage, little-girly way—lots of fifties-style dresses and bright colors—but I'm no less cute than her.

Now is just a bad time for us and sex. Now means we've either exhausted or eschewed all the dyke possibilities in this town, and we are both aching for San Francisco, for a time when sex was good and whole and widely available to both of us. Now means that we drive around the backwoods of Western Massachusetts late at night, blasting Patti Smith on Lola's car stereo and drinking coffee and soda, being really fucking sad and fantasizing about how the butches in San Francisco will sweep us off our feet.

Never mind that in six months I'll be back in San Francisco, and I'll be fucking my fag friends' bi-curious boyfriends, because nerdy gayboys are sexy and surprisingly good lays—and way less drama than Mission hipster dykes who drink too much. Never mind that in six months, Lola will be living in New Jersey, shacking up with a straight metal dude who dyes his hair platinum blonde and listens to Billy Idol and Black Sabbath nonironically. Never mind that shit changes, that your fantasy is *always* perfect in your head, that you can come a thousand times over by touching yourself, but you usually have to show a lover how to do it the first time. Never mind that the first time you do something, even if it's beautiful, even if it's hot, it's also awkward and nervous. Never mind that the nervousness, the awkwardness, is just what makes it so hot. Never mind that real, honest-to-god, genuine surprises are the sexiest thing imaginable.

Forget all that shit. Right now, not six months from now, not a year from now as I sit writing this at three in the morning in December, and it's raining but still balmy outside like it gets here, and I'm feeling *retroactively* sad about how sad I was a year ago—that's before all of this. Before I'm the San Francisco girl with the apartment and the housemate and the friends and the lovers and the job and the community. This is before I'm the girl who can love this city but has complaints about it—the small kinds of complaints that you would have about anyone you loved, but who sometimes still annoyed you.

Right now, there is no margin for San Franciscan error. Right now, this city is *not* where I live. I am in fucking Massachusetts, San Francisco is my escape, and like any good emo girl, I romanticize my escape to its fullest. San Francisco is the city that I fly to every time I whack off. I come hundreds of times in dreams that are always set in this city, my city, home. I dream of faraway lovers' beds. I think about when Lee beat me til my ass turned purple, and made me suck her dick til I gagged so hard I cried, and fucked me slow and sweet in her soft big bed while the rain rocked the trees outside. They scratched at her windows, I swear, just like she'd scratched up my back. Her hands were so full of me. I couldn't come, I was so nervous, so turned on, and then suddenly everything happened at once and I couldn't *stop* coming. I almost cried, a second time in one day, because she was being so sweet. Kissing me, cooing, *Just be a good girl and come for me,* and I was expecting her to hurt me, but I wasn't expecting tenderness, and that was the best surprise.

When we're driving around the woods, caffeinated and horny, Lola always wants me to tell her Lee stories. How I entered a contest at a leather bar because some fag friends cajoled me into it, and because I smile easy and I'm good at selling raffle tickets. That's what's important if you're a girl and you enter a contest at a divey fag bar. They don't have gayboys in Western Mass like they do in San Francisco, and right now, I miss hanging out in fag bars almost as much as I miss marginally sane dykes over the age of eighteen. At the contest, I figured I could do fake dyke–fag flirting with the boys, charm them with my curly hair and cat's-eye glasses and leopard-print skirt. At least a few of them would think it was adorable and fabulous that a femme dyke was there, and they'd buy tickets from me, and I'd have raised some money for the struggling AIDS organization, and I'd get to feel good about that.

And then I saw Lee. Lee and I were two dykes in a sea of fags, and she was butch and at least twenty years older, silver-haired and sweet-eyed. She wore a leather vest over her white T-shirt, there was a hunter green hanky in the left pocket of her jeans, and I thought to myself, *Well, why not try?* I smiled at her, shy, and I asked if she wanted to buy some raffle tickets before I saw that she had a whole roll of them hanging from her belt. "Oh, I guess you won't be buying any, sorry. . . . " I laughed, nervous, and she just stared at me. She held her breath for a split second, and then she said, "Well . . . wait." She asked me, softly, if I did "that thing where you measure someone's inseam with your raffle tickets." I nodded, suddenly speechless, and an enormous grin crept across her face.

Lola loves this part, because she likes stories where women objectify me; I think it's because she imagines herself in them. I can never quite tell if she's thinking of herself as the one being objectified or the one doing the objectifying. For someone as femmey as she is, Lola has a dirty-old-man streak a mile wide. When she's pissed at people, she refers to herself as "Daddy" or "Grampa," in the third person, and tells me to go cut her a switch.

"Lee made me get down on my knees and measure tickets from her inseam to her boots," I tell Lola. "She put my hand right up against her cock, and she held it there." I never meet women like this in Massachusetts—the few older butches I encounter here are way too full of themselves to keep me interested in talking to them, let alone bottoming to them. But this woman, this woman I would bottom to for days. This woman got that my submission was a gift; I could tell that when she touched my hand to her dick. At first, I freaked myself out trying to hold her gaze, trying hard to look charming and cute instead of completely out-of-my-league and petrified. But her hand on mine, and the look in her eyes—suddenly, for that moment, she became my whole world. She told me I looked good on my knees, and that permission was all that I needed. I closed my eyes for a minute, feeling her hardness in my fingers, feeling the rough bar floor on my knees, and I sighed. She helped me up slowly, gave me a kiss on the cheek, and whispered into my ear, "Good girl."

"I found out she was a judge in the contest *after* that," I tell Lola, and Lola hoots and takes a swig of her Cherry Coke. Lee kept flirting with me from the little makeshift stage, and then she spanked me up against the bar—and she spanked all the contestants, but this was different—while a group of drunk shirtless fags cheered. "And while that was awesome," I tell Lola, "that was not even the best part." Afterward, after the pretense of the contest was long over with and we could flirt without being onstage, I sat on a barstool and Lee stood between my legs and held me. Things went from sweet to nasty so seamlessly with her. Her voice was low in my ear, she was telling me how good I was, *What a sweet thing you are,* and then she slid half her hand into my mouth and just fucked me like that. She sucked her breath in when she didn't feel me gag, she sucked her breath in like I was sucking her cock, and for all intents and purposes, I was. Her other hand slid up my skirt, just grazing my thigh, but I was already soaking wet, I wanted to beg her to fuck me right there on the barstool, but I didn't. "That was how we met. I guess that was our first date," I tell Lola.

Lola likes my Lee stories because they remind her of her first butch ex-girlfriend, also a much older woman. "Shannon was taking my bra off, the last time we slept together . . . " Lola says, her voice uncharacteristically wistful, " . . . and she looked at me . . . . Dude, she looked at me like God was in my bra." I can see why—Lola's fierce. I like her stories because they're brave and just a little dangerous, full of this excellent fearlessness I wish I'd had when I was a teenager. Lola talks about sneaking around with Shannon when she was just barely legal, dragging her to her senior prom and getting drunk off liquor that Shannon bought for them, sneaking into the auditorium bathroom and fucking in one of the stalls while some football player and cheerleader were crowned prom king and queen.

Lola and I tell each other these things to keep us going in the now, because we have to keep thinking about some place, some time that is not this. We swap stories about women we've seduced, and we make jokes about people we hate, which gives Lola ample opportunity to use her favorite penis euphemisms, "wiener" and "wanger." Lola also uses the word "gay" the same way that homophobic middle school boys do, but from her, it's endearing. When I broke up with my last serious girlfriend, she took me out for Chinese food and said—the sincerest sympathy in her voice—"Baby, I'm sorry things are so gay right now."

And right now, this now in Massachusetts, is precisely the problem. We are counting the days til graduation, the days til we can move back home. Never mind that Lola moves to San Francisco only to turn right around and move back to the East Coast with the unexpected hesher boyfriend. Never mind that I come back to San Francisco and start to fuck fags and femmes again, but that in a year I could be fucking butches and only butches, and that maybe someday I'll turn into a top, and Lola's boyfriend will be queer like us too.

Never mind that not knowing the outcome is always part of the turn-on. Right now, we blast *Horses* on Lola's beat-up car stereo as we drive through the backwoods at 2:00 AM. *Jesus died for somebody's sins, but not mine. . . . Oh, she looked so good, oh, she looked so fine. And I've got to tell the world that I'm gonna make her mine. . . .* And we keep going, keep talking, keep driving, because it will get us out and move us on to the next thing we'd like to be sure about, but aren't really. Right now, San Francisco is a future that we predict all the time. Right now, San Francisco is the land of milk and honey and silver-haired butch dykes with ten-inch cocks and freshly sharpened switchblades. Right now, San Francisco is where we will go to be femme chicken. Where we will work it, because we sure as hell cannot work it here.

UNTIL IT'S GONE

Shanna Germain

*I*t's a cliché, Maria knows, but still, she can't help but think it, even as Aaron wraps the leather belt around her neck. *You don't know what you've got,* she thinks, and then stops, tells herself to focus on the pull of the leather as it closes in on her skin. She wants to really feel the rough insides of the leather against her veins. The belt is new, as she'd requested. Not expensive. The leather of it doesn't circle her neck in a smooth circle, but in folds, like an octagon. The places where its folds pinch her skin a little, and she focuses there, on the mean throbs in her neck.

She's doggie-style, so she can't see Aaron. If she inhaled, there would be the tanned cow-dirt smell she needs, but also Aaron, who smells, for some reason, of hyacinths and rain.

Not like David, who smelled like leather himself. So she doesn't inhale. Instead, she goes down on her elbows on the bed, lets the leather press into the front of her neck on the way down.

Her movement startles Aaron, who pulls up, probably accidentally, on the belt. There is a second of startled blackness in her brain. It's a blackness her clit recognizes, and speaks to, with steady pulses.

"Ahh," she hears herself say. It's the involuntary sigh of something lost, and nearly found. A gold ring glinting from the bottom of the ocean. If she leans forward into the glint, she might . . .

"Is this okay?" Aaron says, and he might as well have let go of the belt as fast as it brings her back. She opens her eyes, and although the only thing she can see is the dark headboard in front of her, the pillows that probably need to be washed, she can see it all: She is just a woman of thirty-five, ass-up on the bed with a cheap belt around her neck, trying to recapture her youth. Talk about a cliché.

Aaron lets go of the belt, so it goes slack. Anything that had begun to beat in her body shuts down. She pulls the leather off her neck in a single, slick movement. The edge of the buckle catches her shoulder, makes a small mark that she hopes she'll feel later.

She turns and faces Aaron. He sits in the modified lotus position, although she is sure he doesn't know it. His hands are spread on his thighs. Between it all, his short, fat cock sits, half-raised, like a groundhog checking the weather.

"Let's just do it the regular way," she says.

With her words, the glint she saw before, the simmer of hope, dies down, disappears beneath sand. Aaron is happy to oblige—she knows he only does the belt thing for her, anyway—and he pushes her gently back on the bed, leans into her thighs with his mouth. She touches his short blonde hair while he works, does the breathing her therapist recommended, tries to get lost in the way his tongue feels, there and there, small circles. She can almost fall into the sensation, mentally urging him closer to her clit, making small encouraging noises when he gets close. But when he looks up at her, his face covered with juices, his eyes asking her if he's doing it right, she loses focus, has to close her eyes against the question.

As he moves up, over her body, positioning himself to enter her, she reminds herself that he is a good husband, a careful lover, and she should be grateful to have him. Hell, she is grateful. She really is. They have a good life, and she is grateful for that too. Dukkha, is what her therapist calls it, this yearning for something she can't have. These thoughts, even as Aaron parts her, begins his slow slide into her, make her stomach ache.

She tries to focus on her body, the fullness she feels as Aaron enters her, hip to hip. But all she can think of is David; David and leather.

SHE DIDN'T KNOW IT when she met him, but David smelled like sun-warmed soil and leather boots. When she met him, she could only smell the ferment of beer taps and the fry of chicken wings. She was twenty, bartending at the little hometown dive, trying to make her way though college. The bar was past its prime, only frequented by regulars and those who wandered in without knowing any better. The pace gave her time to study, although she mostly took breaks and smoked cigarettes and turned down offers of coke from the guys in the kitchen.

David, who sat in the corner of the bar, was big and dark. She didn't like big and dark. She liked thin and white, pale angles that contrasted her own mocha curves. And so she'd served him his gin and tonics and flirted, but never anything more. Maybe for six months, a year, she knew his name and his drink and nothing else about him, except that he sat there alone. Not "scary" alone, but as a man who needs time to think, maybe, or to not think.

At twenty, she didn't think much. She knew what she had— a lot of ass and a lot of mouth, and she wasn't afraid to use both. She hadn't been dating then so much as connecting men, dot-to-dot, waiting for some picture of her life to emerge.

The first time David asked her out, she'd spent the previous night with a punk rock boy, a friend of her roommate. Great blue eyes, that's what had sucked her in, and skin so pale she could see every vein. But the sex had been fast and fumbling; he didn't touch her except to enter and leave. She wasn't sure how much more she'd needed—she loved sex but wasn't sure she'd ever had an orgasm—so she didn't think she was demanding. But she'd expected more, certainly, than the hip-to-hip job she got.

She was still thinking of the punk, and how badly she'd wanted to kick him out of her bed that morning, when she set David's second drink in front of him. He nodded his thanks, the way he always did, and she grabbed his bill from beside the register. He never had more than two—she liked that about him.

When she set the tab down beside him, he hesitated before he put down the twenty, holding her there.

"Are you free for dinner sometime?" he asked.

Coming from his quiet mouth, it startled Maria, as though the chair had talked to her. Maybe that's why she accepted. Afterward, she would think maybe the reason he'd waited so long and still was to surprise her into saying yes.

His face was round, the cheekbones hidden behind muscle or fat. Even his wrists were large in a way that scared her, made her feel like she'd already been broken.

"Tuesday night," he said. And she wasn't sure whether to be flattered or scared that he knew her night off.

"Tuesday," she agreed.

HE DIDN'T TAKE HER to a restaurant, but to his house, where he made dinner while she sat at the table. It was kind of nice that he didn't talk, or even look at her. The food held his attention, as though it were the only thing in the kitchen. She wasn't used to it, playing second fiddle, but it allowed her to lean back and watch him. His body was big in the room, all shoulders and belly. As he cooked, she could see how he'd come to be as big as he was, the dark skin stretched so tight over his body. Salad with homemade dressing, mashed potatoes with butter, pork chops that he rubbed all over with garlic and olive oil. His big hands made indents in the meat.

She had a drink—red wine, although she didn't know enough to know what kind—and she tried not to chug it. Nervous habit. She wished she could smoke but could imagine his face if she were to ask to light up around this food he was making. After dinner, maybe.

David bent down to the stove, his ass wide in jeans, his back wider. There was something graceful in his movements—a man who knew his own country. It lit some pilot light in her stomach, the flame hot and blue. She let it simmer there for a few minutes and then tried to put it out. But watching him set the table around her, gorgeous blue plates and her napkin just so, she couldn't quench it.

And then he was putting steaming plates and bowls all around, smelling of garlic and cream and oil. She wanted to tell him this wasn't the way to win her, that she was sex and sex. Food was good but just sustaining. There was no way she could look at those mushrooms the way he had looked at them when he'd dug his fingers in, peeled out their insides, stuffed them with something new. But she wasn't sure it was the truth anymore. Maybe she didn't need to love the food, maybe it was enough to watch the way he loved it. She took another gulp of her wine—he'd been refilling her glass in a constant, subtle way that was practiced.

He sat across from her. His face was shiny in the heat and work.

"Shall we eat?" he asked. "Or did you have something else in mind?"

The way he said it, leaning in just a little. Something about his voice, how sure it was of what she really, truly wanted. His hand around her wrist in a way that she thought would be scary, but was not.

"Both," she said. And he let go of her wrist and picked up his fork. Somehow she had given the right answer, even though she didn't mean to.

AND THAT'S HOW IT BEGAN. Sex after dinner, a slow languid affair that left her more relaxed than aroused. His big hands everywhere on her body, feeling her like a topographical map of a place he'd never been. Then stretching her, outside and in, until her muscles ached in that good way, like yoga or running.

Lying on his big bed afterward, watching him sleep, she knew she would leave him early. He was too big for her, too dark. Too sweet and perfect and kind. She already imagined what it would be like if he kept coming in the bar after, or if he didn't come, and there was just his chair, empty.

But then he woke her in the morning by pushing those big fingers inside her. He hadn't even waited to see if she was wet, or even awake. By the time he had two fingers in to the knuckles, she was both, and bucking against his hand in a way that shamed her. She didn't come, but there was a new pulse in her clit that gave her hope.

The belt didn't come until later, maybe a week, maybe two. She can't remember now. What she does remember is this: Her, doggie-style on David's big bed. Him under her, still dressed, his mouth at her clit, one finger inside her ass. The exquisite combination of his warm tongue and his cool finger. The way the top half of her felt lonely, her nipples puckering against the air, her throat and lips alone. And then, David sliding from beneath her. The *shrripp* of his belt sliding out of his jeans. She thought he was getting undressed, but he wasn't. He'd just wanted the belt.

His voice dropped to her ear when he said, "I'm going to make you come."

Her own surprise, the way her face felt hotter on top of the sex flush—she didn't know that he knew. And then he'd put the belt around her neck, around the part of her that had felt exposed, empty. She could smell herself, pungent and sweet, on David's fingers as he fastened the leather, and then the smell of David and the leather mingling. Her neck felt pressure from the belt, like the pressure of his finger entering her ass, which he did now. Rotating his finger, he slid back underneath her, put his mouth back to her clit. His tongue flicked her clit with a steady rhythm that made her afraid, but when she tried to back away from his mouth, his finger in her ass held her there.

She breathed deep the leather, let herself feel the tight pull of the belt around her neck. It was like having David everywhere at once, around and in every part of her body. He kept the steady rhythm on her clit, worked his finger inside her ass, pulling her closer and tighter to his mouth, holding her there. Her head felt like it was filled with some heavy, dark gas. She had trouble holding it up. Her head, her body, none of it felt like it was hers anymore. It belonged to David. And to pleasure.

AFTER THAT, SHE WANTED the belt every time, the way it felt like his hands around her. Sometimes David would oblige, would buy a new belt, expensive or cheap, sometimes with a huge silver buckle that he would wear as a promise, or a threat. He knew how to use the leather other ways, not just around her neck, but against her ass, the sides of her thighs, pinching her nipples between the leather until she'd scream. His belts all smelled like her, and she smelled like David and his belts.

Other times, he'd say no to her pleas, which made her crazy. He'd slide off his belt, hang it on the back of the bedroom door, come to her empty-handed.

"We've got to save something for the future," he'd say. "I can't do everything now and have you bored when we're forty." She liked to imagine them forty, what they might do, what he might do to her, but it wasn't enough to keep her from begging him to get his belt.

When she masturbated, she'd hook a belt around her own throat or run a thin one across her clit. And she'd come, just thinking about what was left, what might happen in the future.

And then she'd fucked it all up. She couldn't wait—she'd found a man on the side, one who'd fuck her with belts and hands. She told herself it was just to hold her over, until David would give her what she needed again. It wasn't the same as David, but it made it easier to bear the wait.

But David found out, and he wouldn't take her back.

BY THE TIME SHE MET AARON, years later, she thought she was over David, over the leather. Sex was just . . . sex. Neither amazing nor awful. Just sex. But lately, it's changed. It's all come back to her. That's why she started seeing the therapist.

Now, with Aaron above her, she turns her head to the side and her cheek comes to rest on the strap of leather. She inhales deep. The tang of shoe polish and hide smells like home to her in a way she can't explain to Aaron, that she can barely explain to herself. The leather rubs against her cheek with Aaron's thrusts. She imagines that it is releasing ghosts. David. Her younger self.

Above her, Aaron makes a sound, low, like an animal and she echoes him. She won't come, not this time, but she can bear it, and that is enough. When it is over, he rolls from her, wraps her body in his arms. She pulls the comforter up to her shoulders. Dukkha. What does it matter? She wants and she wants. Her therapist isn't helping her; she knows that, has known it since the beginning. But when she goes there and he folds his hands in front of him, sometimes she can smell his fingers. Leather and oil filling her nose, until she can finally cry.

SHANNA GERMAIN

ACKNOWLEDGMENTS

Thank you to Don Weise for first conceiving of this project and encouraging the book and me to expand the potential for dirty words. My agent, Lori Perkins, has also helped push me beyond what I think I'm capable of, and she is an unflagging supporter of both my work and the world of erotic writing. Many thanks to Seal Press and Brooke Warner for their interest in this project; I'm honored to have found such a fitting home for *Dirty Girls* and to work with a press whose books have taught me so much over the years. Thanks also to Lori Applebaum, Bess Abrahams, Allison Bojarski, Molly Crabapple, Miriam Datskovsky, Ellen Friedrichs, Shari Goldhagen, Brett and Emily Jackson, Adam Kominik, Sira Maliphol, Judy McGuire, Hitha Prabhakar, Lorelei Russ, Heidi Schmid, Nichelle Stephens, Alison Tyler, Brian Van, and my family for their support and for reminding me that there is life beyond my computer screen.

ABOUT THE CONTRIBUTORS

MARIE LYN BERNARD is a half-Jewish, half-Midwestern farmer's-daughter freelance aspirant. She blogs regularly at This Girl Called Automatic Win (http://marielynbernard .blogspot.com), the L Word Online, and OurChart.com. Among other places, her work has appeared in *The Bigger the Better, the Tighter the Sweater: 20 Funny Women on Beauty; Body Image & Other Hazards of Being Female; Best American Erotica 2007; Best Women's Erotica 2005; Marie Claire;* nerve.com, CleanSheets, Suspect Thoughts, Fresh Off the Vine, Conversely, Desdmona .com, *The Sarah Lawrence Review,* and ElitesTV.com. She graduated from the University of Michigan in 2003 with a very handy degree in English literature. She lives in Harlumbia, believes in St. Elmo's Fire, and occasionally fools around with a website called www.marielynbernard.com.

SUKI BISHOP has most recently been published in *Best Lesbian Erotica 2007, Painted Bride Quarterly,* and *Blithe House Quarterly.* Her story "Where the Story Lies" was a finalist for the 2006 Rauxa Prize for erotic fiction and has been nominated for a Pushcart Prize. Suki lives in Pittsburgh, Pennsylvania.

L. ELISE BLAND never travels without her diary. Dominatrix, stripper, naked actress—she's done it all and has lived to write about it, in both fact and fiction. Her most recent publications include *Secret Slaves: Erotic Stories of Bondage* (Alyson), *Naughty Spanking Stories from A to Z 2* (Pretty Things Press), *The Best American Erotica 2006* (Fireside/Touchstone), and *First-Timers: True Stories of Lesbian Awakening* (Alyson). Learn more about her writings at www.lelisebland.com.

TENILLE BROWN's writing is featured online and in several print anthologies, including *Caught Looking, Ultimate Lesbian Erotica 2007, A Is for Amour, D Is for Dress-Up,* and *The Greenwood Encyclopedia of African American Women Writers.* She obsessively shops for shoes, hats, and purses and keeps a daily blog on her website www.tenillebrown.com.

ANDREA DALE lives in Southern California within distance of the scent of the ocean. Her stories have appeared in *Best Lesbian Erotica,* Fishnetmag.com, *Ultimate Undies,* and *The MILF Anthology,* among others. Under the name Sophie Mouette, she and a coauthor saw the publication of their first novel, *Cat Scratch Fever*, in March 2006 (Black Lace Books), and they have sold stories to *Sex on the Move, Sex in the Kitchen, Best Women's Erotica*, and more. In other incarnations, she is a published writer of fantasy and romance. Her website can be found at www.cyvarwydd.com.

GINA DE VRIES is extremely happy to be living a sweetly debauched life in San Francisco but wants to state for the record that she's less bitter about Massachusetts than her narrator in "The Next Thing." She is also the coeditor, with Diane Anderson-Minshall, of *[Becoming]: Young Ideas on Gender, Identity, and Sexuality*. You can find her stories and essays (some smutty, some not) anthologized in *Five-Minute Erotica 2, Tough Girls 2: More Down & Dirty Dyke Erotica, TransForming Communities, Baby Remember My Name: An Anthology of New Queer Girl Writing, First-Timers: True Stories of Lesbian Awakening, That's Revolting!: Queer Resistances to Assimilation*, and *The On Our Backs Guide to Lesbian Sex*, among other places. Check out her blog at http://queershoulder.livejournal.com.

KATE DOMINIC is a Los Angeles–based erotica freelancer whose solo book, *Any 2 People, Kissing*, was a Foreword Magazine Book of the Year finalist. Under a variety of pen names, she has published more than four hundred short stories, including recent works in *She's on Top, Luscious, Garden of the Perverse,* and both volumes of *Naughty Spanking Stories*. Look for her column, "The Business End," at the Erotica Readers & Writers Association, www.erotica-readers.com. Kate can be contacted at kate@katedominic.com.

MADELYNNE ELLIS lives in the United Kingdom with her partner of more than fourteen years. She is the author of three novels for Virgin's Black Lace imprint: *A Gentleman's Wager*, *Passion of Isis*, and *Dark Designs*. The latter won the best male–male category in Scarlet Magazine's 2006 Erotic Fiction Awards. For news, excerpts, and other details, visit her at www .madelynne-ellis.com.

SHANNA GERMAIN has written her bio so many times that she asks you to please stop her if you've already heard this one. When she's not sitting behind a computer dreaming up sexy scenarios, Shanna can be found walking the streets, eavesdropping at cafés, and indulging in hand-crafted microbrews. Her poetry, fiction, and essays have appeared in publications like *Absinthe Literary Review, Best American Erotica, Best Bondage Erotica, Caught Looking, Cowboy Lover,* and *He's on Top*. Visit her online at www.shannagermain.com.

MELISSA GIRA (http://melissagira.com) is a blogger, a writer, an editor of Sexerati: Smart Sex. (http://sexerati .com), and a contributor to *$pread* magazine and the blogs

BoundNotGagged, Gridskipper, and bub.blicio.us, "tracking the web's social economy." An advocate of international sex workers' rights, a mobile media maker, and a shameless sex futurist, she fully unpacked three times in the last year and prefers to work out of her purse-size office: cell phone, wireless keyboard, and DV camera—wherever a cheap GPRS signal and fancy lip gloss can take her.

ISABELLE GRAY has writing in the anthologies *Best Date Ever* and *Iridescence: Sensual Shades of Erotica,* among others. She also has a fondness for Sharpie markers.

MARILYN JAYE LEWIS is the founder of the Erotic Authors Association, the first international writers organization to honor literary merit in erotica writing and publishing. She is the award-winning author of *Neptune & Surf* and is the coeditor of the international best-selling erotic art book *Mammoth Book of Erotic Photography.* Her short stories and novellas have been published worldwide and translated into French, Italian, and Japanese. *Lust: Bisexual Erotica* represents her erotic short stories from 1997 to 2003. The forthcoming *Ribbon of Darkness* (Magic Carpet Books, 2008) is her collected works of short erotic fiction from 1996 to 2007. Anthologies she has edited include *Hot Women's Erotica, That's Amore!, Stirring Up a Storm, Zowie! It's Yaoi!,* and *Entangled Lives.* Her popular erotic romance novels include *When Hearts Col-*

lide and *When the Night Stood Still.* Upcoming novels include *Freak Parade, A Killing on Mercy Road, We're Still All That,* and *Twilight of the Immortal.*

TSAURAH LITZKY writes erotic stories because she knows making love can and does set us free. Her erotic writing has appeared in over fifty books and publications, including the Best American Erotica series eight times. Simon and Schuster published her erotic novella, *The Motion of the Ocean,* as part of *Three the Hard Way,* a series of erotic novellas edited by Susie Bright. Tsaurah is a member of the creative writing department at the New School in Manhattan. Her groundbreaking course, Silk Sheets: Writing Erotica, is now in its ninth year.

CATHERINE LUNDOFF is the author of two collections of lesbian erotica: *Night's Kiss* (Torquere Press, 2005) and *Crave: Tales of Love, Lust, and Longing* (Lethe Press, 2007). Her short fiction has appeared in such collections as *Periphery: Erotic Lesbian Futures, Lust for Life, Garden of the Perverse, Amazons, Caught Looking, Best Fantastic Erotica volume 1, Stirring Up a Storm,* and *Naughty Spanking Stories from A to Z.*

GWEN MASTERS has been accused of writing even in her sleep, a charge she readily accepts. Her stories have appeared in dozens of places, both in print and online. Gwen hides away in a sleepy Tennessee town, writing naughty novels and working on the century-old mansion she shares with her husband and their two kids. For more information on Gwen and her works, visit her website: www.gwenmasters.net.

CAROL QUEEN is the author of *The Leather Daddy and the Femme, Real Live Nude Girl,* and *Exhibitionism for the Shy.* She's also edited or coedited eight books of erotic fiction and sexual essays. She is the founding director of the Center for Sex & Culture in San Francisco (www.sexandculture.org) and works as staff sexologist at Good Vibrations (www.goodvibes .com). Come visit at www.carolqueen.com or tune in to www .carolqueenblog.com.

SOFÍA QUINTERO is the author of several novels and short stories that cross genres. Under the pen name Black Artemis, she wrote the hip-hop novels *Explicit Content, Picture Me Rollin',* and *Burn.* She is also a contributor to two other erotica collections: *Juicy Mangos,* an anthology of short stories by Latina writers, and *Iridescence: Sensuous Shades of Lesbian Erotica.* Sofía is also the author of the novel *Divas Don't Yield* and has contributed novellas to the "chica lit" anthologies *Friday Night Chicas* and *Names I Call My Sister.* As an activist, she cofounded Chica Luna Productions (http://chicaluna.com), a nonprofit organization that seeks to identify, develop, and support women of color who wish to create socially conscious entertainment. She is also a founding creative partner of Sister Outsider Entertainment, a multimedia production company that aims to create edgy but quality entertainment for urban audiences. To learn about her works in progress, public appearances, and latest rants and raves, visit http://black artemis.com, http://sisteroutsider.biz or http://www.myspace .com/sofiaquintero.

THERESA "DARKLADY" REED is a professional writer, event impresario, and web radio personality specializing in free speech, alternative sexuality, and all aspects of the adult entertainment industry. She hosts the annual Portland Masturbate-a-thon and manages to almost effortlessly piss off extremists from both the left and right wings. She is editor of YNOT.com and her reviews and features appear monthly in *Adult Video News* and *GayVN* magazines. Her erotica can be found in such anthologies as *Naughty Spanking Stories from A to Z, Best Bisexual Erotica 2, Best SM Erotica,* and *Five-Minute Erotica.* She is a member of the Free Speech Coalition and liaison to the adult industry for the Woodhull Freedom Foundation. Learn more about her plans for world conquest at www.darklady.com.

TERESA NOELLE ROBERTS's erotica has appeared or is forthcoming in *He's on Top, She's on Top, B Is for Bondage, E Is for Exotic, F Is for Fetish, H Is for Hardcore, Chocolate Flava 2, Best Women's Erotica 2004, 2005,* and *2007,* and many other publications. She is also half of the erotica-writing team called Sophie Mouette, author of *Cat Scratch Fever* (Black Lace Books 2006).

LILLIAN ANN SLUGOCKI, an award-winning feminist writer, has created a body of work on women and their sexuality that includes fiction, nonfiction, plays, and monologues that have been produced on Broadway, Off Broadway, Off Off Broadway, and on National Public Radio. Her work has been published in books, in journals, in anthologies, and online, including on Salon.com. She has been reviewed in *The New York Times*, *The Village Voice*, *Art in America*, *The New Yorker*, *The Daily News*, and the *New York Post;* and recently in London, in *Time Out*, *The Guardian*, the *Telegraph*, and the *London Times*.

DONNA GEORGE STOREY's erotic fiction has appeared in *She's on Top*, *He's on Top*, *E Is for Exotic*, *Love at First Sting*, *Garden of the Perverse: Fairy Tales for Twisted Adults*, *Sexiest Soles*, *Taboo: Forbidden Fantasies for Couples*, *Best American Erotica 2006*, *Mammoth Book of Best New Erotica 4, 5*, and *6*, and *Best Women's Erotica 2005, 2006*, and *2007.* Her novel set in Japan, *Amorous Woman*, is part of Orion's Neon erotica series. Read more of her work at www.DonnaGeorgeStorey.com.

MADDY STUART arrived in New York City from the wilds of Western Canada and spends her days painting and programming computers. Her writing has appeared in *Sexiest Soles: Erotic Stories About Feet and Shoes* and *Secret Slaves: Erotic Stories of Bondage,* both in the Fetish Chest series. Read more of Maddy at www.maddystuart.com.

Called a "trollop with a laptop" by the *East Bay Express* and a "literary siren" by Good Vibrations, **ALISON TYLER** is naughty and she knows it. Her sultry short stories have appeared in more than seventy anthologies, including *Sweet Life* (Cleis), *Sex at the Office* (Virgin), and *Glamour Girls* (Haworth). She is the author of more than twenty-five erotic novels and is the editor of more than thirty explicit anthologies, including *A Is for Amour, B Is for Bondage, C Is for Coeds,* and *D Is for Dress-Up* (all from Cleis). Please visit www.alisontyler.com for more information.

SAGE VIVANT (www.sagevivant.com) is the author of *Your Erotic Personality* and the owner of Custom Erotica Source (www.customeroticasource.com), where she and her staff of writers create tailor-made erotic fiction for individual clients. She is also the writer and voice on David Courtney's music erotica, CD Sex with a Stranger. She has edited several erotica anthologies with partner M. Christian—including *Garden of the Perverse, Amazons,* and *Confessions*—and her work has been published in dozens of anthologies. Her first novel, *Giving the Bride Away,* will be published in fall 2007.

SASKIA WALKER (www.saskiawalker.co.uk) is a British author who has had erotic fiction published on both sides of the pond. You can find her work in many anthologies, including *Best Women's Erotica 2006; Red Hot Erotica, Slave to Love; Secrets, volume 15, The Mammoth Book of Best New Erotica,* *volume 5; She's on Top;* and *Kink.* Her longer work includes the erotic novels *Along for the Ride* and *Double Dare.*

KRISTINA WRIGHT's erotic fiction has appeared in over forty anthologies, including four editions of the Lambda-literary award-winning series *Best Lesbian Erotica,* two editions of *Best Women's Erotica,* two volumes of the *Mammoth Book of Best New Erotica,* and three editions of *Ultimate Lesbian Erotica.* Her work has also been featured in the nonfiction guide *The Many Joys of Sex Toys* and in e-zines such as Clean Sheets, Scarlet Letters, and Good Vibes Magazine. Kristina holds a BA in English and an MA in humanities. For more information, visit her website, www.kristinawright.com.

ABOUT THE EDITOR

RACHEL KRAMER BUSSEL is a prolific erotica writer, editor, journalist, and blogger. She has edited or coedited more than twenty anthologies, including *Caught Looking: Erotic Tales of Voyeurs and Exhibitionism, Hide and Seek, He's on Top, She's on Top, Yes Sir, Yes Ma'am, Crossdressing: Erotic Stories, Best Sex Writing 2008, Spanking Stories from A to Z* (volumes 1 and 2), *First-Timers, Up All Night, Glamour Girls: Femme/Femme Erotica, Ultimate Undies, Sexiest Soles, Secret Slaves: Erotic Stories of Bondage,* and *Sex and Candy: Sugar Erotica.* Her first novel, *Everything But . . . ,* will be published by Bantam in summer 2008. She hosts the monthly In The Flesh erotic reading series, serves as Senior Editor at *Penthouse Variations,* and wrote the Lusty Lady column for *The Village Voice.*

Her writing has been published in more than one hundred anthologies, including *Best American Erotica 2004* and *2006, Everything You Know About Sex Is Wrong, Single State of the Union,* and *Desire: Women Write About Wanting,* as well as *AVN, Bust,* Cleansheets.com, Cosmo UK, *Diva,* Fresh Yarn, Feministing, Huffington Post, Jewcy, Mediabistro.com, Memoirville .com, *Newsday, New York Post,* Oxygen.com, *Penthouse, Playgirl, Punk Planet, San Francisco Chronicle, Time Out New York,* and *Zink.* Rachel has appeared on *The Berman and Berman Show, Family Business,* NY1, *Naked New York,* and *In the Life.* In her spare time, she hunts down the country's best cupcakes and blogs about them at http://cupcakestakethecake.blogspot.com. Visit her at www.rachelkramerbussel.com.